SHADOWS
OF
THYSIA

Copyright © 2026 by C.C. Martinez

All rights reserved.

No part of this publication may be reproduced, distributed, or transmitted in any form or by any means, including photocopying, recording, or other electronic or mechanical methods, without the prior written permission of the publisher, except as permitted by U.S. copyright law. For permission requests, contact C.C. Martinez

The story, all names, characters, and incidents portrayed in this production are fictitious. No identification with actual persons (living or deceased), places, buildings, and products is intended or should be inferred.

Book Cover & Illustrations by Annguyeart

First edition 2026

IBSN 979-8-9938781-0-2 (paperback)

IBSN 979-8-9938781-1-9 (hardcover)

To all curious eyes peeking behind wardrobes and brave hands
reaching for strange rocks, hoping it leads to another world.
This is for you.

Shadows of Thysia is a full length fantasy romance with material that may be difficult for some readers. It includes violence, blood, occasional gore, vulgar language, emotional trauma, grief over the loss of loved ones, and moments of physical and psychological assault. Characters struggle with war, power imbalances, and moral gray zones. If any of that feels heavy for you, please take care while reading.

Cedarvale
Wispwoods
Holl[ow] Mount[ains]
Veris
Elderstone
Stonehaven
Brinehold
Seastrand
Evomor
Misewharf
Stormcove
Sanc[...] Sc[...]

Molten Reach
Anotalia
Infernis
Scorchmere
EMBERHOLD
Aerilon
Skylume
Lyravisia
STRATOS
THE WORLD OF
THYSIA

CONTENTS

1

NIGHT SHIFT

"I should've been a stripper," I muttered, clocking into what was already a full-blown ER dumpster fire. Strippers were paid better and walked away with actual tips. The only tips I ever saw usually came from the end of an old man's saggy pen—

"Eleni, you made it!"

Emma, the daytime charge nurse, appeared beside me at the nurse's station, yanking me back to reality. Her messy bun told me everything I needed to know about how the shift was going. "You left your bedroom door open this morning and looked utterly dead. I was worried you'd sleep through your alarm."

"Working four shifts in a row can do that."

Emma and I shared a two-bedroom apartment minutes from the hospital. It was a blessing, considering Denver's high gas prices. "You can actually thank my Gram's constant phone calls for waking me up. All of which I ignored." I glanced at the tele-monitor, where alarms were going off in every room.

Gram and I weren't on speaking terms. Not since I told her I didn't want to come home for my birthday. I wanted to spend it with my friends—the few I did have—and she went on about "family obligations" and "tradition" and blah-blah. The conversation ended with me hanging up and swearing I'd never let her guilt-trip me again.

"It's not healthy to keep this bottled up." Emma sighed, the way only someone who'd said the same thing a hundred times could manage. "She's your only family."

"Not interested," I said flatly, nodding toward the monitor packed with patients still waiting to be triaged. The ER reeked of antiseptic and stress under the harsh fluorescent lights, mixed with a variety of bodily odors in every direction.

"Looks like it's been a fun shift."

Emma shot me a side-eye glare. "We've used the helipad twice, two traumas are still waiting on orders, one guy's in four-point restraints after trying to helicopter his junk, and someone's sweet old meemaw has been shouting every curse word known to man."

"Sounds like another day in paradise," I said, flashing a tired grin. "Tell me we've got admission beds so we can get people upstairs."

"For now. ICU's preparing for the traumas, and the Med-Surg floor has a handful left, but they're filling up quick-ly."

"Better than nothing," I mumbled, grabbing a radio from the desk. "Fingers crossed we don't drown tonight."

I clipped up my curls, hooked the radio to my hip, and I headed toward the cluster of nightshift crew. Sam, our night charge, rubbed her temple in slow, methodical circles as she wrote on the board. "Eleni," she said without looking away, "you're in minor care tonight."

I grabbed a handful of supplies into my pockets. "Perfect."

Besides being a resource nurse, working in minor care was my second favorite role. Quick in, quick out, and patients who usually didn't try to die on me. Honestly, I found it more exciting because it typically involved lacerations, burns, and broken bones.

The night unfolded in its usual up-and-down waves. My patients mainly consisted of burned fingers, mild fevers, rashes, or simply too much free time. An older man arrived later that night, reeking of wine and embarrassment. I found out he tried to make late-night nachos and grabbed the hot pan with his bare hands. He had a surprisingly sweet story about his partner of twenty years, detailing how they met and sharing his monthly ritual of cooking her dinner.

I couldn't help but smile.

Even in their golden years, people could still find love and share those sweet, unexpected moments. It made me hopeful that one day I would find someone willing to risk getting their fingers burned for me. But with night shifts, online classes, and barely enough time to sleep, how does anyone manage to meet someone with all that going on?

Because I sure as hell couldn't.

It was my last shift of the week, and I was beyond done. All I craved was to slip into my sweatpants and hoodie, crawl into bed, and stay there forever. With only a year left in my BSN program, I spent every scrap of free time studying for my exams.

My phone buzzed in my scrub pocket. *Seriously, Gram?*

Why couldn't she take the hint that I didn't want to talk? Minor care was slammed, and I didn't have the bandwidth to deal with her.

It vibrated again, but only once.

I groaned, tempted to switch it off, but when I checked the screen, the missed call wasn't Gram. It was an unknown number with the same Wyoming area code, not saved in my contacts, and it left a voicemail.

It must be spam.

But then I noticed the time. Spam callers usually didn't ring this late.

Weird.

Before I could think too much about it, my pediatric patient let out a scream and I shoved my phone back into my pocket.

"Eleni," Sam's voice crackled over the radio, "I need you to resource up front when minor care closes." Minor care always closed at one a.m., which meant my shift was halfway over and that much closer to crawling into my cozy bed.

"Copy."

I refocused on the kid in front of me—no older than eight, his cheeks streaked with dried tears and stubborn pride. His wrist was already swelling, the skin mottled with deep purples, reds, and tenderness radiating up into the forearm. Classic signs of a distal radius fracture, likely from his daring leap off a bunk bed turned launchpad. His eyes searched mine, not for pity, but for reassurance that he could endure the pain. I responded with a confident smile.

After closing minor care, I headed back toward the front of the ER. The breakroom was on the way, so I slipped inside, pulled out my phone, and played the voicemail.

"Hello, this is Sheriff Vic from Carbon County…" His voice hesitated, the pause stretching so long it sent every worst-case scenario tearing through my bones. My hand tightened around my cellphone.

"Listen, Eleni—it's about your grandmother Natalie. There was an accident…"

2

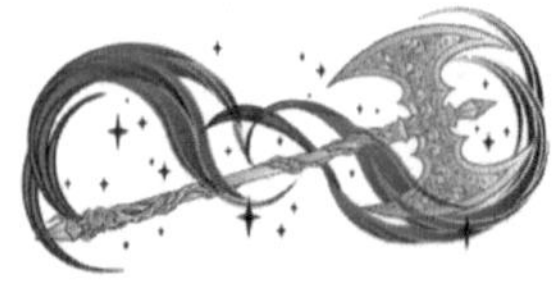

TIME CAPSULE

"Eleni, would you be a dear and fill up my canteen?" Gram asked, buckling the halter on Eddie, our fiery chestnut mustang.

"Sure, Gram," I said, heading back to the cabin, the morning air biting my cheeks. The valley lay under shadows, the jagged peaks waiting to catch the sun. Spring was near, but the cold lingered; even while wearing three layers of clothing, it still refused to let go of its nip. Every minute we delayed felt like a second stolen from our climb up the mountain.

I handed Gram the canteen with a quick grin, eager to get moving. She gave me a sidelong look, eyes dropping to my belt. "Where's your tomahawk?"

I looked down; emptiness greeted me.

"Must've fallen out," I said, retracing my steps.

Halfway there, I spotted it. The blade's reflection caught the early light, still half-buried in the dirt. Heat crept up my neck. We hadn't even left yet, and I was already dropping things.

My fingers ran over the etchings carved into the handle. Its lethal beauty always captivated me. No matter how many times I held it, I never got used to how it felt in my grip. I clipped it back into the leather loop and jogged back to Gram, who was bringing Eddie out of the barn.

"You've done this trail plenty of times," she smiled, holding out Eddie's lead rope. "I think you know the way."

I nodded, feeling eager but nervous too. It was my first time leading us to our secret meadow—the Heart of the Mountain.

Gram glanced down at my tomahawk and tightened the strap. "Remember, if you have to use it, don't just throw it—command it. And it will never miss its mark."

"Yes, Gram." Eddie nudged my shoulder with his nose, letting me know he was ready.

We moved along the trail, the quiet only broken by our footsteps and Eddie's occasional sneeze. As the path narrowed, his pace faltered. One ear flicked back, then the other. He suddenly stopped without warning. His head lifted, nostrils flaring as he tested the air, and his body went rigid as I watched. Whatever he sensed, it wasn't in front of us.

"Eddie?" I whispered, casting a worried look at Gram. Something wasn't right. My skin prickled as silence wrapped around us. No birdcall, no rustling of trees. Dead silence. Gram carefully lowered the bow from her shoulder and stepped forward. My entire body started to shake. This wasn't nerves; it was fear. Real, bone-deep fear.

"Stay alert. We're not alone."

———◈———

The evening chill tugged me awake, brushing against my wind-burned cheeks. My body slumped against the fresh pile of earth, rocks pressing into my back. My neck ached from the awkward angle, and my butt was already numb from the cold earth.

She'd been buried here hours ago, and yet, here I sat, my body refusing to move.

The medical examiner had tried to stall me by citing permits and procedures, claiming I couldn't take her body to bury on my property until then. However, feeling sleep-deprived and quickly losing patience, I decided to remind him of the time I caught him making out with his secretary in the Safeway parking lot two counties over and how his wife would feel if she somehow found out. He signed the paperwork shortly after.

Since working in the ER, I'd gotten good at shutting my emotions down and shoving them into a box. It was second nature at this point. You don't cry when a patient codes. You don't panic when they're bleeding to death. You don't break when a family does. You stay composed, even when everything inside you wants to fall apart.

But sitting here now, the boxes I had packed those feelings into didn't feel as sturdy anymore. I could feel something pressing against them—a slow swelling pressure behind my ribs. Grief had a way of finding me in the stillness. It waited like quicksand, tugging at me beneath the surface no matter how far I tried to step away.

I only meant to sit with her for a few minutes, long enough to pretend I was still in control. But the exhaustion was drowning me, pulling me under before I even had a chance to fight it. I drifted.

I drifted in and out of sleep until a buzzing sound came from my pocket—I ignored it. Again, it buzzed like a tiny gnat that wouldn't go away. Groaning, I dug into my pocket and pulled out my phone. The screen shone in the fading light. My head throbbed as I struggled to focus on the letters and the name that appeared: Emma—Best Roomie Ever.

It was the tenth time she'd called. Every time, I swore I'd answer, but I couldn't bring myself to press the button.

My joints protested as I pushed myself to stand. I'd spent hours awkwardly passed out beside the rocks on Gram's grave and was paying for it. The truck was a few feet away, door still hanging open. I tossed the shovel and the empty bottle into the bed, my gaze drifting back to the mound of fresh earth. "I'll be back soon, Gram."

The door squeaked as I climbed into the old pickup. My hands throbbed as I gripped the wheel, still covered in dried blood and dirt. If Gram had been driving the pickup from town instead of that other junker she had, she might still be here. But knowing how expensive diesel was, I understood why she chose the beater. Still, she should have bought one with working airbags.

The truck rumbled to life. Gravel crunched under the tires as I drove away, the grave fading into the mist behind me. When I reached the barn, I shut off the engine and headed to Eddie's stall.

"Hey, old man."

His black-tipped ears twitched as he popped his head over the stall. Despite how stubborn this mustang was, you would never guess he was a senior. Gram told me she found him wandering our property line, half-starved and limping. She believed he had lost his band, but he had no trouble following Gram to the barn, and she nursed him back to health.

Since he was wild, she always kept his pasture gate open, thinking he would eventually leave. But he never did. He'd often wander up to our porch, pawing at the door like he owned it—usually demanding food or attention, sometimes both. If he spotted coyotes in the upper pasture, he wouldn't hesitate to charge at them, fearless as ever. But what I loved most was how sturdy he was when Gram and I hiked the mountain trails. We never forced him; he just came along, like we were part of his band.

Over the years, Gram eventually got him halter and saddle-trained with some help from our neighbor, Mr. Morris. I always called him Cowboy Morris, mostly because he looked like he'd stepped straight out of an old western: sweat-stained hat, jet-black hair with two tight-knit braids that went past his chest, and boots that had seen some things. He'd show up with his son, who was a mini version of him, and the two of them would walk Gram and me through the steps, patiently showing us how to train and work with Eddie the right way.

Eddie bent over the stall door, sniffing my bandaged hands, and gave them a gentle lick. "She's up the hill," I said softly, rubbing his nose. "A little past your pasture. You can still see her when you walk up there."

He bobbed his head as if he understood.

I filled his hay nets and moved to the other side of the stall, where the back door opened out to the lower pasture. I stepped outside, inhaling the evening air, when I noticed Eddie's gate was closed.

Weird.

Gram never shut his gate.

I walked over, unlatched it, and swung it back open.

"Must've been the wind."

Mist curled low across the ground like a blanket as night slowly crept in. I made my way back down to the cabin. The sight of the cabin gutted me. So many nights we had spent sitting in those old rocking chairs, talking about stories and gossip, while watching beautiful Wyoming sunsets. Now, they sat still, empty with dew glistening on the worn wood.

I stepped inside the cabin and switched on the lights, surveying the room that I hadn't seen in years. Gram's earthy, floral, familiar scent hit me immediately. Everything was as she had left it: her yellow knitted blanket over the armchair, her reading glasses lying on top of the half-cut wooden barrel coffee table, and a blue mug with the last thing Gram drank sitting beside her glasses. Part of me was still half expecting her to be in the other room, hoping she would come out at any moment. But no one came.

Yesterday, I was so focused on choosing her burial outfit that I didn't notice anything else. I wouldn't let myself take it all in. Not until now. The silence hit me harder than anything, and the slow, aching pressure pushed against my ribs a little more.

My throat tightened, fighting back tears. I wasn't prepared for this. I needed a distraction before the quicksand pulled me under. Kicking off my muddy boots, I headed for the bathroom. Knowing the tub would take a while to warm up, I returned to the kitchen for some much-needed food and a drink.

Gram loved baking, which meant the kitchen was stocked with flour, sugar, and about twelve kinds of spices, but nothing I could actually eat. And after topping off the whiskey I'd hauled up earlier to Gram's grave, baking was a lost cause.

"I guess I'm making a run to the store tomorrow," I muttered, shutting the pantry with a sigh and grabbing sunflower seeds.

I took a long sip and glanced down at the pile of mail I'd grabbed from the box. Mostly junk—ads, a contractor trying to lowball us for Gram's land, and the stack of unpaid bills. Utilities. Overdraft warnings. The kind of mail that hits you when you're already down.

I groaned, pressing my fingers to my temple, trying to slow the pounding in my head. Why didn't she tell me she was struggling?

A tight, burning ache of guilt pressed on me. I should have been here. I should have known. Instead, I was gone, pretending I didn't need this place, didn't need her. I let out a shaky breath, frustration burning behind my eyes. "I failed you once again, Gram."

Everything was already a mess, and now this was one more weight added to the pile I was barely holding up.

And the worst part?

I couldn't fix any of it. Not yet. Not like this.

The glass of whiskey didn't cut it, so the whole bottle came with me as I headed back to the bathroom.

The bathwater stung the moment I dipped my fingers in, tiny needles biting into the cuts and open blisters across my palm. Adding Epsom salt to the water was probably the dumbest idea, but fuck it, I was already committed and didn't want the hot water to go to waste.

Sitting and drinking from the WhistlePig, my mind wandered.

It would be easy, wouldn't it? Sell the ranch, take the money, walk away, and pretend none of this ever happened.

But then I heard Gram's voice in my head. *Don't be stupid, girl.*

She loved this place. Every crooked fence, every broken panel on the barn, and every inch of dirt she tended like it was an extension of her heart. She would have fought tooth and nail to keep it, and the thought of betraying that made something twist painfully in my chest. And then there was Eddie and Mooch. My ridiculous, chaotic little family. Who the hell would take them if I bailed?

"Fuck no!" I wasn't selling. I wasn't abandoning them. I wasn't abandoning *her*. Animals or not, they were all I had left.

I leaned back against the edge of the tub, gazing at the wooden ceiling, which was becoming harder to focus on. Exhaling, I took another swig, then struggled to stand, nearly falling and breaking my nose.

"Maybe taking a hot bath while drinking wasn't the smartest choice."

Steam clung to the mirror as I stared at my ghostly reflection. Sleep-deprived eyes, pale skin that hadn't seen enough sun because of my work schedule, and wild brown curls made me look as if I had been homeless.

My gaze drifted to the massive scars across my shoulder and down my back, the skin puckered and uneven, mimicking claw marks. The smaller ones were barely noticeable now, but the big ones were impossible to ignore. The colors didn't match the rest of me, a patchwork of healed damage that refused to blend in. Every time I looked at them, it felt like staring at a warning label stamped onto my skin. I wasn't embarrassed by them, but they served as a reminder that I should have died that day.

A shiver ran through me. Cold weather always found those scars first, digging deep beneath the surface and settling into the bone as if the wound were still fresh, as if some part of it had never truly healed.

After putting on my hoodie and sweatpants, I padded into my old room, the floorboards creaking softly with each step. It felt like stepping into a time capsule. Everything was still as I left it. Dusty ribbons, trophies, and my Breyer horses still lined the shelves on the wall above my desk. I ran my fingers over one of my old trophies, cleaning off the dust that covered the writing—*First Place: Archery.*

The past felt like another lifetime. Four years of being away can do that to a person.

I crawled into bed and pulled out my phone, playing Gram's voicemail again.

"Eleni, are you there? I think it went to voicemail."

The tears finally came as I listened to her voice, each word anchoring me to a life I wasn't ready to leave behind.

"I know we haven't talked in a while, but it would be wonderful if you came home for your birthday. I know your work schedule keeps you busy, but turning a quarter century is a big milestone. Anyway, I think we can plan something fun. You can even bring your roommate, Emma. I can set up an extra bed for her in your room and bake your favorite lemony bites. I know they don't make those in Denver. At least, nowhere I know. Okay, I will keep rambling on here, so I'm going to hang up. Please know that I love you more than the stars in the sky, Eleni."

After the voicemail, I replayed each message, triggering a flood of memories. I'd lost count of how many times I replayed her voicemails, clinging to the sound of her as if it were the only thing keeping me upright. Each message ended too soon, leaving me longing for one more word, one more laugh, anything to stretch the moment a little longer. If only I'd picked up the phone that day, or any of the days I chose to ignore her. Maybe her life's outcome might have been different.

My eyes closed shut as I replayed the voicemail again.

3

TRASH BIN POSSUM

I've never liked driving on back roads after dark. Especially out here, where your high beams were the only things between you and total blackness.

There was a time I would have gotten up at a reasonable hour to go to the grocery store, but night shifts had wrecked my schedule. I was used to staying awake until five a.m. on my days off, and if I didn't set an alarm, I could sleep straight through the day. Which, of course, is precisely what happened. It didn't help that I borrowed one of Gram's old romance paperbacks and stayed up until sunrise, flipping pages like a teenager. As soon as the light crept over the mountains, I knew the grocery store would have to wait until evening.

After tossing the groceries into the back of the pickup, I plugged Gram's iPod into the old pickup's ancient aux jack and queued up one of her favorites. The first notes of Dallas Green's Grand Optimist filled the cab, her ultimate crush, as she always called him. Hearing his voice spill through the speakers brought her back to me for a moment, the familiar tune wrapping around me like a small comfort as I drove home.

I was only fifteen minutes from Hot Pockets and a bath when a flash of red and blue lights beamed in my rearview mirror.

Fuck.

I quickly glanced at my speedometer—65 mph, which meant I was going the speed limit. So why in the hell was I getting pulled over then? I couldn't even remember the last time I had been pulled over. Was it when I had gotten my license and stayed out past curfew? This was a small town. Everybody knew everybody, including the sheriff. Hopefully, it was Sheriff Vic, since we had spoken not too long ago.

Although, come to think of it, he hadn't seen me since I left for nursing school.

The closer I looked at myself in the rearview mirror, the more I straight-up looked like roadkill.

I rolled the window down and forced the best smile I could manage.

"Good evening, ma'am." The voice was low and husky with a distinct country drawl. "Can I see your driver's license and proof of insurance?"

The flashlight in my face made it impossible to make out any features, but the voice? Younger and definitely *not* Sheriff Vic.

"Yes, officer."

My hands shook as I scrambled for my ID and insurance and handed them over. I still couldn't see his face, prompting me to skim to his uniform and the name stitched above his badge: *Morris.*

My eyebrows pulled together. Morris.

Wait a sec.

"Cody?" I asked, squinting toward the light.

The flashlight clicked off. And there he was. Short, jet-black hair, a clean, defined jawline, and that familiar scar on his chin. Probably from when he was kicked by a colt, if I remembered right.

Cowboy Morris's son.

Only he wasn't the lanky kid tagging along behind his dad anymore.

Nope.

This version was the polar opposite—broad shoulders, country-strong, and way too grown up. The only difference was that he no longer had his braids. My childhood friend turned law enforcement.

He looked down at my ID, scanning it like he needed confirmation I hadn't stolen someone's identity. Then his eyes shifted back to mine.

"Eleni?"

I gave a genuine smile this time and nodded. "It's been what—five, six years?"

The last time I saw Cody, he was helping his dad break in young colts and fillies on their ranch. Gram and I had run into his dad at the feed store one day. He'd mentioned Cody had left for basic training with the Marine Corps.

I always believed he'd become a full-time horse trainer, like his dad. He had the patience, the skill, and that calm way with animals that most grown men couldn't fake even if they tried. But he often spoke about this country—his people, the Arapaho Tribe—and what it meant to protect their history, culture, and those he loved.

"It's been about seven," he said, his smile only adding to the definition of those already grown-up features. "What brings you back out to this neck of the woods? Last I heard, you moved to the big city to become a nurse, or at least, that's what my dad told me."

I blinked, caught off guard by how much he already knew.

"He also told me about your grandmother. My condolences, Eleni." His tone was sincere, and I could tell he genuinely meant it.

My fingers tightened their grip on the steering wheel, the sting from my cuts serving as a distraction, anything to avoid sinking into the quicksand. I never knew what to say in response to condolences, so I swallowed the lump in my throat and looked away. "I'm trying to get everything organized with the ranch," I sighed. "Figuring out how I'm going to manage it if I stay in Denver."

I didn't offer more than that. No need to dive into the mess of debt Gram had left behind or how I probably couldn't afford to keep the place if I didn't move back and work somewhere more local.

"If my dad and I can help with anything, please let us know."

His father used to stop by during harsh winters to check on Gram and me, especially when the roads were so bad we couldn't make it to town for groceries. Their old dually pickup could plow through about anything.

"Thanks, Cody. I really appreciate it."

"No, really—here." He reached into his jacket, pulled out a small card, and handed it to me. "Seriously, call me. For anything."

I held onto the card a second longer than necessary, fingers curling around the edges.

Part of me wanted to ask him over for a drink and catch up on the many years that had slipped by. He'd always felt like the older brother I never had, the kind of person you could lean on without asking, someone who felt less like a friend and more like family. But something else kept bothering me.

"Cody, why did you pull me over?"

His shoulders stiffened slightly, as if he remembered this wasn't really a reunion.

"Oh, one of your headlights is out," he said, rubbing the back of his neck. "You know how sketchy these roads get at night. I wanted to make sure you knew."

He remained where he was as he continued to rub his neck. "If you want, I can escort you back to the ranch. Make sure you get home safe."

I should say yes. But the irrational side of my brain, the rude, overly critical, and way too loud, screamed: *Absolutely not. Not while you look like a trash bin possum.*

"Thanks, Cody, but I'm not far. I'll keep my high beams on and drive carefully."

His shoulders dropped, and I felt a little bad.

"All right then. You be safe, Miss Eleni."

I really hoped I wasn't making a mistake by telling him no. The window was already halfway up when he called out, "Oh, one more thing."

I paused. "Yeah?"

"There's a new developer in town," he said. "Been showing up at people's ranches, flashing big checks, and trying to buy them out."

Wonderful.

That sounded like the kind of guy I didn't have time for. The thought of some shiny-shoed developer getting their hands on this piece of land—*my* land—made something in me curl with anger.

"My dad had a few words with him when he showed up on our property," Cody continued. "Told him if he came back, he'd be leaving with one less leg."

I couldn't help but grin, picturing Cowboy Morris saying that with a straight face and a gun in hand.

"I didn't meet him myself, but my dad said his name's Tom Strator. He's trying to build some ski resort or luxury community out here. Already bought two ranches near yours."

"I'll keep a lookout. Thanks for the heads-up."

"Seriously, if he shows up on your doorstep—call me. I'd like to meet this *Strator* in person." There was something in his eyes then. A spark of steel that hadn't been there before. It caught me off guard, and I stared a second too long until he noticed. And in an instant, that spark of steel vanished. Slipped behind that polite smile as if it had never been there.

"Get home safe, Miss Eleni."

4

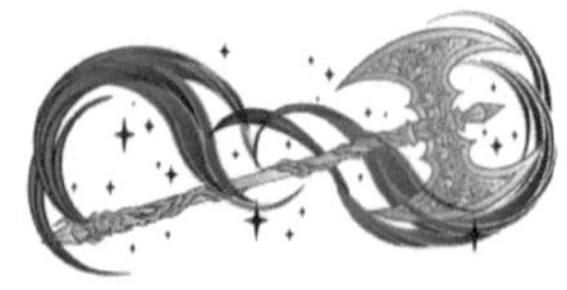

HIDDEN TREASURES

I sat in my car and stared at our old barn. Weathered, warped, and missing some panels, it still stood firm. Gram had told me before I left for Denver that she was saving up to fix it, but from the way it looked, that never happened.

Our ranch sat tucked away in the rural belly of Wyoming, cradled by rolling hills and dense pine forests. Out here, the sense of isolation was quite normal. Our closest neighbor, Jones, was five miles away. He was a retired rancher who rarely left his land, let alone visited town. Cody and his dad lived on the next ranch over, which still meant they were miles away by road.

Eddie was already in his stall, his head turned toward me as if he'd been waiting. The creak of the barn door sent skittish rodents darting from their hiding spots. I stepped inside, searching for the light switch, when I heard a raspy meow. When I finally found it, our barn cat, Mooch, sat atop a hay bale like a queen. Clearly, none of the rodents that ran past impressed her.

"Well, hello to you, too, Mooch."

She stretched, her tail flicking lazily, her uneven stripes shifting across her gray coat. She hopped down and padded over to me. A copper and a blue eye watched me as I crouched to pet her. That feral-looking stray appeared one day and never left. Gram said she was a mooch, stealing food and attention without giving anything back. I'm surprised she's lived this long, since she's been around our property for as long as I can remember. Mooch must be in her twenties by now, which, last time I checked, is quite rare for a cat.

She brushed my hand gently, her purr rough yet soothing. "You missed everything," I said softly, stroking behind her ears. Her purring grew louder, grounding me in that small, familiar way that brought comfort, knowing she hadn't forgotten me.

After Mooch finished her fill of pets, I walked over to Eddie. "Hi, handsome." I rubbed behind his fuzzy ears. His head leaned into me, savoring the touch.

After a few more indulgent rubs behind the ears, a cold chill swept through the breezeway, raising goosebumps along my arms. "That's my cue to go, handsome," I breathed. "I will see you tomorrow."

Though we had electricity, we lacked central air conditioning or a heater. Gram told me it was better for our bodies to adapt to the seasons, as it strengthened the immune system and mind. Our wooden fireplace was the heart of this home, and I was longing for its warmth right about now. I guess I got spoiled being away, living in an apartment that had the luxuries this place didn't. I collected some firewood stacked by the side of the cabin and got to work.

As the cabin warmed up, the dancing flames revived its wooden structure. The fireplace's steady crackles echoed across the room, casting a soft glow and filling the air with the earthy scent of burning wood. The space felt cozy again, dispelling the emptiness it had held during my absence.

How could I sell this place? There were so many cherished memories and comforts tied to it. If that contractor showed up, maybe I could greet him at the driveway with Gram's bow. The mental image brought a slight grin to my face. The big, bad investor meets an unhinged nurse with a weapon. But the grin faded just as fast. I hadn't touched the bow since before I left. My aim was probably trash now.

After a hot bath, I slipped into my hoodie and sweatpants and sank onto the worn couch, its cushions seeming to welcome me as if they missed the company. I held a glass of Wild Turkey 101, the amber liquid burnished in the firelight as I sipped it, its rich caramel and cinnamon aftertaste flowing through me like an extra layer of heat.

I reached for one of Gram's books, *The Wolf and the Dove* by Kathleen E. Woodiwiss, from our small library of stacked books against the wall. A giggle escaped me as I ran my fingertips along the worn cover. This book was one of my favorites in her "forbidden section," the one she had declared off-limits to me during my childhood. Naturally, those restrictions only made them more enticing. Little did Gram know, I had secretly devoured all her romance novels, sneaking them to my room to read under the covers with a flashlight. The thrill of breaking her rule made those secret reading sessions even more exciting.

It wasn't the intimate scenes that drew me in—I wasn't interested in love at the time, and reading those scenes made me feel awkward. It was the badass heroines, the drama, and the fight against impossible odds that captivated me. Gram's books provided my first glimpse into stories where women could be both strong and vulnerable, where fighting for what you believed in didn't diminish them but made them braver.

I smiled, placing it beside me to read later. Stretching out on the couch, I pulled the yellow blanket over me and sank further into the cushions, the familiar scent of wood smoke and floral wrapping around me. My phone rested on my chest. I didn't have any memories of my parents; they died when I was still a baby, and whatever pieces of them existed in stories or photo albums never felt real. They were ghosts I never knew. Gram wasn't. Gram was everything—mother, father, grandmother, the entire universe in one stubborn woman. She was the one who mattered.

I hit play on her voicemail.

Then again.

And again.

If I'd answered, maybe I could've persuaded her not to drive that day or take the old pickup instead. We hadn't exactly been on speaking terms, but she made an effort. She reached out. And what did I do?

I let her calls go to voicemail. Let her texts sit unread.

I'm such an idiot.

The fire kept the cabin warm most of the night, but when it died out, the early morning chill crept in. I shivered as I rubbed the sleep from my eyes. The yellow blanket was discarded on the floor, probably pushed off during the night. Dawn's light was beginning to break through as I rolled off the couch to look out our living room window. I stood up and stretched my arms, still gazing beyond the glass at the burial site on the pasture.

The clock read 6:42 a.m. Gram would already be up with a coffee in hand, tackling the day's chores. Just thinking about coffee woke me up. In colder months, she would let me sleep longer, waiting until the cabin's warmth spread through the rooms before waking me. I rarely needed to set an alarm myself; the smell of Gram's coffee was usually my wake-up call. Especially with this pounding hangover I had now.

My gaze drifted back to the burial site. From this angle, it was nothing more than a lopsided pile of rocks. It was depressing to look at.

There must be a way to make it look less depressing. Something that feels like *her*. I'd already left the lucky arrow on her grave, so why not her bow as well? It had always been hers, never mine. The bow belonged there more than with me, a fitting tribute. I hardly touched it, always favoring my tomahawk. Besides, if I were going to be realistic about defending this place against that contractor, having my tomahawk made more sense.

My sleepy eyes drifted toward Gram's room, and my body reluctantly moved in that direction. The door stayed shut, a silent barrier between me and the part of the house that still felt like hers. I had only gone inside to grab clothes to put on Gram, but I hadn't lingered then. The pain in my chest was still too fresh, her absence too unbearable. Now, even standing outside, my fingers hovered over her doorknob.

Childhood nights came rushing back, nights when I'd crawl into her bed, trembling from bad dreams or the shadows in the dark. Her arms had always been welcoming to me, her voice soothing, and her presence was never something I had to question.

My hand crept toward the doorknob. I turned it, the soft sound of the hinges breaking the stillness. The space inside was familiar, untouched, as if time had paused here. Everything was as she'd left it—her comb and hair ties arranged on the dresser, a glass of water sitting on her nightstand, now slightly cloudy from days of neglect. Above her lamp, her bow hung on the hook.

It looked the same. The black limbs, the white bowstring, and the small carved symbol etched above the grip. Gram's hands had smoothed the edges over the years. She'd had this bow longer than I'd been alive. My thumb brushed the riser, tracing the familiar groove. This was the bow that had saved my life. If that arrow hadn't flown true that day, I would be dead.

I walked to her bed, my legs feeling unsteady, and collapsed face-first onto the mattress.

"*Ughh.* I forgot how comfy you were." My voice muffled into the sheets.

I outstretched my arms, craving something of hers; even her pillow's scent would suffice. It overwhelmed me, the unmistakable essence. My chest buckled, and tears spilled before I could stop them, soaking into the fabric as I clung to what was left of her.

Don't fall into the quicksand.
Don't fall into the quicksand.
I repeated it like a lifeline, even as I slowly sank away.

The sunlight streamed through her window when I heard Gram's landline ringing from the kitchen. I shot upright, my heart rate suddenly rising, causing the bed frame to groan beneath me, along with a dull thud from below.

What was that?

I crouched down when the phone blared again. "I'm coming, jeez," I huffed, trudging to the kitchen. I had no idea who would be calling this number. Gram barely had friends, and the landline was mostly for emergencies.

I picked up the receiver. "Hello?"

"Hey, Miss Eleni. It's Cody." His voice sent a jolt through me, and, stupidly, I found myself leaning in toward the phone. "Hey."

"Sorry to bother you," Cody said, his voice crackling softly through the static. "I would've called your cell, but . . . I never got the chance to grab your number before you left last night."

Warmth settled in my chest. I didn't realize how much I'd missed hearing a familiar voice until now. "Oh, no worries. Honestly, I'm surprised you still even have this number."

"I didn't." He chuckled on the other side of the line. "I asked my dad if he still had your grandmother's number."

Had he gone out of his way to check on me?

That feeling hit strangely soft in my chest. Cody must've really matured over the years because the version I knew was still the menace who put frogs in my boots and tousled my hair until it resembled a bird sanctuary.

But then again, after my accident, Cody visited me almost every day in the hospital. He sat with me even when I wasn't fully conscious. He apologized for things I don't even remember what for, since I was high on drugs most of the time. And ever since then, he'd treated me differently.

"I was actually calling because I forgot to give you back your ID and insurance card."

"*Oh!*" I grabbed my wallet off the counter to check. "So no background check? Disappointing. I thought you would be thorough."

"Oh, who said I hadn't done that already? Had to make sure little Gibson wasn't wreaking havoc in Denver."

There was the Cody I knew, the one who made everything feel normal for five seconds. God, I missed that more than I realized. The tension in my body loosened enough that I found myself twirling the phone cord around my fingers, leaning against the wall with a stupid little smile I couldn't fight off.

"Actually, since technically you can't drive without them, I figured I'd drop them off. If that's okay."

"Only if you bring a blue slushy and scratch-off from Sinclair's," I dared, fully aware that he was permanently banned after breaking the slushy machine and getting caught stealing scratch-offs behind the counter.

Fred never pressed charges, but he promised he would if Cody showed his face there again.

"You're never going to let me live that down, are you?"

"Never," I said, grinning into the phone.

"I get off at six. Gotta grab a few things on the way, so I should be there around seven, if that works?"

"Yeah, that does," I said, looking at the clock on the wall. "I'll be around."

"Alright. I'll see you then."

"Looking forward to my slushy."

Before I could hang up, I heard Cody's voice. "I almost forgot! Happy Birthday, Eleni."

How did he—

"You cheated and looked at my ID, didn't you?" I accused.

All I could hear was laughter before he hung up.

Typical Cody. Maybe he hadn't fully grown up after all.

A small smile escaped me, but as I peered out the kitchen window, it disappeared.

Today was the day Gram wanted me home. Today I could've woken up to stuffed pancakes, lemon bars cooling on the counter, her soft humming drifting through the cabin. She would have had the whole day planned—full of warmth, full of her.

But instead, I woke up to the echo of her absence. No pancakes. No humming. Just silence. And I'd decided pretending the day didn't exist was easier than facing that space she used to fill.

But with Cody coming over, maybe my birthday wouldn't be such a black hole after all. Perhaps he was exactly the distraction I needed before the quicksand swallowed me again. I squeezed my eyes shut, shoved the mess of emotions back into their box.

"Thanks, Cody."

I walked back into Gram's room, stood there for a minute trying to remember why I came back in, then saw the bed.

Right.

I crouched and peered under the bedframe, squinting into the dim space where something dark caught my eye. I reached for it, expecting some lost trinket Gram had dropped and forgotten, but the moment my fingers brushed it, I realized it was fixed to the floor.

Weird.

Grunting, I shoved the bed frame aside, the legs scraping across the wooden boards, until the shape came fully into view—a small, dark handle built right into the floorboards.

What the—

Never in my twenty-fou—wait. I was twenty-five now.

In my twenty-five years, I had never realized that something was there. I took pride in being good at discovering things. I was sure I had crawled under her bed multiple times when hiding or playing.

I tugged at the small iron ring on the floor. The hinges creaked as it opened, revealing an assortment of stuff, including bundles of cash.

Is this where Gram hid her money?

It didn't make sense. If she had all this money, why did she hide it here? She could have easily paid everything off with it, including the unpaid bills.

Beneath the pile of cash, soft green fabric caught my eye. Carefully, I moved the money aside and lifted the material. It was soft and colored in lush green and natural shades that mimicked the forest.

What kind of dress was this?

The thought tugged at me. She was always connected to nature, the kind of person who found beauty and meaning in simplicity. Yet, she always carried herself with quiet regalness. I could picture her in this dress, standing barefoot in the middle of a meadow, all the flowers in full bloom, dancing under an open sky. It felt like something she would have chosen, true to her spirit and love for nature.

As I peeked deeper into the hidden compartment, my fingers brushed against something solid.

"Now what do we have here?"

I ran my fingers over a mysterious box with a lock. I glanced around the hidden floorboard, hoping for a key, but nothing caught my eye. "I'm going to get you open, one way or another."

The bow could wait in Gram's room for now. Now, my sole focus was to discover this hidden treasure beneath Gram's bed.

After rummaging through the barn's drawers, I found an old pair of cutting pliers. "These will suffice." I clamped them around the lock and squeezed. Nothing. Not even a wiggle.

"Stubborn little lock, aren't you?"

I reset my grip and leaned my whole weight into it, my scabbed-over hands throbbing as metal bit into metal. Still no give. Not even a polite crack.

"Okay, you little turd," I hissed under my breath. "I'm putting on my big-girl panties, and you're going to open, one way or another."

The box was left on the counter as I hurried to the front door, my eyes fixed on the barn in the distance. Once inside, I went to the tack room. A thin layer of dust and cobwebs covered everything, except for a few well-used tools and the little table where we used to sit and fix things. I slid open a drawer, grabbed a pair of bolt cutters, and headed back toward the cabin. But as I turned, I froze. Eddie's body was halfway out of his stall, his head held high, ears pointing forward and alert, fixed on the top of the hill. Something was up there, fussing through the grass near the mound of rocks I'd arranged.

"What are you looking at, old man?" I squinted into the sunlight, shading my eyes with my hand. At first, I thought it was the wind causing shadows to shift, but then I saw a figure with four legs and pointed ears moving behind the rocks.

"*Shit!*"

Panic propelled me toward the rocks, my boots crunching on the muddy ground. My heart hammered against my ribs as a dozen frantic thoughts scrambled through me, including the possibility of a coyote or a fox, both opportunistic scavengers. I thought I had dug deep enough; I had even taken precautions, like researching the recommended depth for a grave. Maybe, in my inebriated state, I misjudged the depth.

"Hey!" I shouted. "Get away from there!"

I hurled the bolt cutters towards the mongrel. "Leave her alone, you damn turd bucket!"

The bolt cutters hit below the target, giving it a startled yowl—wait. A *yowl*? Wild animals don't make that noise.

I stopped, catching my breath, as the figure straightened and stepped into the sunlight. My fear morphed into disbelief. "Mooch?"

The cat regarded me with her mismatched eyes, her expression the epitome of feline indifference. She flicked her short tail once, unimpressed by my outburst.

"Oh, for crying out loud," I yelled, bending over to brace myself. "You scared the shit out of me, you little terror!"

Mooch stared at me for a second longer, then started pawing at the rocks again.

"Mooch, stop it. What are you doing?"

I scooped her up and held her close until her meowing quieted. "She's gone, Mooch. You can't get to her. Why are you acting like this?"

Her mismatched eyes met mine with a worrying stillness. I sighed, shaking my head. Cats can't understand you. Or maybe they can; they just want you to think they are incapable of understanding.

She meowed again, a soft sound of a half apology, half demand for attention. A reluctant smile tugged at the corner of my mouth. I knelt and gently set her down. The soil was undisturbed, but I added a few more rocks around the edges, just in case. Mooch sat nearby, watching me the entire time. Her head tilted in that knowing, judgmental way only cats could manage, as if she were critiquing my work.

As the breeze picked up, it carried with it a faint trace of floral sweetness. The same sweetness that smelled like Gram.

I inhaled, lifting my gaze toward the mountain. Were her favorite flowers blooming in the meadow?

It was tradition to hike up to the place she called *The Heart of the Mountain.* It was our sacred little ritual. And every birthday, she'd make me climb it with her, no matter how much I complained.

Thinking about it made my stomach queasy. The last time we took that journey, I didn't come back the same. I could still feel my back tearing open. The horrible cold air touching bone. The helplessness that tightened my throat until I couldn't breathe.

That was the day my life changed. That was the day the mountain stopped being home and became a monster. And I never set foot up there again.

Eleni, you cannot let fear win. It will take root in your mind until you let it consume you. Rise to it. Face it. And you will see there is nothing to fear.

She spoke of wisdom, but at that time it felt hollow. Like words meant for someone braver, someone stronger, someone who wasn't me.

But standing here now, feeling the shakiness in my bones from how afraid I was.

I would face it head-on. And this time, fear can kiss my ass. I'm going up that mountain.

I'm picking Gram's favorite wildflowers, and I'm putting them on her grave.

I peered down at Mooch. "I'm doing it. I'm going to conquer this damn mountain today." She stared up at me for a moment, judging as always, "But first, that mystery box."

Eddie met me at the edge of the lower pasture, ambling toward the fence from the open stall door on the side of the barn. His private enclosure lay behind it, separate from the upper pasture that stretched up toward the hill with Gram's grave. His ears perked as he approached, his nose reaching over the wooden fence, sniffling my pockets.

"Hey, old man," I said, holding my palms up. "Sorry, no treats this morning."

Eddie didn't seem to mind, following me back down to the barn. That was one thing I loved about him—his puppy-like devotion. He followed me wherever he could and leaned into every pet with a contented sigh. He was a love bug through and through. I couldn't help but smile as I remembered when Gram would lie with him in the pasture, treating him like a fifteen-hundred-pound lapdog. You only had to be careful when he stood up since his hooves could pack a punch if you weren't paying attention.

I stepped back into the cabin and got to work on the lock. After a few minutes of finagling, the lock finally broke free.

Inside was a carefully arranged collection of jewels and coins. Each piece was unlike anything I'd ever seen. I brushed my fingers over the contents in the box, my mouth parting in wonder.

"Dang, Gram. Since when were you into *this* kind of jewelry?"

Delicate bracelets with strange etched symbols I didn't recognize. Thick, hand-worn rings that looked as though they belonged to an ancient bloodline. Everything appeared old, loved, and lived-in, like they carried stories far larger than this tiny cabin could ever hold.

Why didn't she ever show me any of this? Was any of this my mother's? Is that why she hid it?

I didn't know, and that's what stung.

And now, all I had were these beautiful pieces and a thousand unanswered questions.

One gemstone was bigger than the others, a deep sapphire blue with tiny specks of gold inside. It had no chain or setting—just the raw gem itself—heavy in my hand and oddly warm.

As my hands reached the bottom of the box, my eyes fell on a unique necklace. At its center was a nickel-sized emerald-colored stone. Its uneven surface made the stone appear as if it had been carved from a rock. It would have looked new if it weren't for a jagged crack splitting across its vibrant green surface. The fracture didn't diminish its beauty; if anything, it deepened it, giving it a haunting, vintage elegance. Surrounding the gemstone was an intricate frame resembling roots that had grown and twisted together with natural, delicate grace. Whoever made this did so with great care.

At first, I thought someone had created the frame from another type of stone. But as I turned it over, the smoothness and striations weren't stone at all.

Is this bone?

It shone softly as it wrapped around the cracked gem, as if protecting something sacred, even in its state of disrepair.

What is the story behind this necklace?

The emerald's deep green hue twinkled with an otherworldly iridescence, shifting like oil on water—flecks of gold, teal, and violet reflecting beneath the surface, never holding the same color twice.

My hands then moved to the chain. The clasp was bent open, something that could be easily fixed with some pliers, which meant going back to the barn.

I grabbed the necklace and headed to my room, rummaging through my dresser until I found an old T-shirt and a pair of worn-out jeans. On the edge of my dresser rested my tomahawk, its dark steel blades catching the light filtering through the window.

Gram once told me it was an old tomahawk given to her when she first moved onto the ranch. She said it came from the previous owner as a gift. The original feathers had long since disappeared, but the worn leather and hand-strung beads still clung to it, weathered but strong—like they had stories of their own to tell.

I stepped out onto the porch with the tomahawk strapped to my belt. The hike up the meadow would take a few hours, give or take, depending on whether I even remembered the path, but that still left me enough time to get back, wash the dirt off, and try to look somewhat human before Cody showed up.

A smile formed at the thought of Cody. But the smile quickly vanished when I heard tires crunching up the driveway.

A sleek car tore through the dirt, kicking up rocks. They scattered across the driveway, pinging off fence posts and crunching under the tires. It was some sort of sports car. I didn't know much about cars, but I knew that anyone driving one of those out here had money. It screeched to a stop, cutting off my path to the barn.

Yeah, they definitely weren't from around here based on his park job.

A man stepped out of the driver's side, shutting the door with a bit too much flair. He wore a perfectly clean western hat that looked more like a costume than practical wear and a sharp navy-blue suit that seemed untouched by dirt. Hanging around his neck was a bolo tie with a yellow gemstone attached. He reminded me of a peacock, deliberately flaunting his riches in my face. Immediately, I got bad vibes.

"Can I help you?"

He was older, possibly in his mid to late forties, with short-cropped hair and piercing eyes. They were cold and calculating. The kind that cut instead of comforted.

"Good day," he said, smiling like a man used to closing deals. "I believe you're Mrs. Gibson?"

"Mrs. Gibson was my grandmother. I'm her granddaughter."

"Oh. My apologies." It sounded rehearsed and fake as hell. From what Cody told me, I had a feeling I already knew who this peacock was.

He walked toward me, his cologne overpowering my senses as he extended a hand. "My name is Tom Strator."

Called it. I didn't take his hand.

I stared him down, giving him the best resting bitch face only a nurse who's worked too many shifts in a row can achieve.

"Whatever you're selling, *Tim*, I'm not buying. So do us both a favor and get off my property." His expression shifted. Just a trace, but it was there.

Someone doesn't like rejection.

"It's Tom," he said, with that salesman smile barely holding. "If you hear me out, I'm only here to offer you a generous opportunity."

Opportunity, my ass.

"I understand your grandmother was in some financial difficulty, and I'm here to help solve all of that."

He said it like they'd met before. Did they? Was there a connection between the money Gram was hiding and him?

"Mr. Strator," I warned, my fingers unbuckling the strap over my tomahawk. "Not interested. Now, please get off my property before I call the police."

His hands went up in mock surrender and took a slow step back. "My apologies, Miss Gibson. I'm only here to offer some help." He reached into his pocket, and I tensed, fingers tightening around the tomahawk. But all he pulled out was a business card.

He crouched, set the card on the ground, and placed a rock on top. "If you change your mind," he said, straightening up, "give my office a call."

I didn't say a word. I kept my hand on my tomahawk until he climbed back into that shiny, overpriced car and finally backed down the driveway.

My shoulders sagged. "Glad I didn't have to hack him into little pieces."

I stepped over to where he had laid his card, kicked the rock away, and stomped on it with my boots.

Eddie stood outside his stall facing me. "You're not coming, old man." He snorted, tossing his head like he'd already decided for both of us.

"Fine," I muttered. "But if you slow me down, no treats for a week."

He gave another snort.

Back in the barn, I dug out the necklace from my pocket and grabbed a pair of pliers from the workbench. The chain had bent out of shape, but it didn't take much to ease it back into place. Once it looked right, I slipped it over my head.

The moment it touched my skin, a jolt of static electricity shot through me.

"What the hell was that?"

Goosebumps ran over my skin, raising the hairs on my arms. I remained still, waiting to see if that strange feeling would happen again. Maybe my touching something caused that shock. But there was nothing. Pushing that bizarre feeling aside, I turned, grabbed Eddie's tack, and headed up the mountain.

5

SILENT GOODBYE

Holy mother of fit gods, I was severely out of shape.

My lungs burned. Each breath came in wheezes, and my legs were shaking like Jello.

Bent over and panting, I struggled to keep up with Eddie. This senior mustang was effortlessly climbing, and I felt humiliated as he glanced back every few steps, silently questioning my stamina. Encouraging him to continue, I waved him on. The trail was easy to follow, with familiar etchings that guided us along. At twenty-three, Eddie's energy surpassed mine. I scoffed as he basked in his lead.

"If I die here on this mountain, Eddie," I yelled up to him, "at least carry me back down to Gram's grave. I would very much not like to be eaten up here." Even though I was trying to be playful, it was becoming harder to hide my anxiety. The rustling in the brush behind us kept pulling my attention. Rabbits and squirrels darted out every so often, their slight forms harmless, yet something else bothered me. I had an uncomfortable feeling that we were being followed.

But Eddie remained unfazed. His ears twitched, more focused on swatting away flies than any lurking threat. He was my barometer for danger, his instincts better than mine could ever be. If he weren't worried, I wouldn't be.

Eddie finally came to a stop and shifted his ears forward. I followed his gaze and saw the meadow spread out before us, bathed in the warm hues of the setting sun. I stared at it in bliss. It was more breathtaking than I remembered. The wildflowers swayed in the breeze, their colors a dazzling mosaic of purples, yellows, and whites. I hinted at a smile. "I finally made it, Gram. Hope you're proud."

I took my shears and leather bag from the saddle and strolled into the meadow, my fingers gliding over the soft petals. Each flower seemed like a small gift—each petal evoking cherished memories of Gram as I inhaled their scents. I arranged lupine, her favorite, which was plentiful in the bouquet, for my bag.

Eddie stood in a patch of sunlight, his eyes half-closed as he dozed.

Impulsively, I threw the bag onto his back, startling him and prompting a moment of frantic calming. "Whoa, boy!" I raised my hand out, trying to soothe him. "It's okay. It's me." My hand ran along his neck, my voice soft and apologetic. It wasn't like him to spook so easily. His ears—usually attuned to even the slightest sound—should've picked me up long before I got close. Maybe his age was catching up to him.

As we made our way back down the mountain, the hairs prickled the back of my neck. The shadows grew longer, and the sun was dipping below the peaks faster than I'd anticipated. A subtle, unexpected snap echoed through the woods, like a twig breaking underfoot. It stirred the underbrush, cutting through the usual forest sounds. That feeling—that creeping sensation of being watched—grew more evident. Eddie seemed to sense it too. His ears snapped forward as he lifted his head alertly, muscles tensing beneath his coat.

"What is it, Eddie?" My breaths grew shallower as panic edged closer.

And then came a low growl.

Its guttural sound left me frozen. Before I could react, a flash of tawny fur exploded from the brush. The cougar struck, landing on Eddie's back with such force that it knocked me to the ground. Eddie released a high-pitched whinny—a raw and primal sound that boomed through the forest. He bucked and kicked, his powerful legs flailing to get the cougar off. A gush of blood came out from where the cougar's claws dug into his flesh, its teeth sinking into his back.

"Eddie!" I scrambled to my feet as my hands flew to the tomahawk at my belt, fumbling at first, then gripping it with a white-knuckled desperation. My eyes darted to Eddie; his body jumped and twisted, each motion an attempt to throw the cougar off. The cougar snarled, its eyes blazing and its stare locked on its prey. I shouted desperately, but neither seemed to hear me. It was a violent, uncontrolled, vicious onslaught.

"Get off him!" My voice tore through my throat. With trembling hands, I hurled the tomahawk, my body moving with the momentum. Every ounce of strength I had left went into the throw. The motion felt familiar, muscle memory kicking in despite the years that had passed.

It cut through the air with deadly speed, the whistle of its blade lost in Eddie's cry. The weapon struck the cougar's shoulder with a sickening thunk, burying itself deep into the muscle and knocking the predator off Eddie's back. The beast let out a furious roar, its body jerking as it staggered backward, trying to shake the embedded axe until it dislodged from its shoulder. Blood oozed from the wound, dark and glistening as it soaked its fur and dripped onto the ground.

The cougar wavered, muscles trembling, as it took several steps backward. Hope surged in my chest, wishing it would retreat, but that hope evaporated as fast as it came. The cougar's growl grew louder, and its golden eyes locked onto me. A cold, sinking fear told me I had become its new prey.

It lunged, its muscles coiling, but Eddie blocked the cougar before it could strike. With all his strength, he reared up, his hooves rising to the sky before crashing down. His head stretched forward, ears pinned flat back, and he clamped down on the cougar's tail with his teeth bared in a furious attack. He was dragging it away from me, using every ounce of his weight to force the predator into submission.

Eddie's front hooves slammed down, each blow aiming to crush. The cougar cried out, its body recoiling to counterattack, jaws snapping onto his muzzle. Blood sprayed as sharp teeth dug into his flesh, but Eddie didn't let go. With a mighty lift, he heaved himself upward, then slammed the clinging cougar back into the dirt with staggering force.

My hands went to my mouth as I watched in horror what was happening. I had never seen him act this aggressively before. This protective.

Eddie reared once more, the creature's tail still clenched in his teeth, and with a surge of momentum, he came crashing down again. This time, the beast faltered. Its claws slowed, raking at the ground, attempting to escape.

Relentless stubbornness and pure determination drove Eddie onward. His body trembled, his strength fading with every motion, but despite that, he didn't stop. The cougar's body finally went still, but Eddie's strikes didn't waver, as if his instincts still hadn't registered that the creature was dead.

"Easy, boy," I said, reaching for his neck to calm his nerves and mine. I fought to keep the lump in my throat down as I assessed his wounds. They were bad. Real bad.

"We need to get you home, okay?"

Eddie didn't protest as I took the lead rope after grabbing my tomahawk, his movements slow and labored, his once-strong body teetering with each step. His exhaustion emitted through the rope; his uneven steps grew worse by the minute. If I didn't get to the barn soon, he might not make it.

"You'll be okay," I whispered, my words trembling as they left my lips. "Just a little further. There's a warm stall waiting for you, with all the carrots and apples you could ever want."

Shame on me for not being more prepared. At the very least, I should have brought a first aid kit. I should have brought my cell phone, even if there was poor service up here.

I looked down at the gaping holes in Eddie's face.

They were worse up close. One of the holes was so deep that it punctured through his sinus, causing blood to shoot out every time he took a breath.

I needed to figure out what I would do once I got to the barn. The nearest vet was over an hour away, which meant I would be on my own for the next few hours. Gram should still have a whole drawer packed with medical supplies. If I could clean the wounds and stop the bleeding, he would make it. He had to.

I placed my hand on his neck, stroking him gently. "I'm not going to lose you, old man. You are too stubborn to quit on me now."

⋅⋅◆⋅⋅

The soft glow of the front porch light flickered like a small beacon, illuminating the darkening sky. The last streaks of sunlight had faded, making the trail harder to see.

"We're almost there, Eddie."

Each step felt like an agonizing struggle. His limp grew heavier and more uneven, and the sound of his hooves dragging through the dirt twisted my stomach. I clenched the lead rope, matching his pace, desperate to keep him moving.

We finally reached the clearing; the barn's shape grew more apparent against the fading light, but Eddie's steps faltered.

"Come on, old man. I know you can make it." His head was dropping lower—too low—and his limp worsened. His ragged breaths strained, and I could hear the effort in each one as he battled each inhale.

"Only a few more steps." My voice cracked as I spoke, struggling to maintain my composure.

As we reached the pasture, Eddie's steps shifted to the left, away from the barn. My hand tugged on the rope, pressing my shoulder against him, trying to direct him to the barn, but he wasn't budging. His battered body, now covered in open wounds and blood, seeped into my clothes and hands.

"Eddie, stop! The barn is not this way!" I pleaded, using all my strength to push him towards the barn. He still wouldn't budge, his injured frame stubborn against my efforts. My frustration grew as I tried to figure out why he was going in this direction until he finally came to a stop.

I stepped back, confused, trying to make sense of what was happening. His head hung so low now that it brushed the ground, his nostrils flaring as he sniffed the soil—the soil I had dug up and replaced with my bare hands not so long ago. My heart dropped as I realized where we were. He had brought us to Gram's grave. The rocks I'd placed were now stained with his blood, pooling alongside the dried remnants of my own.

I leaned against him, trying to support his weight, my arms wrapping tightly around his neck despite the blood coating him. Tears streamed down my cheeks as I buried my face in his sweat-matted fur. "Eddie," my voice broke. "Why?"

I couldn't believe this damn mustang, even in his final moments, had chosen to be near Gram.

Then, as if he had finished fighting, Eddie's legs buckled beneath him, and he collapsed to the ground, his body folding with a heaviness and exhaustion.

"No, no, no, no!" I sobbed. "Not you! Please, not you too. I can't lose you, I can't!"

I knew when he turned against that cougar and sank his teeth into its tail, he wouldn't walk away unscathed. Yet Eddie fought. He chose to defend and protect me.

I had always envied the bond between Gram and Eddie. Gram had said he could be mine, but deep down, he was hers. They shared a connection I could never touch, a quiet understanding that bound them together. As much as she insisted he was mine, I knew better. He was hers, heart and soul. And because I loved her, I never wanted to take that away.

His breathing grew shallow, the wheezing sounds becoming more pronounced with each breath. In this moment, I knew I was going to lose him, too. His heavy eyes, filled with something that felt like peace and sorrow, blinked at me one last time.

I was lying there next to him, hugging him tighter, my fingers gripping his neck as if that alone could hold him together. "Please don't leave me."

With one final exhale, Eddie's chest fell still.

Grief hit me like quicksand, pulling me down before I could escape. Anger, frustration, and that hollow, hungry emptiness tore through my chest and ripped open all those boxes I had carefully locked away. All-consuming as I screamed into the darkness. My fingers curled into the soil, dirt mixing with Eddie's blood on my hands.

I lost him. It was all my fault. All because I wanted to pick flowers and stop being a coward.

My blurry vision drifted to the saddlebags, where a small bundle of lupine and other flowers peeked out, disheveled. The sight of them sent a pang through me. They were the reason we had gone up the mountain in the first place.

My bloodstained hands reached out, opening the flap. The flowers were crushed, their delicate stems broken and beyond repair. I stared down at them. I felt defeated in every way someone can feel.

In the distance, a sound reverberated through the haze, but I couldn't tear my eyes from the crushed lupine.

"Eleni!"

It reached me like a voice underwater, warped and far away, fighting to break through the drowning quiet in my head.

"Eleni!"

I turned toward the sound. In front of the cabin, the bright headlights of a sheriff's vehicle lit up the clearing.

Cody.

Between the pain and the panic, I'd lost track of time. Of everything. Cody hadn't, though. But even as relief wavered through the pain, something shifted.

An intense energy made the hair on my arms stand on end. The earth trembled beneath my feet. The vibrations began faintly, almost unnoticeable, but escalated into a violent quake. A deafening roar drowned out the pounding of my heart. My breath caught as I turned to see the surrounding rocks levitate.

What's going on?

A pair of eyes glowed in the distance, watching me from the shadows near Gram's grave. They glinted unnaturally, reflecting the moonlight like twin embers, filled with all the colors around me. My pulse quickened as I stared at the glowing eyes, as if I were in a trance.

"Eleni, I'm coming!"

I turned toward the sound of my name again. Cody was sprinting up the hill, closing the distance between us and whatever phenomenon was happening around me.

Before I could process any of it, the soil ignited into a burst of light. So bright that I had to shield my eyes. It scintillated with colors: reds, blues, purples, and yellows, each shade bleeding into the next like liquid fire. I felt a static energy surge through me, a force unlike anything I'd ever experienced. It was a terrifying, untamed chaos.

"Cody! What is happening?" I tried to yell his name, but it was lost in the loud rushing noise of the light.

My hands fell into the blood-soaked soil, frantically searching for anything to hold onto, but as they touched, I felt something pull me deeper, wrapping around me in a powerful embrace. The colors became brighter and more vivid until the world disappeared in a blinding display of light.

And then, I was falling.

6

ESCAPE

I twisted as my limbs flailed wildly, searching for anything to grab onto.

But there was nothing.

No solid ground, no handhold. Just a swirling vortex of bright, shifting colors around me, like ribbons of light pulling me deeper into the abyss. The wind howled in my ears as I was falling, and my insides churned.

Was this what it felt like when you get stuck in that in-between place of life and death? But if I was, then why was I panicking? Why could I still feel the pull of gravity as I fell?

I closed my eyes and tried to focus on my breathing. There was no escaping this. I was either sliding toward the gates of Hell or some other afterlife. I braced for the inevitable impact, my body tensing against the thought of splintering pain.

Then I hit something.

The collision knocked the wind out of me as the world kept spinning along with my limbs, over and over, tangled with whatever I had landed on. I only realized I had stopped when stabbing pain shot through my ribs, as if someone had driven a spike through my side. My ears throbbed, each pulse a drumbeat of agony, and I gasped for air, desperate to fill my lungs.

Did I die? Was this it? Should death hurt this much?

As my breathing gradually stabilized, I felt a wave of relief, realizing I wasn't a crumpled heap on jagged rocks. I wasn't a smear of blood and broken bones. I was wholly and actually alive.

What on Earth just happened?

Daring to move, I shifted my body and quickly realized there was something solid underneath me, moving between my legs.

It wasn't grass that cushioned my fall—it was *someone*.

"Cody?" I croaked, still trying to piece everything back together. The world around me was dark, cloaked in shadows, with only the pale moonlight breaking through the night. "Are you alright?" But as my eyes focused, I noticed the person's features were completely different.

Long black hair fell across his face, partially obscuring the rough edges of his features. His jaw was shadowed with stubble, and his nose appeared broken, with fresh blood trickling down from the side. Between strands of hair, a pair of bright, golden eyes shone with life.

This wasn't Cody.

Not even close.

"I'm so sorry!" My heart started racing as my brain continued buffering on the situation.

The man appeared equally as stunned, as if neither of us had expected such an aggressively intimate collision, with me straddling him.

His expression seemed to mirror mine: wide-eyed, caught off guard, and very much, *what the fuck just happened?*

But then his expression quickly darkened. In a split second, his hands lunged forward, grabbing my shoulders with an intensity that sparked a wave of fear. In one swift motion, he slammed me onto my back, like a heavyweight tossing a featherweight across the ring. The air left my lungs all over again.

I needed to escape, but how? He was much bigger and stronger. Then, suddenly recalling why I took all those self-defense classes, I understood it was for this moment. I planted my foot and shifted my hips, aiming to create space.

"Get *off* of me!"

He leaned his weight to counter my movement.

Dammit.

My hands desperately tried to push his body away from mine until a cold pressure touched the hollow of my throat. The sensation was sharp and metallic, sending a chill through the humid air that clung to my skin.

"W—what the hell is wrong with you?"

"Who are you?" he growled. I could hear he had an accent; I would've been more curious about where, but I was more concerned about my own life. He hovered closely as blood trickled from his nose, landing on the side of my cheek.

The stranger's dark hair fell like a curtain around his sharp features, partially obscuring his face. Yet the pale moonlight illuminated enough to see the right side of it. Jagged scars ran down from his scalp, past his jawline. Those didn't look like your typical scars because they also bore the unmistakable texture of burn marks, the kind that was traumatic and violent. His golden eyes glowed in the night, fixed on me with an unnatural intensity.

He didn't look angry; he looked dangerous.

"Answer me!" His dagger pressed further into my skin, and I felt warm liquid trickling down the side of my neck.

Is this asshole really going to kill me?

"I—I can't," I gasped. His grip on my wrists tightened, keeping me immobilized. The dagger's edge dug deeper into my skin, causing more blood to drip down my throat with each swallow. The warmth of it sent a sickening chill through me.

Yep. This asshole is going to kill me.

My body tensed as fear gripped me tighter. "I—can't—breathe," I rasped.

His grip loosened enough for me to draw a shaky breath. His anger shifted, the intensity in his eyes fading. "Who sent you?"

"No one!" I snapped, still breathless. "I just fell out of the freaking sky and crash-landed on you—which, by the way, was *not* on purpose."

"Do you think me a fool, girl?"

"Maybe," I croaked. My vision blurred, and my chest heaved under the weight of his arm. "I don't believe you." He leaned in closer, his scarred face becoming more visible from this distance. "Then tell me, *who* sent you?"

"No one." I spat back, gritting my teeth. I needed to get free.

My survival instincts took over, cutting through the fog of fear clouding my thoughts. His weight pinned down my upper body, but with his knees braced on either side of mine, he left a vulnerable opening. I shifted my hips and drove my knee upward, aiming straight for his groin with every ounce of force I had left.

A choked sound escaped him as his body jerked, and he released my wrists. His dagger moved away from my throat, and he rolled off me, clutching at the spot where I'd hit him.

My lungs burned as I took a breath and scrambled to my feet, adrenaline propelling me forward.

I briefly scanned the area, hoping Cody was nearby and that there was a familiar face I could run to, but all I found was the stranger, still clutching his man parts where my knee had rammed him.

I needed to put as much distance as I could between myself and this person. I sprinted across the landscape, noticing the trees were completely different. Their leaves were massive, easily as big as my torso, with edges curling into delicate spirals.

Is this real?

Did I hit my head hard enough that I'm seeing things now?

The ground beneath me was soft and lush, and the atmosphere was filled with the fresh aroma of rain-soaked soil. It smelled alive and rich with so many unfamiliar scents.

It also felt off. Foreign. Almost like walking into someone else's dream where the rules were different, and reality bent at the edges. This whole place hummed with unusual energy, sending goosebumps up my arms.

There were no pine trees or jagged mountain peaks. The air wasn't as thin as it was in Wyoming and Denver at high altitude; it was heavy with humidity and warm against my skin.

Perhaps Cody had fallen somewhere else and was still unconscious, or he was sprawled on top of one of those peculiar trees.

But there was only silence, broken up by the relentless buzzing of insects.

There was an odd lightness in my steps, like gravity had less of a hold on me. My body moved effortlessly, each step propelling me farther and faster than I believed I could go.

Why wasn't I tired yet?

Or more importantly, where the hell was I that would make me feel this way? Did that blinding light do something to me?

I took in my surroundings, trying to spot anything familiar, like roads, houses, or any sign that I wasn't completely lost or losing my mind. But in the darkness, with only the moonlight to guide me, I couldn't see a damn thing.

Movement on the far side of a clearing halted my steps. A group of people stepped out of the shadows, and relief flooded through me.

Maybe they could help.

But hearing their voices and peering at what little I could see, I realized they were all men.

Something in my gut told me this was wrong. Their clothing didn't look normal at all. Was that armor? I squinted at the puzzling attachments hanging at their sides.

Wait.

Were those . . . *swords?*

Who *were* these guys? Renaissance Fair rejects? Dungeons & Dragons cosplayers?

I shook my head, thinking the armor was overkill, until another figure stepped out of the trees. Taller than the rest, with long black hair.

It was *him.*

The same guy I'd nailed in the nuts with my knee. And he was with them.

This is not good.

I stopped in the middle of the clearing, panic overtaking me as I searched for a hiding spot until I saw a tall thicket to my left. I hurried over, crouching down among the underbrush. My heart raced as I peeked through a narrow opening in the thicket.

There were five of them, each clad in the same dark uniform. As they closed the distance, I caught glimpses of intricate designs etched into their chest plates, though they were still too far away to make out clearly.

One of the men caught my attention when he let out a deep, booming laugh. He had darker skin and wild, curly black hair that framed his face. He held his sword, swinging it in a slow practice motion.

In any other situation, I would've assumed I'd stumbled onto a movie set or crashed a session full of sword-wielding nerds living out their best fantasy lives. But these guys?

No. They were *fit*, like *soldier-fit*. Their swords screamed *real*. And their armor? Definitely not from a Halloween store.

These weren't dudes I could stroll up to and say, "Hey, I'm super lost. Any chance you can point me toward the nearest police station?"

Nope.

My body lowered closer to the ground as I tracked their approach. I searched for the one I'd collided with, but he had vanished.

Odd.

I could've sworn he was there.

I leaned through the brush to get a better view, but my necklace caught on a low branch. I twisted, my fingers fumbling as I tried to free it. Suddenly, a surge of electricity tore through me, making me lose my balance as a branch broke under my weight.

One of the men halted and turned in my direction.

Fuck.

I sprang to my feet and bolted across the clearing, adrenaline kicking in. Shouts erupted behind me, their words drowned out by the rush in my ears. Escape was the only thought driving me forward, so focused that I didn't notice the pressure tightening around my waist.

One moment, I was running, and the next, I was abruptly pulled back and slammed onto the ground. I tried to suck in a breath and scramble up, but something was holding me down.

I looked at my body and stifled a scream. Darkness slid around me like living serpents, its touch unnervingly cold and pulsing with a mysterious energy. It carried a metallic scent, reminiscent of cold iron, mingling with damp earth. The darkness squeezed tighter, pressing against me as if testing my strength and resistance. A prickling sensation crawled along my skin where they wrapped around me—neither solid nor air, but something in between.

I was struggling against something intangible that I couldn't grab, attack, or comprehend. My body jerked in frantic attempts to escape, but stilled when I realized the men I'd been fleeing from surrounded me, swords pointed at my throat.

Fan-fucking-tastic.

7

GOLDEN CUFFS

The soldiers closed in, surrounding me, leaving no chance at escape. Their swords pointed directly at me, catching the moonlight's reflection. Every step they took warned me *not to move*, like twitching could get me killed.

Was this really how I was going to die?

By D&D cosplay rejects with real swords? After the day I was having? Absolutely not. I refused to give them the satisfaction.

I locked eyes with the closest one. If I was going down, I wasn't going down without a fight.

But his focus suddenly shifted over my shoulder.

I turned to where their attention had moved. The soft moonlight barely illuminated him, yet I instantly recognized those striking eyes.

"Velorn," one of the soldiers said as he lowered his sword.

Velorn? Who would name their child that?

Out of the corner of my eye, I noticed the shadows moving around him. But unlike the ones restraining me, they didn't attack. They coiled fluidly around his hands, responding to his movements like an extension of his will.

Internally, I was *losing it.*

The inky tendrils writhed around me, and my brain couldn't settle on what the hell they were supposed to be. Were they snakes? Eels? Shadowed spaghetti? They shifted softly at the edges, but their grip was terrifyingly strong.

This had to be a nightmare.

But in nightmares, you don't feel pain.

There had to be a logical explanation. Maybe it was military tech. Advanced gear. Prototype nanobots or something. Some secret experiment I accidentally crashed. I mean, that made way more sense than *shadow tentacles obeying some moody stranger with a resting bitch face.*

Velorn stepped closer. Close enough that I could smell musk, smoke, and blood. That metallic tang idled between us, most likely from his busted nose.

Wait a minute.

I squinted, trying to make sense of what I was seeing.

His nose wasn't crooked or bleeding. There was no swelling, no bruising, no*thing*—except for a jagged, burn-looking scar slashing across the bridge.

I blinked hard, hoping that might reset whatever weird optical illusion was messing with me. I *saw* it broken, *felt* the blood from it. There was still dry blood crusted on my cheek to prove it.

What the hell?

He must have reset it into place while I was making my escape.

His presence was intense as he loomed over me. I wasn't particularly short—a pinch over five feet eight—but I felt like an ant next to him. The way he carried himself made his presence not just commanding but also overwhelming and dominating.

I wanted to run, but the ridiculous, shadowy things held my legs. Maybe for the better, since running was precisely what got people killed in horror movies.

Whoever this man was, this *Velorn*, he wasn't normal. He was something else entirely.

"Does she belong to a House?" The soldier with the wild curly hair asked.

Velorn was so close to me, which made his already ominous presence even more unsettling. His large hands reached out for mine. I reflexively tried to pull away, but he was faster.

He held my wrists tightly, inspecting them with a scrutiny that made my skin crawl. His fingers were coarse, tracing the lines of my palms before moving up my arms as if searching for something. His touch wasn't gentle, but it wasn't rough either, just purposeful.

"Do you belong to a house, little *Viri*?"

Viri?

I met his stare, and damn, those eyes.

They looked like they had seen some serious shit. The kind that wouldn't blink before ending me if he thought it was necessary. My brain scrambled, racing a hundred miles an hour, trying to come up with a rational explanation for all of this. Were they asking if I was homeless? I mean, technically, I wasn't. It was more like a cabin, but close enough.

"Yes," I finally spat out.

"Then why aren't you marked?"

I had no idea how to respond, mostly because I had no freaking clue what they were even asking about. But one thing I knew was that if I told them too much about myself, it might not end well.

The curly-haired man interrupted with a grin. "You know, the Riftbloods are getting creative these days. We should strip her down to be sure she doesn't bear the mark of a traitor."

"The fuck you will."

The words were out before I could stop them, heat flaring in my cheeks as I realized my mistake. Even though I had no idea what they were looking for, there was no way I was going to let *them* see me naked.

"We should ash her." Another soldier grinned.

"Enough," Velorn hissed. "She doesn't bear the mark of any house. Put her in with the rest of the others."

Panic crept into my veins as one of the soldiers moved forward, passing a set of golden iron cuffs to the curly-haired man.

They're handcuffing me. Seriously?

Where was Cody when I needed him? He'd put these low-life idiots in their place. But as my eyes darted around the clearing, there was no sign of him. And even though I ached for a familiar face, some part of me hoped he wasn't here. My gut told me these guys didn't play by the same rules Cody did, and that meant his life would be at risk.

Velorn turned without another word, slipping into the shadows as if our whole interaction had been nothing more than a mild inconvenience. His weird, shadowy things—which I still couldn't figure out—uncoiled around me until they too disappeared into the night. I tried to shake it off, but the feeling lingered, crawling over my skin.

The curly-haired man stepped close, narrowing the gap with a smug grin that sent a ripple of unease through me. He was about my height and lean.

The cuffs he carried were definitely not normal—not even close. The metal gleamed with peculiar etchings, the kind of thing you'd only see in a medieval dungeon.

"You are not putting those on me." I bit out, jerking back and fighting against their grip. But the soldiers were stronger. Rough hands grabbed my arms, holding me in place until the cold bite of the cuffs clicked shut around my wrists.

Suddenly, all the strength drained from my body. My limbs felt heavier, and my movements grew sluggish.

What kind of cuffs were these, and why did I feel like I had been drugged?

"I'm sure she'd clean up well." Another soldier said as he approached. He had longer brown hair and a slight limp when walking.

My fingers twitched, itching to drive them straight into his throat.

"She's a pretty thing," he muttered, fingers digging into my jaw as he forced my face up. "Shame she's not marked. Smells like rotten blood, too. A complete waste of—"

"Don't touch me!"

The moment the words left my mouth, it was a mistake.

His expression hardened as his hand struck the side of my face, causing my head to jerk to the side.

Heat flooded through my veins. Usually, I prided myself on staying calm in stressful situations, but right now, all I wanted was to beat the shit out of him.

I spat blood onto the ground at his feet. "That's all you got?"

His hand lifted again, ready to strike, when the curly-haired man interrupted. "Enough, Arkos!"

Arkos. A name I promised not to forget.

"I think you should let this one go before you end up doing something stupid." His tone was light, but his expression carried a warning.

Arkos scoffed. "Unmarked elementals should be put in their place, is all, Garron."

"No," Garron argued. "The Blood Seer will decide."

A swarm of words buzzed around me, like relentless gnats that I couldn't swat away.

Elementals.

Unmarked.

Riftblood.

Blood seer.

What the hell did all these words mean? Who were these people? And most importantly, where the hell was I?

"I doubt any House will want her," Arkos snorted, folding his arms as he leaned back with a smug expression.

That too. What did they mean by House?

"Perhaps," Garron replied, walking ahead of us. "But until the seer decides, no touching. Do you understand?"

We approached a large horse-drawn carriage with an iron cage enclosing it. Inside, at least a dozen people sat hunched on the floor. Their clothes were filthy, and some were so torn they were nearly naked. Most appeared to be young teenagers, but a few might've been around my age.

Are they human traffickers?

Panic slammed into me so hard my legs locked, rooting me to the ground. My body refused to move. No way was I getting in that.

Arkos grabbed my arm, wincing at how tight his grip was, and shoved me into the cage. "Welcome to your new home for the next few days."

I stumbled going inside, my balance faltering on the uneven floor.

"You can sit next to me," a young woman said, her voice quiet and as though she was afraid someone might overhear. She leaned against the bars, her thin frame hunched forward.

But I wasn't focused on her. I was too focused on the narrow gaps between the bars and the suffocating, tight space between bodies that left little room. I pushed the rising fear back down, swallowing hard before it could spiral into a full-blown panic attack. I couldn't afford to lose control—not here, and definitely not now.

Suddenly, I felt a pair of hands grasp mine. Startled, I looked over to see the frail young woman gazing up at me. The moonlight illuminated her dark, gaunt face, highlighting the hollows under her eyes. Her black curls, tangled and streaked with dirt, clung to her dark skin. Her shoulders shook as she spoke. "Sit here."

Her clothes were torn and filthy, hanging loosely over her petite frame. She wore the same golden cuffs around her wrists. Her eyes darted nervously, scanning the cage and the soldiers outside.

"Thank you."

I took a deep breath, trying to piece it all together—the cage, the people trapped inside, the guards, and then Velorn, with those shadowy things he controlled as if they were alive. No matter how I turned it over in my head, the only thing that made any sense was some experimental military tech. It had to be, because the alternative option was too crazy. I'd stumbled into the wrong place at the wrong time. Except . . . why the hell did they have *swords*? Wouldn't guns make more sense?

And even if they were soldiers, why was I treated like a criminal, slapped in cuffs, and shoved into a cage that horses were pulling instead of being placed in a car with people who didn't even dress remotely the same? Not even close.

None of it added up.

Since landing in this place, I'd been threatened, chased, humiliated, beaten, and imprisoned.

How was I supposed to get home from here? I didn't even know where *here* was—only that wherever I landed, it was already proving to be, without a doubt, a special kind of hell.

8

RATIONS

The smell inside the carriage was foul, carrying a pungent mix of unwashed bodies, rusted iron, and sweat. Over the years, I had grown accustomed to unpleasant, debilitating odors while working in the ER, but this was next level. A mask wouldn't even hide it. All I had was my shirt with dried blood to cover my nose.

The cage was packed tightly, with nearly a dozen of us crammed together on the rough floor. We sat shoulder to shoulder, our legs forced into confined positions, barely able to stretch.

My body rocked forward as the carriage abruptly halted, jolting us into different positions. The young woman, who had been kind to me when I was thrown in here, stumbled into me, her thin frame pressing against my shoulder. Her sweat-ridden hair spilled halfway across her face as she scrambled to right herself.

"I'm so sorry," she mumbled as she eased herself back into her cramped corner, tucking her messy curls behind her ears.

"I've got shoulders of steel." I tapped my shoulder, which earned me a hesitant smile in return. It didn't quite reach her eyes, but it was something.

When they captured me in the dead of night, everything had been a blur—darkness and fear clouding my senses, making it impossible to take in my surroundings. But now, with daylight creeping in, I could finally see everything.

The more I assessed the others, the clearer it became that our clothing was completely different. Their attire, distinctive yet simple, was made of rough, practical fabrics in subtle earth tones. The girl next to me sported a worn dress with uneven patches of fabric roughly sewn into the skirt. Nearby, a boy wore a tattered tunic and trousers, frayed at the edges as if they'd been handed down one too many times.

A few people stole glances in my direction, probably because my clothes didn't match theirs, but no one said a word. I appreciated that. I didn't know them, and they didn't know me. The less we knew about each other, the safer it felt.

I kept scrambling for explanations, any scenario that would make sense. But those colorful lights? The ones that moved like a waterfall and yanked me through the ground last night? Yeah, there was no rationalizing that.

The only conclusion that didn't make my brain short-circuit. Some evil force had abducted me. And for some reason, they'd dumped me on another continent because there was no way I was still in Wyoming.

The atmosphere felt rich, almost sweet. Colors appeared more vivid, painting the landscape in bright shades of green that flourished. Leaves as broad as my torso swayed gently in the breeze, their edges sparkling with dew from the morning moisture that hadn't dried despite the warmth. Thick roots jutted from the ground, twisting across the forest floor. The smells were intense and rich, layered with the sharp, tangy scent of unknown flowers blooming in bursts of fiery orange and red along the trail. A canopy of leaves partially shaded the sky above, but it felt warm and vibrant where the sunlight broke through.

Thankfully, this foreign place spoke the same language as me, though everyone had an accent. Not dramatically so, but enough to make me feel like I was backpacking through Europe. Part of me wondered how it was even possible that we spoke the same language, while another part spun out wild theories that the beam of light I'd fallen through had somehow rewired my brain. Either way, I understood them, which eased the stress a little.

"Okay, you sullied lot. Out!" a voice shouted. "You've got five minutes to relieve yourselves before I come in and start swinging!" The crack of a whip marked Arkos's nastiness as it lashed against the cage bars. Something I was certain he didn't have last night.

The carriage doors opened with a rusted screech, and Arkos's rough hands grabbed each prisoner, hauling them down one by one. When it was my turn, his gaze lingered too long, giving me the ick. His dark eyes narrowed as I approached, and his lips morphed into a smile that made me want to vomit right on him.

His fingers clamped around my clothes and yanked me out of the carriage. My boots hit the ground awkwardly, catching myself before face-planting into the dirt. Arkos leaned in, his breath hot and foul. "Move it, princess. Or I will drag you by your pretty little neck."

I held my tongue, though the urge to punch him was very tempting.

The soldiers herded us forward until we stumbled into a grove of oversized leaves growing straight from the soil. They looked like water lilies, but instead of floating, each one rose on a thick brown stem that reached my waist. Above them was a single pink flower, its petals rounded and shining like glass droplets. My curiosity piqued as I took in every detail, wishing I had my cell phone to capture a photo.

If I weren't shackled to this marching circus, I'd probably be on my hands and knees right now, nerding out over foreign plants.

They herded us behind the tall lilies to relieve ourselves. The plant stems clumped together but offered little privacy. It was embarrassing, but I couldn't help feeling a grim kind of gratitude, and at least it meant I didn't have to pee myself in the cage.

Back in line, a soldier pushed a heavy leather jug to the prisoner in front, each taking a sip before passing it down. I looked over the path we were on and noticed it was a heavily used dirt road, judging by the wear. Was this a main route? If so, where were the travelers, the cars, or anyone at all? Roads meant traffic, didn't they?

Yet I hadn't seen another soul since we started. My thoughts scattered when the jug was thrust against my chest. I'd almost forgotten how water felt against my lips. The liquid flowed down my throat, soothing and invigorating, much like the feeling after a long run when you finally get that first taste of water. I could have gulped down the entire jug at that moment. But as I lifted it for another sip, the soldier snatched it from my hands and shoved it toward the next prisoner.

"No hogging the water," he warned. "Unless you want to watch the rest of those behind you suffer. You should be grateful we didn't kill you, unmarked lot."

There was that word again, *unmarked*. I turned it over in my head, trying to decipher its meaning.

He jerked his chin toward the other captives. Some prisoners appeared irritated, while others showed quiet desperation as they waited. I hadn't even thought about the fact that the water was being rationed.

Idiot.

The girl from earlier sat beside me again. "This is all we get. If we are lucky, we might get scraps from whatever food they don't finish."

"Well, aren't they generous," I mumbled. Not only was I being held captive, but I also faced the risk of starving or dying of dehydration. I really needed to start planning how to get the hell out of here.

I lifted my arms, twisting the cuffs, trying to angle them off my wrists in some miracle Houdini way.

Nothing.

If I could dislocate my thumb, possibly . . . but nope. I fully accepted that I was too much of a coward to break myself like that intentionally.

Alright. Plan B.

If I couldn't escape these cuffs, perhaps I could escape by learning more about where I was and where they were taking me. Knowledge was leverage. And leverage meant maybe, just maybe, I wouldn't die here.

"I never got to thank you for helping me last night."

The young woman glanced at me before turning her eyes away. "When they captured me and threw me in here, no one helped me," she said softly. Her eyes darted toward the others, who were gathered for warmth or comfort. "None are from my village."

"How come you're the only one?"

She shook her head. "Everyone in my village was ashed."

I frowned. I had heard the soldiers say that word, too. "*Ashed?*"

"Burned." Her voice cracked on the word.

My stomach lurched at the image of people being burned alive. I'd seen plenty of deaths in the ER, but nothing like that. Nothing so intentional, so cruel. My throat tightened, and the unease in my gut grew.

What kind of place would do this to its own people? What kind of government would allow it? My skin crawled with anger. This wasn't brutal. It was barbaric.

She couldn't have been more than a few years younger than me. Yet, her hazel eyes revealed a different story. One of loss and experiences no one should ever have to witness, especially someone so young.

"What's your name?"

"Vyria," she said, lifting her chin. "Vyria Narvo."

"I'm Eleni."

That got the tiniest genuine smile out of her. "Eleni? That's an unusual name."

I couldn't help but smile back, leaning in a bit to her. "So is Vyria. But who am I to judge?"

That earned me a giggle. A few of the others glanced our way, and she quickly dipped her head.

I gently grabbed her hand. "Don't worry about them."

She nodded but didn't say more.

I hesitated, then asked the question that had been gnawing at me. Bugging me since the moment I fell into this hellhole. "Where are we?"

She gave me a puzzled look. "You mean besides being locked in a cage?"

I nodded.

"Veris."

"*Ver-is?*" It sounded unfamiliar. A place I couldn't remember learning about in geography class.

"And do people here control black liquid? Or an inky substance-like material that moves and has smoke radiating off it?"

It sounded absolutely insane, but I had no other way to describe it.

Vyria blinked at me, undoubtedly confused.

I glanced beyond the cage bars, trying to spot him, but he was nowhere to be seen. I turned back to her, gesturing with my hands above my head. "The tall, broody one—Velorn. Long black hair, golden eyes, and scars down his face? He had smoke all around him."

That caught her attention as her eyes widened in alarm. "Shhh," she hissed, glancing around nervously. "Don't mention the *Tracker*. He might kill you for saying his name."

Tracker?

My eyebrow arched, skepticism fully engaged, but before I could press her with more questions, she raised a finger to my lips. Her voice dropped, barely more than a whisper. "His elemental magic isn't like the rest of ours. His shadows only bring death when he is near, so we don't speak about it."

What did she mean by his *shadows*? It was something I wanted to understand, but the fear on her face told me it was best not to bring it up right now.

She finally lowered her finger, and I leaned in slightly. "What do you mean, *elemental magic?*"

Vyria arched a brow, like I'd asked if water was wet. "You really *are* an unusual one. I'm guessing you are unmarked. Like the rest of us?"

I hesitated—then nodded. Mostly because I had no idea what else to say, and partly because the soldiers said I was unmarked when I first landed here, too.

It made me feel uneasy.

"For educational purposes," I said, choosing my words carefully, "let's say I'm not exactly familiar with this whole elemental magic thing you're talking about. What does it entail?"

Vyria looked at me as though she was trying to decide whether I was messing with her or genuinely stupid.

I tried to sound like I wasn't entir*ely* out of my depth. If I wanted any chance of getting home, I needed to start understanding what I'd gotten myself into.

"There are four Houses in Thysia," she said finally. "The House of Earth, the House of Water, the House of Air, and the House of Fire, which currently rule all of Thysia." She paused, eyes flicking toward the soldiers posted outside the cage before continuing. "Each House wields elemental magic tied to its namesake. When our magic awakens, it decides which House we belong to."

And just like that, I was lost all over again.

She'd mentioned *Veris* earlier, but now she was talking about *Thysia.* Was Thysia the name of this world? And Veris was what—a state? A province? A kingdom?

My thoughts kept snagging on the word *magic, though.* Was there actually *real* magic here? Did that explain the inky strands or *shadows* from before, or were they tricks of the mind?

Vyria's brows furrowed, as if she was also wondering why I was asking these questions.

She opened her mouth, but a metallic clang against the bars drew our attention to Arkos strolling by with a dagger, smirking at Vyria and me as he licked his lips.

God, he gave me the creeps.

Vyria must've felt the same, because I caught the slight curl of her lip.

I may not have known her very long, but I already liked her.

Eventually, Arkos moved ahead, and Vyria let out a quiet breath. She closed her eyes and leaned back against the metal bars.

I wasn't so lucky.

My brain wouldn't stop replaying it—that blinding light, the crackling surge of energy, as if chaos itself had reached out and dragged me into the ground. I remembered Cody running and shouting my name. But the more I thought about it, he'd been too far from the light. He hadn't gone through. Which meant I was completely and utterly alone.

The more I thought about it, the more dread started to set in. What if I never make it back? What if I were stuck here forever?

And if I couldn't find a way back, that piece of shit Strator would figure out how to get his hands on Gram's land.

I couldn't let that happen. I had to find a way home.

9

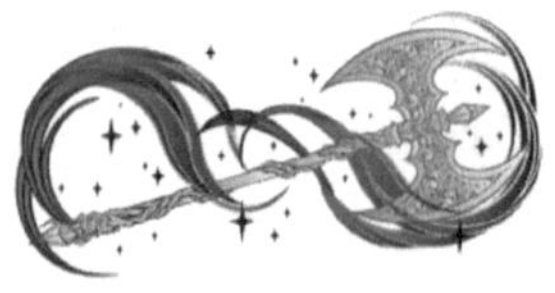

CAGED COMPASSION

Holy hell—the stench in the cage was worse today.

It had been two days since I'd fallen into this godforsaken place. Two days since I had bathed. The rank odor of unwashed bodies clung to everything, mingling with the sharp, metallic tang of blood and the sickly-sweet scent of decay.

At the far end, a young boy sat slumped in the corner, unmoving. His frail body curled inward as if sleep had taken him. But his face was waxy and pale, his half-closed eyes cloudy and staring into nothing.

I had witnessed life fade from a person's body countless times in the ER and had stood beside the deceased long after their final breath. I knew a dead body when I saw one.

The other prisoners refused to look at him, their gazes fixed on the floor or anywhere else, as if ignoring his presence would somehow erase the reality of it. No one spoke about or acknowledged him.

I couldn't help but wonder if he was like Vyria, the only one taken from his village. Was that why no one seemed to care?

Death was an unpredictable thing. Most people don't often see death, but when they do, they tend to fall apart. But here? There was an air of indifference as though an untimely death were expected. As a nurse, I related to that more than I cared to admit.

When Vyria finally woke, her eyes landed on the body across from us. Her shoulders locked, every muscle tightening in her body. She didn't need to say it; I could see the fear of being next rolling off her.

"When you mentioned elemental magic earlier," I asked, trying to shift her attention away from the dead boy. "Do you mean like someone controlling water? Or moving air with their hands?" All I could think of was some anime show my coworkers kept talking about. I'd never watched it myself, but they were hardcore fans who discussed it nonstop—something about powers and elements.

Yeah, this was giving off the same vibe.

"Sort of," Vyria said, slowly moving her attention to me. "It depends on the strength of your core—how much energy you can produce. Everyone's ability varies."

I nodded, but honestly, I was still having a hard time taking this stuff seriously.

Magic? Real, honest-to-God magic? I'd seen zero proof, unless you counted the smoke tentacles Velorn used to pin me like a bug. And okay, *that* was freaky. But the rational part of my brain, the one raised on science and evidence, wasn't quite ready to roll over and accept elemental Hogwarts yet.

Vyria kept her gaze on me, and little by little, her shoulders eased, the tight line of tension softening as she relaxed.

Good, my distraction was working.

Part of me wanted to tell her everything—that this wasn't my world, I had somehow ended up here against my will, and I wanted to find a way back home. But the words got stuck in my throat. Would she even believe me? Was it even safe to tell her?

Instead, I clung to another question that had been festering in the back of my mind. "You mentioned the unmarked. Why do the others see them as such a threat?"

Vyria stiffened, her shoulders going rigid, and for a second, I regretted asking. I opened my mouth to apologize, but she cut me off. "If you're unmarked, they assume you might be Riftblood," she said. "And that's worse. Because being Riftblood is basically the same as being branded a traitor to Thysia."

Okay, so being unmarked was bad, but being a Riftblood was worse? What was the difference between the two? I opened my mouth, but the words were lost as the carriage suddenly stopped.

A soldier finally let us out to relieve ourselves, and when we were shoved back into the cage, I noticed the boy's body was gone. They must have dragged him away while we were outside.

The longer I thought about him, the more I wondered—was that going to be me? Would I rot away in this cage, forgotten, like he had been?

No.

I refuse to die. I'm not some helpless victim. I'm a stubborn, scrappy, strong-as-hell woman, and I'm getting out of here alive.

Somehow.

Vyria sagged into me as soon as we sat back down, her head barely resting on my shoulder before she was out cold. Something wasn't right. I pressed the back of my hand to her forehead.

"Damnit," I whispered. She was burning up.

I pressed two fingers to her wrist. Her pulse raced beneath my touch.

These were all classic signs and symptoms of sepsis.

This wasn't good.

She needed care quickly. I lifted her shirt to help cool her down, fanning her every few seconds. Her time was running out, and I had to figure out how to get us out of here.

That evening, or what passed for evening, the carriage jolted violently, causing the entire cage to sway to one side. Bodies collided, and a loud, guttural scream pierced through the chaos. I turned to see a young girl crumpled on the floor, clutching her arm to her chest. She trembled, her face pale beneath streaks of dirt and sweat. Her elbow jutted out at a sickening angle.

The other prisoners shuffled away from her, muttering under their breaths, but no one moved to help. She needed care, but that seemed to be a rare luxury in this place.

Without hesitation, I pushed toward her, crouching low in the cramped space.

"Let me see," I murmured.

Her wide, tear-streaked eyes met mine. For a moment, I thought she would push me away, but then she slowly extended her arm, biting her lip against the pain. Her elbow was severely swollen, and her skin was red and inflamed. I fought to keep my hands steady as I examined it, careful not to jostle her further.

"I can't fix it properly," I said, "but I can make it easier to manage." I scanned the cage, searching for anything I could use. My eyes landed on a tattered cloth draped over a pile of discarded belongings in the corner. It wasn't much, but it would have to do.

"This will help keep your arm up. It's not perfect, but it'll take some pressure off and might help the swelling." It wasn't my best work of a sling, but it was better than nothing.

The young girl winced as I looped the sling around her neck, securing her arm within it. Her breaths came in short, shallow gasps, and I paused momentarily, meeting her eyes.

"I know it hurts, but keeping it elevated like this will help." She nodded weakly, tears pooling in her eyes. Her breathing had slowed slightly, the sling doing its job.

I leaned back against the bars as exhaustion took over. My limbs felt heavy, and my head was light—signs that the lack of food and water was beginning to take its toll. Every movement drained what little energy I had left.

I will not die here.

Vyria will not die here.

The scenery beyond the cage started to fade as night approached. Sleep became more elusive, slipping further away with each hour. I longed for my own bed, the comfort of lying down with soft pillows supporting my head, instead of being slumped upright against these uncomfortably rigid bars.

I thought about the ranch—about how I'd give it a DIY makeover. Fix up the cabin, repair the barn, and give Eddie a proper burial beside Gram. I thought about Emma and whether she would be mad that I hadn't returned any of her calls. I thought about Cody. Would anyone besides him even realize I was gone? Or was time different here?

What if the memory of me just . . . vanished? Like I'd never existed at all.

No.

I refused to accept that. Cody saw me. He was running toward me. But I'd been pulled away before he could reach me. I had to cling to that hope. The belief that he was out there doing something. If anyone could figure this out, it was him.

Either way, I won't let this place, *Thysia*, consume me entirely.

I was about to close my eyes when something caught my attention.

At first, I thought it was merely a trick of the light. However, I soon spotted him again, half-hidden in the darkness, with only a glimpse of his scarred face barely visible.

Velorn.

He stood beyond the cage, leaning against a tree, motionless in the dark, watching. His golden eyes flickered from the campfire, locking onto mine.

Dread sank in my chest and settled in the back of my throat. It took everything I had not to look away. If he thought he could intimidate me, he had another think coming. He was the reason I was here. If it weren't for him and his damn shadows, I might have already found a way home.

A surge of irritation burned through me, sharply contrasting with the helplessness I felt in his grip days earlier. I could've fought back and found a way to escape. But in the heat of the moment, I felt like a deer caught in headlights.

I slowly raised my hand through the bars and flipped him off, holding it up like a banner of pure defiance. He might not realize what the gesture meant, but I sure as hell did, and oh, I wanted him to see every ounce of anger behind it.

Bastard.

His expression didn't change, but his brows drew together slightly.

Good.

Ponder on that, asshole.

He lingered there for a beat, then turned and melted into the night, swallowed by the darkness as if he had never been there at all.

10

NEW PRISONER

I was going to lose my mind if I had to stay in this cage any longer.

Another day had passed—another day with barely any food or water. My emotions were on a constant loop, shifting from sorrow to panic to outright frustration. The scraps they threw at us were a joke, hardly enough to qualify as a meal. It was more of a tease—enough to remind your stomach what hunger felt like, but never enough to fill it. Vyria wasn't improving, but she wasn't getting worse either, which I saw as a good sign.

I needed to distract myself to keep from falling apart.

"Where are they taking us again?"

"Hollows Mountain," Vyria said, her voice raw and barely holding together.

"And what do they do in this Hollow Mountain?"

"*Hollows* Mountain," she corrected, raising a brow. "It's the only land bridge between the East and West Kingdoms. Because of that, it's the only place where trade and official exchanges are allowed."

"And why would they be taking us there?"

"I'm not sure. I had never been there before."

The words *trade* and *exchange* echoed in my mind, and my stomach twisted.

Were we being sent there to be traded?

"Any idea how much farther it is?"

Vyria glanced out through the bars, scanning the passing landscape. "It looks like we're near the Wispwoods, which means we aren't very far." Her tone wavered with uncertainty, but at least she had some idea.

"Do you know what they're going to do—"

Clang. "Quiet in there!" One of the soldiers barked, slamming his sword against the metal bars.

My jaw clenched as I glared at him. My patience with this captivity was wearing dangerously thin.

I gazed out beyond the cage when restless movement caught my attention. Soldiers shifted about, murmuring. A few stood guard around us and the supply cart, while others investigated the commotion.

Minutes passed before they finally returned, dragging someone with them—a new prisoner. At first, it was hard to make out details since it was nearing night, but as he drew closer, the dim light revealed more. A tall, broad-shouldered man, looking close to my age, was shoved into the cage with us. He stumbled, catching himself on the bars before he fell.

I never liked to stare. Hell, I hated it when people stared at me. But after being caged for this long, modesty had been thrown out the window.

The moment he turned, his eyes caught me off guard. They were an arresting shade of green, so vivid they seemed unnatural, like fresh-cut emeralds catching the light. They didn't look at me; they *held* me, locking me in place with an intensity that felt invasive.

It was perplexing; they felt so foreign yet completely familiar, and I couldn't figure out why.

He moved, searching for a place to sit. The shifting light traced the contours of his muscular frame, emphasizing the defined strength he carried.

A gust of wind swept through the cage, cutting through the stale air with a crisp, clean smell of oak after rain. It wrapped around me, teasing at something deep in my chest, and suddenly, without reason, I wanted to be closer.

Meanwhile, I probably smelled like a wound dressing that hadn't been changed in weeks.

He didn't say anything when he sat down across from me, just scanned his surroundings, like I had when I was shoved in here for the first time.

Should I say something?

Just thinking about it made my fingers twitch, restless with indecision. My mouth parted slightly, but no words escaped. In the end, I was too much of a coward to speak. Partly because I also hadn't brushed my teeth in days. I could only imagine what that smelled like.

Instead, I stayed in my corner, quiet, letting the moment pass by.

He watched the other prisoners; his gaze shifted from one to the next until it settled on me. When our eyes met, I didn't look away.

Was this what *déjà vu* felt like?

My heart skipped a beat, and suddenly my palms were clammy, forcing me to look away. I clenched my fists; I couldn't afford this kind of distraction. I blamed it on the lack of food and water.

I closed my eyes and leaned back against the metal bars as the carriage started moving again.

———◆———

By morning, whispers drifted from the guards.

"…why the Wispwoods?" My eyes were too heavy to open, but my ears strained for every word.

"I'm not sure. This is my first time with this group," another soldier replied. "But I overheard Garron say rebels destroyed the bridge crossing. They haven't repaired it yet."

I forced my eyes open, my vision a little blurry as I watched their figures retreating.

When I turned my head back, the newcomer sat upright, his gaze fixed on me.

A trace of unease settled within me as I arched an eyebrow.

"Have we met before?" His voice was deceptively calm.

"No."

"You sure?"

"Yes."

He stared at me for a beat too long, his eyes narrowing. "I've never seen clothes like yours. What village do you come from?"

My body stiffened. Should I tell him?

I glanced around the cage, catching the attention of too many curious eyes. "A village far from here."

"And what is the name of that Vill—"

The carriage pitched forcefully, the sudden jolt throwing everyone inside off balance. His hand shot out, bracing against the bars, jaw tightening as he glanced toward the shifting shadows outside. He looked annoyed, like the interruption had cost him something. But he didn't turn back to me.

I followed his lead, craning my neck to see what lay ahead. At first, there was nothing but the road and distant tree lines. But then, beyond the hills, vibrant trees with silvery bark stood out, seeming to catch and reflect the hidden light, like they were glowing. Their branches stretched upward in elegant, twisting patterns, and their leaves hung in cascading layers of deep, glowing sapphire, fiery crimson, and sparkling gold. They appeared to shift and glisten as if the forest came alive with every breeze. It was mesmerizing but troubling. The colors were too vivid and perfect.

As exhausted and lethargic as I was, the creeping chill running down my spine jolted my adrenaline. The air felt different here, too, heavy with an unnerving stillness. My skin tingled with awareness.

"Son of a *hellsfire*, this place makes my skin crawl." One of the soldiers said.

"I heard you can thank the rebels who destroyed the bridge crossing for that. It's the only route until it's rebuilt."

"Ancients cursed Wispwoods." Another soldier spat. "You don't actually believe those old superstitions, do you? We'll be fine. By tomorrow, we'll be in Hollows Mountain, with ale in our hands and a pretty woman on our laps."

But the man beside him didn't look convinced. His posture remained rigid, and even the others' bravado cracked. Their focus bled into darting glances at the trees, shoulders drawn tight. The forest itself seemed alive, watching and waiting. And despite their bluster, I could see it in their faces—they were afraid of this place.

Everyone, including the other captives, appeared to sense the change in the atmosphere. They all grew more alert and conscious that something peculiar was occurring.

Ahead, beyond where the soldiers walked, thick mist weaved through the silver trunks. It glided over the forest floor, curling around the roots as if it were alive.

The soldiers didn't seem to notice.

But I did.

The mist didn't drift aimlessly like ordinary fog; it moved with purpose, silently coiling around some of the soldiers' feet. It clung to them, winding higher with each step, as though testing, tasting. For a second, it seemed like something moved with the mist, but in a blink, it was gone.

A chill ran down both of my arms.

This wasn't normal.

"Keep moving!" one of the soldiers yelled.

The deeper we ventured, the more the forest seemed to close in. The trees, once standing tall and indifferent, now leaned inward, their gnarled branches twisting together above like the ribs of a massive, skeletal cage. Shadows stretched around us, shifting where they shouldn't.

There was that flash of movement lent again at the edge of my vision. I blinked again, rubbing my eyes.

My mind is playing tricks on me. It had to be exhaustion.

Then, a bloodcurdling scream resonated outside the cage. The sound froze me in place. I watched in horror as the mist swallowed a soldier whole, leaving nothing behind but empty space.

"*Ambush!*"

Panic erupted from outside the cage. More soldiers vanished into the mist, their cries abruptly silenced.

Without warning, figures dropped from the trees, landing soundlessly among us. Their bodies were covered in streaks of paint, the colors blending so seamlessly with the twisted bark and creeping mist that they appeared to materialize from the forest itself.

Their movements were fluid, calculated predators stepping into the open. They wore no armor; there weren't missteps as they moved, only quiet, controlled efficiency.

Fights erupted from every direction. The soldiers guarding our cage faltered, stepping away to defend themselves. I gripped the bars tightly.

Who are these people?

Were they here to save us?

Hope ignited within me. I glanced around at the other prisoners, who appeared just as confused as I was. The new captive sprang to his feet and shouted at one of the attackers.

A young figure darted toward us with incredible agility before stopping in front of the cage.

He gestured to a soldier clutching a ring of keys. "They've got binding cuffs on us."

The stranger nodded, and with a flick of his hand, a piece of rock flew, hitting the soldier right in the back of the head. He collapsed to the ground, allowing the stranger to grab the keys and toss them into the cage.

Well, that answered one of my questions.

The new prisoner was already in motion, his fingers working swiftly as the cuffs around his wrists clicked open. The faint metallic clatter barely registered before something else stole my attention. His veins. They began to pulse with a green glow radiating from his hands and slowly moving up his arms.

Okay, that's . . . different.

Maybe there was actual magic in this world.

"You're that Earthshaper they've been hunting," someone in the cage whispered.

Earthshaper?

What did that even mean?

The prisoner looked up. "The name's Ehlark. Please, don't be afraid. We're here to help you escape."

I fought the urge to cry, not out of fear, but from the overwhelming, surprising wave of relief.

Whoever this Ehlark was, he might be my ticket home.

He passed the keys to the next captive. "Once you're free, head back down the trail we came in on," he instructed. "Others are waiting beyond the outskirts. Save your powers for when you need them."

The others nodded, determination flashing in their eyes. I did too, though for a different reason. I didn't have powers—not like they did, but I was definitely ready to get the hell out of here.

If I could escape and find the people Ehlark was talking about, then I could figure out the rest. I could figure out how to get home.

Ehlark tore open the cage door, the hinges snapping under his grip. His arms glowed with a vivid, neon green light, reminiscent of a sci-fi scene. Lines of green energy coursed through his veins, branching out in intricate patterns beneath his skin. The light was pulsating rhythmically up his forearms.

Ehlark moved like a force of nature, leaping from the cage with an agility that defied his size. He landed in a low crouch, the green glow still pulsing from his fingers, casting soft flashes of light against the dirt.

Then the earth responded.

Within seconds, the soil stirred, and thick roots surged upward, twisting and moving like living creatures. They struck with ruthless precision, lashing out at the two soldiers charging toward him. The men barely had time to react before the vines coiled around their limbs, yanking them off their feet and hurling them backward forcefully.

I stood there, mouth hanging open like a fish out of water.

I guess that's what they meant by *Earthshaper*.

My brain was firing on all cylinders, trying to make sense of what I'd seen. This must be what Vyria was telling me about.

The other prisoners hurried after Ehlark, desperately trying to escape. As soon as their cuffs hit the ground, their veins started to glow, too. Some pulsed with deep greens; others shimmered in shades of blue. Cuts and bruises that clung to them like second skin faded. Their raw, scraped-up bodies were healing right before my eyes, color returning to their cheeks as if someone had hit a reset button.

Life itself was pouring back into them.

I remained stunned in the cage, watching the impossible unfold.

A clang rang out beside me, snapping me back to the present.

I turned my attention to Vyria, who was struggling with the keys, her hands shaking so badly she couldn't insert them into the lock. Her petite frame trembled with shallow breaths, and her knuckles were white as she clenched the metal.

There was something in these cuffs that suppressed everyone's magical abilities.

It made sense now why I felt like I was drugged when they were first put on me.

I moved to Vyria's side, gently taking the keys. "Take a deep breath. We *will* get out of here."

The cuffs clicked open and fell to the ground with a dull clang. She exhaled shakily, then reached for the keys again, her fingers steadier now as she worked on mine.

When my cuffs unlocked, a static sensation coursed through me, rippling beneath my skin like a dormant current suddenly coming to life.

I flexed my fingers at the feeling. I still felt dehydrated and hungry, but not as weak as I did with them on.

Vyria and I were the last to scramble out of the cage. As I helped her down, my gaze swept across the battlefield and the sheer ferocity of the fight.

Flames streaked through the air, small fireballs sizzling as they exploded on impact, knocking rebels back. The same eerie glow that had pulsed from Ehlark's hands and the other captives was emanating from the soldiers, but in different shades of red. Their arms shone with raw energy, veins glowing like rivers of lava.

Water surged through the chaos, twisting and colliding with fire in a violent hiss of steam. A rebel with a sapphire glow raised her hands, sending a spear of water hurtling toward an incoming fireball, extinguishing it before it could land.

High above, nestled halfway up a tree, another rebel struck. A spear of ice had impaled a soldier mid-charge. The man barely had time to react before frost overtook him, encasing his body in jagged crystal until he fell to the ground.

Part of me screamed to get away from the danger, to survive. But another part, quieter and deeply ingrained, told me to stay. The part of me that had responded to code blues and crash carts, to run toward screams, not away from them.

But before I could move, a small hand gripped my arm.

"Eleni, we need to get away from here!"

I barely turned when Vyria let out a sharp, high-pitched cry. She was thrown backward, her fingers slipping from my arm as she hit the ground with a sickening thud and a choked gasp.

"Where do you think you're going?" Arkos stood over her, his sword raised and ready to strike.

Instinct took over as I slammed into him with everything I had, catching him off guard. His balance wavered for a second, but it was enough.

"Run!" I yelled at Vyria as she hurried to stand up.

Before I could move again, Arko's arm wrapped around my neck, yanking me backward. My breath came in shallow, desperate gasps. My hands flew to his arm, nails digging into his skin as wild panic rushed through me to break free.

"I'm going to enjoy killing you," he growled against my ear, with hot breath that reeked of rotten meat. His arm tightened, cutting off my airway.

I had to break free, or he was really going to kill me. Gripping the arm locked around my throat, I swung my body up with all the force I could muster and brought my heel crashing down on the arch of his right foot.

A sharp grunt tore from his throat as he loosened his grip.

I twisted to the side and drove my elbow into his ribs, targeting his weak side. He staggered, his grip loosening as he swayed unsteadily on his other leg—his bad leg, where I had noticed the limp days earlier.

Quickly pivoting, I backed off enough to kick his right knee. The force knocked him off balance, and he crumpled to one side, cursing as his leg gave out beneath him.

"You little *skath*," he snarled.

He tried to lunge at me again, but his movements were slower now, and his limp was worse. I stepped back, forcing him to overextend, and then drove my knee into his stomach with all the power I could muster. He broke out in ragged gasps as he doubled over, clutching his side.

I thought I had beaten him, but then his veins glowed a deep red. Arkos swung wildly and struck me on the side of my head. Black spots burst in my vision as I staggered backward, ears ringing. He grabbed my arm tightly, yanking me to the ground.

"You think you can overpower me?"

Arkos pressed his weight onto me as he straddled my chest. His hands wrapped around my throat, squeezing with terrifying force. My vision blurred, dark spots creeping into the edges again as I clawed at his wrists, desperate for air.

This was it. This foul-breath bastard was going to end me.

Out of nowhere, a force like a sledgehammer slammed into Arkos, knocking him off balance and sending him sprawling to the ground.

I rolled to the other side, coughing for air. My vision blurred as I tried to focus, my body quivering and struggling for clarity. Through the haze, a figure stood a few feet away behind Arkos.

It was Vyria. Her small frame radiated defiance, and her hands were outstretched, glowing a brilliant dark blue; determination burned in her eyes.

She moved her hands in slow, controlled circles. Droplets formed around her, forming from the moisture in the atmosphere, merging into a swirling sphere of water between her palms. It pulsed with a beautiful glow, illuminated like liquid silver, shifting and churning as if alive.

Arkos heaved to his feet, his sword igniting in flames that licked hungrily along the blade. The firelight cast jagged lines across his face, twisting his expression into something monstrous. Vyria threw the sphere of water towards Arkos, hitting his sword dead center and snuffing out the flame.

His face contorted in rage as he lunged toward her, driving his sword into Vyria's side. Her scream pierced the air, a sound that made my blood run cold. She dropped to her knees, fingers trembling as they gripped the sword buried deep in her body.

For a fleeting second, our eyes met.

Wide, filled with agony and desperation, but there was something else there, too. A silent plea. A question I couldn't answer.

The world slowed around me.

We hadn't known each other very long, but in that cage, she was the only one who reached out. The only one who spoke to me. The only one who made me feel like I wasn't completely alone.

A hollow, gut-wrenching crack echoed within. I stood there, numb, staring at her crumpled body. A moment earlier, she'd been alive. So vividly, fiercely alive. I could hear her voice, see the pain in her eyes, and feel the weight of her hand pulling me to safety.

Now . . . nothing.

My hands stilled. Not from shock. Not acceptance.

No.

This was the kind of stillness born in the eye of the storm, when the rage runs so deep, everything else falls silent. I didn't feel anger. I became it. It ripped through me like wildfire, consuming every other thought until nothing else existed.

I pushed myself up, my hands curling into fists, when a sudden warmth emanated from the necklace I had forgotten. It had become another weight on my skin, hidden under my shirt, ignored amid exhaustion and the fight for survival.

But now, I felt it.

A sensation I couldn't ignore, the same one I felt the moment I was pulled into this world, radiating through my bones. A surge of energy ripped through me, crackling in my veins and igniting every nerve. It wasn't just warmth; it was raw, unrelenting power, flooding deep to my core.

The searing warmth tore down my arm, erupting into a green blaze that danced across my skin like lightning, channeling energy through my veins. My lips parted as I watched, wide-eyed, as the brilliant light gathered and shaped into a solid form.

A double-bladed axe appeared in my hand, crackling with power.

Its metal gleamed with an otherworldly sheen, inscribed with symbols I couldn't decipher, their lines pulsing as if the weapon itself was flowing with power. It was heavy and bigger than my tomahawk, but the balance and grip felt right. Tightly twisted roots were woven into the handle, making it feel as though it were molded to my grip. Its balance was so precise that it seemed to move with me, not against me. It wasn't my tomahawk, but it might as well have been. This felt like something forged for me, something connected to my very being.

After my accident, fear consumed every part of me. I kept having nightmares of the monster ripping open my back again. I feared it would tear through my spine and leave me paralyzed.

That's why Gram gave me the tomahawk.

"This tomahawk," Gram said, closing my fingers around the handle, *"is your spirit given shape. Let it be your weapon against the dark, your voice when fear steals your breath. It will carry your courage, your intent, your truth. You are its heart, and it is your hand. Aim true, and it will always find the mark."*

I remembered all the times I had thrown my tomahawk at targets back home. I could hear Gram's voice, patient yet firm, as she corrected my stance, drilling me endlessly on my grip and technique. *"Again,"* she'd say, watching me like a hawk. *"You're not just throwing it. You're commanding it."*

I hadn't fully understood everything she meant back then, but I did now.

Arkos charged at me, sword back in hand as flames erupted from it. The world around me seemed to disappear as I focused on my target.

I raised the axe high above my head and, with a guttural scream, let it fly.

A raw surge of energy coursed through me as it tore through the battlefield. It moved with lethal accuracy, carving through the space like a predator targeting its prey.

It struck with explosive force, the sound cracking outward violently.

The blade cut clean through Arkos with a sickening sound, splitting him in two as if he were nothing more than paper.

Blood erupted in a hot, sticky spray, painting the ground in deep crimson. His body barely had time to register the impact before he collapsed.

I stood there, chest heaving, my breath ragged and uneven. The rage that had burned so brightly moments ago drained from me, replaced by a creeping, hollow shock. My fingers twitched involuntarily, adrenaline still coursing through me, and that's when I felt the weight of something warm and familiar in the palm of my hand again.

I looked down, and there it was—the glowing axe. My grip tightened instinctively, and my heart raced as I tried to understand what was happening.

The weapon felt heavier; the blades were stained with blood, streaking down their edges, but the glow still pulsed to life, waiting for its next target.

I examined the axe in my hands, struggling to understand. My gaze drifted to Arkos, sprawled in a growing pool of blood beneath him.

Holy shit.

It took me a long, surreal moment to fully register it.

I had killed someone.

No, not just killed, but torn them in half with a single throw of *this* axe.

My fingers flexed around the handle as I stared at the weapon.

The image branded itself into my thoughts. The way it had felt so natural in my grip.

Fear and shock gnawed at the edges of my thoughts, trying to worm their way past the haze of adrenaline.

How is this even possible?

Did the axe really come from the necklace? Gram's necklace?

I looked up and realized I wasn't the only one stunned. Soldiers and rebels had halted mid-battle, their weapons lowered, their faces showing a mix of fear and disbelief. The chaos that had taken over the battlefield moments ago was now completely silent. But it wasn't me they were looking at; they were staring at what lay beyond Arkos's body.

I gulped.

Dozens of trees were split in half, with their trunks torn apart and bowing, as if a massive force had ripped through the forest. The axe not only struck him down but also left a trail of destruction through everything in its path.

And somehow the axe had come back to me.

Scattered among the fallen timber were the bodies of soldiers and rebels, caught in the sheer force of whatever power had been unleashed. Some lay motionless, while others groaned in pain, their armor shredded and their bodies battered by the weapon's devastating impact.

I took a hesitant step back, my legs trembling as fear replaced my shock.

Suddenly, the weight of the axe in my hand changed. Once solid and weighted, it now somehow felt lighter. My fingers twitched as I felt the static charge fade, the electric hum in my veins disappearing as the weapon vanished. Its edges dissolving into nothing, like mist burned away by the sun.

But the humming sensation wasn't gone; it had merely shifted.

My gaze lowered to my chest, and there it was—my necklace. The glow from the pendant flickered as if it had breathed moments ago and was now settling back into silence.

Goosebumps prickled down my spine as I still felt the remnants of the power I had experienced.

Is this necklace somehow connected to the magic here?

How was this possible? Why was Gram hiding so many secrets from me?

As I lifted my gaze, searching for answers, anything that could explain what had happened, my eyes locked onto a pair of golden ones.

Velorn stood at the far edge of the battlefield, his silhouette outlined by the dead bodies around him. His shadows curled and thrashed, feeding off the barely contained fury etched into his face. His golden eyes blazed, brighter than fire, focused entirely on me. He looked as unhinged as I felt right now. Terrifying and dangerous, yet somehow, I couldn't look away.

Until a pair of hands pressed against my back.

I spun around quickly, raising my fists in defense as a pair of glowing green eyes stared back at me. The glow slowly retreated like dying embers, settling into a deep emerald hue.

It was Ehlark.

My shoulders sagged slightly. His expression remained unreadable, but his eyes held something else. Not fear, not anger, but something deeper.

"We need to go."

But I couldn't move. My feet felt anchored to the ground, still in complete shock.

Ehlark's grip tightened around my hand. "Now!"

He yanked me out of the trance and pulled me forward. My legs finally obeyed, stumbling into motion as I followed his pace.

11

FIELD TRIAGE

After what felt like a ten-mile sprint through the forest, Ehlark finally slowed. His breaths had become shallower and more strained.

Something was wrong.

"We need shelter."

"What about the others?" I asked, still trying to catch my breath.

"My friends will make sure they will be okay, but we need to be hidden by darkfall." He paused to scan the surrounding area. "It's too dangerous to be left exposed in the Wispwoods at night."

He pointed to a massive boulder that jutted out ahead, half-hidden among the twisted roots and thick underbrush. Just beyond it, barely visible through the shadows, was an opening.

"There is no way I'm getting in that cave." Tight spaces and I did not get along.

Hell, I hated elevators so much I'd rather climb fifteen flights of stairs than feel that coffin-on-ropes vibe. So, the thought of crawling into a dark, narrow cave?

Hard pass.

"We don't have a choice," he shot back. "Unless you'd rather get caught again or let something out here eat you alive."

Ehlark's breathing was now more labored than before.

Something definitely wasn't right.

"We'll hide in here," he said, though his voice lacked its usual strength; the edges of his words sounded rough. "I cannot go any further until I heal."

I moved in closer, my eyes tracing the lines of his face. Dirt clung to his skin, smudged into the dried blood across his cheek.

Was that his blood?

Before I could get a better look at him, he gripped my wrist and pulled me into the cave.

The cool stone brushed against my fingertips as I steadied myself. It was damp and eerily still, muffling the sounds of the forest outside. It felt like stepping into another world where the insanity of the day couldn't reach us.

As we rounded a corner, a small glimmer of light caught my eye.

Ehlark tensed immediately and stepped in front of me, his stance rigid, ready to strike. But nothing came.

The drip of water echoed deep inside, each drop sounding like the ticking of a distant clock, marking the passing seconds as we moved deeper into the cave.

The dim light filtering through a narrow crack high above cast dancing shadows along the jagged walls. It wasn't much, enough to push back the overwhelming darkness, but even that sliver of illumination felt like a lifeline.

I exhaled again, my body sagging with exhaustion. The stone beneath me felt cold and unwelcoming, and every part of me begged to get out of here. I hated the cave, the dampness, the darkness, and the way it pressed in from all sides. But for now, at least, nothing was chasing us. For now, we were safe. And that small piece of safety was enough to keep me from falling apart completely.

A cool, sweaty hand suddenly laced between my fingers. Instinct took over, and I jerked back, ready to fight. But when I turned, it was Ehlark. His hands gripped mine, his brows furrowed in confusion between our entwined hands.

"Where's your power?"

If there were an award for the dumbest expression in existence, my face would've taken first place.

Power?

Did he mean the necklace? Because if so, he was screwed.

I had no clue how to work the thing. And I had absolutely no clue how to explain that to someone like him. So I stood there, wide-eyed and motionless, like a deer about to get hit head-on.

His eyes fluttered, barely holding on, and before I could react, he collapsed, pulling me down with him.

His face was pale, almost gray, and his breathing was worse. Sweat clung to his skin despite the cold air in the cave. "Hey, stay with me, Ehlark." I shook his shoulders, trying to get his attention. "I need you to open your eyes."

My nursing instincts kicked in, pushing aside the rising panic.

I scanned him for injuries and found the source almost immediately. The gash along his side was worse than I had realized. His shirt was soaked in blood, the fabric clinging to his skin.

He's losing too much blood. If I don't do something now . . .

I tore the remnants of his shirt away, my hands surprisingly steady as I exposed the wound. It was deep layers of fat and muscle tissue exposed beneath the slick crimson. It was worse than I thought.

"Damn it," I muttered, yanking off my shirt. I quickly folded it and pressed it firmly against the wound. Warm blood seeped through immediately.

Think, Eleni.

I didn't have any usual emergency room supplies. No gloves, no gauze, no sutures. Just me, a cave, and whatever I could find.

I glanced around, the dim light revealing little more than damp stone walls and patches of moss.

Okay. If I can wrap the shirt tightly enough to slow the bleeding, I can stabilize him. Then, I need a fire.

My thoughts quickened as I ran through my options.

Cauterization. I need something metal—anything that will hold heat long enough to seal the wound. I shifted slightly, pressing harder on the wound to control the blood loss.

"Ehlark," I said again, trying to steady my voice as much as possible. "I need you to put your hands on this shirt and press down as hard as you can, okay?"

His lips moved, but the sound was barely audible.

"What?" I leaned closer.

"I need your power—to heal."

This time, I understood him. I leaned in, keeping my mouth close to his ear. "I don't know how to do that."

His eyes blinked open again, this time locking onto mine as if surprised. Maybe it was the pain, or perhaps it was the realization that I wasn't what he thought I was, but whatever expression he gave me, it wasn't exactly warm.

I chose to ignore it.

"Do you have anything metal on you?" I asked, trying to pivot.

He didn't answer, just kept staring like I'd grown a second head.

"Ehlark!" I snapped my fingers in front of his face, trying to pull him out of whatever thought he was stuck in. His gaze finally shifted. "My boots," he mumbled. "There's a knife inside."

I yanked off both boots, my fingers fumbling in my rush. A small, flat dagger tumbled out, no larger than my hand.

"I need to figure out how to start a fire," I muttered, glancing around the cave, only to find wet stone and damp moss.

"The end of the handle can create sparks when struck with dry stone."

I turned it over in my hands. Sure enough, a rough, flint-like strip was embedded in the back of the handle, mildly worn from use. "Well, isn't this convenient?"

I examined him and noticed the trace of green light at his fingertips. It pulsed weakly, barely there, like dying embers struggling to remain alight. His hand twitched against the dirt, fingers dragging sluggishly as he tried to grasp something.

"Ehlark," I said, leaning closer to his ear, "I need to start a fire, but I can't do that if I'm holding pressure on your wound. Can you press your hand there instead?"

His eyelids fluttered, struggling to focus, but after a long, tense moment, he gave a slight nod.

With everything being so damp in the cave, my only option was to search for dry wood outside. The soldiers might still be out there, but I had to help Ehlark.

I stood and slipped out, scanning my surroundings for any sign of movement. The forest stretched around me, silent, except for the distant chirping of birds. No immediate threats. At least, none that I could see.

I hurried into the trees, gathering whatever I could—dry branches, brittle leaves, anything that would burn. My arms filled quickly, and I turned back toward the cave.

A prickling sensation at the back of my neck raised my defenses—the unmistakable feeling of being watched.

I held my breath and moved slowly, scanning the shadows between the trees, searching for movement, but there was nothing.

Then, a sudden breeze stirred the trees to life, and a heavy rustle sounded in the darkness a few yards away.

Nope! Not today.

I didn't wait to find out what it was. My legs moved on instinct and bolted for the cave, nearly tripping over myself as I threw the bundle of wood inside.

The walls seemed to close in again, pressing against my skin until my heart raced. I hated tight spaces like this. They dragged up memories I'd buried deep, memories I wanted to forget. My pulse quickened, panic grabbing at the edges of my thoughts.

Focus, Eleni. You have a patient who needs you.

I forced the words through my mind like a lifeline, shoving the fear back down where it belonged.

Approaching Ehlark, I saw his breathing was worse than before; he was tachypneic, which indicated he was going into shock.

After stacking the wood into a small pile, I grabbed the knife and the driest stone I could find, positioning them right. Holding my breath, I struck them together—once, twice—nothing.

Gritting my teeth, I tried again and again. My arms ached, frustration mounting as the dull clink of metal against stone echoed uselessly through the cave. "Come on, work, dammit!"

On the seventh strike, a spark landed on the brittle leaves. My pulse leaped as I dropped to my knees, cupping my hands around the tiny ember. Carefully, I blew on it, coaxing the fragile flame to life. The leaves smoldered, curling black at the edges—then, suddenly, a small fire came to life.

A huge smile stretched across my face. "Yes!"

Feeling quite proud of myself, I sat there, staring at the small fire.

All those years living in the backcountry, all those trips in the mountains, Gram had drilled survival skills into me, making me practice over and over until I could perform them half-asleep. At the time, I thought it was excessive. Now, all I felt was gratitude toward her for teaching me.

I closed my eyes, grabbing her necklace.

Thank you, Gram.

After a painstaking five minutes, the blade glowed softly with a red-orange hue. I turned back to Ehlark. His breathing was still rapid, but his eyes flicked toward me, then to the blade.

"Do it," he said, his focus never leaving me.

Carefully, I moved his hand and peeled away my now blood-soaked shirt from the wound. The bleeding had slowed from the pressure—*good*, but not good enough.

"This is going to hurt," I warned. "Take a deep breath, okay?"

He gave a slight nod as he clenched his jaw tightly, muscles tightening in anticipation.

"I'm going to count to three, okay?"

He didn't speak, just gave a single nod.

"One, two," I didn't finish saying three as I pressed the hot knife to the open wound. A loud hiss filled the cave, and the sickening scent of burning flesh curled into my nose. Ehlark's body went rigid, a strangled sound ripping from his throat. He gritted his teeth, barely holding back a scream, his fingers digging into the dirt beneath him.

Seconds stretched unbearably, but when I finally pulled the blade away, the bleeding had stopped completely. The raw, cauterized wound was ugly, but it would keep him alive.

I exhaled, only now realizing I'd been holding my breath.

I glanced over at Ehlark, his body finally still, his chest rising and falling in a steady rhythm. He must have passed out from the sheer shock of it all. I didn't blame him. If I had to go through something like that, I would've blacked out too.

With a slow exhale, I slumped back against the stone wall, my muscles aching from exhaustion. Every inch of me burned from the frantic sprint through the forest and the stressful moment of what had happened.

Okay. Not dead. That's a win.

I'd escaped. I was free—free to finally figure out how the hell to get out of here.

Sadness washed over me upon realizing that the only friend I had made here was now gone.

I hope you are at peace now, Vyria.

I glanced back at Ehlark.

Could I trust him? He did help me escape.

There was something in his eyes, something familiar, that made me want to trust him. But in the end, he was still an outsider. A stranger with glowing veins and very extraordinary powers that still gave me goosebumps. I glanced down at his chest, observing the slow, even breaths that indicated he was asleep.

The glow of the fire and the quiet breathing wrapped around me like a lullaby. My body was nearing its limit. My eyelids grew heavier with each passing second, and my vision was darkening.

I leaned against the stone, its cool surface soothing the heat sticking to my skin. Gradually, my muscles relaxed. I couldn't fight it any longer. Exhaustion was winning this round.

12

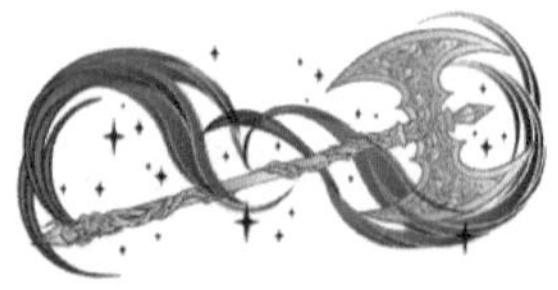

BLOOD CONTRACT

There was a scent of wet stone and earth mingling with something sweet that I couldn't quite place. It was subtle yet comforting, like the smell of my grandmother's house after cooking.

When I turned over, I noticed the ground beneath me was uneven and rough, far from the soft mattress I had envisioned. The blanket covering me was thin and short, a poor substitute for my oversized comforter.

Then I heard the crackling of fire. My groggy mind struggled to make sense of it.

Had I fallen asleep on the couch again?

My eyes fluttered open, the haze of sleep fading as the fire's glow filled my vision with a young, *very* attractive, shirtless man sitting beside it, staring right at me.

I sat up quickly, perhaps too quickly, and the sudden chill against my skin reminded me of what I wasn't wearing. My shirt was gone, leaving me in my pink sports bra and torn-up jeans.

"I didn't want to disturb you," Ehlark said, clearing his throat. "And, well, since you used your shirt to stop my bleeding, I thought I could at least cover you with mine. Even though…" He glanced down at where I was holding his shirt now. "It's bloody too."

I spotted my shirt draped over a rock near the fire, drying beside a medium-sized, banana-shaped piece of food he was gradually roasting.

That must've been what I was smelling in my sleep.

I pulled his shirt higher over my chest, suddenly acutely aware of how cold it was without one. The fabric felt rough against my skin, but I didn't complain. I glanced at him, his face partially illuminated by the small flames. I couldn't help but let my eyes slowly drift downward, taking him in.

Tanned skin. Broad shoulders. A very fit body and dried blood where his wound was.

Wait a minute. I leaned in, believing my eyes were deceiving me.

My eyes searched for where his wound used to be, the one I cauterized hours earlier. Now, it was gone. In its place lay nothing more than a faint scar.

"Your wound! It's healed?"

Ehlark seemed puzzled by my response, then followed my gaze to his now-healed skin. He flexed slightly, testing it, before exhaling.

"Well, almost. It still hasn't repaired the deeper parts, but thanks to you, I was able to heal after you stopped the bleeding, mostly.

I probably wouldn't have made it through the night otherwise." He met my gaze, his expression softening. "For that, I'm indebted to you."

I blinked at him.

Did he really heal on his own?

Similar to when the prisoners were escaping. Was it because of their magic? Could this place really accelerate healing properties?

Great. Just great.

As if feeling out of place wasn't enough, now I had to deal with superhuman recovery on top of it. I scanned my own cuts and bruises, hoping maybe it was this place or the environment that could somehow grant instant healing, but every cut and scrape on me was still there. A reminder that I wasn't healing any faster than normal. I felt like a fish thrown onto dry land.

I scooted closer to the fire, allowing the warmth to seep into my skin and drive away the disappointment and goosebumps still visible on my arms.

The silence between us was already awkward, but what made it worse was the way he kept staring. These weren't the subtle, shy glances of a stranger; they were the kind of looks that said, *I swear we've hooked up before, but I was too drunk to remember it.*

I wanted to say something, but every time he looked at me with those familiar eyes, I lost my will to speak. That had never happened to me before. I chalked it up to exhaustion and forced myself to focus on the fire.

Thoughts kept circling back to Ehlark's glowing green veins and how the earth had moved beneath his command. His power was unlike anything I'd ever seen; not even movies could make something like that look cool. I wanted to ask him about his magic and how it worked, but he was staring again.

"Do I have something on my face?"

"Three."

I blinked, confused. "There are *three* things on my face?"

"No," he replied flatly. "You said you would count to three, but you only counted to two."

Of all the things he could have focused on—*that* was it?

"I'm trying to figure out if you're illiterate, or if not having powers also means you never learned how to count."

I gave him a deadpan look. "Wow. First of all, I *do* know how to count, even without powers. And second, it was my way of distracting you before using a scorching hot piece of metal to sear your flesh."

"Well, thank you for being considerate," he mumbled.

"You're welcome," I said, matching his tone. The silence returned. But this time, we were both looking at each other. His gaze had shifted again. Softer now. Or maybe just curious. In that quiet, probing way.

"You said earlier that you don't know how to use your powers?"

My heart stuttered. What could I even say to that?

I went over everything that had happened again. The bursts of power from everyone around me, the chaos, the fear. And then there was the axe. I concluded it came from the necklace because there was no way the axe had come from me.

Back home, something like this would've been impossible—unreal, like part of myths. Yet, here it was, appearing out of nowhere, drumming with a power that didn't feel entirely mine. It had given me strength I'd never believed I had.

Oh my god.

I killed someone.

My breath faltered, my hands trembling as the memory re-played in vivid detail. The axe cutting clean through flesh, the spray of blood, the body splitting apart, like it had never even been whole.

I sometimes acted without thinking; it was a habit that even Gram had mentioned on one too many occasions. Especially when I let my emotions overwhelm me, but this . . . this was something entirely different. The rage had been instantaneous and overwhelming, as if a force outside of my control had taken hold and refused to let go. That wasn't normal. That wasn't *me*.

Or was it?

Then I thought back to Vyria and how Arkos had plunged his sword through her. Anger and frustration rose again. I clenched my fists, forcing myself to swallow against the nausea.

Something else stirred in my memory.

The raw power I felt with the axe. My fingers reached for Gram's necklace, holding it gently and feeling its familiar weight. There it was, that hum of energy running through it, subtle but undeniable.

I met Ehlark's gaze, surprised he was still silent.

"If you have no powers, how did you come across a weapon like that?"

I stiffened.

Another question I didn't know how to answer.

Hell, how could I, when I didn't even understand it.

"I think," I paused, glancing down at my chest, "it came from my necklace."

Ehlark glanced at the pendant, and his expression shifted again. He was quiet, but I felt the intensity of his thoughts as his eyebrows moved.

And suddenly, I wasn't sure if my answer had made things better or much, much worse.

Ehlark moved closer, his oakmoss scent following him. "May I?"

Reluctantly, I slipped it off and handed it to him.

He turned the necklace over in his palm, holding it up to the firelight. "It looks like an ordinary gem from the outside," he said. "But I can also feel something is alive in there."

"How do you know?"

"I don't know how to explain it. A feeling, I guess." His words only deepened my confusion. Nothing made sense; the more I learned, the less I understood.

He handed the necklace back, his warm fingers brushing briefly against mine. "If you don't have powers, like you said, it must be because you are unmarked."

There it was again—that lovely word *unmarked*.

"Or could it be possible that you are . . . *Riftblood?*"

Vyria had told me that being unmarked meant you were seen as a threat or a traitor, but I hadn't gotten the chance to ask her what it meant.

"I keep hearing that term. What is a Riftblood?" Then I quickly added. "Not saying I am one. Just curious."

Ehlark glanced at me before poking at the fire. "Riftbloods are elementals whose powers don't belong to any of the four main elements. Their bloodline is tainted, at least according to the Houses. It comes from the Rift War, a long time ago. Some Houses see them as dangerous and want them eradicated."

He must've noticed the confusion on my face because he kept talking. "Back then, another species invaded Thysia. They had powers we'd never seen before. When the fighting started, some of their blood mixed with ours. No one realized it at the time, but generations later, their descendants were born . . . different. That's why they're called *Riftblood*."

So, another species had also ended up on this planet? I couldn't help but wonder if they arrived the same way I did—through that bizarre liquid light.

His attention shifted, suspicion dancing in his gaze. "This is a common story that every elemental should know."

Time to change the subject.

"What House are you from?"

The muscles in his jaw clenched, and for once, his eyes darted away from mine.

"I was supposed to be marked to the House of Earth."

"What do you mean, *supposed* to be? Are you unmarked too?"

"The House of Earth doesn't exist anymore." There was a subtle but unmistakable pain in his voice.

So, he *was* unmarked.

For a split second, something flashed across his face. Then it was gone, concealed behind the gaze he had directed at me earlier.

I had so many questions I wanted to ask: questions about this place, Veris; about the unique powers everyone seemed to have; and about the different Elemental Houses. However, something told me that if I kept pressing, it might reopen old wounds.

And I, for one, didn't like reopening old wounds.

"If I told you I wasn't from your world—that where I come from, magic doesn't exist the way it does here—would you believe me?"

Ehlark's brow furrowed as he glanced back at me, puzzlement playing across his face before something else settled there.

"I saw you wielding a weapon that no ordinary person could."

"No," I attested.

"I can't explain it, but that wasn't me. It had to be the necklace. Or this place. But I'm telling you for certain, those powers weren't mine. Look at what I'm wearing. Clothes like mine don't exist here. You noticed that yourself the first time we met."

Ehlark studied me again; this time his gaze drifted to my pants and then to my bra. Heat rushed to my cheeks.

"Where do you come from, then?"

"Wyoming. Have you heard of it?"

Ehlark shook his head slowly, his expression unreadable as he attempted to process what I was saying.

"Well," I continued, forcing the words out, "I come from a world called Earth," I said, exhaling slowly. "A place where there are no powers, no true magic. Just individuals trying to get by with what they can. Mostly with bad decisions, overpriced coffee, and a crippling reliance on the internet."

"So, you're telling me you are not from Thysia?" His expression twisted into something between suspicion and disbelief.

Great. The last thing I need is him thinking I'm lying.

I shook my head slowly.

"Then you're a *Noztari?*"

"Noz—what? No. I'm human. Do you even know what that is?"

His skepticism softened, but only slightly. "No. The only species ever recorded from another world was the Noztari."

"Well, I'm human. That's what we're called where I come from." My pulse kicked up. The way he stared at me made this feel less like a conversation and more like an interrogation. I took a deep breath, trying to keep the frustration down.

"Do you know how you got here in the first place?"

"All I know is that some brilliant, colorful light beamed me here. Then I landed on that guy with those creepy shadows, who's also a complete dick, and then was immediately kidnapped." I exhaled. "So no, I have no idea where I even landed. But if I retrace their footsteps, I can probably figure it out."

I scrunched my brows, trying to piece together every detail of that night, searching for something useful. But the problem was, I hadn't had much of a chance. The moment I hit the ground, I was running for my life. To make matters worse, it was already nightfall.

So many things were working against me.

I felt a headache forming and rubbed my temples methodically. Then another sinking thought settled in my chest.

What if I never find my way back? What if I were stuck here until I died?

I quickly shook the thought out of my head.

No.

I'm not going to give up. I will find a way.

"Okay. Let's say I do believe you."

Hope flooded back into me at his words.

"I have someone back in my village," he continued, turning over the food still resting over the fire. "Who might have the answers you're searching for."

My heart leaped at his words, but before I could speak, he lifted a hand, cutting me off.

"You might have already figured this out by now, but the rebels who attacked the convoy?" He went on. "They're with me."

"Okay—"

Ehlark exhaled. "We were on our way to Hollows Mountain to rescue some of our captured comrades. That was our mission, until we came across your convoy instead."

I frowned, not liking where this was going.

"There's a place beneath Hollows Mountain," he continued, "where they take prisoners and those who are unmarked. That's where they were taking you."

"And what exactly do they do with the prisoners?"

"It's a place where they bring you before the other Houses, who will either make you pledge to one, where you will spend the rest of your days as a slave, banish you, or execute you as a traitor."

"Wow," I muttered. "Sounds like a gem of a place."

Ehlark's expression was inscrutable. Clearly, sarcasm eluded him.

"Since we arrived at your convoy first, the other convoy with my comrades should already be at Hollows Mountain. However, the battle slowed us down. One of my comrades, who can transport others over long distances, most likely used up her strength to help those with you escape. Which will mean she and the rest of her group will need to lie low until their powers recharge."

I raised an eyebrow, already sensing where this was heading.

"We may only have a day or two before my comrades will be sentenced."

"So, what you're saying is—"

"If you want any chance of getting home," he said matter-of-factly, "you'll have to come with me to Hollows Mountain first."

"No. Absolutely not." I interrupted. "You said it's a place where people get enslaved or executed. Neither of those is on my to-do list." I stepped back, with my hands raised. "And what good would I even be? I don't have magic like you. I can't just wave my hands and poof, the ground does tricks for me."

His gaze dipped to the necklace at my throat, and a slow smile tugged at his lips as he rubbed his chin. "You have something special around your neck. Something that could protect us if needed."

He looked way too confident for someone who didn't realize I had no idea how I summoned that axe in the first place.

"You're still a stranger. What if this is some elaborate trap? What if you betray me and leave me there for your comrades? You don't know me. How am I supposed to trust your word?"

"You seemed to be forgetting," he said calmly, "that I saved you earlier. If this were a trap, you'd still be wearing those cuffs."

Okay. Fine. He had a point. But it still diverged from my plan.

"What if we make a contract?"

"A contract?"

"Yes. Where both of us get what we want."

I narrowed my eyes, studying him. "How would this contract be worth anything to me?"

"You want to find a way to get back home?"

I gave a short, reluctant nod. "Yes."

"If we make a blood contract," Ehlark said carefully, "you help me free the prisoners, and I'll ensure you get back home."

My brain immediately went to those movies where someone cuts their hand open, lets the blood drip into a bowl, chants a few creepy lines, and poof, instant spell. Was that what he was talking about?

"Why a *blood* contract?" I asked skeptically.

"A blood contract guarantees that we both follow through on our word. Otherwise, there are consequences."

That gave me pause. I chewed on the inside of my cheek, considering my options, not that I had any good ones.

Going off on my own? Yeah, that'd be a death sentence. I had no idea how to survive in this world. Hell, I didn't even know where to go. And if what he'd said was true, I'd barely escaped something worse than death. If I had any chance of making it out of here alive, it was probably with him, especially with those powers of his.

Which could come in handy later.

But what about my end of the deal? If I agreed to this contract and couldn't summon the axe again, would he turn on me? Or worse, leave me for dead?

"What if I *can't* summon the axe again?" The words tumbled out before I could stop them. He needed to know how unsure I was because, honestly, I wasn't so confident in myself.

He went quiet, rubbing his chin.

"I'm confident that when the moment demands it, you will use it. I have a good feeling about you."

I blinked. "You're trusting me based on a *feeling*?"

"Yep." He said confidently.

Glad one of us had faith.

My gaze swept over him again—the broad shoulders, the steady stance, the calm way he carried himself. He wasn't much taller than me, but he looked like someone who knew exactly what to do in a fight, someone who didn't spook easily. Logically, sticking close to him wouldn't be the worst idea. And if he believed the axe would reappear, perhaps I shouldn't doubt myself so quickly.

It happened once.

Who's to say it couldn't happen again?

"Fine," I muttered. "Let's do this *blood* contract."

Ehlark stepped closer, his broad frame filling the small space between us.

Actually, now that I looked at him more closely, his features seemed more youthful, like someone I would run into on a college campus. Which meant he had to be somewhere in his early twenties.

Even with dried blood streaked across his face and dirt smudged along his jaw, he still had a striking presence. His tan skin and short reddish-brown hair that curled at the tips complemented his look. His vibrant emerald-green eyes sparkled with energy and held a depth of beauty.

I half-expected him to pull out the dagger I had used to cauterize him, slice our palms, and shake hands like witches doing a spell. But then his grin widened, and so did his canines.

Wait.

Are his teeth getting longer?

My stomach flipped. "W—what are those for?"

Ehlark's confusion lasted only a second before he let out an amused chuckle. "These?" He bared his teeth even more. "They're used for intimidation—or, in this case, for making a blood contract."

I blinked. "Why can't we use *your* dagger?" Because that made way more sense than him biting me like some deranged vampire.

Is he a vampire?

"That dagger won't seal the deal the same way," he said, shaking his head. "A true binding contract requires a special blade or a blood seer, which we do not have. "This," he tapped one of his elongated canines. "Is the next best thing."

I stared at the tooth in question, unsure if I wanted to pass out or sprint into the nearest tree. "Okay, just for my own sanity, you're not some blood-sucking vampire, right?"

His brows shot up. "I take only a few drops of your blood," he countered, "but this word *vampire* has no meaning to me."

I dragged a hand down my face. "Okay. Never mind. You're not a vampire."

He nodded once, as if I'd declared him free of some horrific disease.

The thought of putting someone else's blood in my mouth was disgusting enough, and didn't anyone here care about blood-borne diseases? The revulsion twisting my face must have given me away. "Don't worry. My blood won't kill you." He extended a hand, waiting.

"Your arm, please."

Every instinct screamed this was a terrible idea, but what choice did I have?

Either risk swallowing someone's blood and possibly contract some foreign disease, or trust him and risk being betrayed and left behind so the soldiers could find me and finish the job.

Reluctantly, I offered my arm.

His grip was surprisingly gentle and warm as his fingers wrapped around my wrist. His thumb brushed over my skin, as if he were examining it more closely.

Then his teeth sank in.

A sharp sting of pain flared, enough to send a jolt through me. Warmth spread from the bite, a slow, trickling sensation that quickened my pulse.

"I don't suppose you have canines like mine?" He smiled widely, obviously proud of them.

"Definitely not." I shot back, flashing him a wide grin, one that showcased years of braces and a relentless dedication to flossing. *Perfectly normal human teeth, thank you very much.*

Ehlark huffed a quiet laugh. "Alright, we'll try it this way." He lifted his forearm and bit down until blood trickled to the side.

I watched in stunned silence as he was able to puncture himself without losing his composure. Then, without missing a beat, he extended his arm toward me.

"You have to drink."

"I have to what now?"

"For the contract to work, we must take in each other's blood. Hence why it's called a *blood contract*."

"But you said a few drops. Not actually drink it."

"Did I?" He said, placing his other hand behind his head.

This was not how I envisioned my day would go. But if this was what it took . . . *ugh.*

Reluctantly, I leaned forward, taking his forearm in my hands. My lips barely brushed against the warm, crimson streak before my tongue touched the blood.

To my complete shock, it wasn't coppery or metallic, as I had expected. Instead, it was warm and earthy, similar to the first time I smelled his scent in the cage.

I slowly released his wrist, swallowing the questionable sensation lingering on my tongue.

Ehlark studied me for a moment, something unreadable in his expression. Then he spoke.

> *"By blood and soil, bound by oath,*
> *I swear to get you home.*
> *My word to yours, and yours to mine,*
> *Only in betrayal, death will follow."*

"Wait, stop right there." I lifted my hand. "What do you mean by that last part, *only death shall follow?*"

Ehlark shrugged. "It guarantees that neither of us breaks the contract, or—" He dragged a thumb across his throat in a clear *you're dead* gesture.

I stared at him with wide eyes. "I never agreed to *death!*"

"It's only a formality," he said dismissively. "You won't really die. Probably."

"*Probably?*"

"Well, I've never actually seen someone die from breaking a contract." His voice trailed off with the last word.

"I can't do this. This is completely ridiculous."

I turned to walk away, but Ehlark caught my wrist, his grip firm but not forceful. "Listen, you wanted a guarantee; this is it. So, it's either the blood contract or you take my word for it."

I faltered, racing through any other rational option.

If this contract *truly* worked, it could be my only assurance of getting home. And as much as I strongly disliked the idea of this whole blood contract thing, trusting a stranger's word in a world like this felt even riskier.

All I have to do is keep my word.

I groaned, rubbing my temples. "*Ugh*, fine."

Ehlark's smile slid back into place. "Repeat after me," he began. "*By blood and soil, Bound by Oath—*"

I echoed his words:

"By blood and soil, bound by Oath,
I vow to help you,
My word to yours, and yours to mine.
Only in betrayal, death will follow."

After I finished the last part, my arm started to tingle with warmth where his lips had touched.

Something shifted between us, a force that felt both foreign and familiar. An invisible thread tightened around me, anchoring me to him. The puncture wounds on my arm throbbed with heat, the feeling radiating outward, and then, slowly, the warmth cooled as if the pact itself were sealing into place.

The sensation felt unnatural; it wasn't painful, nor did it feel forced, but something deep inside me knew I couldn't escape this, couldn't escape him, even if I wanted to.

But I had to accept it.

No matter how uneasy this bond made me feel, it was my best chance of getting home. And Ehlark was my *guarantee*.

"By the way," Ehlark said, breaking the silence. "I never got your name."

"Eleni. Eleni Gibson."

His eyes glimmered in the firelight as he repeated it.

"Eleni."

My name coming off his lip, for some reason, made it sound personal, sending a chill down my arm.

"Welcome to Thysia."

13

WILD ANIMAL

Why can't I work in Denver, Gram?" I argued, my voice trembling with frustration.

Gram stood by the sink, her back to me as she rinsed a dish, her movements steady. "Because it's too far away, and I need you here on the ranch."

"Yes, but it's supposed to be one of the top hospitals there," I pressed, gripping the edge of the kitchen table.

"You can work at the local community hospital." Her weathered hands held a faded dish towel. "They have a decent Emergency Room, and you can stay with me. The winter is going to be a harsh one this year, Eleni. I'll need every bit of help to get this place ready. I'm sorry, but my word is final."

Her tone was like a stab in the chest. I opened my mouth to argue again, but the look in her eyes stopped me. It wasn't anger; it was something more profound—worry, regret, love. The weight of her words settled on me like the chill of an early frost.

"But Gram," I whined. I wanted to say more, to fight for what I wanted, but the words never left my lips. The kitchen light above us flickered slightly, the warm glow softening the lines of her face. The scent of her fresh-baked bread drifted in the air, wrapping around me like a blanket. For a moment, it felt as if everything would be all right.

But then the edges of the scene began to blur, the comforting warmth slipping away. Gram's face faded, her features dissolving into shadows as the golden light dimmed, replaced by a cold, damp darkness.

⚬

That memory stirred emotions I had desperately tried to bury. It was the day I resented Gram for holding me back, for not letting me pursue what I wanted. I ended up applying to the hospital in Denver.

I should have talked to her and told her how I felt. But at the time, I resented feeling trapped on the ranch. Getting accepted felt like my chance, my shot at something bigger. A taste of the world outside of country living, of something different. By the time she found out, it was too late. The contract was signed, and I was already heading out the door.

That decision triggered one of the worst fights we've ever had. Afterward, I cut her off, stopped answering her calls, and ignored her voicemails for years. I let resentment take over instead of trying to understand her point of view. Now, I wish I hadn't ignored her or deleted the hundreds of messages she left on my phone. If I could go back, I'd listen to every single one. But all I had now was the last one, the final message she left me.

I pushed myself upright against the cave wall; the cool stone was a surprising contrast to where I had slept. I looked down at the necklace resting against my chest, feeling its warmth.

Did the necklace's magic keep me warm? If so, what else was it capable of?

My fingers traced the edges of the bone framing the gem, and a heaviness settled in me.

Why did you hide this from me, Gram? And more importantly, how did she ever end up with something like this?

After sealing the blood contract, Ehlark and I were both exhausted and agreed it was best to stay in the cave a little longer. Unfortunately, whatever Ehlark had scorched over the fire for dinner left me with a severe case of cottonmouth.

A toothbrush and some toothpaste would be great right about now.

And, of course, I also had to pee.

Ehlark had warned me about the dangers outside and told me to wake him if I needed anything, but I couldn't bring myself to do it. He needed rest. So I let him sleep, convincing myself it wouldn't take long.

The cool morning air welcomed me as I stepped outside. Dawn was nearing, and the soft light coated the forest in muted shades of gray and green. It was serene, reminding me of mornings on the ranch.

I treaded carefully through the unfamiliar terrain.

Years of hiking with Gram taught me to be more aware of my surroundings, and I found myself slipping back into those old habits as I ventured deeper into the woods. The sound of water drew my attention—a faint but promising trickle—and hope rose at the thought of finding a stream to drink fresh water from.

Before heading toward the rushing sound, I ducked behind a thick bush. Given my recent luck, the last thing I needed was to get caught in an awkward situation, or worse, attract some magical creature with a keen sense of smell. Years of hiking with Gram taught me how to stay downwind and be careful not to let my scent drift into the trees.

After I emptied my bladder, I adjusted my clothes, feeling somewhat more human again.

With that settled, I made my way towards the sound of water. It was steady, growing louder as I moved closer.

The stream's clear surface gleamed in the light as it wound between moss-covered rocks. My throat ached at the thought of drinking, of finally tasting something other than burnt ash. I bent down, my hands reaching toward the water, scooping handfuls to my mouth when something across the river caught my eye. Everything in my body froze, instinctively crouching lower to stay hidden. My eyes narrowed where the movement was.

At first, it was subtle, the movement in the landscape blending so seamlessly with the trees and light. But then, it stepped forward. Breaking through the tall brush on the far side of the river was a horse, or at least, something that resembled one.

Its silvery coat caught the light and changed color with the shadows, making it seem to blend into the forest. A creature woven from mist and moonlight rather than flesh and bone.

I remained still, not wanting to spook it.

Its form seemed unreal as it stood there, regal and stunning even from this distance. Then, its appearance started to change. Its coat shifted, transforming into shades of green and brown that blended seamlessly with its surroundings, making it nearly invisible. The effect was mesmerizing, like watching sunlight dance through a canopy of leaves. Its head turned toward me, and its ears pricked forward.

That's when I saw the mark on its forehead. It looked like a star, though the bottom point extended further than the others, trailing down toward the bridge of its nose like a delicate streak of light.

Its mane was long and black, flowing over its neck in a cascade of darkness. Then the coat faded back into the original silver. The transformation was smooth and effortless, as if it came naturally. It stood there, its gaze scanning the area with a calm intelligence.

What are you?

Any normal person would stay low and hidden, away from potential danger. But for some reason, something was pulling me forward.

Typically, you'd never get this close to a wild horse; they were notoriously aggressive and quick to charge if they sensed any threat to their herd. But this one was alone.

I didn't sense wild hostility or fear. It was loneliness. There was no herd, no others in sight—just him, standing in serene solitude.

His head shot up abruptly, his ears swiveling in my direction.

I stiffened as my pulse hammered through my chest because I had unintentionally stood up from my spot.

He snorted, nostrils flaring as he tried to catch my scent, his gaze fixed on me. But he didn't move, and neither did I. We stood there, watching each other. His posture wasn't hostile, and I made sure mine wasn't either. He seemed curious, not aggressive.

Then, to my surprise, he took a few cautious steps. My heart thundered, instincts not to startle him. I slowly stepped back. He was a wild animal, and I wasn't willing to take unnecessary risks.

The creature seemed to notice my retreat. His head dipped slightly as he licked his lips, which, for horses, was a sign of calm. Still thinking it was some type of horse, I didn't dare turn my back on him. I stayed still, maintaining a relaxed, non-threatening stance.

Without warning, his head shot up again, ears swiveling quickly. His body tensed, and as I observed, his shimmering coat blended again with the forest until he disappeared entirely.

How incredible, I mused, amazed by how effortlessly he vanished.

However, the awe was short-lived.

A crunch of leaves behind me heightened my senses, sending a jolt of awareness through my body.

Realizing I had left myself vulnerable, I quickly turned back toward the cave, but something stopped me. A crushing force engulfed me. My limbs wouldn't respond; my body was frozen as if invisible chains had snapped tightly around me. Then I dared to look down at what was restraining me.

Panic set in as black smoke-like wisps swirled around, revealing a towering figure in my view and bringing me face-to-face with it.

With *him*.

Before I could react, everything around me plunged into darkness.

14

REUNITED

Strong hands gripped my arms, holding me tightly as the suffocating darkness receded. No, not darkness, but shadows.

They retreated into Velorn and the dark corners of the forest where the pale morning light broke through. My instincts were to pull away, but my body wouldn't budge. Velorn stepped closer, his presence hitting like a storm you could feel in your bones. From a distance, it was beautiful and impossible not to watch. But up close? It would tear you apart.

Being this close in daylight also meant I could see his scars more clearly. There were five jagged marks, as if someone or something had tried to kill him and failed.

Something that hit closer to home than I expected.

"Where is it?" His voice was low, rough, and laced with something dangerous.

"Where's what? Your charming personality? Because it's sure as hell not here."

"The axe."

I yanked my arm away from his grip and tried to break free, but he lifted me effortlessly, pushed me against a tree, then seized both of my wrists, shoving them above my head and holding me there. His body caged mine, heat radiating off him in waves, and I suddenly forgot how to breathe.

If his goal was to terrify me, he was certainly doing a damn good job. Still, I refused to give him the satisfaction.

"Ohhh. *That* axe," I managed. "Yeah, no clue what you're talking about. Maybe check up your ass?"

He leaned into me, closing the already too-close gap between us. "There you go again, letting lies slip past that mouth of yours," he seethed. "If you are an unmarked House of Earth, there will be consequences."

Consequences? What the hell is he talking about?

Ehlark told me that the House of Earth no longer existed. So how could I be tied to something that was supposedly gone?

"If you value your life, little *Viri*, you will hand it over. Otherwise, the Blood Seer will decide your fate."

"First of all," I bit out, twisting against his iron grip, "my name is **Eleni**, not *little Viri*, whatever the fuck that means. You wanna threaten me? At least get my damn name right."

His expression remained cold, but there was the slightest arch in his brow.

"Secondly," I lifted my chin to glare back at him. "I don't know where the axe is."

That caused the slightest twitch in his scarred face.

Good.

"And third," I hissed, struggling harder against the bark digging into my back, "even if I knew where it was, do you really think I'd hand it over to you all willy-nilly?"

His hand tightened around my wrists as he silently stared, studying my face.

"You'll regret this decision."

Oh, I knew I would regret every word, but the last thing I wanted was for him to see how damn terrified I was inside. He let go of his grip, and I fell to the ground. He stood up to his full, imposing height and looked down at me as if I were a speck of dirt on his boot.

"Very well, Blood Seer it is."

He turned as the shadows reappeared around me, swallowing the light and draining every last bit of warmth from the forest.

Fuck, not again.

I tried to scream Ehlark's name, but something massive clamped over my mouth, cutting off the sound before it could escape.

⸻ ◆ ⸻

We reached the base of a massive mountain, its jagged peak disappearing into a veil of clouds above. The temperature suddenly dropped, piercing my skin and sending shivers throughout. The air was thinner, colder, and completely the opposite of what we had come from.

Every so often, I stopped to look around and take in the new scenery, but I was cut off when I felt a hand behind my back. "Move."

Velorn somehow whisked us here in a matter of seconds. One moment we were in the woods, and the next—darkness. I felt the rushing wind and the sensation of being pulled through a void that left me feeling disoriented and nauseous. I'd be perfectly fine never experiencing that again.

My stomach growled loudly, and I pressed a hand to it. If it were anyone else, I might've asked for a snack, but I highly doubted Velorn was the type to carry granola bars and mercy.

The farther we traveled, the more the path shifted. Torches lined the mountainside, their flames casting jagged shadows that danced against the rocks. The trail grew wider with each step until stone pillars appeared, guiding the way forward. Just ahead, two men stood at the base of the mountain, waiting.

Velorn grabbed my arm to stop me in front of the soldiers who were standing next to a massive gate engraved into the rock, towering above us. "She's the last one."

Last one?

What did he mean by that? Did the escape fail? Was everyone captured and dragged here, like me?

A horrible feeling settled in my stomach. I opened my mouth to demand answers, but his grip tightened on me, forcing my silence.

Asshole.

"Send her to be cleaned and prepped for the Blood Seer."

Cleaned and prepped?

Was I a sacrificial offering? Was this Blood Seer planning to eat me or something?

The soldier nodded before turning to open the gate.

I glanced around, frantically searching for any way out. What if Ehlark was out there somewhere, hiding, ready to swoop in and save me? But the sudden drop in temperature and the lack of trees told me otherwise. We were nowhere near the Wispwoods. But if this was where Ehlark's comrades were, then he would be coming this way eventually.

Velorn's grip lingered on my arm long enough to remind me there was no escape.

"Karma's a bitch, Velorn."

He gave no reaction, no hint of emotion behind that cold stare. He was a wall.

The soldier grabbed my arm, squeezing painfully before giving a quick nod to Velorn.

At least I won't have to deal with him anymore.

The gate ahead groaned loudly as massive stones shifted inward with a deep, rumbling sound that echoed through the mountain's belly.

Before me lay a tunnel carved straight into the center of the mountain, so wide and dark that it felt less like a passage and more like a mouth ready to swallow me whole.

"Move," the soldier barked, his fingernails digging into my skin. I turned back again, trying to escape into the light, but the stone door was already closing.

Torches lined the walls, dancing in a flamboyant pattern along the stone corridor and casting long shadows that shifted across the jagged rocks. As we rounded a corner, I saw narrow windows and ledges cut into the cliffside high above us. They spiraled in uneven patterns, so high that the mountain seemed to swallow them whole. Were they guard stations? Holding cells? Watch-towers? It was impossible to tell since there wasn't a single soul in sight.

Eventually, we reached a white stone archway. Its surface was smooth, adorned with intricate, swirling symbols etched so finely they appeared to emerge from the stone itself. The soldier beside me reached out a hand, fingers crackling faintly with a yellow glow. As they rested against the stone, the symbols on the arch flared to life, glowing with a ghostly light that pulsed outward.

This whole world really couldn't run on magic alone. Could it?

Then again, watching the soldier's hands glow with a yellowish hue, and it bleed into the wall, seemed like magic. Perhaps it was common practice. Using magic was like pulling out a phone or turning a key—just something you did.

"In you go," the soldier said, pushing me through the doorway. I turned back to give him some not-so-pleasant words, but the heavy doors groaned shut. Panic took hold; my hands frantically reached the stone, but the massive doors were already sealed, and the bright symbols dimmed once more.

This was not good.

Tight, enclosed spaces and I did *not* get along.

I took a deep breath and forced myself to face the corridor again.

One step.

Then another.

Deep breaths, Eleni. Keep it together.

Each echo rang loudly in the silence, and my pulse pounded as I braced for, well, anything. Then, the narrow hallway finally revealed a room.

Soft, golden light flooded the space, while the atmosphere grew warm and humid, rich with the aroma of herbs and a hint of floral notes. Steam curled along the floor and ascended in spirals from the expansive, shallow pools built directly into the stone.

Is this a bathhouse?

Of all the things I was bracing for, this was *not* one of them.

I expected to be thrown into a dank dungeon, shackled to a wall, and possibly stripped of whatever dignity remained. Not a daytime spa.

The polished stone walls glistened with moisture, their smooth surfaces etched with delicate artwork of vines that twisted around celestial patterns, symbols that appeared entirely foreign. Steam curled upward from large sunken baths opened into the floor, making it feel like a millionaire's bathroom.

Damn, this was nice. Probably the best thing I've seen since landing here.

I stepped further in until my eyes caught movement. A figure moved in one of the tubs, and when she lifted her face toward mine, my heart stopped.

Was I seeing a ghost?

Sitting in the warm water in front of me was a young woman with long, curly black hair and hazel eyes.

"You're alive!" I gasped, standing there staring at Vyria.

"Eleni!" Vyria cried out, splashing out of the water without a shred of modesty. She was completely naked as she hurried toward me, nearly slipping as she threw herself into my arms. We collided, laughing and sobbing at the same time, clinging like survivors separated at sea. Tears streamed down my cheeks as I held her tighter, overwhelmed by the simple, impossible fact that she was here, alive and not dead.

When we finally pulled away, I stared at her in awe, wiping my face. "But how? I saw the sword go right through you."

My eyes drifted to the spot where the blade had pierced her. There, above her chest, was a small, pale scar. It was fully healed, like Ehlark's wound.

"I thought I was dead too," she said softly. "But then shadows surrounded me. Everything went dark. And when I woke up, I was in the healing quarters here."

Shadows and *darkness.*

Velorn.

The guy who nearly choked the life out of me and threatened to turn me over to some ominous Blood Seer. The one who stood over a pile of dead bodies. Surely, she couldn't be talking about him. I shook my head.

No. There's no way.

"They were able to patch me up," Vyria continued. "Said I got lucky."

"I'm just glad you're alive." I pulled her in for one last squeeze.

"Where are we? And why is it so nice?"

"Oh," she blinked, recalling our location. "We're in the purifying rooms. It's where you get cleaned up before seeing the Blood Seer. At least, that's what the healer told me when she brought me in."

I raised an eyebrow. "*Purifying* room?"

"Yes," she nodded, a little sheepishly. "Apparently, the water has magical properties. Supposed to draw out any impurities before your meeting. It's the ritual you must do. Every village with a Blood Seer does it, though I've never gone through one myself."

The baths appeared to be nothing more than stone tubs. But then again, this world did seem to rely heavily on magic.

"Come on, Eleni," Vyria insisted, her eyes bright with insistence as she took my hand. "You'll feel so much better once you're soaking in it. Trust me."

As much as I craved a hot bath to wash away the dried blood, dirt, and the overall smell of not having bathed in a week, all I could really think about was how to escape this place.

"I know what you're thinking, and no, there's no way out of this room. I already tried," Vyria said. The way her eyes darted toward the walls told me she meant it.

"Eleni, trust me," she added gently. "Once you step foot in the water, you'll see."

I hesitated, scanning the room once more for any hidden exits or cracks in the walls. Anything I might have missed, but there was nothing: just polished stone, swirling etchings, and steam.

"Okay, fine. Only because you said so."

One by one, I slowly peeled off each layer of clothing, leaving only the necklace on.

These clothes were my last real tether to Earth, to home. They served as a reminder of who I was and why I had to survive this place. I folded them carefully, bending down to place them in the corner of the room, when a loud gasp escaped from Vyria's lips.

I turned quickly toward the door, anticipating danger—

But she wasn't looking at the door; she was staring at me. Her expression was wide-eyed, frozen somewhere between awe and fear.

Right. I didn't need to ask what she'd seen.

The large, jagged scars across my back stood out sharply against my skin—scars I was blessed with over six years ago.

"S-sorry, I didn't mean to make such a noise, but what happened?"

"Animal attack," I said, walking back to the tub. "It happened a lifetime ago. I don't even notice them anymore."

But I *did* notice them.

Every time I stepped out of the shower and caught a glimpse in the mirror or wore a tank top, people would stare, then look away in pity. The scars were always there—a constant reminder.

I detested talking about them. Not because I was ashamed, but because the moment I said it out loud, I'd *hear it* again.

The guttural growl. The tearing of flesh. The sound of claws and teeth raking down my spine like it wanted to rip it straight from my body.

So, I didn't talk about it.

"What kind of animal does that?"

"The grizzly kind."

Vyria looked at me with confusion. She still didn't know that I wasn't from this world, and explaining what a bear was would probably make things more complicated. Luckily, she didn't push the topic further.

The heat seeped into my muscles, melting away the tension I hadn't even realized I was holding as I fully immersed myself in the bath. The steam curled around me, fragrant with an herbal scent—something similar to eucalyptus. Whatever it was, it worked. My nerves relaxed, lifting the constant pressure in my chest. I lifted my arm, expecting to see the usual mess of scratches and bruises. But instead, the wounds I had days ago slowly faded, and the discoloration lightened. The cuts were smoothing over, and my skin was repairing itself.

My body, moments ago sore and battered, suddenly felt . . . *whole.*

Did it also heal my old scars?

I turned to examine the back of my arm, but there it was, in the same spot, with the same jagged line. That meant the scars on my back were still there.

As quickly as hope flared in my chest, it deflated.

Vyria must have seen the disappointment in my face. "Sadly, the baths can only wash away recent wounds."

My eyes drifted to my wrist, the place where Ehlark had bitten me. Those marks remained.

I wonder if the magic recognized what it was and left it untouched.

I leaned back against the side of the tub, exhaling slowly. The heat cradled me like a weighted blanket, and for the first time in days, I felt a sliver of peace.

Vyria was right. I did need this.

After a few quiet moments had passed, I turned to her. "How long do they let us stay in here?"

"Not sure." She took a deep breath and sank deeper in the water until only her face was visible.

"Vyria?"

"Yes?" Her eyes stayed closed as she answered, as if she, too, refused to let the peace of this moment slip away.

"What do you know about the Blood Seer?"

Vyria's eyes opened slowly, but her gaze didn't fix on me. Instead, she watched the steam rise from the water, her expression distant. "When you come of age, your powers awaken. Those powers can be wild and dangerous. And if they aren't placed in the right House, they can destroy you. Belonging to a House helps control your magic and keeps you grounded. The Blood Seer's duty is to determine which House you're best suited for."

Okay, that didn't sound *too* terrible. Like applying to college, but instead of choosing a school, you get matched with a House based on your elemental powers. Same concept except, you know, with life-or-death consequences.

"Then why is it that whenever someone mentions the Blood Seer, I get this pit in my stomach?" I pressed. It wasn't just me; I'd noticed it every time the soldiers, Vyria, and even Velorn mentioned the name. Unease shifted in their eyes.

"They are figures of both reverence and fear," Vyria said softly. "Some have more authority than others. And those types can do more than assign you to a House. They can also judge you." She said the last words as if they tasted bitter.

"Judge you?" I reverberated.

This time, her eyes met mine. "When my brother came of age, my mother took him to a Blood Seer. When she returned, she was alone." She drew in a shaky inhale. "A single drop of blood is all it takes. If the Seer deems you a threat to Thysia's future, they take you away. And you don't come back."

"They took your brother?" My voice cracked with disbelief. These so-called Blood Seers had *that* much authority?

One drop of blood, and they decided your entire fate? It sounded so cruel.

"I was thirteen," Vyria said softly. "My powers hadn't awakened yet. My mother was terrified that what happened to my brother would happen to me. She never took me to the Blood Seer. That's why I remain unmarked."

I couldn't believe what I was hearing. These Blood Seers had the power to take children from their families forever, all over a drop of blood. Ire simmered inside me at the thought of Vyria's brother being taken and her village being destroyed. The captives in the carriage, the young boy, all of it came crashing down on me.

Did that mean her mother, too?

I hesitated, unsure if I was pushing too far, but I had to know.

"Vyria, why did they destroy your village?"

"Because my village loved and worshipped the Matriarch of the House of Earth, and they refused to align with any other. Because of our loyalty, they saw us as threats to the king." Her eyes welled up with tears, spilling over before she could blink them away. "My mother was ashed, like the rest of them in my village."

Vyria's hands flew to her face, her head sinking into them. My eyes burned, and before I could stop them, tears rolled down my cheeks. I moved to her side, wrapping my arms around her, holding her as tightly as I could.

Words had never been my strength when it came to comforting grief, but I'd learned in the ER that sometimes silence carried more weight than anything you could say. So, I held her while she wept. Wept for her mother. Wept for her brother and for their entire village that refused to back down to a tyrannical ruler.

The moment was shattered when the door creaked open, and a female soldier stepped into the bathhouse. "The Blood Seer is ready."

Heat flowed through me, a wave of anger I couldn't explain. Then I noticed it—the warmth against my skin. My gaze dropped to the necklace on my chest. The gem pulsed with a soft glow, barely noticeable, but it was there, and it felt . . . *alive.*

15

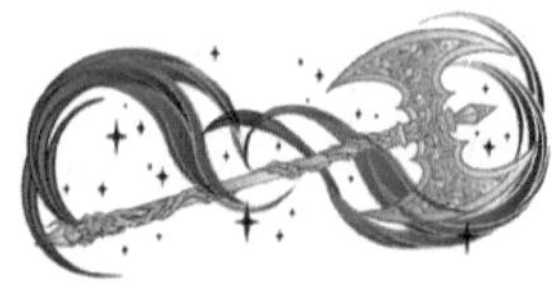

BLOOD SEER

The soldier was a woman of few words as she handed us plain robes. The fabric felt soft and luxurious, woven from a material I couldn't quite place. The loose fit hung awkwardly on my frame, and the absence of underwear and a bra made me acutely aware of my body.

I missed my clothes and wanted them back, but after days without washing and being covered in dried blood, sweat, and other substances, I understood why.

We were led down a long corridor as people walked past us, keeping their distance. Vyria kept her head down, but I couldn't help but notice everything.

Everyone seemed normal. No one looked starved or frightened; they were simply minding their own business.

"Child, where do you come from?"

Vyria came to an abrupt halt as a tall figure stood before her. She wore a deep hooded cloak, but her face was visible. Her skin was as dark as midnight, smooth and luminous like polished obsidian, but her eyes were a shade of blue I'd never seen in any human before. Not electric blue, not ice blue, but more like the color of a distant, undiscovered planet. They were otherworldly.

And I was staring like an idiot.

"Do not be afraid," the stranger assured. "Your hand, please."

She extended her hand toward Vyria, who hesitated before slowly placing her trembling hand into the woman's. Then, almost as quickly, Vyria let out a startled yelp as she jerked back, and I noticed the cut on her finger.

"What did you do?" I stepped in front of her, placing myself between them.

The woman's gaze slid to me. Looking into her eyes was like staring up into the boundless sky. They were stunningly beautiful yet terrifying. My instincts urged me to look away, but I kept her gaze. Cloak or no cloak, this woman exuded power. If this came to a fight, she'd wipe the floor with me.

"Please step aside," the soldier ordered, her hand resting on the hilt.

The stranger's focus remained on Vyria and me, completely ignoring the soldier's demand.

"I like your spirit."

Her smile held no warmth, only a challenge.

I was torn between punching her or running when she lifted a slender, finger-sized dagger. I hadn't even noticed her holding it.

Slowly, she raised the blade to her lips.

What the—

The woman tasted Vyria's blood, then wiped the blade clean before tucking it beneath her robes. "I mean no harm," she said evenly. "I was merely curious. You may continue your path."

Curious about what? My brows furrowed, and I looked at Vyria, who also seemed confused.

"Move, ladies." The soldier barked, urging us forward.

We were about to pass the stranger when suddenly she pivoted. Her hand shot out and grabbed Vyria's wrist—the same one she cut moments earlier. Her fingers tightened, and she murmured something softly under her breath.

It lasted only a second. When the soldier turned, the stranger had already disappeared. Vyria stood wide-eyed and unfocused. "Hey." I placed a hand on her shoulder. "Are you okay?"

She blinked herself out of whatever spell she'd been in. A small, shaky smile wavered at her lips. "I think so."

Vyria and I entered an impressive hall, its walls adorned with intricate designs and the same symbols I noticed at the mountain's entrance. The room buzzed with conversation, and people wore a vibrant mix of flowing robes, layered fabrics, and exotic designs that seemed unique to each individual.

We were led into another room where a long, imposing table stretched across the front. Seated behind the table were figures dressed in elaborate, jewel-toned robes with deep crimsons, yellows, and blacks, all decorated with metallic thread and embossed with unique symbols.

They carried themselves with a kind of authority that made my stomach tighten. When Vyria and I stepped forward, the crowd of faces turned, their gazes pinning us like insects under glass. Heat crawled up my neck, and I fought the urge to retreat.

Some whispered behind raised hands, their voices hushed but conversation unmistakably focused on us. A few remained silent, but their eyes—their eyes were worse than words.

There wasn't an ounce of pity behind them.

Beside me, Vyria shifted nervously, the tension in her shoulders mirroring my own.

After a long, painful eternity of everyone's stares, a voice rose above the sea of murmurs, silencing the room. I turned toward the source of the commanding voice.

"Let's begin, shall we?" said a man at the end of the table. The female soldier shoved Vyria and me forward, putting us front and center.

A slow *tap, tap, tap* echoed through the room.

I turned toward the sound as an elderly woman emerged from the far side, moving with unhurried purpose.

She was short, barely reaching my shoulder, and hunched slightly as she leaned on a long, gnarled staff decorated with old, weathered beads and tiny stones that softly clicked with each step. Despite her frail frame, there was an intimidating presence that silenced the crowd around her. Her pale eyes, sharp with unsettling clarity, scanned the room with a focus that made it feel as though she already knew everything there was to know.

This had to be the Blood Seer.

I was still skeptical, especially when looking at the woman in front of me now. Her presence reminded me of an old patient back home, one of those sweet, unassuming elderly women who could charm anyone with her gentle voice and soft smile, until she didn't. She had that same deceptive appearance. At first glance, it seemed innocent, but I couldn't shake the feeling that once the light faded, she would turn into a devil with a smile.

I glanced at Vyria, noticing how her eyes remained fixed on the Seer. I reached out and took Vyria's hand, squeezing it. "It's going to be okay." Even if I wasn't entirely confident myself.

The Blood Seer stopped before Vyria, her gaze calculating as she studied her. Vyria stood stiffly, her chin raised, though I felt her hand squeezing tighter in mine.

"Do you know who I am, child?" Her voice sounded ancient, and she carried herself with the hint of someone who disliked their time being wasted.

Vyria nodded.

The Blood Seer's lips curled into a harsh smile. "Good." Then her gaze went to me. "And you, child, do you know who I am?"

I gave a silent nod, mirroring Vyria.

"Very good."

She stepped forward, the beads on her staff rattling softly with each movement. "You two stand before me unmarked. That is a crime in the eyes of the Houses across Thysia. No mark means no House. No House means no protection, no purpose, no place among our people."

Her tone had grown colder, more formal, like she'd repeated this many times.

"I do not care what tragedies have befallen you, nor the reasons your village's Blood Seer did not mark you. That is the past. Here and now, your path is decided. You are brought before me to determine whether you are worthy of joining a House." Her eyes gleamed as the torchlight highlighted the cloudy gray of her irises.

She was blind.

"Or a threat, and should be taken to the dungeons and tried for your transgressions for not joining a House."

Well, I was screwed.

I didn't belong to any House. I didn't even learn about the Elemental Houses until days ago. And magic? I didn't have any.

Well, except for the axe. But that wasn't even mine. It was the necklace. If this Seer searched me and found nothing, would she immediately send me to the dungeons? Or worse, would she have me executed on the spot? A sense of unease twisted within, pulling me toward the worst outcome, until a flashback surfaced.

Ehlark mentioned freeing prisoners. Were the prisoners here? If so, that means he and his rebel group would be coming this way. Relief flared inside me.

If I could find a way to reach them first and help them escape, then I'd be fulfilling my part of the blood contract. This meant Ehlark would be obligated to keep his promise. He'd have no choice but to ensure I'd get home.

My mind raced as I tried to piece together a plan, but the Blood Seer's voice interrupted my thoughts.

"Your hand, child."

Vyria gave my hand one last squeeze before hesitantly pulling away. She lifted her chin and offered her hand to the Seer.

The woman reached out with gnarled fingers tipped with nails like obsidian shards and sliced Vyria's palm. She flinched but didn't pull away from her grip. The Seer brought Vyria's bleeding hand to her mouth and drank. The room seemed to hold its breath, waiting for the Blood Seer's response.

The way she savored Vyria's blood and the faint hum in her throat sent a shiver down my spine. Ehlark had never reacted like that when he drank mine. Then again, I'd tasted his blood, and it wasn't bad.

The Seer's face remained pinched, her eyes half-closed and squinting. Finally, she spoke, her voice echoing so everyone could hear.

"She does not pose a threat to any House."

The Seer's eyes snapped open, gleaming as they swept over Vyria from head to toe.

Maybe she wasn't completely blind.

"However, she belongs to the House of Water." Murmurs moved through the room, apprehension giving way to clear disappointment.

I didn't understand it. Was the House of Water a problem?

"Her powers are still young," the Seer continued. "She has time to learn and adapt to whatever House she is bound to, if someone chooses her."

The Seer let go of her hand, and I saw it—that glimmer of relief in Vyria's eyes. She hadn't been marked a traitor like her brother.

"What's her age?" asked a man at the table.

"Your age, child."

"Eighteen," Vyria replied softly.

"Young enough for your brothel, Lord Fren," one of the other men sitting nearby commented.

"Lord Fren," the Seer said, her voice cutting through the conversation. "Would you like to claim her? Even though her powers are not aligned with the House of Air?"

My stomach sank in horror.

"How could I say no to such a pretty face?" Lord Fren drawled, lounging in his chair as his eyes roamed Vyria. "Especially one with the potential to fetch a high price. If she's still pure, she'll bring even more. That's why I'm here. That's why we're all here.

To see what opportunities we can seize from those who refused to pledge willingly to their Houses."

He spoke as though we were cattle, as if our lives and our bodies were commodities to be sold to the highest bidder. They were treating us like slaves.

And the way he spoke about Vyria's virginity made my blood boil. There were many things I could tolerate. But men who preyed on young women? Who viewed innocence as a profit margin? That was where I drew the line.

The last thing I was going to do was watch Vyria be dragged off to serve in some lecherous brothel, her body used for someone else's disgusting greed.

"You know the rules, Lord Fren," the Blood Seer continued. "Their own House has the first right to claim them. If they pass, then you may bid with the others."

Lord Fren sat back down. "You and I both know, no one from the House of Water comes here."

It made me sick.

I wanted to punch this man and wipe that disgusting smirk off his face, but a voice called out from the crowd.

"My apologies, Lord Fren," a familiar voice said. "But I will be taking this young woman with me. She is, after all, part of *my* House."

A woman stepped forward from the crowd. Her skin radiated against the deep blue of her regal gown, with the fabric catching the dim torchlight like moonlight on water. Her hair flowed down her back in glossy braids, and her presence immediately changed the energy in the room.

She was the stranger from earlier.

"Lady Anira," Lord Fren said, visibly surprised. "Didn't expect to see you here, of all places."

Everyone seemed to shift uncomfortably in her presence. I didn't blame them. She was a sight to behold—tall, strong, and appearing to be the most powerful one in the room. Even the Blood Seer adjusted her stance.

"I was informed there were unmarked elementals taken," she said evenly, her gaze moving to us before returning to him. "I've come to ensure the ones belonging to the House of Water are returned to me, properly."

Why was this woman hiding her identity earlier? Was she not welcomed here because of the House she belonged to? Judging by everyone's reactions, it certainly seemed that way. I peered at the soldiers, their hands resting on their hilts as they adjusted their stances.

Who was this woman?

The Blood Seer stepped forward. "Lady Anira of the House of Water, as you know, unmarked elementals must first be brought here for trial. To determine whether they are traitors to Thysia."

"I'm aware," Lady Anira replied. "That's why I am here now, to collect all water elementals belonging to my House, including any prisoners who have not yet been executed." She spoke with such confidence that even the Seer blinked in surprise.

"Lady Anira," the Seer continued, "you know the law. Once an elemental breaks Thysian law, they must face justice."

No one else spoke. No one dared to challenge the Seer, except Lady Anira. She didn't flinch or even blink at the display of power. The longer I watched, the more the soldiers shifted on their feet, gripping their weapons tighter. Whoever Lady Anira was, she exuded something that twisted the room around her, a kind of power that people didn't want to test.

I was starting to like this Lady Anira.

Finally, Lady Anira gave a slight nod. "Very well."

"As is required by law," the Blood Seer announced, her tone clipped, "she must be officially marked before leaving Hollows Mountain. She must be bound to you, Lady Anira, before departure."

"I am aware," Lady Anira replied as she stepped forward.

Out of the corner of my eye, I glanced at Lord Fren. His smug expression vanished entirely, replaced by the unmistakable look of a man who had been denied what he believed he was entitled to.

Good. Slink back to your hole, you disgusting creep.

Lady Anira stood before the Blood Seer and Vyria, with the tension in the room clearly visible as the Seer moved forward again.

This time, something appeared in her hand.

From her palm, an obsidian-black blade emerged, gleaming like glass forged in darkness and shining with a ghostly light, deadly at its edge.

It reminded me of when the axe appeared in my hands. The same eerie suddenness, the same presence. Only this one didn't feel familiar.

I watched in silence as the ritual unfolded. The Seer spoke her words peculiar and lyrical, in a language I couldn't understand.

She made a swift cut across Vyria's wrist, then another on Lady Anira's. The two women reached for each other without hesitation, grabbing onto each other like a lifeline. The Seer kept chanting, and that's when I suddenly felt the temperature drop.

The power in the dagger crackled softly, humming low as if it were coming to life.

Their joined hands glowed, triggering a burst of glowing blue light from their skin, each hue slightly different. Vyria's was a radiant aquamarine, while Lady Anira's was a deep, pulsing sapphire. Her sapphire glow was spreading up her arm, spiraling and winding like living rivers. The older woman's veins blazed bright for a moment, then, slowly, Vyria's veins did the same thing.

The entire process was mesmerizing.

Their power hummed off them in waves, as if the magic itself were pulsating out like a heartbeat. And for the first time since I met Vyria, there was peace in her eyes, a hint of joy, even. She seemed to embrace the person she was binding herself to.

Then, slowly, the glow in their veins faded. They disappeared into Vyria's skin, becoming faint impressions, until they were gone.

The Seer's chant ceased as the energy and power around her faded.

For a heartbeat, I'd forgotten why I was there.

Then, the Seer stepped toward me.

I was in such deep shit.

16

RIFTBLOOD

"Now, you, child."

Her cloudy eyes pierced through me, suddenly making me feel exposed.

Once she drinks my blood, she'll know.

She might even realize I'm not from this world. And then what?

Interrogation? Probably.

Torture? Most likely.

Death? Definitely.

Come on, Eleni. Think, dammit!

Okay, best-case scenario? She would find nothing valuable and send me to a prison cell with the other captives. Maybe that's what should happen. Those were the people Ehlark was trying to save. If I ended up with them, I would have a better shot at escaping.

Bracing myself, I extended my hand toward her, trying to hide the trembling in my hands.

The Seer's fingers were like ice as she took hold of my wrist. With one swift motion, she dragged a nail across my palm. I flinched at the sting, but it wasn't as bad as I expected—more heat than pain. Then she brought my hand to her lips and drank.

The feeling was repulsive.

What is up with these people and their fixation on blood?

Her mouth was dry, and I could feel the pull of something deeper than blood, as if she was tasting my deepest, darkest secrets. Her face twisted as her brows furrowed together. She jerked her head to the side, then the other, as though fighting something invisible.

I held my breath, begging the universe not to let her see it. That glint of something not born of this world, that strange truth that didn't belong here.

The necklace against my chest hummed. It was soft at first, then grew stronger, emanating a low pulsing warmth that vibrated beneath my skin.

It wasn't loud, not like a sound. It was more like a presence that filled my ears and under my skin. I looked around, but no one else reacted, including the Seer.

Am I the only one hearing this?

Her eyes snapped open, and the warmth from the necklace vanished immediately. She stilled, her expression blank for a heartbeat, then she refocused on me.

"W-what are you?" she whispered. "I ... I cannot see anything. *Nothing.*"

The spark of hope and an instinctual sense of safety disappeared. Abruptly, she clutched my wrist tighter, her razor-sharp nails digging into my skin. Her face twisted with confusion and suspicion.

"Who have you seen before me, child?"

"No one," I stammered, the truth spilling out too fast.

Her eyes narrowed to slits. "You are cloaked, shrouded in something ancient. You are hiding what you are. And there is only one kind that can do that."

She leaned in closer, sniffing at my skin. "You are *Riftblood*. I can smell it on you."

Everyone in the room gasped. A wave of horror spread through the crowd, followed by the sudden rise of anxious murmurs.

Riftblood.

Ehlark mentioned the massive war involving the Riftblood and how they were seen as even worse than the unmarked. If they thought I was one, that meant I'd be in deep shit.

"If she truly is *Riftblood*," a voice from the table hissed, "she is a threat to all Houses. Especially since we do not know what magic she's capable of." The Blood Seer's gaze snapped back to me, and there was no mistaking the fury blazing in her milky eyes. She looked at me like I was a disease that needed to be eradicated.

I tried to yank my hand free, but she held it tightly. Her fingers were like iron bands, and her strength was surprisingly strong for someone who looked so old.

I couldn't break free.

A sudden, cold sensation curled around my hands, and my breath caught as I dared to look down. From the places where the Blood Seer's nails dug into my skin, thin wisps of ink snaked upward, delicate and stealth-like, slithering around her wrists and then upward on her arm. She was so preoccupied that she didn't even notice what was happening. Then I remembered her cloudy eyes.

The old hag was blind.

Her mouth opened to speak again, but the shadows moved faster. In an instant, they rose upward, slipping past her lips and into her mouth. She gave a sudden cough that grew more consistent and violent with every passing second. Her milky eyes were wide as she grabbed at her throat, trying to speak.

"Rift—blood."

Finally, her grip finally broke as she hunched eye level to the ground.

"R-Rift—."

She kept trying to force the word out, like saying it might somehow stop what was coming. A warning, perhaps. Maybe even a plea. But it was already too late. One moment, she was gasping, and the next, she collapsed to the floor.

I stood there watching in stunned disbelief.

"Seize that murderer!" someone yelled from the crowd.

Chaos erupted in the room as people jumped from their chairs. Some ran out, while others hid behind the soldiers approaching me. Panic exploded in my chest like a firecracker. I needed to get out of here. *Now.*

I searched for Lady Anira and Vyria for help, but in the midst of the chaos around me, I couldn't find them.

Soldiers surged forward, readying their weapons. Their expressions twisted between confusion and anger. I didn't even realize I was retreating until my back slammed into something solid.

Expecting another soldier, I turned around but froze when I saw a tall man now standing inches from me. His long, light blonde hair framed a sharp, rugged, deeply intimidating face.

His masculine presence, combined with intense dark brown eyes, made my stomach churn with unease.

"You can lower your weapons." The man's voice was calm but authoritative. The room seemed to settle with his words as everyone stopped scrambling around, and soldiers halted their advance toward me. Whoever this man was, he held power, which I wasn't sure was reassuring.

"This, *Riftblood*," he announced, "will be a valuable asset to the House of Fire."

A wave of murmurs spread across the room, but no one dared challenge him.

His dark eyes locked onto mine with intimidating force as he stepped in close enough so only I could hear. "If you want to leave here alive, you'll do exactly as I say."

I swallowed hard. I didn't trust him, but what other choice did I have?

"What about the Blood Seer?" someone called out from the crowd.

"It appears it was simply her time to pass into the afterlife," he said evenly.

But I knew what had really happened.

And I had the feeling he did too.

He turned to face the crowd again, lifting his voice so all could hear. "Since our Seer is no longer present to perform the binding, we'll settle this matter with a contract instead. To assure those who question their safety that she will not cause harm."

My stomach sank.

Are you kidding me?

My thoughts instantly went to Ehlark and to the blood contract we'd made in that cave. The echo of his words still lingered in my memory.

What is sworn shall not be broken.

I remembered the warmth of his breath before his lips brushed my skin, the sharp pressure of his bite, and the heat that followed. I could still feel it.

And suddenly, I missed his safety.

Perhaps it was the contract. Maybe it was something else entirely. But the pull toward him hit me with unexpected force.

What would happen if I entered into another contract?

Would it break the first one? The bond I'd made with Ehlark? Or worse, would it tear me apart trying to serve both?

The idea of binding myself to someone else made my skin crawl. I couldn't explain it, but it felt like I was betraying Ehlark somehow. I was so tired of people slicing into me as if I were a sacrificial goat at some altar. There had to be another way.

"I refuse."

He leaned in closer again, his breath uncomfortably warm against my ear. "If you don't accept my offer, everyone in this room will kill you."

I forced myself to look around the room. The soldiers surrounding us stood at attention, blocking any escape routes, their swords still drawn.

Dammit, blondie was right.

They would kill me if I tried to run. Right here, completely bypassing me, going down to the dungeons, leaving me with no other option.

"Fine."

If I hadn't been in this situation and had seen him walking down the street talking with someone else, I would have thought he was normal. However, the way he spoke to me was anything but friendly. His smile wasn't genuine, and neither was the act he was putting on for everyone in the room. Something in my gut told me this guy was bad news.

Blondie smiled with a slow curl of his lips. "Velorn."

Velorn?

Oh, you've got to be kidding me.

Just hearing his stupid name made heat flare up in my cheeks.

Velorn emerged from the corner, watching and waiting. He didn't appear; he unfolded like darkness taking shape. One moment, the corner was empty, just another patch of dimly lit stone, and the next, he was there—solid, composed, and utterly still. Given the murderous shadows, I knew he couldn't be far since he discreetly killed the Blood Seer, and I was being blamed for it.

Fucker.

I hated him even more now than before. I really thought I was never going to see him again, but nope. Karma decided to bring him right back to me.

He moved with quiet, predatory grace, making the air feel heavier with his mere presence. He wasn't wearing the armor as before. Instead, he wore a dark tunic that hugged his frame. His black pants were tucked neatly into worn boots, each step purposeful and silent. There was nothing flashy about his clothes, just a presence that seemed to swallow the space around him. I wasn't the only one who noticed it. The soldiers nearby also adjusted their stances.

Apparently, I wasn't the only one uncomfortable with Velorn.

His eyes moved to mine as he approached. They contained no kindness or emotion, only a piercing calculation.

Velorn bowed slightly toward the tall male. "Prince Malakar."

So, the blondie was called *Malakar*. And did he say *prince?*

"I need you to bind a contract with her."

My head jerked so fast it was practically trying to detach from my neck. "Oh, hell no." I threw my hand out in a sweeping gesture that encompassed all six-foot-whatever of Velorn's sullen, shadow-drenched nightmare self. "There is *no way* I'm doing a blood contract with this asshole!"

He was *literally* the reason I was here in the first place. If it weren't for him, I'd still be . . . well, anywhere else but here.

And even if we forgot that minor detail, I had zero interest in contracting myself to a murderous psycho who, I'm pretty sure, *enjoyed* killing people right in front of me. A man whose eyes promised ruin, misery, and possibly a slow, painful death.

"Velorn is my most trusted ally and tracker," he said as if that was meant to comfort me. "He'll ensure no harm comes to you while you're here. I wouldn't trust anyone else for this contract."

I glared at Velorn, unable to hide the disgust on my face. He didn't flinch or blink. He merely watched me as though I were a fly on the wall.

"I have private matters that you cannot be involved in. When we arrive at my fortress in Emberhold, we'll finalize a proper binding contract."

I closed my eyes and took a slow, shaky breath. "So, this contract you want me to do with him is temporary?"

"Yes."

I didn't like this. Not one bit.

"What are the terms?" I finally asked, the words burning my throat like fire.

Malakar's smile returned. "Simple. You'll remain at Velorn's side until we reach Emberhold."

He made it sound so easy, a simple transaction that had no consequences.

I hated this—all of it.

I wanted nothing to do with Velorn. I despised him and wanted to steer as far away from him as possible. But what other options did I have? It was either a temporary contract or pretty much die right now.

"Okay." I managed, though it felt like swallowing tar.

"Excellent. Now—"

"Wait," I interrupted. "I have terms of my own."

If I were going to be stuck in another contract, I should have a say.

"He," I gestured, pointing to Velorn, not wanting to look at him. "Must swear in this contract to ensure nothing happens to me. No harm. No accidents. Nothing."

Malakar stood still, his eyes narrowing as he considered my words. "So, you want his protection then?"

I nodded once. Malakar might not notice, but I saw it. Every time Velorn looked at me, even with those cold, calculating eyes, there was something darker beneath. Something that hinted that if I made one wrong move, he wouldn't hesitate to kill me in my sleep. And the worst part? He might actually enjoy it.

"Then it's a deal."

Before I had time to second-guess myself, Velorn stepped forward, closing the distance between us. His tall frame practically engulfed the space around me. My reflexes tensed automatically, expecting that same cold intensity he always carried, but when I met his unforgiving amber eyes, it wasn't bitterness staring back at me.

Was that *annoyance?*

He may be just as hesitant to take on this contract, which could work to my advantage.

"Your arm." My eyes darted to the marks from Ehlark, still fresh in my mind. No way was I going to offer that one.

I extended my other arm instead.

His grip was firm but not painful as his canines slowly extended. They were longer and more threatening than Ehlark's, catching the light enough to make my stomach twist into a tight, nervous knot.

I really hoped Ehlark was right and they were only meant for intimidation, because those looked like the kind of teeth designed to tear someone apart. My instincts wanted to pull away, but I stayed still, trying not to flinch as he placed my wrist in his mouth.

The sting was immediate and brutal, like fire burning through my veins. I bit back the pain, my teeth clenched so tightly that it hurt to hold back a scream. This wasn't like Ehlark's bite. There was no warmth or grounding pull from the earth, only raw, ripping agony.

His lips lingered too long, brushing against my skin in a way that sent an unwelcome shiver down my spine. Goosebumps prickled from my arm to the rest of my body.

His expression tightened, like something about me didn't quite make sense.

He pulled back unexpectedly, blood still dripping from his lips. His eyes weren't glowing; they were *blazing*, lit from within.

Velorn remained frozen in place. Whatever he'd taken from my blood seemed to have ignited something in him.

Then Malakar cleared his throat.

Velorn blinked once, then again. Just like that, his face returned to its usual mask of indifference.

But something changed.

When the glow in his eyes faded, they took on a honey-colored hue. A color I'd never seen in them before.

I was so caught up in the sudden shift of his irises that I didn't even notice Velorn's wrist hovering near my mouth.

I stared at it, confused, until realization struck—he thought I had fangs.

Ha!

Of all the times I might've wanted to hurt him, this would've been perfect. But of course, I didn't have long canines like them. Still, he didn't need to know that.

Gritting my teeth, I leaned in and bit down as hard as I could, eager to draw a drop of blood. Instead, all I managed was a bruise and a sore jaw. It was pathetic, honestly.

I glanced at him, expecting a smug comment or a biting insult, but his face stayed unreadable. No smirk. No taunt. Only that infuriating indifference.

His eyes flicked down to my weak attempt, narrowing slightly in suspicion.

He raised his wrist to his mouth, puncturing it with his fangs. Blood welled up immediately, trickling down in thin rivulets before he thrust his wrist toward me.

I looked at his face, then at his bloodied wrist.

Am I really about to do this?

A long breath escaped me.

Fuck it.

I took his wrist, bracing myself for the coppery tang of blood. But when my lips met his skin, the taste was not what I expected. Warm, with a floral undertone. It caught me off guard, and for a moment, I was somewhere else entirely, standing in the sunlit meadow up the mountain back home, the air sweet with wildflowers.

Why, out of all memories, did that one pop into my head?

When I finally released my grip, Velorn's hold on my wrist only tightened. Then his eyes glowed again, flaring with the same fierce intensity I'd seen moments earlier. He straightened, his voice resonating as he spoke.

"By fire and ash, bound by blood,
Will keep you from harm until you reach Emberhold.
My word to yours, and yours to mine,
In betrayal, only suffering follows."

I exhaled shakily, noticing that his words differed slightly from Ehlark's.

"By fire and ash, bound by blood,
Will remain at your side until—"

I hesitated, the final words catching in my throat. Every instinct urged me to stop, to say nothing, but I forced myself to continue.

"—until we reach Emberhold.
My word to yours, and yours to mine,
In betrayal, only suffering follows."

The silence that followed was overpowering. Everyone observing us stayed motionless. Velorn's hold on my wrist stayed firm.

Then, his shadows appeared. They surged from the ground like a living tide, pouring into the space around us. Within seconds, we were completely encircled by his power. The soldiers around us faded into the blackness, their outlines engulfed by the swirling darkness.

Velorn's magic enveloped me, and I braced for the icy, bone-deep chill I had felt the first time they touched me—the cold, choking terror of being trapped in something I couldn't control.

But this time, his shadows felt warm, their magic brushing against my skin like a protective embrace. My muscles loosened against my will. The sensation wasn't exactly comforting, but it wasn't frightening either. His powers shielded me from the room's hostility. I swallowed hard, trying to push aside the realization.

If Velorn must protect me, then his shadows do as well.

Velorn's gaze never left mine.

. . . *Will protect you.*

His voice echoed internally, soft and unsettling all at once, those three words looping over and over like a broken record I couldn't stop playing.

. . . *Will protect you.*

Around us, the shadows shifted again, slowly retreating and loosening their invisible grip as they slithered back into him. Light gradually returned to the room, brushing over pale faces and uneasy stances. The soldiers had moved further away from us. Their expressions were taut. Whatever they'd witnessed during the binding had rattled them more than they were willing to admit.

Velorn finally stepped back, putting space between us. "The contract is sealed." His voice was indifferent, maybe even a bit annoyed, but his eyes lingered a heartbeat too long, as though I'd become a problem he hadn't planned for.

170

17

SHARED SPACE

I followed Velorn down a narrow hallway that opened into what could only be the kitchen—if the piles of mismatched bowls and the overflowing sink of dirty dishes were any indication. The warm scent of something freshly baked hit me, and my stomach let out a loud, traitorous growl.

I was starving.

Honestly, that burnt piece of whatever Ehlark had cooked up didn't cut it.

I thought that after the contract, he would drag me to Ember-hold right away so we could be done with this ridiculous contract. But he brought me here instead.

I wanted to thank him, but his scowl, which drained the warmth from the room, suggested maybe another time.

A small group of workers froze in place, hands hovering over pots and knives paused mid-slice. All eyes turned to Velorn.

"Out."

They didn't question him.

Without exchanging glances, the workers abandoned their tasks and filed out quickly. The only sounds were utensils hitting countertops and a bowl shattering on the floor.

Velorn approached a tall counter where a stack of bottles was arranged. He grabbed one from the top, poured its contents into a cup, drank it in one gulp, and then poured himself another.

I stood by the counter, watching him.

Part of me expected him to explode, perhaps throw something, or show a trace of emotion after agreeing to the blood contract. But the familiar tension in his posture and the piercing glare in his eyes were gone.

Was this really the same Velorn?

The same man who had grasped me by the throat and stood over a pile of bodies, shooting deadly looks. Because right now, he didn't look like a monster. He looked like a man running on empty, someone who had barely survived a brutal twelve-hour shift. And that frightened me more than I'd like to admit.

My hand instinctively moved to my stomach as another loud growl echoed through the space.

"Your stomach has been growling since I brought you here. So, eat before I force food down your throat."

"Wow. You truly are charming. Your parents must be so proud," I shot back, even as my mouth watered like a traitor.

I went to the counter and grabbed the first thing that was remotely edible—bread and what I hoped was cheese—and shoved both into my mouth.

The taste was absolute *heaven.*

After days of starvation and stale scraps, this was borderline euphoric.

I kept devouring anything that smelled edible. If it wasn't nailed down, I was ready to stuff it in my face.

Would I regret this later? Probably.

Did I care right now? Absolutely not.

After shoving another piece of bread into my mouth, I saw Velorn sit down at a table. Perhaps this was the perfect opportunity to start fresh, but I needed to be cautious.

I grabbed a cup off the counter and sat down, pushing it toward him. He glanced at it, then back at me, before he filled it.

"Look," I started, trying to swallow a piece of bread. "I believe it's clear neither of us wants anything to do with each other or this contract."

Velorn took another slow sip but remained silent.

"So, why'd you do it?" My voice stayed low, careful, testing the waters before he could shut me out.

He drained the rest of his cup before setting it down. "Malakar ordered it."

"I am aware he ordered it. But what does he want with me? Why did you kill the Blood Seer? Why are you keeping me here and not taking me to Emberhold now?"

His hands stilled, and his face went back into that harsh exterior. The change was so sudden that I immediately knew I'd pushed too far.

Shit.

"Do you always ask this many questions?"

"Only if I'm kept in the dark."

"Malakar has his reasons."

Was he going to keep circling back to *Malakar*?

Ugh. I was getting absolutely nowhere with this.

I took my cup and knocked the whole thing back in one go, praying whatever was in it would take the edge off or at least dull the urge to throw it at his face.

My eyes shot up in surprise . . . delicious. Bright and tangy, like a cross between pomegranate and raspberry, with the faintest fizz at the end.

I took another sip, then leaned back in my chair. "You're really good at evading questions, you know that?"

He didn't look up from whatever he was pretending to focus on. "I answer the ones worth answering."

"Oh, so mine aren't worth answering?" I tilted my head, feigning offense.

"Last time I checked, we weren't friends. And no, before you even ask, I have no interest in getting to know you."

"Well, good thing I have no interest in you either. But like it or not, we're stuck with each other. I'd at least like to know who I'm stuck with."

They say you should keep your friends close and your enemies closer. Velorn was definitely in the enemy category, but if I could find even a small crack in his armor, I could use it as leverage later.

"How old are you?"

Silence.

"What are your favorite hobbies?"

Still nothing.

"Which House do you belong to?"

He didn't budge an inch.

Fine. New tactic.

"Are you and Malakar in the same one? Is that why you jump every time he snaps his fingers—like a trained dog?"

Velorn shot up from his chair. He loomed over me, gripping my robe with his fist as he pulled me close, his face inches from mine.

I guess I found his sensitive spot.

"Careful what you ask, little *Viri*," he replied sharply. "I may have a contract to protect you, but remember, it's only *temporary*."

I wanted to keep pressing those buttons until he broke. If this contract really did its job and he couldn't hurt me, I could basically ask for anything and get away with it.

Before I could push any further, he released my robe.

"I grow tired of this."

He turned for the door, then paused, glancing back over his shoulder. "I suggest you follow."

"Why should I?" I protested.

He didn't answer.

I let out a heavy sigh, took a final sip, and followed.

⁘

By the time we reached the doors and the endless staircase be-yond, whatever I'd drunk earlier was catching up with me. My steps felt too loose, and my balance was tilting enough to make every climb a gamble. I fought the urge to giggle, but it kept bubbling up, slipping free in little bursts no matter how hard I tried to suppress it.

That drink didn't even taste like alcohol.

It was one cup. One.

I was usually capable of knocking back multiple shots of hard liquor before I would get a buzz. And yet here I was, feeling strangely light, a little too warm, and way too confident.

Velorn opened the door, and a cool breeze swept through as it creaked inward, carrying the scent of stone and smoky wood. Based on their treatment of me, I had expected a cramped pantry, but the sight that greeted me completely shattered that expectation.

The room was enormous. In the center was a grand fireplace, its flames casting a warm glow and dancing shadows that seemed to breathe life into the stone walls. To the right, a cozy furniture arrangement caught my eye—a leather-worn sofa, two light beige chairs, and a low table, all invitingly close to the fire. On the low table, there was also food. My stomach rumbled at the sight, and I couldn't help but grin.

Hope you heard that, Velorn.

On the left, a massive bed dominated the space, draped in layers of dark gray sheets and blankets, with plush pillows I wanted to throw my whole body onto because they looked so inviting.

The ceiling stretched high above, arched at uneven angles where it bled into the mountain, and the rough-hewn stonework gave the room a natural, cavern-like feel. It made me realize how far we must have climbed; we were likely high up in the mountain now, and all those stairs finally made sense.

At the far end of the room, a window stretched across the wall like a framed portrait. I couldn't help thinking how strange it was to see an actual window built directly into the side of a mountain.

I don't know if it was the giddiness or the liquid encouragement, but suddenly, this place didn't seem so bad. The walls didn't feel as oppressive, the shadows less ominous, and I even spotted some pleasant details. The rugs were soft enough to tempt me to remove my boots, and a subtle scent of spice and wood smoke lingered, which I found somewhat appealing.

It still wasn't home, but I hated it a little less.

I wish you were here, Vyria.

The thought alone made my chest tighten, and I could only hope Lady Anira was treating her well.

Footsteps shuffled behind me, and when I turned, Velorn walked toward the door.

Relief swept over me. All I wanted was privacy. A chance to finally shed this damn robe, sink into that enormous, comfy-looking bed, and forget about today's events.

Velorn was still facing the door when I heard a soft *click.* The door stayed shut with him in the same spot, still inside the room.

Oh no.

No, no, no.

"What are you doing?" The words tumbled out messier than I intended, slurred with panic and too much breath.

"Our contract states that you stay near me. This ensures you do."

"No!" I said, as if I could will him out of here. "Don't you have another room you can sleep in?"

"This is actually *my* room," Velorn said. "Yours would have been in the dungeon, but given the contract, I prefer a more restful place."

My gaze skimmed to the luxuries around us: the roaring fire casting golden light on the polished stone, the untouched tray of food, and the ridiculously soft-looking bed that might as well have been calling my name.

"You're more than welcome to try and leave—if you can." He challenged.

If I left, I would sacrifice this comfort, but what I needed most right now was privacy, especially since I was finding it increasingly difficult to pronounce words without slurring.

Screw it.

I turned and strode toward the door, my fist clenched with determination.

As my hand reached for the handle, his arm shot out of nowhere, slamming against the door and blocking my path.

"Seriously?" I tried to push his arm away, but he didn't budge. It was like trying to move a damn wall.

"Get your stupid, muscular arm off the door," I warned. "You and I both know we want nothing to do with each other."

His eyes met mine as he stepped closer, crowding the space between us. "If you walk out that door, you will only feel pain. Do you want to test that?"

If he thought I was going to back down, he was dead wrong. "Let's find out, then."

He moved swiftly, faster than I could react. One arm wrapped around my waist, yanking me back as I twisted, causing my elbow to slam into his ribs. He grunted but maintained his grip. This time, I drove my heel into his shin, forcing him to shift enough for me to slip free. Almost.

His hand clamped around my wrist like a vise, spinning me and slamming my body back against the door. He pressed his body against mine, trapping me between the door and solid muscle. I tried to shove my knee back up at his precious jewels, but my movements were sloppy. He took my delay as an opportunity and pressed his knee between my legs high enough that I was now straddling it, lifting me off the ground and pinning me in place.

I swung wildly with my free hand, but everything was happening in slow motion. He caught my wrist mid-swing, pinning it above my head. With one hand, he held both of mine there, his forearm pressing against my collarbone. His breath brushed my ear, his voice dipping low, each word a dangerous caress across my skin.

"*Wild* little thing you are."

"Oh, you have no idea," I hissed, then sank my teeth into his forearm.

I half expected him to release his hold on me. He didn't.

He remained utterly still, letting me bite down like a rabid animal until my jaw ached and my pride started to crack.

It was a battle of wills, a test of my now drunken stubbornness. But my body began to give out as I felt my grip and my muscles loosen.

"Are you done?"

My jaw finally slackened as I realized it was a lost cause at this point. He eventually released me but remained blocking the door.

Fucking asshole.

I didn't give him the satisfaction of a glance as I stood up, stormed across the room, and then collapsed face-first onto the bed, letting the cozy softness of the blankets swallow me whole.

18

TWISTED LOYALTIES

Warm sunlight kissed my face as I peeked out from under the covers. Usually comforting, but right now it stabbed through my skull like a jackhammer. My head throbbed, and my mouth felt drier than the damn desert. Whatever was in that drink was deceptively strong and caused horrible hangovers.

I'll avoid that drink from now on.

I moved my legs over the side of the bed until they touched the cold stone. The dresser beside it held a neatly folded set of clothes. My heart sank as I picked them up and saw they weren't the ones I came with.

I looked around the room to see if anyone else was there, but only the soft morning light outside kept me company. Food and a pitcher of what I hoped was water sat on the living room table.

I padded towards the pitcher and drank straight from it. Etiquette be damned.

My bladder was about to burst, so I instinctively headed to the bathroom. As I opened the door, hot steam poured out toward me. Beyond it, a tall figure stepped out of a massive tub. Every thought ceased as my brain caught up with my eyes.

Water dripped from his long, black hair, clinging to his neck and broad shoulders before sliding over his sun-kissed skin. His chest was shadowed with hair, yet it didn't conceal his well-defined muscles, which were marked by scars crossing his sides and abdomen—stories etched into his body that I wasn't sure I wanted to uncover. My eyes had a mind of their own, tracing the thick lines of muscle down his arms, veins bulging as he twisted water out of his hair. Every movement amplified everything, making it impossible to ignore.

My eyes drifted downward, tracing the defined V-shape and his—

Blood rushed to my cheeks. "What are you doing?" I blurted, my gaze focused on the stone ceiling.

"Drying myself off."

Was that a hint of annoyance?

"Why are you still naked?"

Of course, he would be naked; it's a bathroom, for God's sake.

"Is this how you like to spy on others, little *Viri*?"

Why does he keep calling me that?

Even from across the room, I sensed the unspoken challenge in his presence.

He walked toward me, closing the distance. "I'm not a spy." I shuffled to the side, trying to create enough space from him. "And the name's *Eleni*. Not little *Viri*."

"Only a spy would say that."

"Why don't you believe me?" I seethed. "I told you the truth then, and I'm telling you the truth now—I'm not a spy!" The edge in my voice slipped out before I could reel it back. I wasn't sure if it was the hangover or the blood contract, but Velorn didn't scare me anymore.

He just really pissed me off.

He stepped closer, and—

Oh, for the love of—

His towel dropped.

Bastard.

Before the heat in my cheeks could explode, I quickly turned on my heel and slammed the door behind me.

Fuck. I still have to pee.

⸻◆⸻

Getting ready took way longer than it should have. The outfit they left for me was nothing but layers and fancy lace with zero instructions. I couldn't tell which piece went where, and after a frustrating round of trial and error, half of it inside out, and a few pieces discarded entirely, I finally managed to get the whole thing on. The kicker? It was a dress.

I've never been much of a dress person. The last time I wore one was years ago. I put one on to impress Cody when he and his dad came over to help with training Eddie. Big mistake. He laughed, and that laugh stayed with me. After that, dresses left a bad taste in my mouth. My wardrobe back home was simple: scrubs or jeans. I could count the dresses I owned on one hand, and every single one was from Gram, pulled out of the closet for weddings or "special occasions" I couldn't argue my way out of. At least this place provided comfy underwear—small victories, I suppose.

Velorn stood by the door, leaning against it with his arms crossed. His gaze grazed over me, and I could tell from the set of his jaw that he was annoyed again, probably because I had taken so long wrestling with the stupid dress.

"Do you always take this long to get ready?"

"Oh, my bad. I didn't realize we were on such a tight schedule. Maybe you could've, I don't know, *actually* said something? Your communication skills are a bit lacking."

He didn't say anything further as he opened the door, stepping aside to let me pass. I followed him into the hall, muttering to myself about the ridiculous dress.

By the time we made it down the endless flights of stairs, I'd tripped over myself more times than I cared to admit. I was ready to rip this dress off and set it on fire. And the shoes? Don't even get me started. Stylish, perhaps, but about as practical as a paper towel in a rainstorm.

"What's the plan for today? Are you going to *whisk* me away to Emberhold? Is this dress really necessary?" The muscles in Velorn's jaw worked, but he said nothing.

He pushed open a towering set of doors, revealing a vast courtyard alive with motion and sound. Though we were still deep within the mountain, the ceiling above had been opened to the sky. Jagged stone framed the edges like the mouth of a giant cavern, letting in shafts of sunlight and casting the silhouette of a distant bird flying above. The clash of steel rang out as two soldiers sparred with each other, bringing my focus back down to them. Every movement was honed, brutal, and efficient. There was no wasted energy, no hesitation. The sheer force behind their blows sent a jolt through my bones. This wasn't like the cushioned mats and polite corrections of my self-defense classes.

This was real. Dangerous.

"We are testing your skills." Velorn's voice interrupted, my hand instinctively flying to my chest. I hadn't even realized how close he was to me.

"And what skills are you referring to?" Because I was pretty sure wearing this dress would only highlight my talent for tripping.

"The axe kind."

This wasn't good. Of course, Velorn wanted to see my skills with the axe. He was there that day to witness its full destruction under my rage. A cold prickle crawled up my spine.

Was that why Malakar wanted me?

As we crossed the courtyard, one of the soldiers stopped mid-motion, his focus entirely on me. Curly hair, dark skin, and light brown eyes. *Garron.*

My blood boiled the instant I saw him. He was one of the soldiers who cuffed me, who stood by without hesitation as they locked us away. He didn't lay a hand on me directly, but he was there, watching while I suffered, while the others starved. And that was enough.

His opponent seemed to notice the sudden distraction. With a quick pivot of his feet, he lunged with his blade and drove it into Garron's shoulder.

I gasped, my hand flying to my mouth. For a terrifying second, I thought I had witnessed his death. But then Garron's eyes moved upward, locking onto the tall blond soldier who now stood over him, dropping onto one knee.

"See?" the blonde said. "This is what happens when there are pretty distractions. You lose focus, and then—" he gestured lazily toward the wound. "You get stabbed."

I recognized the voice instantly.

Malakar turned to look at me, then turned his gaze to Velorn.

My focus stayed on Garron's stab wound. Every nerve in me screamed to stop the bleeding, pack the wound, and do something. But then Garron's hands glowed with a soft, pulsing yellow. The light bled upward through his veins like liquid sunlight, tracing a path until it reached the open wound.

I blinked in surprise.

The bleeding slowed until it eventually stopped.

Before my eyes, the torn skin slowly healed itself until the gash was gone. All that remained was a smear of dried blood and a faint scar. Their healing abilities were truly astonishing. But the longer I watched, the more questions surfaced. Maybe it wasn't about healing quickly. Perhaps severity mattered. Or the amount of power used. Or both. Was that why Ehlark asked for my help back in the cave? Had he exhausted too much of his magic and become too weak to heal completely on his own?

Garron rolled his shoulder, then stood up and raised his sword again. "Ah, nothing like a casual stabbing to kick off the morning routine." He glanced at the blood on his tunic. "Really pulls the whole outfit together."

I tried to keep my face neutral, but my mind was whirling. That kind of healing challenged everything I knew. It was beyond science, beyond reason. And yet, all I wanted was to examine it more closely.

"You are going to wind up dead on a battlefield if you keep getting distracted," Malakar said, placing his sword back in its sheath.

"Sorry. Won't happen again," Garron said, straightening with a grin. "Just hard to stay focused when there's something pretty to look at."

I rolled my eyes.

If we were back in Denver, I'd peg him as a total player—someone who thought every woman would swoon over him with his presence.

Velorn crossed his arms tightly over his chest, jaw muscles working as his gaze flipped from Garron to Malakar. He remained quiet, but something else stirred behind those eyes.

Malakar turned and walked toward Velorn and me. His crimson shirt fit snugly around his frame, catching the light with a subtle shine. Gold embroidery traced the sleeves and neckline, curling upward like licking flames. The fiery patterns seemed to move with him, alive with each subtle shift. His black pants were tailored to perfection, complementing his lean, muscular build, and tucked into boots so polished they could've reflected the battlefield. The design was built for both command and combat.

Something about his outfit seemed oddly familiar, though.

I looked down and realized the lacework on my dress resembled the flames on his, and the crimson shade was the same.

Were we matching?

"You were supposed to be here before training."

Velorn held the silence long enough to make it uncomfortable. "It won't happen again."

"No, it won't." Malakar's attention shifted to me. His eyes traveled the length of my crimson dress, lingering far too long and making me feel even more exposed and uncomfortable in the damn thing. His gaze dropped to the hem, where the fabric was torn in several places, either from snagging on rough edges or courtesy of my tripping down the stairs more than once. A hint of disapproval crossed his face. "I see you do not take good care of the things that are gifted to you."

I guess that explains why we're matching.

"How about next time you could *ask* what I like to wear instead of assuming all women are the same size and actually enjoy being stuffed into dresses." The words escaped before I could stop them, and my mouth went ahead of my brain, as always.

An amused smile curved at the corner of his mouth. "I like to look at pretty things."

Why did I feel like he wasn't being genuine? My gut twisted, as it always did, whenever someone was hiding something. He definitely had ulterior motives. It couldn't only be because of the axe. He wasn't even there that day.

Unless Velorn told him.

Malakar looked at Garron and the other soldiers. "Training is done for the day. You may leave." The soldiers all bowed in unison, then turned and filed out of the courtyard, their footsteps fading until only Malakar, Velorn, and I remained.

"Velorn has informed me that you can summon a rather unique weapon."

So, my hunch was correct.

He moved closer to me, reaching out toward one of my curls and gently pinching a strand between his fingers. The touch felt too personal, and I instinctively took a step back. Malakar's lips twitched at the corner.

"Velorn described to me in vivid detail what he saw. And if my suspicions are correct, you wield a weapon of extraordinary power."

"If I did, I don't have it anymore."

Why were they so interested in the axe? Was its power something unfamiliar here? I didn't even know what it was or how I summoned it in the first place, but one thing I did know was that if it fell into the wrong hands, it could be catastrophic.

"Are you certain about that?"

"Yes."

Malakar's gaze went to Velorn. "Well?"

"I haven't seen the weapon since that day."

"Is that so?" Malakar dragged his fingers along his chin. "Are you familiar with the elemental relics?"

I raised a brow. "No."

"There were four relics forged by the Ancients, our ancestors, during the height of their power. These weren't ordinary weapons, you see. Each one was crafted using the pure, undiluted essence of its respective element and drawn from the core of Thysia itself. They weren't only tools of war; they were living extensions of their wielders, bound by blood, spirit, and will."

Why was he telling me this? Did he think this axe could be one of those weapons?

"The relics didn't just enhance elemental power," he continued. "They amplified it. Transformed it. In the hands of the worthy, they could reshape the battlefield, manipulate storms, split mountains, and summon tidal waves. But the relics are sentient in their own way. Only a few were ever chosen to wield their power."

He tilted his head slightly, his eyes narrowing as he studied my reaction, which I had none, since this was the first time I had heard about all of this.

"Over the centuries, the relics stopped awakening. Their powers faded not because they were broken, but because the Houses had become unworthy. The relics went dormant, transforming from symbols of power to mere ceremonial trophies." He turned his attention to Velorn. "But decades ago, they vanished—all of them. There were accusations that the House of Earth had somehow stolen them. As for their reasons why, no one knows since the House had been dismantled."

I finally understood why asking about the House of Earth cut so deeply for Ehlark. Living through that kind of loss must have been unbearable. To have his people accused by the other Houses of stealing the relics on top of everything else must have felt horrible.

"Did they ever find proof that House of Earth actually stole the relics?"

"No," he replied. "Just rumors. The relics are still missing, believed to have been destroyed along with the House of Earth."

It was unsettling how an entire House could be destroyed solely because of a rumor. It made me feel sorry for the poor souls who were involved or even killed because of it.

"That is, until you summoned a very unique and powerful axe."

So that was it. That was why he'd kept me alive. He thought I had one of the missing relics. But how could that be? How could a relic from this world have ended up in mine?

Then again, Gram had kept a hidden box from me for years—a box I didn't even know existed until recently. And now that I think about it, ever since I put on this necklace, weird things have been happening. One of those being, you know, getting *yeeted* into this world. But more importantly, how did Gram get hold of this necklace? She hid it for a reason. Was it because she knew what it was? If so, she must have come to this world. Was the necklace the key to getting me back home then?

"Velorn told me that the axe you wielded not only glowed a bright green essence but also split the earth open beneath your feet. That is something no ordinary weapon can do."

His words hit hard, each one breaking down my denial. If what he said was true, the heaviness I felt in my hands that day wasn't just anger but something else, something more ancient and powerful.

Powerful enough to transport me to this world.

"Eleni, it is urgent that I know if you truly possess an axe with this kind of power, because if you do, your very life depends on it."

My life?

I mean, I've *been* trying *not* to die since crash-landing here, so it wasn't exactly new information. But the way he said it made it feel like we were close friends who could share secrets. Which we were not. I didn't trust him one bit, even if it might take me longer to figure out how to get home. There was no way I was giving up the only thing that could potentially send me back home.

"What I mean," he continued, "is that if the other Houses discover you do possess one of the relics, they'll assume you know where the rest are, and they will stop at nothing to take them back."

I hadn't thought about that. Malakar was so convinced I had one of the relics, all because Velorn said so. But if the relics hadn't shown a hint of their power in centuries, how would anyone even know what the real one looked like anymore? And if they were stolen decades ago, would anyone even recognize them now?

"Unless, of course. You pledge to the House of Fire. Under my House, you are promised protection and safety. Something you will certainly need if you want to survive here. Especially since you are currently not marked with any House."

"Why are you offering me this?"

Malakar lifted his head toward the jagged opening in the sky, his expression distant. "The Houses have been restless. On edge since the relics have gone missing." His voice was calm, but the words were anything but. "The relics are their core. The one thing that gives them order and purpose. Without them, the Houses destabilize. And unstable Houses always break. And when Houses break, war will follow."

His attention stayed fixed on the mountain's opening, and against my better judgment, my eyes followed. The stone arch yawned above us like a massive, waiting mouth, ready to swallow anything that wandered too close.

War.

A cold shiver ran down my spine, something I'd prefer to avoid if I could. "I'm offering this," Malakar said quietly, "war is coming. And when it does, it will matter what House you stand with."

I raised an eyebrow. Deep down, the thought of being stuck somewhere on the brink of war only confirmed one thing: I needed to figure out how to get home sooner rather than later.

"If you truly can wield the axe," he continued, finally settling his gaze back to me, "if it truly responds to you, then you give me an advantage the other Houses do not have. A safeguard, so to speak."

There it was. Leverage.

So that was his angle. Use my connection to the axe as a shield against the other Houses. My stomach twisted as the realization set in. But why? Was the relic truly that much more powerful than everything else here? Or was he afraid of what it represented?

"And what if I don't have it?" I dared to ask.

Malakar took another step, closing the distance between us. His hand rose to my chest, brushing lightly against my skin before lifting the necklace. "I think you do have the relic, Eleni," he said. "Which brings me to Velorn."

He let the necklace drop back against my chest and strode to Velorn. "While I settle my affairs here, I want you to make sure she can demonstrate the relic's power."

"Yes, Prince Malakar," Velorn replied, dipping his head in a way that felt more rehearsed than respectful.

Malakar turned to leave but paused mid-step. When he looked back, his smile was polite, but his eyes remained emotionless.

"It is imperative that you show me the relic. It would be quite *unfortunate* if you can't."

19

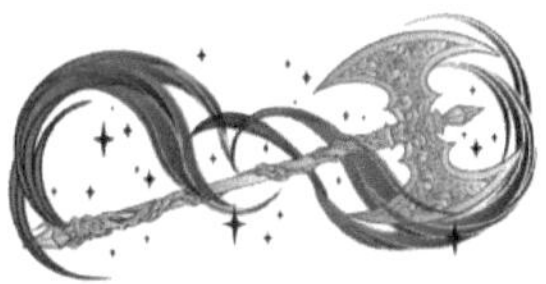

SANDWICH

After Malakar left, I needed space. Not this cramped courtyard. Anything to slow the disarray stampeding through my head.

I couldn't stay here if war broke out. I wouldn't survive it. I didn't grow up in a world like this. I grew up in a place where the biggest conflicts were people suing over spilled coffee and loud neighbors. How the hell was I supposed to face something like war?

My boots scuffed against the stone as I paced the courtyard, back and forth, chewing at my nails. "I can't be here."

I hurried toward the edge of the courtyard, but shadows moved across my skin, wrapping lazily around my arms and waist.

"Let me go!" Their weightless touch still threw me off, mainly because I couldn't for the life of me figure out the damn things.

"Giving up already?"

"No." I bit out.

All I could think about was getting out of here, trying to keep from spiraling into a panicked state.

"Then where are you going?"

"Somewhere, I don't have to see your face," I shot back. I didn't realize what I had said until I noticed the shift in his stance. "Does my face offend you?"

"That's not what I meant. I just—" I realized too late I couldn't take it back. I knew better. It wasn't the scars on his face that bothered me; it was everything else about this place, this whole world I was trapped in.

"Sorry to disappoint," he bit out, "but as long as this contract stays in effect, I have to protect you and make sure you can summon the relic."

His shadows finally retracted back into the dark as he loomed over me. "But let's get one thing straight. The second you set foot in Emberhold, this contract ends. And I can finally be rid of you."

"Can't wait." I retorted.

"Good. Glad we're on the same page. Now, are you capable of summoning the axe?" He folded his arms over his chest and looked down at me.

Not a chance in hell was I going to try to summon the axe in front of him. For all I knew, this was a trap. Contract or not, I didn't trust any of them. Not one.

"No."

He arched an eyebrow. "No?"

I copied his posture, folded my arms, and lifted my chin to meet his challenge. "No." The edge of fear I'd felt whenever he was near had vanished. I'd thought it was a fluke last night, just liquid courage, but standing in front of him and meeting his glare, I felt none of it.

Was it because of the contract?

He opened his mouth to interrupt, but I stopped him with my finger.

"Let's get one thing straight. You've done *nothing* to earn my trust. A contract that binds you to follow me doesn't make you trustworthy. For all I know, this is a setup to get rid of me sooner." I let the words hang before continuing. "But hear me, *Velorn*." I let his name roll from my lips like a warning. "No one is forcing me to do anything." I stepped in close enough to see the amber in his eyes. "Not Malakar. Not some damned Blood Seer. And especially not *you*."

He stared at me for a long moment, and I could've sworn the corner of his mouth twitched before his mask slipped back into place.

"Even if your life depends on it?"

"Yes," I said with certainty.

The amber in his eyes flickered briefly before settling back into a soft honey hue. "Very well, then." He turned and exited the courtyard. I followed, my footsteps echoing his.

Velorn was silent through the corridor, broken only by the shuffling of our footsteps and the occasional person rushing past. Each time someone crossed our path, they either darted in the other direction or gave us such a wide berth that I thought they might melt straight into the walls. I knew Velorn had an intimidating presence, but damn, I hadn't realized it was this bad.

I even heard what sounded like a grunt from him when one poor soul passed too close. The man nearly face-planted in his hurry to bow and scurry away.

As I followed Velorn, a troubling thought kept bothering at me. If I were stuck with this contract until we reached Emberhold, couldn't I see it through and then find a way back?

I shook my head. That was a dangerous assumption. I didn't even know where Emberhold was. For all I knew, it could be on the other side of the continent.

I was stuck with Velorn whether I liked it or not. Even if I somehow figured out how to get home, what then? What if Velorn was forced to return to my world because of the contract? What would I do to him? Convince Cody to arrest him for, oh, I don't know—kidnapping and mass murder?

I sighed, rubbing my eyes, as the weight of everything sank in. I was utterly defeated.

Once inside the room, my eyes drifted to a bottle on the table.

If that was the same drink I had last night, I knew how it would make me feel, and it wasn't good. Then again, it took the edge off.

I poured myself a glass and sat at the table. I reached for a fresh slice of bread, grabbed some chunks of meat, and something that looked suspiciously like cheese to make a sandwich.

With food in my system, my brain finally kicked back into gear.

Why is Velorn such a dick?

He was always annoyed by practically everything I did, and I was pretty sure he was physically incapable of smiling. He hadn't said much since we got back to the room either. Come to think of it, he didn't really talk much at all.

Chewing slowly, I glanced over in time to see Velorn slip into the bathroom.

At least Ehlark had shown me kindness; he was also the only one willing to help me get home. My hand drifted to the bite marks on my arm, a quiet reminder of our contract.

The prisoners were somewhere inside this mountain. Maybe I could persuade Velorn to give me a tour. Casual. Harmless. And perhaps I could steer the conversation toward where the prisoners were being held.

I needed to figure out how to convince him.

I took another bite, savoring the taste, right up until a thought started to form.

Outside the bathroom, I held a plate with another sandwich, took a deep breath, and pushed the door open.

"Ever heard of *privacy*? Usually applies when the door's closed." Velorn was sunk neck-deep in the oversized tub, hair tied back in a bun that only made his features stand out more. Stubble shadowed his jaw, except in the places where the scars cut the growth short.

"Listen, you don't like me, and I definitely don't like you." I walked over to the bathroom sink and set a plate on the counter.

"But this contract means we're stuck together. We can either make it hell for both of us, or we can call a temporary truce until it's done. Then you can go back to brooding in a corner, or whatever it is you do with your magic."

Velorn's eyes remained on me. Steam drifted, clinging to the edges of the tub. The water was clear, and I was doing my best not to let my gaze wander where it really, *really* shouldn't.

"Are you suggesting I trust you? That we become friends, frolicking through a meadow holding hands?"

A quiet snort escaped before I could stop it because now my brain was cursed with the image of Velorn frolicking in a field of flowers.

"Let's call it a temporary alliance."

The usual hostility in his eyes had disappeared. He remained silent, watching me.

"Look, all I want is for us to get along. If I ask you a question or need help with something, you don't refuse or give me a one-word, grumpy answer. And vice versa. We don't need to hold hands everywhere we go, but we should get along."

He leaned his head back against the tub, exhaling slowly. "If I agree to this, will you leave me in peace?"

I nodded.

"Fine." His words came out more like a reluctant sigh than anything, but a small smile tugged at my lips.

"You can go now," he said, "unless you want to see all of me again when I get out of this tub."

My gaze almost slipped where it shouldn't have, but I jumped down from the counter and made for the door before it was too late.

"Make no mistake, little *Viri.*"

I froze, my hand on the door.

"There's a reason I don't trust others. Don't make me regret trusting you."

I turned, nodding toward the sandwich on the counter. "My peace offering." Then I slipped out before he could say another word.

My heart was pounding faster than I expected. That took way bigger balls than I'd given myself credit for, but I pulled it off.

The next step was to figure out where the prisoners were being held.

But I will take this small victory for now. I lifted my arms in a silent little *woohoo* of triumph and instantly caught a whiff of my armpits. Right. I'd forgotten how much I'd sweated climbing all those stairs in that stupid dress.

After what felt like an eternity of waiting, the bathroom door creaked open. Velorn stepped out, his dark hair tied back. The only clothing he wore was a pair of loose black trousers. Then I noticed what he was holding in his right hand. The plate with the sandwich I'd left. He didn't even take a bite.

So much for my peace offering.

Disappointment tugged at me, but at least I'd tried. Feeling defeated, I headed for the bathroom.

Heat permeated my sore muscles, washing away the tightness in my limbs as I sank into the deep tub. It was bliss. Pure bliss. Leaning back, I let the water cradle me, my eyes fluttering shut as the warmth enveloped me like a protective cocoon. No shouting. No running for my life—just peace.

I stepped out of the bathroom, feeling refreshed and human again. My hair was tightly braided to keep my curls in check, and the soft black tunic draped comfortably over me, falling above my knees.

I glanced over at the table where Velorn was sitting and noticed the plate with the sandwich was empty. It shouldn't have mattered whether he ate it or not, but for some reason, it did. Only a smidge. The tiniest, microscopic speck of happiness filled me.

He lounged on the sofa, his feet propped up and a book in hand, completely absorbed.

For someone who could control darkness like living weapons and who bore scars that seemed born of pure violence, seeing him quietly reading was oddly disarming.

His focus shifted from the pages of his book to me. "Tell me, what was that you made?"

I blinked at him. "You've never had a sandwich before?"

"*Sand—wich?*" He said it slowly, like he was testing out a foreign curse word. "Why is it called that? Did you secretly put sand in it?" The edge of annoyance in his tone made me panic. "No, no. *That's what it's called.*"

Although now that I thought about it, I had no idea why it was called that either. I'd have to put a pin in that mystery for later—*if* I ever got back home.

"Do you want another?" I asked. Looking at his size now, I was pretty sure he could put away multiple foot-long subs without breaking a sweat.

"Yes," he said, though the word came out stiff.

Perfect. Nothing builds trust faster than a good old-fashioned food bribe. I went back to the table and started making another sandwich.

"Do you know how to summon the relic?" he asked.

My hands stilled over the bread.

He needs to trust you, Eleni. Be honest.

"I don't," I admitted. "I'm not even sure how I was able to do it in the first place."

Once the sandwich was done, I set it down on Velorn's plate.

"If there's one thing I know about Malakar," he said, "it's that he's true to his word—good or bad. Show him the relic, and he will provide protection."

"How long will he give me?" I wasn't asking for myself. I needed to know how much time I had to find those prisoners.

"His affairs here won't take more than a few days at most. I highly recommend you start figuring it out."

A few days? That was nowhere near enough time. Velorn might have let his guard down a fraction, but he wasn't stupid. I needed to figure out a plan, and fast.

"What happens if I can't figure out how to summon the relic by then?"

"He will use other means necessary to persuade you."

I didn't like the sound of that. And something told me Malakar's "other means" didn't involve a bouquet of flowers.

Velorn polished off the sandwich in a few bites, then stood and started to walk away. Halfway across the room, he paused. "Thank you."

I blinked. Of all the things I expected from him, that was dead last on my list.

A grin tugged at my lips. "So, you do know how to be nice?"

It wasn't much, but it was still progress.

I watched as Velorn made himself comfortable in the bed, pulling the sheets up over his bare chest.

Wait.

"What do you think you're doing?" I asked, striding over to hover at his side.

"Since we're now *friends*," he said casually, "and I can trust you now, I know you won't try anything."

Is he serious right now?

"Absolutely not!" I argued. "If anything, I should be worried about *you* coming on to *me*."

"You don't have to worry," he said, as his eyes slowly drifted down my body and then back up to meet my gaze. "You don't interest me in that way."

Ouch.

Part of me wanted to find out what his *interests* were and then throw it right back in his face. But the more rational part of me knew that it would be pointless. I rubbed my eyes, feeling the exhaustion creeping in, grabbed my pillow, and stormed over to the couch.

Flowers swayed gently in the breeze as I stood over Gram's grave. Yet, something felt off. The air was too stale, and the shadows were too long. My heart raced as I turned, searching for something I couldn't name.

That's when I spotted Eddie. He stood by the old oak tree, his back to me, his posture rigid.

"Eddie?" I called out, but my voice sounded distant and foreign.

He didn't respond.

Instead, I heard a low, rumbling growl that rooted me in place. My blood turned to ice as something dark stepped out, its golden eyes locked on Eddie.

"Eddie, look out!" I screamed, but it was too late. The shadowy figure lunged, its darkness sinking into him as he crumpled.

"No!" I yelled, my voice cracking as I ran toward them.

Anger and fear surged through me, spreading over me like wildfire. A sudden warmth burned in my hands. It felt intense and electric. I looked down and saw the axe. It glowed faintly, pulsing with the same fury that filled my chest.

Without thinking, I threw the axe with all my strength. It soared in a blur of green light and hit the dark figure squarely in the side. The beast collapsed, motionless, with the weapon embedded deep in its ribs.

I ran to Eddie and dropped to my knees beside him. "Eddie, stay with me. Please," I begged, but he was covered in too much blood.

Then I heard a snarl. I looked up to find the shadowy figure lunging at me with teeth and claws, ready to kill. I screamed as its weight crashed down on me and tore into my back.

I jolted awake with a gasp, my heart pounding and sweat clinging to my skin. Velorn hovered over me, his hands gripping my shoulders. Only his eyes, now glowing gold, pierced the darkness.

"What happened?" His voice was rough, edged with something else.

I glanced down and saw his magic surrounding me. I should have been afraid, but it felt protective, as if it were concerned for me.

"I—" I swallowed hard, still trembling, and forced myself to nod. "It's fine. It was a dream."

Velorn examined me for a few more moments before the shadows started to withdraw, slipping back into the corners of the room. His glowing eyes faded into the darkness as he returned to the bed.

My hand flew to my chest, half-expecting to feel the sharp sting of claws still raking through my skin. But all I felt was warmth.

The necklace rested there, its green glow pulsing against my skin. Then, slowly, the light faded.

Even though it was only a dream, I couldn't shake the feeling that the axe—the relic—hadn't appeared by chance. It sensed danger and somehow found its way into my dream. I closed my fingers around the necklace. If it truly was the relic, then I needed to figure out how it worked: what triggered its power and why it reacted to certain things.

20

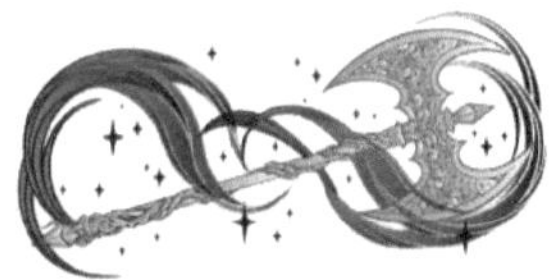

UNWANTED ATTACHMENT

Velorn stood across the courtyard, arms crossed like a coach ready to make me run ten laps. "Are you going to summon the relic, or are we going to stand here all day?"

I scowled at him. Did he think it popped out of my ass on command? I barely knew how I'd made it appear the first time, and that was in the middle of a life-or-death panic.

Sure, I like to think of myself as a strong, independent woman, but I also had no damn clue how to summon this thing.

"I'm working on it," I yelled back.

"You summoned it once. Which means you can summon it again."

"Should I say *abracadabra* and hope for the best?"

One of his brows dipped lower than the other. Clearly, he didn't know what *abracadabra* meant.

"When I saw you during that battle, I saw anger. Rage. You intended to go after that soldier. Go back to those feelings. What was your intent when you saw him?"

So much was happening all at once. Arkos had attacked me, and Vyria stepped in, risking her life. The image of that sword sliding right through her made my stomach knot up. Shock hit me first. But after that, all I wanted was to drive a sword through him.

"I got pissed off."

"Then focus on those feelings and see if you can summon it."

I looked at him. How could I suddenly feel that way? It wasn't like I had a switch to turn it on and off. But I had to try.

I closed my eyes and thought about the scene that played out on the battlefield.

The anger I felt. The rage.

Nothing.

I clenched my fists and tried again, squeezing my eyes shut and focusing harder.

Still nothing.

I took a deep breath and shrugged my shoulders in defeat. This was going to be a lot harder than I thought.

"Can you please tell me why it is so important that I summon the relic *now*?" The question burned at the back of my mind. Why was Malakar so desperate?

"Protection. That's all you need to know." His irritation was evident in his stance and the look he gave me. He moved to the other side of the courtyard, leaning against a stone pillar, and closed his eyes with a long, exasperated exhale.

I hated having an audience, especially one with a face that kept looking at me like it was ready to kill. I glanced over once more to make sure his eyes were still shut and slowly reached out my hand. Instead of focusing on that battle, I closed my eyes and concentrated on the dream—on that wave of anger when the dark figure reached for me and how the axe had suddenly appeared.

How it had felt in my hands.

If the relic did react to my feelings, I needed to dig deep into the fury I felt for Eddie's life.

There was a gentle hum vibrating against my skin. I kept my eyes closed and concentrated. The necklace's magic spread across my chest, flowing like liquid energy beneath my skin. I glanced down, and the green light pulsed brightly, like a heartbeat echoing my own. The hum deepened into a low, resonant vibration, thrumming through my ribs and streaming down my arm like a current of raw energy.

It was exhilarating, electric, like every nerve in my body had been plugged into a storm. Power flowed through me, wild and intoxicating, until I swore my strength had increased tenfold. My muscles felt tighter, my stance steadier, as if it was trying to become part of me, fusing into my bones and blood.

There was a shift around me and the subtle pull of gravity in my palm. My hand slowly felt heavier as energy flowed into my hands, and the axe materialized before me.

But as the weapon took shape, voices and footsteps echoed from the corridor, and I lost focus. In an instant, the feeling disappeared, leaving only empty air and the fading warmth of power in my palm.

"Dammit." I clenched my fists.

So close.

I looked at Velorn, half expecting him to be leaning against the pillar, but he wasn't. He was fully upright, his whole focus on me.

Did he feel it too?

That surge of power.

Soldiers chatted among themselves as they strolled into the courtyard, their voices fading gradually when their attention landed on me. Their judging stares made my insides twist. I couldn't bring myself to try again, not with all of them watching.

With a sigh, I crossed to the far side of the courtyard. Far away from Velorn, who finally lost interest in me as another soldier approached him.

"Would you like some water, Miss?" A familiar voice called from around the corner.

I turned, and from behind the stone wall, a pair of striking emerald eyes met mine—eyes I knew better than I should.

"Ehlark?"

I stepped toward him, ready to embrace him, but he raised a hand to halt me halfway.

"Don't," he warned quietly. "They must not see that you recognize me."

I quickly scanned the courtyard to see if anyone had noticed, but luckily, no one did, including Velorn.

Ehlark extended a pitcher and offered me a cup.

"I've been trying to find you," Ehlark spoke under his breath. "But this mountain is a maze of corridors and hidden rooms."

He tilted the pitcher ever so slowly, filling the cup with water.

"Listen," he continued, "I can't stay long, but where are they keeping you?"

For a fleeting moment, my heart rose. Ehlark had truly come to rescue me. However, when I looked at Velorn, despair washed over me again.

"You can't," I said quietly. "I have a watchdog," I gestured subtly toward Velorn.

Lifting my wrist, I showed him Velorn's bite mark. "I was forced into another contract." I risked a glance at Ehlark. For some reason, I felt nervous about telling him.

His eyes dropped to my wrist and stared at the mark. "This will complicate things."

"Is there a way for me to get out of this contract with him?"

Ehlark hesitated, his expression caught somewhere between certainty and doubt. "I think so, but not here." His gaze slid past me toward the courtyard, but I kept my eyes on him. There was something about him in that moment, steady, protective even, that made him feel like the closest thing I had to a knight in shining armor. A foolish, reckless part of me wished he'd take my hand and get me out of here now. But the rational part of me knew better. Too many eyes. Too many risks.

"I've got to go," he whispered urgently. "Meet me in the kitchen tomorrow if you can."

"I'll try."

I shouldn't have, but I reached out and caught his wrist, my desperation outweighing my better judgment. "Did you find where they're keeping the prisoners?"

For a second, I braced for him to pull away, to remind me this was dangerous. Instead, he placed his other hand over mine. "Yes." He gave me a small smile. Not wide, not showy, but enough to quiet the anxiety inside.

When I met his eyes, they held a promise. Comfort radiated from that gaze, saying, *everything will be okay.*

My fingers lingered before falling away. His footsteps faded into the distance, leaving the space between us a little emptier. I barely had time to collect myself before I turned and found Velorn striding toward me.

Oh, fuck.

My body stiffened with his approach. Velorn's gaze remained fixed on the spot where Ehlark had stood. "Who was that?"

I held the cup in my hand. "You mean the one kind enough to offer me water?"

Velorn remained motionless.

Why isn't he saying anything? Does he know?

I needed to think of something before his silence turned into something worse.

"Question," I cleared my throat. "Do you know how far I can be from you, or is it a feeling?"

His eyes slid to mine, but he didn't immediately answer.

"You want to know?" His voice was calm, but that look was back in his eyes. The one that made it feel like he could see right through me, peeling back every lie and half-truth I'd tried to hide.

This was probably a bad idea. But curiosity, or maybe recklessness, won out. "Yes."

"Remain here." Then he walked away from me until he was out of the courtyard.

There was a strange pull that urged me to follow, but I remained put.

Then I felt it. Pain around Velorn's mark. It was small, a dull throb, but the longer I stood there, the worse it became. The throbbing grew to a burning sensation as it traveled up my arm and then through my entire body.

I gasped and staggered, clutching my arm as the burn intensified. It grew worse—hotter, angrier. Like molten fire coursing through my veins, igniting every nerve ending ablaze.

My knees nearly buckled from the intense pain, and it hurt like a *son-of-a-bitch*.

The soldiers in the courtyard stared as I bent over, trembling, trying not to scream. My pride was shattered. I couldn't take it anymore.

I ran through the courtyard and into the corridors, chasing the invisible tether pulling me forward. With every step, the pain lessened, but it wasn't gone, not until I turned the last corner, breath ragged, and stumbled into the expansive kitchen.

There he was.

Only there wasn't a smug expression on his face. No. There was sweat trickling down the side of his face, his chest rising faster than usual.

Did he feel the same pain I did?

"Do you understand the contract now?" His tone wasn't mocking this time. He wanted confirmation. Whatever had happened wouldn't happen again.

I still didn't fully understand it. But if my theory was correct, I had nearly broken my part of the contract by putting too much distance between us. That could explain the pain. But why was Velorn feeling it too? Was it because of his part of the contract?

No harm shall come to you.

The words kept looping repeatedly.

If I were in pain, then I was being harmed. And if I was being harmed, he wasn't keeping his end of the bargain. The same pain would tear through him as it had through me.

212

21

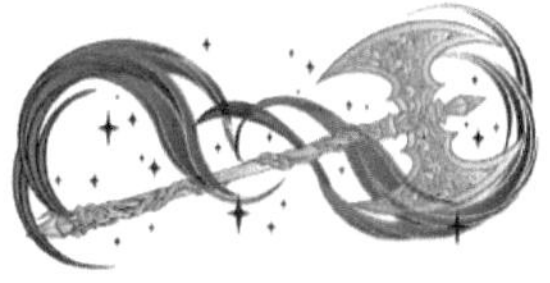

POSSESSIVE MARK

Velorn led me down an unfamiliar corridor. It felt cooler here, laden with the scent of wet stone and iron. I tried not to think about the weight on my wrist or the invisible leash tethering me to him.

That searing, bone-deep pain from being too far away? I wasn't eager to experience that again. Ever.

My eyes wandered, drawn to the signs on the doors we passed, some loosely hanging from hooks and pinned into the stone. Symbols curled across them, elegant but foreign. I didn't recognize a single one. Their language, perhaps.

It looked like scripture—graceful lines woven into flowing shapes, like ink caught in motion. It was beautiful and distracting until I collided with Velorn's back.

He stopped, letting out a slow, overstated sigh. "Do you struggle with basic awareness?"

I scowled at him. "Maybe if you weren't taking up the whole hallway, I wouldn't have run into you."

His shoulders rolled in quiet irritation as he took a slow breath, then pushed open the rich brown door before him.

As soon as I entered the room, I felt like I had stepped into the heart of a living, breathing fashion show. Dresses in every imaginable style and cut adorned wooden racks or draped elegantly over mannequins, their vibrant colors catching the golden light streaming through high windows. Rich silks in deep emeralds and shimmering golds, soft velvets in dusky purples and crimson, and delicate, floral-embroidered fabrics filled the room with undeniable elegance. Scraps of cloth littered the floor, mingling with half-finished designs and loose threads in a chaotic yet strangely organized mess. A nearby table bristled with spools of thread in every shade imaginable, alongside neatly arranged needles, pins, and measuring tools.

Why did he bring me here?

"Hello," a voice chirped, catching me off guard.

A petite, curvy woman emerged from behind a pile of fabric, appearing to be in her mid-thirties. She possessed a striking, unique beauty, the kind you'd expect to see in fantasy movies. Her delicate features were soft, with doe-like eyes, a small button nose, and thick, bushy eyebrows that gave her a warm aura. Her brown hair was casually pulled into a messy bun. Her hands were full of scraps of thread and fabric, evidence of her craft, and her bright smile carried a friendly, disarming warmth. She stepped forward, her gaze sincere and welcoming, until it settled on Velorn, who was looming next to me.

Her expression instantly faltered, the warm welcome giving way to wary hesitation. She glanced at me, then back to Velorn.

"What can I help with today?"

"We need an outfit," Velorn said, his tone unexpectedly formal. "For my friend." The word seemed to catch in his throat, like it tasted horrible, but still—he said it. And that alone was enough to draw my attention to him. "Something suited for better maneuverability. Not formal wear."

I blinked and lifted my eyebrows. Did Velorn bring me here, where I could get proper wear? Not a frilly, trip-over-yourself princess dress? Maybe I'd been wrong about him this whole time. Perhaps beneath all that menace and muscle, he was a grumpy little cinnamon roll with a talent for murder and mayhem.

"I see you're wearing one of the dresses Prince Malakar requested," she said, breaking me out of my thoughts.

She offered a warm smile. "As much as I respect the prince's taste, men rarely get a woman's figure right, let alone her comfort."

The image of his eyes catching mine in the courtyard resurfaced. That slow, measured stare trailing down my body and the cold disapproval on his face when he saw the dress—*his* dress—torn, sweat-stained, and ruined.

It made sense now.

"I'll need you to remove the dress so I can get accurate measurements." She reached for a tape measure before turning her attention to Velorn. "Would you mind giving us some privacy?"

Velorn looked at her, then at me, before quietly stepping back and closing the door behind him.

Silence settled between us as she worked to help me out of the dress. Her hands moved carefully, but her eyes kept darting toward the door, as if she expected Velorn to storm back in.

"Does he follow you everywhere?"

"Yep," I admitted.

She visibly shuddered. "I don't know how you stand it. The sight of Prince Malakar's Tracker frightens most of us." Her gaze darted toward the door again. "People don't say his name here. Not unless they must."

Her words grabbed my attention. Not only because she was discussing Velorn, but also because this was the second time someone had mentioned his reputation as the Tracker.

"Why do they call him that?"

She looked up at me with surprise. "Have you not heard?"

I shook my head.

She glanced at the door once more. "Whatever Prince Malakar sends him to find, he finds it. People. Artifacts. Corpses. Doesn't matter. They say he can find anything. That's why they call him the *Tracker*."

Her voice faltered. "He has burned villages to the ground and slaughtered hundreds of elementals without remorse. His actions only bring ruin and death. He is Prince Malakar's monster that everyone fears."

Dread coiled down my bones, but before I could respond, she spoke again, "And that scar on his face? It's a curse, a mark of what he truly is."

"A curse?"

She nodded. "He killed a Blood Seer after she read his path."

I vaguely remembered that Vyria had mentioned that when their powers awaken, they visit a Blood Seer. Did that mean Velorn was a teenager when it happened to him?

It made sense now why his scars looked old, settled into his face long before the man outside existed. He had to be in his mid-thirties based on his appearance, which meant he'd been carrying those marks for decades—growing up with them, fighting with them, surviving with them. No wonder he was stone-cold and didn't hesitate to kill. He'd been shaped by violence long before he ever became the monster people whispered about.

What if my scars were visible? If people could see them without clothes hiding the damage, would they see me differently? Would they whisper "monster" under their breath, too? Velorn didn't get the choice. His scars lived on his face, greeting people before he ever had the chance to speak.

"Did no one read your path when your elements awakened?"

I shook my head, not elaborating. Considering the circumstances, the fewer people who knew about who I truly was, the better.

I managed to slip off the last remaining layer of the dress, leaving only the thin white undergarment.

"Take that off too."

I did as she asked, standing awkwardly while she assessed me. Her fingers brushed against my wrist, and her expression shifted. Gently, she turned my arm over with a studying gaze.

"You are not pledged to a House." Her observation lingered on the bite marks on my wrist. "And you have *two* blood contracts?"

"How did you know?"

"Well, it's quite simple, really," she said, almost cheerfully. "Marks like these don't stay on the skin unless there's magical binding involved. They're meant to stay visible—to remind you of the contract." She brushed her fingers lightly over Ehlark's bite mark, studying it.

"This one," she murmured, "is much younger." Her hand drifted to Velorn's mark. "Than this one."

"How can you tell?"

She looked at me, puzzled, but continued. "Younger elementals typically cannot bite as deeply," she explained, tilting my arm to inspect the marks. "Their canines aren't fully developed until they've lived at least a half-century. As a result, their marks are shallower and less pronounced."

Half a century? How old were people here?

"This one, though," her fingers traced Velorn's mark. "Whatever contract you made, I'd tread carefully."

"Why?" Unease crept into my voice.

"My dear, has your mother or father never told you? This is basic knowledge—something one learns at a young age."

My body stiffened. I needed to keep a low profile, to blend in as best I could.

"My mother and father passed away when I was a baby," I said carefully. "And I had to fend for myself for many years." It wasn't exactly a lie. My mother had died giving birth to me, and I never knew my father. So, it was easier to let people assume he was gone, too. However, fending for myself only happened when I left to work in Denver and faced a harsh reality check about what adult responsibilities really were.

"Oh, I am so terribly sorry. That explains it," she said. "Then by all means, let me explain it properly." Her attention shifted back to Velorn's bite mark.

"This mark appears to be deeper, which makes the contract stronger and harder to break. However," she hesitated, a sputter of worry crossing her face. "When I touched it, I felt an unwelcome shiver run under my skin, which only means this is also a possessive one."

"*Possessive?*"

"Oh yes. A mark like that isn't made lightly and won't be ignored. Be careful, my dear."

It felt like I was fumbling in the dark, constantly trying to understand rules and customs that made no sense. And now I was tied to the most feared person in Thysia.

A cold dread curled in my gut, telling me I'd sunk too far into this world already, and sooner or later, something was going to come back and bite me in the ass.

My eyes drifted to her wrist, noticing a small, detailed design etched into her skin. It resembled the stroke of a paintbrush, shaped like a *C*, with edges blooming into petal-like forms and flowing lines that curved around it in an elegant arc. It might have been beautiful if not for the deep slash running straight through it. The wound wasn't fresh, but it didn't look as old as the original mark it scarred.

Come to think of it, I hadn't paid much attention to who was marked and who wasn't. Not when I first arrived here. It made sense now why Velorn was looking at my wrists the first time I landed here. This must have been the mark they were looking for.

"Can I ask you something?"

"Of course."

"I noticed a scar across your mark." It was a hunch, this symbol had to represent a House, but I had no idea which one.

"Oh." She paused, the word catching on her tongue. "Yes." The admission was soft, filled with sorrow. "After the massacre and the death of the matriarch of the House of Earth, those who had pledged to it were offered to swear allegiance to another House if we wanted."

My chest tightened.

The House of Earth.

Ehlark's House.

Malakar had told me earlier, but I hadn't realized they had been massacred. "I'm so sorry." I moved closer and rested my hand on her forearm.

"But now I have a contract with the House of Air. They've given me this shop, and I get to create beautiful things." Even though her demeanor changed, I could see that her eyes betrayed her lingering sorrow—sorrow that felt all too familiar.

"Enough talk about Houses. Let's focus on you." She twirled her finger, motioning for me to turn. Aside from the thin underwear clinging to me, I was basically naked.

The sharp gasp behind me broke the silence the instant she saw my back. "Solryn's soul! What happened to you?"

"It looks worse than it feels," I said quickly, waving it off before she started asking more about them. I turned and cupped my breasts. "Do you happen to have anything to support the ladies?"

She blinked, visibly struggling to pull her focus away from my back. After a moment, she nodded and grabbed her measuring tape. "Yes, I believe I have just the thing."

She stepped away and rummaged through a nearby chest. "Here we go," holding a piece of beige bra-like material.

It wasn't a typical-looking sports bra that I was used to wearing, but it would do. At least now I had some support, which gave me one less thing to worry about.

After finishing up my measurements, she handed me a glass of water. "I'll start working on something for you right away. It should be ready by tomorrow."

"Thank you."

"Oh, don't mention it, my dear," she replied and lifted her hand.

"I just realized, I never got your name?"

"Oh, forgive my rudeness. Where are my manners?" She laughed. "The name's Farna, as the sign says outside my door."

"Nice to meet you, Farna. I'm Eleni."

"Eleni?" she repeated, tilting her head slightly. "What a beautiful name. What is your family name?"

"Gibson."

"*Gib-son.* Well, that's certainly unique. One I have not heard before."

I rubbed the back of my neck and let out a nervous laugh. "Yeah, it's pretty unique."

"Well, Eleni Gibson, it is my pleasure to help you out today." She returned a smile and helped me back into my dress, for which I was grateful. I was still hopelessly clumsy with all the buttons and strings, and Farna's skillful hands made quick work of them.

The door opened and revealed Velorn leaning against the wall across from the shop, arms crossed, and eyes closed as if he'd been waiting for hours. I was tempted to say something but thought better of it.

After learning more about his reputation, I decided it was best to avoid any confrontation with him in the future. This agreement between us was only temporary after all.

"We're finished," Farna said to Velorn. Her tone shifted from friendly to formal once more.

His eyes finally opened. "Did you get what you needed?"

"Yes."

"Good." That was all he said before turning on his heel and continuing down the corridor. He stopped when we reached another shop with a carved symbol unmistakably resembling a pair of boots.

After everything Farna had told me, I couldn't help but wonder about the rumors involving him. *He's burned villages to the ground to track what he's after.*

Was he the one who burned Vyria's village to the ground? Did he murder her mother?

My steps faltered.

If he was truly what they said—a stone-cold killer—why was the same guy going out of his way to get me clothes? Because he'd decided we were *friends*. I didn't buy it.

What was his angle?

He was hiding something. The question was—what?

22

GAME PLAN

While we were in the courtyard, Velorn arranged for an extra mattress to be brought to our room. I initially saw it as a kind gesture because the couch was quite uncomfortable, but ultimately, it didn't help.

Even with my own mattress, I slept like complete and *utter* crap.

Velorn's damn shadows decided to make an appearance in the middle of the night, hovering around me and jolting me awake. For one groggy, horrifying moment, I thought his hands were around my waist. But when I sat up and prepared to throw a jab at him, he was asleep on the other mattress.

His face was tense, pained, and the shadows seemed to cling to me as if searching for something or someone, for comfort. It was troubling, like observing a frightened child instinctively seeking the closest source of safety. I didn't know what else to do in that moment other than wait it out until eventually they retreated.

After that, sleep was a lost cause.

Velorn was a walking contradiction, and it drove me crazy trying to understand him. He hardly spoke unless forced. He kept everyone at arm's length. He wore his reputation like armor, believing being feared was easier than being known. But the way he looked last night, that wasn't anger. That was pain. Old pain. The kind you only notice if you know what trauma looks like beneath the surface. Whatever shaped him into this hardened, silent nightmare of a man had not allowed him to find any closure.

I wanted to talk to him, to peel back his hardened layers and discover who he truly was deep down, but I had a feeling he would shut me out.

I had no one here I could talk to. No Gram, no co-workers, not even Vyria. Just me and my spiraling thoughts. I was utterly exhausted, deeply homesick, and to make things worse, I also started my period.

Fan-fucking-tastic.

What did women in this world even use? The thought alone sent me into a quiet panic. The cramps came in waves. I stayed in the bathroom as long as I could, fashioning a makeshift cloth and trying not to cry. My periods had always been on the lighter side, so why did it feel so much worse? Was there something in the environment here that changed me?

I stared into the mirror. "Come on, Eleni. This is nothing. If Florence Nightingale could handle it, then so can you."

The wave of cramps started again.

"What is taking you so long?" Velorn spoke from outside the door.

"None of your business!"

"The entire point of the new clothes was to avoid this drawn-out nonsense every time you get dressed," he barked. The threat in his tone was obvious.

"Just give me one damn minute!"

The wave of pain finally eased enough for me to move. I quickly slipped into the new outfit Farna had made. It was the opposite of flashy—soft brown leather pants and a black tunic that fit without being restrictive. Practical. Comfortable. And completely perfect for me. I would have to thank her if I ever saw her again.

Finally, I stepped out of the bathroom, doing my best to hide the pain.

"You should eat something before we train."

The thought of eating anything right now made me want to vomit. I ignored Velorn's suggestion and walked past him, heading for the door.

"Aren't you forgetting something?"

I froze mid-step, dread twisting in my stomach as I slowly turned to face him.

Velorn stood outside the bathroom, holding out my boots like an offering. Without a word, I marched over, snatched them from his grasp, and shoved them on.

⸻⸻◈⸻⸻

By the time we arrived at the courtyard, I wanted nothing more than to curl up into a ball and disappear.

I tried to come up with different excuses to go to the kitchen, but because of the distance from the kitchen to the courtyard, Velorn would have to follow.

My shoulders deflated.

Back home, a light workout usually helped ease the cramps. I also had the essentials: painkillers, heating pads, sanitary products, and a tub of rocky road.

The longer I felt stuck in this world, the more everything grated on me. I was dangerously close to losing it altogether.

Keep it together, Eleni.

Velorn's presence closed in beside me, only fueling my irritation. "What is wrong with you today?"

"Nothing's wrong!" I snapped. "Just let me do my thing and figure out this axe-summoning nonsense while you go sit by your wall or whatever it is you do."

Well, there went my *keeping it together.*

He didn't move. He stood there, likely searching for a reason as to why I was acting this way.

Did women here even have the same cycles, or was that only my problem? Maybe I could ask Farna. Surely, she'd understand.

But at the same time, I wasn't sure what was appropriate to discuss here in Thysia. The only person I was with rarely spoke. Asking him anything felt like pulling teeth.

I turned away before I could say something I'd regret and stepped farther into the courtyard.

The axe. That's what I needed to focus on. I'd done it once; I could do it again.

But of course, I had an audience.

Several soldiers were already spread out across the courtyard—some sparring, some leaning lazily against the walls.

"How pathetic," one of them announced. "Why does Prince Malakar really want her?"

"You know why," another added with eyes roaming my body.

And this right here was precisely why I hated having an audience.

I clenched my fists, trying to block out the soldiers, Velorn, the pain, and the exhaustion.

Focus. Just summon the damn axe.

I closed my eyes and reached inward, grasping at the feeling I'd found before, that surge of power, that fierce connection to it. I knew it was in me. I'd felt it. I'd seen what I could do.

But right now, it felt like trying to start a fire with wet wood. Nothing.

I tried again, pushing harder this time and summoning everything I had left.

Still nothing.

The cramps came in full force again, making me double over. I staggered, legs trembling, barely catching myself before I hit the ground.

I should have listened to Velorn and grabbed at least something before we left. Training on an empty stomach while on my period wasn't the brightest move.

Laughter erupted behind me. "Pathetic," one soldier sneered. "This is why female elementals shouldn't train. They are too weak and merely distract the rest of us."

Irritation coursed through me as I listened to these men talk. I felt my body tighten, focusing on the heat in my core—the same pulse I had felt before in the necklace.

This time, it responded.

Warmth spread across my chest, then down my arm like a wave of fire and lightning intertwined. My fingers tingled, and then—

Dark strands of smoke shot forward, latching around the soldier's throat mid-taunt. His laugh died instantly, replaced by a strangled gasp as the shadows tightened like a noose.

"I'd be very careful with your choice of words," Velorn warned. "Or they will be your last."

The warmth from the axe faded as I watched his magic expand outward. Wisps of shadows billowed across the courtyard, striking at every soldier within reach. In a flash, the entire group stiffened, staring at him like prey watching a predator choose who would die first.

"I could kill every single one of you," he continued, calm in the most disturbing way. "And I wouldn't lose sleep over it. Your lives mean nothing to me." He stepped forward, and shadows obeyed his every move. "The only life I value is Prince Malakar's. If he chose to take her under his care, it is for a reason. You do not question him. You do not question me. You follow. Understand?"

A chorus of frantic nods followed.

I'd seen Velorn intimidating before, but witnessing him act this way made my pulse skip. This was the monster they whispered about—the Tracker everyone feared.

A wave of pain tore through me again, interrupting my thoughts. I clenched my teeth, nearly doubling over as another wave of cramps hit.

Oh, come on! Why now?

My face couldn't hide the pain anymore. It felt like my insides were being squeezed to death. The world was spinning, my vision narrowed, and my knees buckled. Exerting myself on an empty stomach was the worst idea ever.

Get up, Eleni!

Before the world tipped completely sideways, hands caught me, hauling me up from the cold ground.

"Move," Velorn ordered.

For a second, I thought he meant me, but then I heard hurried apologies. "Sorry, sir." My fingers fisted his shirt without thinking. I didn't want to let go.

His grip loosened only when he lowered me onto something soft. A figure stepped closer and pressed something cool to my lips. "Drink. It will help with the pain."

I didn't argue.

A few minutes later, the cramps subsided, and the sharpness faded as my body relaxed. The room's edges blurred and darkened, then I quietly slipped into the abyss.

⁂

I stirred, uncertain of how long I had been unconscious. I blinked up at the unfamiliar ceiling, my body slow to respond. Hovering above me was an older man, his weathered face lined with deep creases, skin sun-kissed and marked by time. There was something about him, his calm presence and the way his kind eyes met mine, that made me feel at ease.

"You're awake. Good."

I blinked again, slowly pushing myself up. "W-where am I?"

Panic started to well up inside.

The courtyard. The soldiers. The humiliation. It all rushed back to me. My hand moved to my abdomen, expecting the wave of cramps that had caused me to spiral in the first place. But none came. In fact, I felt no pain at all. Nor was I sluggish or lethargic.

"You're in the healer's quarters," he said with a kind smile, rising to his feet. He approached a set of shelves lined with glass bottles, each filled with what looked like herbs and liquids in every imaginable color.

"Healer's quarters?" I repeated, taking in my surroundings. "How did I get here?"

"The Tracker brought you here."

I glanced around the room, half-expecting to see him brooding in a corner, arms crossed, wearing that signature scowl of disapproval, but he wasn't here.

My arm burned slightly, meaning he wasn't nearby, but he also wasn't far enough to make it unbearable.

The healer chuckled as if he could read my thoughts. "Don't worry. I kicked him out. He stormed in here all in a fuss, going on about how pale you looked—thought you'd been poisoned or something terrible." He waved a hand as if brushing away the assumption. "But the moment I laid eyes on you, I knew exactly what was going on."

Heat crept into my cheeks, and I looked down, my body still mostly under the sheets.

"Oh, don't fret, dear girl," he said kindly, walking back over with a steaming cup of something floral. "I raised six daughters—six. There's not a symptom or shade of pale I haven't seen before. Trust me, I've learned what to worry about and, more importantly, what not to."

He winked, and I couldn't help but smile as the tension in my shoulders eased.

There was something about the way he spoke, calm and confident, with a spark of mischief, that reminded me of Gram. That same mix of nurturing care and sly humor.

The hot liquid felt soothing as I took a sip. The aroma was a calming blend of floral notes with a hint of citrus and a touch of sweetness. "*Mmm*, this is really good," I said, lifting the cup once more for another taste.

"You can thank my wife for that recipe," the healer replied with a fond smile. "It's her special blend. Eases tension and helps with the cramps too."

As he moved about the room, my curiosity explored the neat rows of bottles, the dried herbs hanging from the beams, and the organic scents that filled my nose. Everything in this space had been arranged with care. I imagined him spending hours perfecting every detail, each one touched with purpose. The thought warmed me more than the drink.

"I've sent one of my daughters to fetch you some proper things to help with your cycle," he added, not making a fuss about it. "In the meantime, rest and finish that tea. I'll go track down your friend and let him know you're awake."

"Sorry, I didn't get your name."

"The name's Bevaro." He gave me a reassuring nod before stepping out, the door closing quietly behind him.

The atmosphere in this room felt peaceful. The kind of peace that wrapped around you like a blanket. Everything here seemed so lived-in and inviting, as if someone had poured their soul into creating it. For a fleeting moment, I didn't want to leave.

I took another sip from the cup, and then the door swung open. I tensed, expecting to see a scowl and brooding glare, but instead, a pair of familiar emerald eyes met mine.

"Ehlark!"

He slipped inside and quietly closed the door behind him.

"Are you hurt?" His eyes scanned me as if he needed to be certain.

"No," I reassured. "I'm okay."

He kept assessing me before sitting on the edge of the bed. "The workers in the kitchen told me you were brought here. Did *he* do something to you?"

My chest tightened at how he said it. "No, he didn't."

His brows drew together, like he still wasn't entirely convinced.

"Listen, I have a plan. One that will better our chances at escaping this place."

From his pocket, he pulled a small vial, no bigger than a perfume sample. "You need to get the Tracker to drink this."

I sat up straighter. "You can't be serious? He's going to know something's up if I hand him that."

"He won't," Ehlark assured. "Slip it into one of his drinks. It's scentless and tasteless."

"Will it kill him?"

"No. It'll knock him out for a while, but it'll give us the chance to kill him."

Killing Velorn didn't sit right with me. "I'm not a killer, Ehlark."

Velorn wasn't exactly in the running for a Daisy Award for friendliness, but that didn't make him irredeemable. The good was there, hidden deep, but it still existed.

"Listen, the only way to break a contract is to either repeat the words voluntarily, or he must die. Those are the only options."

Ehlark's hand reached out and gently touched mine. "I made a contract to get you home. I won't go back on my word. I will protect you until the end, Eleni. There's something about you. I'm not sure what, but," he paused, like he was weighing the risk of saying more. "I feel like we've met before. I can't explain it, but there's a familiarity I can't let go of."

There was a rawness in his eyes I hadn't seen before, a quiet ache buried beneath the steady resolve. It was the kind of look that made heat crawl up my neck.

"If you want to go home. This is the only option." I reluctantly took the vial from his other hand, sliding it into my pocket. I didn't like this plan. I couldn't let him kill Velorn, but how was I going to convince him?

Ehlark's eyes glowed softly in the lamplight. They reminded me of spring after a long winter, like life itself. They brought back memories of someone I had loved with all my heart. Someone whom I would never see again.

Gram.

I had to do whatever it took to get back home.

Grief welled in my throat, wanting to rise to the surface, but I couldn't break now. I had to make it back. For Gram. For the ranch. For everything she fought to protect, and for everything I still had to.

I didn't know how long we remained there, neither of us looking away. He leaned in, enough to close the space between us, and suddenly the room felt smaller.

A young girl stepped through the doorway, arms loaded with folded cloth and small parcels. Her eyes widened the moment she saw us.

"Oh! My apologies," she stammered with flushed cheeks. "I was told you needed some—" She glanced awkwardly between the two of us before settling her gaze on me. "Supplies. For your ailment." She practically threw the items onto the small table by the door, gave a stiff nod, and bolted out of the room.

"*Ailment?*" Ehlark asked, one brow raised.

"Female problems," I mumbled, wincing. Hopefully vague enough to end the conversation.

Shuffled footsteps came from the other side of the door, causing Ehlark's hand to tighten around mine. "I have to go."

His hand stayed on mine longer than it should have. He might not have noticed it, but there was a soothing warmth to his touch, one I wasn't ready to lose. Then he stood and headed toward the door.

"Be ready at nightfall."

23

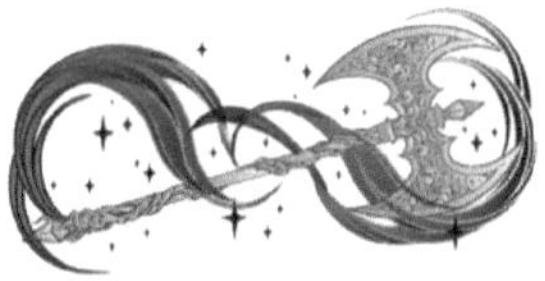

Mix Up

After about an hour in the healer's room, Bevaro finally arrived with Velorn standing outside the doorway, arms crossed, with a surly expression.

I wasn't surprised.

"I see one of my girls came," Bevaro said, spotting the supplies toward the table. "I'm sure you'll know what to do with those once you're back in the privacy of your room."

I let out a short, dry laugh that made the healer blink in surprise. Obviously, he didn't realize that privacy wasn't exactly something Velorn granted me.

The healer handed me three vials, their contents a deep shade of pink. "I took the liberty of getting these from my wife. She's a healer, too, and works on the lower levels with the other female workers. They tend to keep more of this stocked."

"What is it?" I asked, curiosity tugging at my already frayed nerves.

"They'll help with the cramps, take the edge off," he replied. "Make sure to take it in the evening, as they can make you a little drowsy."

Honestly, I'd take anything I could get right now. I thanked him, slipped the vials into my pocket, gathered the rest of the supplies, and headed out. Velorn was still outside, eyes fixed somewhere far away. He didn't even glance at me as he spoke. "Next time you decide to get your cycle, let me know first. We could've avoided all this unnecessary embarrassment."

My head tilted to the side.

"It wasn't your business to know. Sorry if it *embarrassed* you." I knew better than to think he cared, but still—it got to me.

I shook my head and let out a sigh.

His words mean nothing. Don't let him get to you.

We walked back to our room, the vials rattling in my pocket. My gaze drifted to Velorn's back as I mentally listed everything I couldn't stand about him, including having to practically jog to keep up with him.

Maybe if I replayed all the awful things he'd done, I could make myself believe he deserved whatever fate found him. Perhaps I could finally convince myself he *was* the monster everyone said he was. That letting him die would be easier.

He was the obstacle between me and home.

So why did the idea of killing him still feel wrong?

As he turned down the hallway, my eyes dropped to his right arm. At first, it seemed like a smudge or a bit of dirt in the shape of a hand. But the more I examined it, the more it resembled a burn mark. A hand-shaped burn.

"What happened to your arm?"

"Nothing that concerns you."

Okay, someone was in an even crankier mood than usual. I caught his other arm as he passed and stopped him in the hallway. "Velorn, what happened to your arm?"

I half expected him to yank it back or bristle at the contact, like he did with anyone who tried to get close, but he didn't. Instead, he fixed me with that calculating stare of his.

"Malakar."

That was the first time I'd heard him say Malakar without the whole "Prince" formality.

Strange.

"He did that? But why?"

"He expected you to be able to show him the axe today. I told him you need more time. He didn't like my answer."

But why had Malakar burned him? He wasn't the one summoning the axe. Was Malakar punishing him for failing to do his job?

He pulled his arm free and started up the stairs.

"I'm sorry he did that to you." The words came out quietly, but Velorn's steps slowed for a single beat before continuing at their usual pace. By the time we got to the room, he walked directly into the washroom.

The sun was setting, stretching long shadows across the walls. Night was approaching, which meant Ehlark would be here soon. I had to come up with a plan quickly.

My eyes fell on the table. There was a pitcher of water and a few stone-colored cups neatly arranged beside it. I walked over and reached into my pocket for the vial, the one Ehlark gave me.

But the moment my fingers touched the glass—no, glasses—my stomach plummeted.

Oh no.

I pulled out not one, but four vials. I had shoved all of them into the same damn pocket without thinking. I lifted each vial to the light, hoping at least one of them stood out from the rest, but they all appeared unique. Each bottle displayed a subtle variation from the others. One was a shade lighter than the rest, while another was a shade darker.

I popped open the first one and sniffed, then the second, third, and fourth. Nothing stood out. They all were scentless.

"Okay, don't panic," I whispered to myself, which was precisely what someone did when they were, in fact, absolutely panicking. I repeated, as if maybe the fifth time would magically cancel out the full-blown internal meltdown occurring in my brain.

Then I heard the bathroom door creak.

Screw it.

I uncorked all four vials and poured them directly into the pitcher. The liquid blended seamlessly, vanishing into the dark green glaze of the glass.

I stepped back, my heart racing, trying to look casual as Velorn emerged from the bathroom, drying his hair with a towel.

If I wasn't already freaking out mentally over the fact that I'd made a potentially dangerous cocktail and served it like a casual refreshment, I might have taken a closer look at Velorn's half-naked body. But I had no time for that. I was too busy trying to keep my cool.

I darted out of his way the moment he walked toward me—nope, correction—toward the table. Toward the pitcher.

I couldn't look.

If I looked, the full-blown fear etched on my face would give me away in an instant. So, I did the only logical thing: I threw myself into fake drawer organization as if my life depended on it.

I started sifting through the pitiful selection of clothes, all the while tracking Velorn in my periphery. He sat down with a quiet sigh, the kind that said *I hate everything, but I'm too tired to murder anyone right now.* Then I heard the soft clink of water being poured.

I should've looked away. I should've kept my eyes glued to the drawer my hands were pretending to be busy with.

But no, of course not.

I glanced over in time to see him lift the cup to his lips and pause. Thankfully, the cup was the same dark glaze green as the pitcher, so even if there was some color, it wouldn't be obvious. Or at least I would hope not.

Drink the water.

Drink the damn water.

Our eyes found each other, and my breath stopped mid-inhale. I couldn't move or blink. Time slowed.

This was it.

The moment.

The climax of my terribly thought-out plan.

With a gulp, he drank the contents down in one go. Then lowered the cup from his lips and looked straight at me.

Shit.

He knows.

Say something. *Anything.*

"Do you ever have any regrets?" The words came out awkwardly because my regret was currently swimming around in that damn pitcher, and I had to buy myself some time before the effects kicked in.

"Doesn't matter," he said after a beat. "It's not something I like to dwell on."

Vague and dismissive. But at least there wasn't any suspicion in his tone.

"Why?"

Never mind. There it was.

"You know," I said, as my fingers fidgeted with the hem of my sleeve. "That's a great question, actually."

I paused, scrambling to come up with a reason. Any reason. But the first thing that came to mind wasn't the pitcher or the awkward silence—it was *Gram*.

The regret hit me like a deep ache in my chest. Out of all the mistakes I had ever made in my life, losing my connection to her was the only regret I had.

"I used to think the one thing I wanted most was to be the best nur—erm, healer—I could be. To heal, to advocate for people who couldn't speak for themselves. I wanted to hold their hands when no one else would, to remind them that someone cared." I paused, glancing at Velorn to see if he noticed my slip-up, but he remained silent, taking another sip. "I gave everything to that dream, prioritizing everyone else over me, even over the person who loved me more than life itself."

A small crease formed between his eyebrows as he rubbed his thumb along his jaw, but he still said nothing.

"Now it's too late." My voice came out quieter than I intended. "I had so many chances to fix things with my grandmother, but

I wasted them. And now she's buried in the earth, and I'll never be able to apologize enough or tell her how much I love her."

I took a shaky breath, only then realizing the pitcher was half empty. "I know you have regrets, Velorn. I've seen the way you look sometimes, like the weight of something old still follows you. Maybe it happened long ago, but that doesn't mean it stopped hurting."

Something wavered across his face. Not his usual sharp edges, not that cold mask he wore like armor. It was something sorrowful.

"Regret won't bring anyone back. Trust me."

I could see it hidden in the silence that followed, in the way his shoulders tensed and the muscles in his jaw tightened. Something had happened. He did lose someone. And maybe he hadn't let go of it nearly as much as he claimed.

His expression changed again, but this time, it wasn't in response to my question.

He looked down at the cup, his eyes narrowing this time. Then he glanced at the pitcher, then back down to his cup, and brought it to his nose.

Dread curled in my gut as I watched his knuckles blanch with pressure until the glass shattered in his grip.

Shards fell to the floor as his expression darkened, eyes burning with an ire that locked onto me like hell was ready to erupt.

Oh, I was completely and utterly fucked.

I've never been a good liar. So, I was pretty sure my face at that moment showed something like, *"Yes, I absolutely did the thing, and I regret all my choices; please don't kill me."*

"What's in this?" He growled, striding toward me with that *I'm-going-to-murder-you* look.

"I—I don't know what you mean," I stammered, instinctively backing away. I frantically searched for anything that might shield me from his wrath.

His shadows lunged at me, wrapping around my arms and torso, pulling me off my feet before shoving me halfway onto the bed, leaving me completely immobilized.

Then he was right on me, towering and glaring down, his intense stare burning into mine. His body was so close that I could feel his heat against my skin. Or maybe it was my own fear radiating off me.

"What did you put in the water?" Sweat dripped from his forehead, small drops landing on my face. His voice remained alert, but I could see his body weakening. His mouth opened as if speaking had drained him. He swayed, struggling to maintain his focus.

I was a bit surprised it was working so quickly. But then again, I had dumped four random vials into that pitcher.

Who even knew what kind of messed-up alchemy I had brewed?

Still, that didn't change the fact that he looked absolutely terrifying right now.

"W-what have y-you done?"

His voice slowed, each word forced painfully from his throat with visible effort. Yet, his arms remained locked on either side of me, muscles tight, as if only rage kept him upright. I could hardly breathe, only able to watch and pray he wouldn't kill me right then.

His whole body shook, but his shadows continued to hold me, binding me to the bed as if they didn't quite care that he was losing control. I tried to move, but I was trapped beneath the weight of both his body and his magic, still clinging to me.

Then slowly, they disappeared, gradually letting go of me.

His breath caught. Once. Then again—shallow, rapid, as if he were trying to hold on to something slipping away.

Then, with one last shuddering exhale, his entire body fell onto me.

24

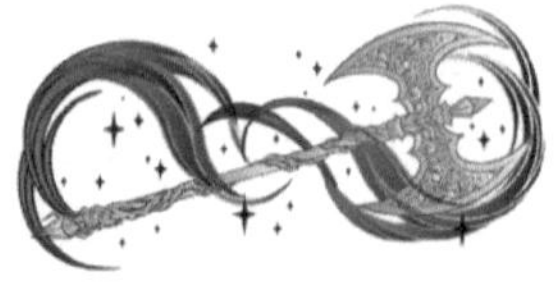

PREDATORY STARE

As I stared at the ceiling under Velorn's body, two thoughts crossed my mind:

One—was he really asleep, or had he dropped dead from an overdose?

Two—how in the hell was I supposed to get out from underneath him?

When he collapsed, his entire body landed across mine, pinning my arms to my sides and most of my legs under his absurd weight.

I squirmed.

Nothing happened.

I tried shimmying side to side, but no luck.

"Damn, Velorn," I grunted, wriggling again. "You weigh as much as a five-ton elephant." There was no response, only a soft exhale from his nose to confirm he was dead asleep.

My elbow dug into his side, trying to lever myself out. He didn't budge. Not even an inch. "This is fine," I muttered to myself. "Totally fine. Don't panic." After what felt like an eternity of awkward writhing and whispered curses, I finally managed to slide one hand free, then the other. Bit by bit, I slithered out from beneath him like a disgruntled earthworm until I flopped onto the floor.

"Freedom," I said, feeling victorious. It hadn't been more than a few minutes when a soft knock at the door jolted me upright.

I glanced over my shoulder—*yep, still out cold.*

I walked to the door and cracked it open enough to peek outside. A hooded figure was standing there. They looked up slowly, and as they pulled back their hood, I saw a pair of familiar green eyes.

"Perfect timing."

He stepped inside and immediately froze. His gaze drifted over to the bed, to where Velorn's unconscious body sprawled across it.

"Oh," he whispered, eyebrows raising as he scratched the stubble on his chin. "I thought that dose would make him groggy enough for me to take him out quietly. Looks like you did all the hard work for me."

If only he knew the truth and that I'd dumped four vials into the pitcher without thinking. I was glad that I didn't kill him. But then Ehlark's hand went to his side, where a dagger hung from his belt.

"Wait." I stepped in front of him, stopping him from going any further. "We can't kill him."

Ehlark frowned at me. "And why not?"

"Because we can't. We need to find a way to get him to come with us. Please." I didn't have any solid reason to tell him, but I'd seen different sides to Velorn—glimpses that showed he wasn't all bad. There had to be some goodness buried inside him. Maybe he also needed to get away from here. Away from Malakar.

Ehlark crouched by the bed, took his fingers, and flicked Velorn's forehead. I almost had a heart attack, but Velorn didn't stir.

"He didn't try anything, did he?"

"No. He didn't." However, looking at Velorn's half-naked body might have suggested otherwise.

"Good." Ehlark stood and rubbed his chin. "Wait here. And grab him a shirt."

Getting a shirt onto someone who was essentially dead weight became a challenge in itself. By the time I finished, Ehlark had arrived with a tall cart. It was covered by an animal hide draped over the top, hiding what was underneath. Ehlark lifted it, revealing a small stash of supplies neatly tucked beneath bundles of linen. In the cart, he reached in and pulled out a pair of handcuffs.

Golden cuffs.

I immediately recognized the etching. It was the same one they used when we were taken prisoner.

"You two will hide in here," he explained, gesturing to the cart. "I'll take you down to the prisoner levels. There's usually only one guard after nightfall, and I've already planted a little surprise for him." He approached Velorn and moved his body halfway off the bed. "But we must move fast. Grab his legs."

Together, we lifted Velorn's body into the cart. He was so damn heavy, and every muscle in my arms burned as we maneuvered him into place. His head lolled slightly to the side, but once he was settled under the pile of linens in there, he almost looked like a bundle of supplies.

I climbed in afterward, positioning myself awkwardly on Velorn, the sharp angles of his body pressing uncomfortably against me. It wasn't exactly the most dignified escape plan, but I wasn't about to complain.

"Wait," I said, peeking out from under the linens. "How are you planning to get this thing down all those stairs?"

"There's a hoist at the end of the hallway," he explained. "I've got someone waiting at the bottom to keep watch."

I ducked under the linen as the cart started to move. Every creak of the wheels echoed in my ears, and each bump on the floor jostled me against Velorn's unconscious form. His heat seeped through the fabric between us, and his steady breathing filled the tight space.

Being so close to Velorn was becoming an unsettling pattern. Even his muted presence made my heart race. A confusing mix of nervousness and something deeper, something I couldn't quite name.

My curiosity betrayed my caution as I lifted a hand to his scarred face. My fingers brushed over the uneven ridges. They were deep, violent, and familiar. They felt like mine. It felt like I wasn't just touching his pain but my own. Perhaps for the first time, I realized we shared something: wounds that never fully healed, marks we could never escape. I wanted to ask why they hadn't healed, why his skin hadn't mended like other wounds. But then I remembered what Farna said—these weren't scars.

They were a curse. Maybe that's why they looked so brutal, so permanent. And maybe that's why, when my gaze lingered on him, something inside me ached with the quiet, forbidden thought that he wasn't the monster the world wanted me to believe he was.

I let my fingers trail lightly over the scar cutting across his eye.

He looked at peace, as if the endless war inside him had finally gone quiet. For a selfish, fleeting second, it made me happy. Happy that, even if I'd practically drowned him in potions to get us here, at least it gave him this rare, fragile stillness. If that was the price for peace on his face, I couldn't regret it.

The cart hit something rough, jarring me out of my thoughts. Faint whispers drifted from outside the cart.

"Do you have the package?" a feminine voice asked. Her tone was familiar, one I'd heard before but couldn't quite place where.

"Yes."

"I checked below. Seems like the soldier's still unconscious."

"Thank you," Ehlark whispered. "Truly."

The cart shifted again as Ehlark pushed. Every bump and turn sent fresh waves of anxiety rippling through me. My body couldn't relax; each jolt magnified in the claustrophobic space, along with the grinding of the wheels against the uneven stone. If we were caught, there would be no way out—for either of us.

Finally, the cart came to a stop. The linens above me rustled as Ehlark pulled them back, his face illuminated by the light. His hand reached down, helping me up as my eyes slowly adjusted to the darkness.

Five prisoners stood before me, huddled behind iron bars that appeared to be forged from the mountain itself. Their eyes were sunken and shadowed, yet still held quiet defiance. Their faces were pale, skin stretched tight over sharp cheekbones, a look caused by too many days without food or sunlight. I didn't recognize any of them. None were from the convoy I was taken with. They were strangers, but not unfamiliar in their suffering.

Golden cuffs bound their wrists, the metal catching the dim torchlight with a cruel glint. The memory of them weighed heavily. How they dug into my skin, how they made every movement feel like dragging chains through mud. Even without having magic like theirs, I had felt it: the suppression, the silence inside me, the aching stillness where something should have been.

Even in worlds as different as ours, the system of violence wasn't all that different from where I came from. The realization hit me. This was the system Velorn and Malakar upheld. This was what they enforced.

Frustration flooded through me at the thought that any of this was allowed at all. Maybe Ehlark was right, and we should kill Velorn. End it before he could cause any more damage. But every time I imagined his death, something inside me pulled back. The hair on the back of my neck prickled, a quiet warning that it wasn't right.

I wasn't a killer. I was someone who helped others, and right now, I needed to help Velorn.

A soldier was lying a few feet away, his chest rising and falling in a slow rhythm. I crouched down and took the keys from his belt. The metal felt cold and heavy in my hand as I unlocked the cell door.

"Hold still," I whispered, moving quickly to uncuff the prisoners. When their shackles fell, the veins in their hands started to glow. Some were the same vibrant green that Ehlark had; others were a beautiful blue, spreading through their veins, knitting wounds and washing away fatigue, like what Vyria's were. I couldn't help but stare, even though I'd seen it before. The magic still amazed me.

"We cannot use all of our powers to heal; otherwise, we won't have enough to escape," one of the men remarked.

"Do what you can," Ehlark replied. "I'll start working on the hole."

He turned toward the back wall; his hands radiated the same vibrant green I had seen before. The glow in his veins traveled up his arms, pulsing like a heartbeat as the soil responded to his magic. The earth shifted, roots awakening and twisting to life as they did when we faced those soldiers in the Wispwoods. It was mesmerizing and terrifying to witness that raw, unstoppable power once again.

Within minutes, a gaping hole formed, with the roots twisting and turning like a giant blade slicing effortlessly through the soil. The others, bolstered by whatever power they'd absorbed, joined the effort, smashing rocks and clearing away clumps of dirt with practiced efficiency.

Without power like theirs, I knew I would be dead weight if I tried to help. Instead, I remained near the cart, near Velorn.

My eyes darted between the dark corners of the cell. Even though Velorn was knocked out cold, I couldn't shake the feeling that his shadows were still somehow watching me.

The sudden sound of hurried footsteps echoed down the hall as one of the lookout prisoners appeared in view.

"They've sounded the alarm!" he shouted. "We have to move now!"

The tunnel seemed deep enough to serve as an escape, but could it accommodate all of us? And what about the cart—would we even be able to navigate it through?

"Why is the Tracker here?" a prisoner hissed. "Leave him here with the guard," another bristled.

"We can't," Ehlark said firmly, his gaze briefly met mine. "She is bound to him."

"Then leave her too," another prisoner snapped. His eyes met mine with full-on disgust. "She's an unknown; we don't even know what she has. She could be a spy for all we know."

Why does everyone in this world assume I'm a spy? I started to protest, but Ehlark slammed the prisoner against the cell bars, making everyone stop suddenly.

"We do not leave her behind, Terryn. She comes with us. Therefore, so does he. Do you understand?"

The prisoner hesitated, then nodded stiffly. "Does anyone else want to question me?" No one responded. Everyone remained silent. Tarryn backed away as Ehlark released him, but not before giving me a final look.

"Everyone inside the cell," Ehlark ordered.

I pushed the cart forward, Velorn's body shifting slightly as I maneuvered him into the already cramped space. The distant sound of boots grew louder until one of the soldiers saw us.

"There!"

The light of the approaching flames stretched across the walls, their shadows dancing like phantoms. The soldiers stopped beyond the bars, their fires illuminating their grim faces.

"Find the keys!" another soldier shouted.

They searched the guard's pockets, and their frustration mounted when they came up empty. "Fetch Prince Malakar," one of the soldiers ordered, sending a soldier back up the stairs.

If Malakar were coming, we would be in trouble. We were running out of time.

"Is it deep enough yet?"

A voice yelled back, "Not yet!"

The soldiers didn't move as they watched us, like they were waiting for orders, which made it even more nerve-racking.

"Ehlark, please hurry!" I shouted down, my voice cracking enough to reveal how truly not okay I was.

I didn't know what terrified me more: Velorn waking up and turning into a rage monster, or Malakar showing up and doing something worse. I hadn't seen what Malakar was capable of, but the few times I had been around him, he felt dangerous. The silent kind of dangerous you wouldn't notice until you were already dead.

The soldiers outside the cell suddenly turned toward a figure as it came into view.

I guess I had my answer.

Malakar descended, his presence consuming the room like a heatwave that pricked my skin. He moved with unhurried confidence, the loose black robe he wore billowing slightly, its open front revealing the muscles of his chest. His dark eyes met mine.

"Eleni."

The glare he was giving me now made it clear that I was in way over my head.

"Where is Velorn?"

I gripped the side of the cart tighter. "With me."

"Is that so?"

His hands lifted slightly, red veins glowed up his arms, and embers sparked to life with a slow, simmering intent. "I'll offer you one chance," he continued. "Bring him out of the cell, and I'll forget this *unfortunate* incident. No harm will come to you."

"And the prisoners?"

His expression hardened, all pretense of civility melting away. "They've broken our laws. They will face their punishment."

"Then no."

Malakar's expression narrowed as the red glow traveled further up his arms, flooding his veins, until it ignited his eyes. Without warning, a ball of liquid lava shot through the bars, striking one of the prisoners. The man barely had time to scream before he was consumed by liquid and melted to the ground.

I jerked back, the blast of the heat scorching my skin even from several feet away. The world seemed to tilt, with a sickening feeling, as I looked down at the remnants of the prisoner who had been there moments ago. My eyes widened in horror at the sight.

This was Malakar's true nature.

He was the monster.

"The bars themselves repel powers, Eleni," Malakar stated. "But they don't stop what passes between them."

"Ehlark!" A desperate shout echoed down the tunnel from the other prisoner beside me. "We need to go now! The prince killed Worro!"

Malakar's fiery gaze remained on me. Watching, waiting for my next move. His eyes, once a deep, smoldering coal, now blazed with a vivid, otherworldly red that seemed to burn into every inch of my soul.

"Release Velorn back to me, or I will burn down everyone around you. One by one."

Malakar would keep his word; I had no doubt. He would slaughter every last prisoner in this place to drag Velorn and me back.

"Go," I said sharply to the other prisoner beside me. "I'll hold them off as long as I can."

The prisoner nodded and then hurried down the hole.

I wouldn't let him take another life. Not now. Not while I was still breathing.

I narrowed my focus to the necklace, listening for the hum beneath my skin, the steady warmth of magic. It had always been there, waiting for me to reach for it. My breath quivered, but the hum kept rising.

My fingers loosened at my side, shaking as I felt the magic unfurl from the necklace in a sudden rush, spreading through my chest and down my arm until it reached my palm, pooling there, the pressure humming through my bones, electric and powerful.

A surge of bright green light burst from my hand, so intense it left streaks in my vision. The weight followed—a heavy, grounding presence that felt familiar in my grip. The axe materialized: solid and unwavering, its emerald glow pulsed with energy that seemed both ancient and angry. The fear remained, but my anger dominated my thoughts. It felt raw, wild, and entirely mine.

"Is this what you wanted to see, Malakar?"

Malakar's unshakable composure faltered as his eyes widened.

If he could strike through the bars, then so could I.

I raised the axe high, every muscle in my body tense and shaking as I narrowed my focus on the target, then hurled it between the bars.

The weapon tore through, aiming at the prince, but Malakar was faster and dodged to the side as it struck the soldier beside him, sending out a shockwave in its wake. The axe slammed into the wall behind them, cracking the rock. The mountain groaned as debris fell from above, jagged chunks crashing down on the soldiers. Screams roared as soldiers scattered, some diving for cover, others retreating toward the exit in panic.

Malakar was on his knees, the red glow retreating from his face. "Glad to see you can summon the relic."

The axe reappeared in my hand, feeling even more powerful than before. Like it was feeding off my anger, drinking in everything I felt.

Whatever this feeling was, I wanted more.

"Get a good look, Malakar, because it will be your last!" I raised the axe again, but Ehlark rushed to my side and grabbed my arm. "Eleni, if you throw that thing again, the whole mountain could collapse. We need to leave. *Now!*"

Before I could argue, he yanked me into the tunnel. Dirt and debris rained down around us as one of the prisoners pressed his glowing hands against the walls, the earth trembling under his command. The ground groaned as the entrance collapsed, sealing the way behind us.

The last thing I heard was Malakar's voice echoing down the tunnel.

"I'll be seeing you again soon, Eleni."

25

SOFT PROMISE

The tunnel was pitch-black, except for the glow emanating from the ground, guiding us as we were pushed deeper into the earth. Amid the chaos unfolding behind us, I hadn't thought much about how long we'd been underground. At first, I kept my mind occupied, thinking about home. The feeling of clean sheets and sunshine. The taste of a greasy cheeseburger, ice-cold soda fizzing on my tongue. Silly things. Comforting things.

But the deeper we went, the harder it became to pretend.

"How much further?" one of the prisoners moving the soil behind us asked, his voice tinged with exhaustion.

"Based on the distance we've carved out, we're a little more than halfway," Ehlark replied.

Halfway?

We'd been at this for hours, and I could see the glow in the once bright ground gradually dimming. They were losing strength, and we hadn't thought to bring water.

Brilliant planning.

To make matters worse, Velorn kept shifting in the cart. The effects of the drugs were fading, which shouldn't have been possible. But then again, Velorn wasn't exactly normal.

His movements were subtle, but they were enough to set my nerves on edge. The last thing I wanted was to be stuck underground with him conscious. Even in those cuffs, he would still be dangerous.

"Ehlark, we need to hurry," I said. "I think the drugs are wearing off."

"Listen, missy, we're going as fast as we can," the prisoner with the disgusted look from earlier snapped. "Some of us don't have the luxury of sitting back and watching while we do all the work."

"Stop it, Terryn," Ehlark shouted.

"What?" Terryn argued. "Does she even have any abilities?"

"She just saved your hide, so maybe show some gratitude."

"No, he's right," I said, interrupting the escalating argument. "What if I used the axe to help cut through the soil?"

All eyes turned to me, their expressions a mix of doubt and curiosity.

"What if her axe causes the tunnel to collapse?" Someone asked with concern. "We'd all be buried alive. The entire escape would be ruined!"

A murmur of agreement followed.

"Look," I said. "I may not have magic like the rest of you, but you can feel it, can't you? Yours are fading. And as fast as you heal from wounds, it doesn't seem like your magic bounces back the same way."

A few heads nodded in quiet acknowledgment, while some ignored me.

"Let me try," I pleaded. "Give me a chance. We're running out of options."

Everyone paused, considering whether to take the risk with me or to rely on all their abilities. Then, they turned to the one person they seemed to trust the most. The one who kept risking his life to help us escape.

Ehlark gave a slow, firm nod. "Do it."

"Stand back," I warned, stepping forward.

I closed my eyes and reached for the emotions I had felt before: the surge of anger, the rush of power, like electric currents flooding my veins. I needed to find it again. To hold it.

The necklace pulsed to life, coursing through me in a wave of energy. It traveled down my arm until it materialized in my hand. Its vibrant glow bathed the tunnel in radiant green light.

"What in Solryn's soul is that thing?" One of the prisoners whispered. Every gaze fixed on the axe.

"A way out."

I positioned the axe carefully at my waist. My fingers tightened around the handle, feeling its power thrumming beneath my skin.

"Here goes nothing," I muttered under my breath.

The blade struck the soil with a resounding force, sending a shockwave through the tunnel. The earth yielded instantly, deepening the hole in front of us. The world above groaned as bits of dirt and rock tumbled down, but Ehlark and the others quickly reacted, using their powers to stabilize the tunnel.

Okay, maybe I'd used a little too much weight in that swing. Let's dial it back.

I reset my stance, not pulling the axe so far back, and swung again. The blade cut cleanly through the soil, but this time, the ground remained still.

"I think it's working!" one of the prisoners exclaimed.

I tightened my grip on the axe, determination fueling each swing. We would get out of here, whether my body broke or not.

Sweat dripped down my face, soaking my shirt and running into my eyes, stinging like fire. My hands trembled with the effort, the ache of exhaustion spreading from my fingers to my shoulders. Each swing of the axe sent shockwaves through my arms, and I felt my grip slipping. I had never held the axe this long before, never tested the limits of its endurance—or mine. But I reminded myself I wouldn't stop. Not until the axe refused my swing and disappeared, but it never did.

Glancing back, Ehlark and the others were faltering. Their movements turned heavy and sluggish as exhaustion clung to their limbs. The glow of their hands glinted feebly, a pale imitation of the vibrant energy they had once commanded. One of them, thoroughly drained, had entirely given up on their powers and now strained against Velorn's cart, pushing it forward with nothing but sheer physical effort.

Don't stop.

Swing.

The words echoed like a mantra as I tightened my grip on the axe. My heartbeat pounded rapidly in my ears, each pulse syncing with the rhythm of my strikes.

I will get home.

Swing.

My arms burned like they were being torn apart from the inside, every lift of the axe heavier than the last. The muscles in my shoulders screamed in protest, and my fingers threatened to give out entirely.

Swing.

But I didn't stop, and the axe didn't disappear. Because somewhere deep in my bones, I knew that if I quit swinging, I'd be giving up my only chance to get home. So I made a choice. I'd rather collapse face-first into the dirt than surrender to exhaustion.

Swing.

The glow of its light and its power felt like a defiance against the darkness surrounding us, a testament to my determination to keep moving, regardless of the cost. One more swing, I told myself, then another and another, as if each strike was the final thread holding our fragile hope together.

"Eleni," a voice murmured behind me, cutting through the fog in my thoughts. I turned to see Ehlark standing behind me. "I think you can stop now." His hand brushed against my arm. His gentle touch and smile eased the tension coursing through my body.

As if responding to that unspoken release, the axe dissolved and retreated into the pendant. Its absence left an odd emptiness and a sense of vulnerability. My legs buckled, and I sank to my knees as exhaustion overwhelmed me now that I had nothing left to fight.

Ehlark stepped forward, placing a hand on the packed soil above us. The glow pulsing from his palm was dim, barely a shadow of the strength I had seen before, but it was enough. With one final push, he coaxed the earth to part, roots untangling and soil shifting away.

A thin ray of light pierced through the cracks, spilling into the tunnel. It felt blinding after so much darkness. I raised a hand to shield my eyes, blinking as my vision adjusted to the stark contrast.

"Let me check it out before we all climb up," he said as he hoisted himself through the narrow opening. His figure was momentarily silhouetted against the light as he disappeared above.

We held our breaths, waiting for what lay above.

26

MISTWEAVER

"All clear."

We climbed out of the hole one by one, the fresh air a pleasant contrast to the dark, cramped space below. The weight of the earth around us disappeared, replaced by a vast sky softly lit with the early morning light. That's when I realized we had been digging all night.

No wonder I felt completely drained.

We had emerged from Hollow's Mountain, and ahead of us loomed the shadowy expanse of Wispwoods Forest. Its twisted trees stood like sentinels, their gnarled branches reaching toward the sky. The sight was both foreboding and strangely comforting, familiar in its wildness compared to the mountain's confines.

"Kaelira is supposed to meet us by the waterfall at the edge of the Wispwoods," Ehlark said, pointing ahead of us.

As his words faded, my mind drifted homeward. Not to the memory of it, but the actual possibility. I was another step closer to getting there.

The possibility alone made me smile.

For the first time in a long while, it didn't seem impossible. It felt real, almost within reach.

Suddenly, a choked yelp snapped my attention behind me. My heart lurched as Velorn stood there, the chains wrapped around Terryn's throat. The man struggled, clawing at the chains, his face growing redder with each passing second.

"Move, and he dies." There was no hesitation in his stance, no bluff in his words.

I halted, my hands slowly rising. "Velorn, let him go. There's no need for this."

Velorn's lips curled into a bitter smirk; his eyes bore into mine with an icy stare.

"No need?" he spat. "You drugged me, chained me, and now you expect me to play along?" His grip tightened on Terryn's throat.

"Velorn, stop," I pleaded and took a step toward him, but Ehlark grabbed my arm.

"And you!" His gaze turned to Ehlark. "You were the prisoner who was caught that night. And it was *you* in the courtyard."

Before Velorn could kill Terryn, the ground suddenly shifted beneath him. Roots erupted from the earth like coiled snakes, wrapping around his legs and pulling him off balance. He stumbled, his grip on Terryn weakening enough that he shoved himself away from Velorn, gasping and falling forward.

A cluster of roots shot upward, wrapping around Velorn's arms and pulling tight. Ehlark's faint green glow flared as he channeled his remaining strength into the ground, his jaw tight with focus. The other prisoners joined in, their trembling hands glowing as they reinforced the bindings, securing Velorn in place.

Velorn thrashed against the restraints. "You think this will hold me?!" He glowered at Ehlark and then at me. Even with the cuffs on, he still fought against the roots holding him, snapping some of them off.

"Enough, Velorn!" I shouted. "We didn't drag you out of that mountain to kill you. Stop fighting us!"

He paused then, his golden eyes searing into mine, sending a sudden wave of unease through my bones. "I expected betrayal," Velorn said, his tone dripping with venom, "but I actually hoped you were different." He spat the words like they tasted foul, the bitterness clinging between us. "Which will make killing everyone here that much more enjoyable."

The way he said it hurt more than I expected. I wanted to explain why I had to do it. Ehlark would have killed him if I hadn't drugged him first, but Terryn stormed ahead and swung his fist. The crack of impact rang through the stillness as his knuckles made contact with Velorn's face, snapping his head to the side.

"Touch me again, and I'll make sure you won't be able to see out of those demon eyes," Terryn warned.

Velorn slowly straightened as a trickle of blood ran from his split lip. He didn't flinch or raise an eyebrow. Instead, he spat a mouthful of blood onto the ground, right onto Terryn's shoes.

Terryn moved to strike again, but Ehlark stepped in, grabbing his arm. "We need to move; if we don't reach the waterfall before nightfall, we'll miss our window, and I don't plan on spending another night here."

The group started to move, the roots wrapped around Velorn's legs and retreated into the ground, but he remained where he was.

"You can walk with us freely, or I'll drag you. Your choice." Ehlark stepped forward, his voice warning.

Velorn didn't move, his gaze shifting from Ehlark's to find mine again.

"Velorn, I'm telling you the truth. I have no reason to lie to you now. It was either kill you or drug you. I chose the latter."

He still looked disappointed, but after a few tense moments, he took a deep breath, held it like he was wrestling his temper back into place, then exhaled sharply and walked.

⸻◆⸻

The edge of the Wispwoods surrounded us, its dense canopy casting long, shifting patterns across the forest floor. The thick undergrowth and towering trees created a protective yet somewhat oppressive presence that seemed to breathe around us. Unlike last time, when survival had been my only focus, I allowed myself to appreciate the forest's remarkable beauty. Vibrant, moss-covered, gnarled roots and clusters of luminescent flowers shone in the dim light. Birds with light, iridescent feathers flitted through the branches, their songs carrying an eerie, melodic quality.

As my eyes wandered deeper into the forest, I froze. There he was again—the silver horse-like creature. He stood still, his dark mane rippling like shadows against his shiny coat. But this time he wasn't passing through; he was staring directly at me, his intelligent eyes meeting mine.

"Ehlark," I said softly, maintaining eye contact with it. "Do wild horses live here?"

Ehlark slowed, following my gaze into the trees. "None that I can recall," he said, his brow furrowing. "Why do you ask?"

"I think I saw one," I said, pointing toward the spot where the creature had been. But it was gone, vanishing like mist into the dense foliage.

"No ordinary creatures live in these woods. The Wispwoods are steeped in Old Magic that keeps most normal animals away."

I turned to him. "Old Magic?"

"Yes, from our ancestors, the Ancients," Ehlark explained, his voice quieter now as if the forest might hear him. "The Wispwoods are still tied to their power, remnants of what they wielded before the Rift War."

He mentioned the Rift War back in the cave, how another species had come here, invading their lands and tearing through them. The details had been hazy then, swallowed by the weight of everything else that had been going on. "What exactly happened during the Rift War?"

"Our scrolls say King Solryn—one of the last surviving Ancients—ended up sacrificing his core to save Thysia. He used the four relics to defeat the Noztari, forcing them back into their realm and closing the rift between our worlds."

"Were the Noztari the ones who came here and invaded?" I asked, trying to piece together the scraps of history.

Ehlark nodded. "Yes. They looked similar to us, but instead of elemental power. Our scrolls mentioned them using foreign metals and armor that were impenetrable."

Impenetrable armor and foreign metals.

On Earth, we had our own bulletproof alloys, materials that could stop a blade or a bullet. What if the Noztari weren't some alien race after all? What if they were people from Earth and dragged through the same strange light that had torn me from my world?

If the rift brought the Noztari here and sent them back the same way, then I must have gone through a rift as well. This means if I could find that rift, I had a chance of getting back home.

"And this Ancient you mentioned . . . Solryn. You said he used all the relics to send them back to their world? Not just one?"

"Yes," Ehlark continued. "He aligned them, bringing their power together until they became one sentient force. Strong enough to drive the Noztari back. But wielding that much power came at a great cost to him and to this world. At least, that's what the scrolls tell us."

Questions crowded my thoughts—about the war, about their ancestors, and about how anyone could bear that kind of power and still command the relics. The same relic that now rested against my chest. If those scrolls truly held proof of the Rift War, then maybe they also held something even more important: the truth of how the rift had opened and what had slipped through.

My gaze returned to the spot where that creature had been moments ago, now vacant. But strangely, it still felt like it was watching me.

"There are stories," he said quietly. "Legends of beasts, the Noztari once rode into battle. When called upon, it granted its rider power beyond measure. Wings vast enough to darken the sky, a horn brimming with arcane force, and scales that morphed into their surroundings until the creature vanished from sight."

The hairs on my arms rose, casting a wary glance back into the forest. "What is a creature like that called?"

"A Dreros," he said at last. "But no one's seen one since the Rift War. Like so many creatures tied to the Old Magic, they were either killed during the war or sent back into the rift. Now, they're nothing more than myths, stories told to entertain children and fill the silence of long nights."

I thought about the creature's shimmering coat and how it seemed to shift colors like ripples in water. But it didn't have wings or a horn. Whatever it was, though, it was no ordinary animal.

We finally reached the waterfall, its thunderous roar a welcome reprieve from the Wispwoods. Mist swirled around us like a veil, and from the rocks, a figure emerged.

I recognized her instantly. She was the elemental who had helped us escape when we were trapped in that cursed cage. Petite and ghostly in the dim light, her pale complexion appeared translucent, starkly contrasting with the freckles adorning her face. Snow-white hair cascaded loosely over her shoulders, catching the gleam of the water's reflection.

She rushed to Ehlark and threw her arms around him in a fierce embrace that conveyed a closeness deeper than mere camaraderie.

It shouldn't have bothered me. Hell, I barely even knew the guy. So why did seeing that hug make something twist inside me?

I guess I shouldn't be surprised. A guy like him probably already had someone he cared about. And she was beautiful. She also seemed genuinely concerned for him.

"Thought you were dead there for a moment," she teased, taking a strand of his hair in her fingers.

"We almost were, Kaelira," Ehlark smiled.

You know what? Good for him.

Staying here was temporary anyway.

Kaelira's sunlit eyes swept over the group, her expression softening until her gaze landed on me. Her smile faltered, darkening before she turned back to Ehlark. "Where's Worro?"

"He didn't make it."

Kaelira's composure cracked momentarily, her eyes revealing a flicker of grief. Then her expression hardened. "All right," she said. "I'll take two at a time."

I frowned, confused by what she meant.

Terryn and another prisoner appeared to grasp her statement as they moved forward, gripping her arms tightly. "I hate this part," he muttered, squeezing his eyes shut like a child preparing for something unpleasant.

Kaelira smirked. "You're such a baby." The thick mist swirled around them, growing denser by the second until the three figures disappeared entirely.

My heart leaped into my throat as I stood there stunned, my eyes widening. "What the—what happened?"

"She's a Mistweaver," Ehlark explained.

"A what?"

"A Mistweaver. She can summon mist and use it to transport people to different locations. This is her elemental ability."

I stared at him, still trying to wrap my head around what I had seen. "And you couldn't have mentioned that before?"

Ehlark gave a slight shrug. "Seemed like the least of our concerns at the time."

My disbelief remained as I looked back toward where the mist had swallowed them. She had the same magic as Velorn, but instead of darkness swallowing you in the abyss, hers seemed a bit more on the pleasant side.

"When Kaelira returns, Lorrak and I will go," Ehlark said, his eyes wavering briefly to me before settling on Velorn. His expression sharpened, the glow of his waning power still pulsing through his tense frame. "Then you and Velorn will follow." He stepped closer to Velorn, his voice dropping to a lethal chill. "Try anything, and I will kill you."

The remaining roots binding Velorn's arms slowly retreated into the earth, leaving only the golden cuffs.

Velorn met Ehlark's threat with a cold-hearted stare.

The tension remained between the three of us until Kaelira emerged from the mist. Her pale form appeared spectral, her movements silent as she stepped into the dim light. She said nothing, her expression calm but focused as she waited, ready to guide Ehlark and Lorrak.

Ehlark turned to me, his expression softening as he stepped closer. His hands gently gripped my shoulders. "I promise that once we're back in Cedarvale, I'll do whatever it takes to get you home."

I nodded, unable to find the words. His hand on my shoulder eased the guilt that had been eating away at me since I betrayed Velorn. Out of everyone here, he was the only one who had shown me genuine kindness, the only person still trying to help even when I was falling apart. I was grateful to have someone like him on my side.

He walked toward Kaelira. Her attention was still fixed on me, her expression anything but friendly. When Ehlark took hold of her arm, her gaze softened as she turned her focus to him.

Whatever tension she'd been holding seemed to dissolve in his presence.

The mist swirled around them until it completely swallowed their forms in an ethereal haze. When it finally cleared, silence lingered, leaving Velorn standing beside me.

Unease crawled back under my skin as we stood alone in the fading edge of the trees.

He was the *last* person I wanted to be alone with right now.

"If you value their lives, you'll uncuff me and return to Malakar," Velorn warned.

I heard him but refused to respond, my eyes scanning the Wispwoods, hoping to catch a glimpse of the creature again, but the forest remained still.

"Listen to me," Velorn continued. "Malakar will stop at nothing until he gets what he wants. Even if that means killing those you care about."

It shouldn't have gotten under my skin. I was so close to finding a way home, but the way he talked about Malakar and what I'd seen in the Mountain left me feeling troubled.

Would he really kill anyone he had to in order to get to Velorn and me?

He stepped closer, his towering frame bleeding into the dim light, making his presence impossible to ignore. "Malakar has spies everywhere. You're playing a dangerous game, little *Viri*—one you will lose."

"Velorn, I want to go home," I said, my words cracking under the weight of frustration. "Do you even know what it feels like? To be out of place? To not belong anywhere?"

"More than you know."

I studied his face, searching for cracks in his hardened mask. "How?"

"I am unmarked." There was no emotion behind his words, no empathy or concern. "I will never belong to a House."

My eyes dropped to his arms, searching for a bite mark or the symbol I had seen on Farna, but there was nothing. Only old scars traced his skin, including the burn mark that still looked fresh from yesterday.

How did I not notice this before?

I stepped back. "But I thought—"

"You thought wrong." The edge in his tone cut through the space between us. "Because of my contract with Malakar, I'm tolerated in the House of Fire, but I am not marked."

If Velorn was also unmarked, why was he so eager to kill and capture others like him? How was he okay with this? Was it related to his contract with Malakar?

It had to be.

"Make no mistake," His words brought my attention back to him. "The moment we leave here, their deaths will be on your hands. Do you want that?"

"Of course not. How can you say that?" My frustration and shock reached their boiling point. "They are unmarked like you. Don't their lives mean anything?"

"They don't."

The cold indifference hit like a slap in the face as I stared up at him, disbelief and disappointment colliding within me. "You don't care about anyone but yourself, do you?"

"When you've been treated like a monster your whole life, when the very people who were supposed to care for you betray you and cast you out . . ." His voice trailed off as he took another step closer. "I do not care enough to value anyone else's life."

The space between us disappeared, his presence now a wall of heat and shadow, inches away. His scent clung to the charged air like smoke, musk, and something darker, thick enough to make even breathing challenging.

"You're lying, Velorn."

His head tilted with one eyebrow arched. "Oh? Am I?"

"You pretend you don't care about anyone. Pretend to be this *monster*." I said, stepping closer despite every nerve in my body telling me it wasn't a good idea. "But that's your way to keep everyone at arm's length."

A dangerous smirk left his face. "And what brilliant insight gave you *that?*"

"I know you saved Vyria."

His smirk vanished.

"She didn't know who brought her to the healer's quarters after Arkos stabbed her. She only remembered a pair of hands and darkness everywhere."

I swallowed hard. He was so close to me, close enough that I could smell him, close enough that he could kill me if he really wanted to.

"Shadows that moved like they had a mind of their own." I knew it had been Velorn who saved her, though at the time I didn't understand why. If he were truly the monster everyone claimed, he wouldn't have gone out of his way to save her life.

That had to mean something.

Footsteps sounded from behind, but before I had the chance to turn, Velorn grabbed my wrists. He pulled me close enough that his body heat pressed against my skin, close enough that I could smell the soap he washed with.

"Last chance, little *Viri*." His voice dipped into a challenge. "Come with me now or seal their fate."

My stomach twisted so hard, I felt as if the ground was collapsing beneath me. I couldn't. I was so close to getting home, and if I went back with him now, I may never get another shot. I would hope that wherever we were going next was hidden enough that we would never be found. And prayed I wasn't making the wrong choice.

Kaelira appeared, her expression scrutinizing us before she extended her arms. "If Ehlark weren't so forgiving, I'd have left your disgusting romp here to rot."

Velorn ignored Kaelira as he kept his attention on me, waiting. He was giving me this choice, letting me decide my fate.

I reached for Kaelira's arm to indicate my answer. A small, terrified part of me whispered, *Please let this be the right decision.*

Thick mist swirled around us, its icy touch creeping over my skin like a cold, unwelcome embrace. It clung to me, dense and oppressive, and I found myself comparing it to Velorn's shadows.

His shadows, for all their darkness and cruelty, had warmth—like a protective shroud. But this mist? It was unforgiving, biting, and hollow.

My body shook uncontrollably as the cold seeped deeply into my bones, draining what little strength I had left. My vision blurred, and a wave of dizziness hit me. The world tilted violently, my stomach lurching as if the ground had been ripped away beneath me.

Before I could cry out, something yanked me upward with a force that twisted my body. The mist turned into a chaotic, violent vortex, spinning me faster and faster. The edges of my awareness frayed, and the world dissolved into a swirl of blinding light and bitter cold. This was much worse than Velorn's shadows. My breaths came in shallow, frantic gasps as I felt myself falling. Only a pair of hands shielded me, stopping me from screaming.

27

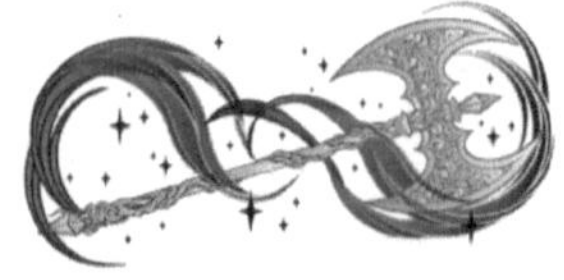

FAMILIARITY

"It is not my fault she didn't know," a female voice cut through the fog in my head. "Didn't you tell her to put her feet down when you slowed up?" A male voice retorted.

My head throbbed as I blinked into consciousness; the voices circled above me like restless crows. At first, the figures around me were blurry shapes, their outlines swirling in my vision. Gradually, they came into focus as a group of people huddled close, their faces reflecting concern and curiosity.

"She's coming to. Shoo, shoo—give her some air," an older woman ordered. She stepped closer, her lined face framed by wisps of silvery hair, and peered down at me with bright, gleaming eyes. "How are you feeling, child?"

I pushed myself up, my body protesting with every movement. My hand instinctively went to my forehead, where I found a tender bump.

"What happened?" I croaked, sounding like sandpaper.

"You took a bit of a fall," she replied, smoothing a blanket over my lap with practiced care.

"I can feel it," I mumbled, glancing at my hand to check for blood. Thankfully, there was none. "How long was I out?"

"Not too long, child." She handed me a small glass bottle filled with dark amber liquid. "Here, drink this. It'll help."

I slowly reached up and grabbed the bottle, its contents emitting a strong herbal aroma. As I cautiously took a sip, my gaze wandered around the room.

I was no longer outside. The room was small but warm, with walls of rough-hewn wood that showcased the trees' natural grain and knots. The soft glint of a lantern hanging from a wooden beam illuminated the space, casting shadows across shelves filled with jars and bundles of dried herbs. The bed I sat on was draped in thick patchwork quilts, their colors faded, and a worn woolen rug covered the floor, its edges fraying as though it had seen many winters. A small wood-burning stove crackled softly in the corner, filling the space with cedar and woodsmoke.

It felt like a cabin—cozy, secluded, and filled with a rooted warmth that reminded me of home.

"Where am I?"

"You're safe," the woman said gently, her weathered hand resting on mine.

My eyes wandered over her skin, each deep line a testament to years of endurance and resilience. The flickering light danced across her bracelets—intricate bands of hammered copper woven with braided material, their surfaces adorned with delicate patterns of leaves and vines.

My gaze lingered, drawn to the subtle details, until it landed on something unmistakable: the symbol etched into her wrist.

It was the same mark Farna had.

The House of Earth.

A chill ran through me, cutting through the warmth of the room. My mind scrambled for clarity, but my stomach let out a loud, impatient growl before I could piece together what it might mean. The savory, rich aroma swirling around me demanded my attention.

The woman chuckled. "I figured you'd be hungry when you woke, so I made some stew." She set a steaming wooden bowl before me. The aroma hit me with a savory blend of herbs and slow-cooked vegetables, with a touch of smoky richness. My mouth started to water.

"Eat," she urged, "it'll do you good."

I didn't need to be told twice. Gripping the warm bowl in my hands, I let the heat seep into my palms before dipping the spoon. The first taste was a burst of flavors—hearty and rich, like every sip was infused with the essence of the forest. The broth was thick, flecked with thyme sprigs, and chunks of root vegetables that melted on my tongue.

"There's someone outside who's been waiting to see you," the old woman said, her voice hinting at quiet amusement. She rose from her seat and crossed the room, her bracelets jingling softly with each step. With a creak, she pulled open the wooden door.

Ehlark stood leaning against the frame. He straightened abruptly, a sheepish yet mischievous grin spreading across his face as if he'd been caught eavesdropping. His clothes were different now—a loose, white linen shirt that appeared soft and well-worn, opening to reveal part of his chest. Below were beige pants that fit snugly around his hips and then fell into a relaxed drape over his boots. He looked less like a warrior and more like someone at ease.

"Ehlark."

He stepped inside, closing the door behind him. Without waiting for an invitation, he walked over and sank onto the bed beside me, the mattress dipping slightly under his weight. His warm eyes met mine, and the room seemed to close in around us.

"How are you feeling?"

"I've had worse." I offered a playful smile, though my heart raced at his closeness.

"I'm glad. You had me worried there."

For a moment, all I could think about was the warmth of Ehlark's hand. There was something achingly familiar about him, something that wrapped around the frayed edges of my thoughts. I didn't understand it, but I didn't want to let it go.

"Where's Velorn?" I asked quietly.

"We placed him near a tree outside." His body shifted, as if there was something else on his mind.

"What is it?"

He exhaled slowly, the tension in his gaze unmistakable. "Eleni, I spoke with our Eldryss. She wants to meet with you."

"Eldryss?"

"She's the elder of our village," he explained. "But more than that, she's seen more than anyone still living here. She comes from the Sanctum of Solryn."

I shot him a raised eyebrow, and he must have caught the confusion on my face because he went on. "The Sanctum of Solryn is where all our scrolls of history and knowledge are kept. It's the one place every House agrees to leave untouched, a neutral ground protected by Seers."

The hairs on my arms stood up, and I felt the blood drain from my face. "This elderly woman you want me to see . . . she's a Seer?"

"Yes," he admitted, "but not of blood or prophecy. She's different. She carries knowledge. Knowledge that might help you find a way back to your world. Not the kind that tastes your blood to determine your fate."

Relief loosened the tightness in my body. "She's the one you told me about back in the cave, isn't she?"

He nodded. "She also understands contracts and how to break them." He paused for a moment before continuing. "The only way to free you from the tracker's hold is to kill him."

My stomach dropped.

As much as I wanted to hate Velorn—his threats, his shadows, his cold indifference—there was still part of me that recoiled at the thought of his blood on my hands.

Or anyone's, really.

This world made it feel too easy, as if life could be weighed on a scale of convenience.

Say yes, and someone dies.

Say no, and you live with the consequences.

But that wasn't who I was.

Back home, I dedicated my career to saving others. To ease pain, not cause it. I held the hands of strangers in their final moments, whispered comfort through tears, and fought to keep hearts beating that most had already given up on. Even the worst among them deserved a chance.

"I—I can't let you do that," I whispered, my gaze dropping to the floor. "There has to be another way."

Ehlark frowned. "There is, but he won't agree."

"What is it?"

"You'd have to perform the ritual again," he said carefully.

That sounded easy enough. "Fine. Then let's do that."

Ehlark shook his head. "He already refused."

Why did he refuse? It didn't make sense. He was the one who wanted me to get to Emberhold as soon as possible so he could be rid of me, so what was the hang-up?

"You're telling me he'd rather die than break our contract?" I said, my voice edged with panic.

What kind of idiot would rather die than break the contract?

"That's why the Eldryss believes it's best to end this now," Ehlark said. "The Tracker has killed so many of us. Most of the villagers here lost someone because of him. A fight nearly broke out when they saw him. If we let him live, you could be at risk too."

I set the bowl on the small table beside me. "Let me talk to him."

"You can't," Ehlark stated. "You took quite a fall. You're not ready to be out of bed."

I pushed myself up, ignoring him. A wave of dizziness hit me suddenly.

Ehlark caught me, his arms firm beneath my own. "You need rest."

"I'm fine," I muttered, steadying myself. "Let me talk to him."

I didn't give him time to argue. Determined, I stepped out the door.

The forest welcomed me with its vastness, the trees towering so high they seemed to pierce the heavens. Their trunks were massive, their bark gnarled and old, etched with patterns that indicated they had been around for centuries. Turning back, I saw the cabin for what it was. A home built into the very tree itself. Its wooden walls merged seamlessly with the trunk, as though it had grown there naturally. Around me, I noticed more homes hidden among the trees, scattered like whispers of a forgotten world.

My mouth dropped open at the sight. "Wow."

The whole area was concealed, an elaborate network of life and shelter interwoven with the forest. The view was stunning, a flawless balance of nature and survival.

Was this the place that Ehlark told me about back at the waterfall? Was this Cedarvale?

Across from me stood a smaller tree, but still massive by any standard measure. Velorn sat beneath it, knees drawn up, one arm lazily draped over them, his figure shadowed by the towering trunk. Two men flanked him, their stances rigid, hands hovering near their weapons.

I pushed myself forward, each step a battle against the dizziness that made everything tilt and sway. The guards moved to block me before I could get close, their hands raised, but then Ehlark motioned his hand to lower their weapons.

My eyes were fixed on Velorn as the question spilled out. "Why don't you want to do the ritual to break our contract?"

He didn't respond. He didn't even spare me a glance. His gaze was fixed somewhere beyond the trees, distant, as if I didn't exist.

I squatted down in front of him, moving my face into his line of sight until his eyes finally met mine.

"Velorn, did you hear me?"

"I did."

"Then why won't you?"

There was a glimmer of doubt crossing his face before he answered. "I have my reasons."

That was it. No explanation. No apology. Only cold, impenetrable words. My dizziness worsened, and the world tilted as if the ground beneath me was shifting. I swayed forward, my hands instinctively reaching out, but Velorn's hands caught me before I tipped over.

His grip was firm yet gentle, sparking a strange sense of déjà vu, like that moment in the courtyard all over again. Only this time, he didn't lift me from the ground. He stayed there, holding me, letting me sink into the safety of his embrace.

"Eleni!"

Ehlark's voice interrupted the haze as the guards shoved Velorn away from me. He rushed toward me, wrapping his arms around me before lifting me. My head spun; the dizziness turned into a sickening whirl, and I gripped his shirt to steady myself. "We need to get you back inside."

I wanted to fight the nausea, to push through the dizziness, and stand my ground, but I couldn't.

As Ehlark carried me, I glanced back over his shoulder at Velorn.

His expression wasn't stern or angry. His brows furrowed, his lips pressed into a thin line, but his eyes revealed an emotion I couldn't quite identify.

It was the most human I had seen him.

28

NEW RULER

I felt the warmth of a hand gripping mine. Blinking against the soft light filtering through the wooden slats of the cabin, I turned and saw Ehlark. He was slumped in a chair beside the bed, his head resting on his arm, with his brown hair tousled in a way that made him seem uncharacteristically unguarded.

The lines of quiet determination that usually marked his face were absent, replaced by an expression of tranquility.

As I observed him, I was taken aback by how different he appeared—calm, almost vulnerable. Tentatively, I tried to wriggle my hand free, but his grip instinctively tightened, his fingers warm and snug around mine.

His eyes fluttered open, emerald green and hazy with sleep; their usual sharpness dulled as they focused on me.

"You're awake."

"I am."

"Do you still feel dizzy?"

"I think I'm okay now," I replied, as I lifted myself up. My body protested with a dull ache, but the nausea from the previous day seemed to have passed.

If I had a concussion from hitting my head, I should have been more careful.

"Good. I'll get the healer to bring some medicine, just in case." He stood and straightened, his hand reluctantly releasing mine. "There's bread and water on the table. Eat something. When you're ready, we'll go see the Eldryss."

The Eldryss, who was also a Seer. I had to admit I was curious to learn more about her.

Ehlark carried a quiet urgency, yet his eyes lingered, as if he needed to reassure himself that I was genuinely okay. When he finally felt satisfied, he turned and left the room, leaving me with the trailed scent of the forest and the echo of his fading footsteps.

⸻❈⸻

We walked along a narrow, well-trodden path that wove through towering trees, their massive trunks worn with age and their canopies so dense they filtered the sunlight into a soft, warm glow. Ehlark strode beside me in silence, his presence grounding, while Terryn's was the complete opposite as he flanked Velorn, his eyes never leaving him.

The path steadily ascended a large hill, offering views of sprawling fields embedded in the slope, dotted with crops of varying colors. Some shimmered with silvery leaves, while others were crowned with jewel-toned fruits. The land felt alive, its richness palpable beneath my feet, and the heady fragrance of flowers I couldn't name swirled around us. Their blooms resonated under the dappled light, as if nature had imbued them with a quiet, radiant magic.

Gram would've lost her mind over this place. Maybe she already had. Every question in my head kept circling back to her and that damn hidden box. Those trinkets and the dress that were with the necklace. Seeing how people dressed here, they weren't similar. They were the same.

Gram had been in this world.

But for how long? How did she escape? And why the hell did she take the relic? The answers felt out of reach, like trying to grab something impossible to catch.

My heart ached as her absence weighed heavily on me, knowing I might never fully understand what happened. A sudden emptiness swept through my chest like a hollow wind. Despite how magical this place was, it only made me miss her more—miss home and my life back in Denver.

When we reached the crest of the hill, we saw a breathtaking view of ancient stone pillars, worn smooth by time, standing like sentinels. They were adorned with intricate carvings of swirling symbols and patterns, captivating in their mysterious designs. My gaze fell on the corner of one pillar, where I recognized a familiar symbol of the House of Earth. The others bore similar half-shaped C designs, yet each exhibited a unique variation.

These must have been the symbols of the other Houses.

Beyond the pillars lay a beautiful garden, its carefully tended plants bursting with life. An elderly woman stood hunched over, pruning the delicate leaves.

"Eldryss," Ehlark said softly, breaking the quiet. The woman straightened slightly and turned toward us.

Ehlark dipped his head in a formal greeting.

"Oh, child," she sighed, slipping off her gloves. "How many times do I have to remind you? Call me Eryndra."

I couldn't help but smile. She had the same tone that Gram used with me when I annoyed her with trivial stuff.

Her voice was sincere, carrying a lifetime of wisdom. Her freckled, weathered face held a warm presence, and her faded auburn hair seemed to bear the weight of many years under the sun. Despite her stooped posture, her presence had an unmistakable strength, deeply rooted in this land like the ancient trees themselves.

"And this must be the young woman you were telling me about," Eryndra said, her gaze settling on me. She stepped closer, but her attention shifted beyond my shoulder. Her expression tightened slightly, and her lips pressed into a thin line of disapproval.

"And I'm guessing that's the Tracker?"

Ehlark nodded.

The woman sighed before slipping her arm through mine, her grip surprisingly firm. "Come, child. I have some freshly brewed herbs for tea." Her voice softened, but an undertone left no room for argument.

She glanced back over her shoulder. "The Tracker can stay outside."

Terryn nodded, standing guard.

We strolled through the lush garden, filled with the fragrance of thriving herbs and vibrant flowers. Beyond the garden stood a quaint little cottage, its walls weathered yet charming. Clusters of white blossoms framed the windows like a natural garland, their petals softly shining in the light.

Inside the cottage felt like stepping into a scene from an old, comforting tale. A cozy fireplace nestled in one corner, its embers crackling softly, while a small wooden table stood beside the window, covered with a simple cloth. On the other side of the room, a modest bed rested near the fireplace, its quilt neatly folded at the edges. Everything about the space radiated warmth and simplicity.

"Would you like some tea?" Eryndra asked, already moving toward a small cupboard.

"Oh, um, yes, please."

She placed a tray on the table, setting down a pot of tea and three mismatched cups. We each took a cup; the tea's aroma was sweet with subtle notes of vanilla and honey. The heat of the cup seeped into my hands as I took a careful sip, the delicate flavor soothing my senses.

We sat there for a while, the quiet calm of the room broken only by the soft clinking of cups and the occasional pop from the fireplace. In this moment of peace, the tension slowly released from my body with each calming sip.

"What name do you go by, child?" Eryndra asked, holding her tea with a steady hand.

Halfway through raising the tea to my lips, I paused and gazed into the cup before setting it down. "Eleni."

"*Eleni,*" she repeated, allowing the name to hover on her tongue. "That's a pretty name."

"Thank you."

"What is your family's name, Eleni?"

"Gibson."

"*Gib-son.*" She let the word roll off her lips like a foreign taste. "That is certainly an unusual name. And not one with any known roots in our history."

"I wouldn't expect it to," I replied.

"Ehlark tells me you are not from our world." Her eyes studied me with quiet curiosity. "Tell me then—where do you come from?"

"A place called America, specifically Wyoming," I said, hope edging into my voice. "Have you heard of it?"

She shook her head slowly. "No, I have not."

She set her cup down and rested her arms on the table. "Give me your hands."

I placed my hands on the table while I watched her rough, worn fingers gently turn my palms. Despite the calloused skin, her touch felt tender as she traced the bite marks on my wrists. "I see you have not one, but *two* contracts."

My brows furrowed as I remembered what Farna said about the bite marks.

"I suppose this one belongs to Ehlark, and the other one to the Tracker."

I nodded in confirmation.

"Ehlark mentioned you might be able to help me find a way back home?"

She moved her fingers along the creases of my blistered palms, still raw from swinging the axe in the pit.

"You don't heal like us, and your accent is strange," she murmured, more to herself than to me. "Do you remember how you got here?"

"There was a blinding light of colors shifting and merging like liquid fire. It felt charged, pulsating with energy I'd never experienced before." I paused, my grip tightening around the teacup at the memory. "Then everything changed. The ground disappeared, and I was weightless until it pulled me through the light. The colors spun around me like ribbons, and the atmosphere turned hot. Not painful, just . . . overwhelming, like reality was unraveling around me."

I glanced at Eryndra, her gaze on me as she absorbed my story. She sat there, deep in thought, with only the crackle of the fire breaking the silence. "Was there anything you saw around the light? Anything at all?"

"Actually, yes," I murmured. "I remember a pair of eyes. They looked animalistic, but the way the colors changed so quickly—it didn't seem natural. It felt otherworldly. And as I started to fall, they vanished."

Eryndra released my hands, and her fingers slid back around her teacup. "A Kortika. Though it shouldn't be possible, since they were believed to be extinct after the Rift War."

A Kortika? Ehlark never mentioned them before.

I gripped my teacup tighter. "What are they?"

Eryndra sighed, her gaze growing distant. "They are creatures that possess a unique ability to open portals between worlds. Their presence in Thysia dates back to the time of the Ancients." She paused, weighing her words. "At first, they were considered harmless—mischievous, yes, but not dangerous. Some even became companions, admired and revered for their intelligence and grace."

I leaned in, captivated by her words.

"But," she continued, "everything changed when one Kortika opened a door to another world, a world from which the Noztari came."

Was this the creature I saw? Did the Kortika that opened a portal to my world and brought me here?

"Were there others like me who could've gone through these portals?" I asked, trying to keep my voice steady. Deep down, the question wasn't about *others*. It was about Gram.

"Yes," Eryndra said. "Long ago, some of the Houses sought to misuse the Kortika's power. Instead of carriages or horses, they wanted to create portalled roads and pathways that could shorten distances and carry someone across kingdoms in seconds."

That had to be it.

Maybe one of those roads accidentally opened into Wyoming, pulled Gram through, pulled *me* through. Perhaps this wasn't some freak accident, but something as simple as a road that accidentally led to my world.

"Could that be how I ended up here?" I pressed. "One of those portal roads opening into my world?"

Hope rose within me at the thought.

"That would be impossible," she said flatly.

"Why?" I sputtered. My hand tightened around my cup.

"The last portal created by the Kortika opened the day the Noztari invaded our lands. There have been no others. The roads were sealed, destroyed, forbidden."

Damn.

The glimpse of hope inside dimmed, shrinking like a dying storm, because that was hundreds or possibly even thousands of years ago. Gram wouldn't have been alive then.

If the portal roads didn't exist anymore, then how did Gram get here?

How did I?

"Solryn, the ruler at the time, fought to seal the portals the Kortika had opened," she said. "They succeeded, but the cost was immense. After Solryn's sacrifice, the Ancients decreed that no portal road could be used, which also meant no Kortika could be allowed to survive. Even one could reopen the pathways and bring ruin to Thysia all over again."

She exhaled slowly, the thought of old memories evident on her face. "And so, they were hunted. Driven to extinction." She paused, resting her hand under her chin.

"But if they were extinct, how could one have brought me here?"

"That, child, is the question that troubles me most."

"But that's just a story," Ehlark interjected, "A tale for the fire gatherings to entertain children."

Eryndra's head tilted slightly, "Is that what you think? That the firelight only casts shadows of make-believe?" Her tone was calm, but it carried weight. "Stories, child, are how we remember, how we warn. The truth lives in their bones, even when we choose to forget."

"So, you're telling me a creature thought to be dead for centuries somehow survived and brought her here?" Ehlark asked, still sounding doubtful.

Eryndra exhaled deeply, her eyes never leaving his. "If a Kortika truly brought her here, then either not all of the portal roads were destroyed, or not all of the Kortika were killed."

I stiffened at her words. "If that's the case, shouldn't we find it?"

"Yes, child. But it's not that simple."

"Why do you say that?"

"Every time a Kortika opens a portal, it loses most of its power. It will regenerate, but it can take time before it can be fully up to its original form to reopen."

Ehlark turned to glance at me. His expression, usually so steady, now flashed with concern.

"If a Kortika does indeed still exist and it opened up a portal, Eleni, it would've gone into hiding, somewhere remote to recover."

She took another sip from her cup before continuing.

"My best guess is the Wispwoods. It's wild, untamed, and veiled from the eyes of most. If something were hiding, that's where it would be."

Eryndra rose from her chair and crossed the small room to the sink, carefully filling the teapot. Her gaze drifted to the window, where the light illuminated the wrinkles of her face.

"Your Tracker might be able to locate the Kortika, if he's willing to help."

Velorn was the last person who would want to help. Especially since I betrayed him and didn't go back to Malakar, but still . . .

I glanced over at Ehlark, whose knuckles around the teacup turned white.

Eryndra settled back into her chair, her gaze changing between us. "Ehlark also mentioned you wield a rather unique axe."

"I do."

"Hmmm." Her eyes slowly drifted from my face to my neckline. Her gaze stopped and narrowed as it settled on the chain partially tucked beneath my shirt.

"Ehlark also told me about a necklace you wear," she held out her hand.

"May I see it?"

Instinctively, my hand moved to the necklace, fingers curling tightly around it.

After a moment, I slowly slipped it off and placed it into her outstretched hand, my heart thudding in my chest as I watched her examine it.

Will she recognize it?

Eryndra lifted the necklace toward the light, tilting it so the gem caught its reflection. Her brows creased together.

"It can't be." When she finally looked at me, her voice trembled. "Do you have any idea what this is?"

"I was told it might be one of the relics." Malakar was the one who told me what he thought it was, and now that Eryndra had seen it, my stomach sank knowing that what I held was, in fact, the *Heart of Mountain* axe.

The relic that belonged to the House of Earth.

"How did you come into possession of it?"

Should I tell her the truth or share my theory about how my grandmother came to possess this relic before me? I wasn't sure how much she should know, and part of me still wanted to be careful.

"I found it under my grandmother's bed."

Eryndra stared at the necklace, as if she were in a trance.

"And who was your grandmother, child?"

That was the first time anyone had asked me about her since she died—the first time someone hadn't offered condolences and moved on. Memories came rushing in all at once, warm and bittersweet, crowding my mind with moments I'd held close for years.

If I told Eryndra about my grandmother, maybe she would meet her, and she could tell me more information and clue me in on how my grandmother came here in the first place.

"My grandmother was Natalie Gibson. Does that name ring a bell?"

I searched Eryndra's face, hoping for even the slightest trace of recognition, some sign she had heard the name before. But looking at her face, my heart sank.

"I'm afraid that is not a name known here. Which means your grandmother must have gotten the necklace from someone else. Possibly someone who crossed into your world by mistake."

What Erynda didn't realize was that ever since I fell into this world, I'd been replaying every possibility in my mind. Who could've given Gram that box? That dress? The relic?

But every path led back to the same answer.

It had to be her.

Eryndra softly laid her weathered hand on my arm. "Does the relic respond to you?"

I managed a slow nod.

"Can you show me?" she asked, carefully placing the necklace in my hands.

As soon as the relic touched my skin, immediate warmth rushed through me. Its presence made me feel at ease again. My body still felt sluggish after the last few days. Every muscle in my body ached. But tired or not, I had to try.

Taking a steady breath, I extended my hand and concentrated on the gentle hum beneath. The familiar energy flowed into my palm, and in seconds, the axe appeared. It felt effortless this time, as if summoning it had become second nature.

It was the first time I summoned the axe without immediately having to swing it, the first time I could truly look at it and take it in.

Up close, it was breathtaking. The handle wasn't wood; it was a braid of living roots that had molded into my grip. The twin blades gleamed with ancient markings and designs that seemed unfamiliar until I saw the curved shape *C*. It was the House of Earth's symbol. And it was etched on each blade.

The Heart of The Mountain.

My eyes studied its beauty. My attention only shifted when I heard a chair fall. Eryndra staggered to her feet, her face as pale as her hands, which grabbed the edge of the table for support.

"Solryn's Soul," her voice quivered, "It is *true*." She fell to her knees; her hands trembled as tears fell down her wrinkled cheeks. Ehlark jumped out of his seat to steady her. "Only the worthy."

A chill ran down my spine. "I don't understand."

My fingers tightened around the axe. Eryndra stepped closer, her eyes fixed on the relic as if it were the first time she was seeing it.

"This relic has not awakened in hundreds of years," she spoke carefully. "If it answered your call, then it has deemed you worthy."

My throat dried. "Worthy of what?"

Her gaze lifted to mine as tears streamed down her face. "The Heart of the Mountain has chosen you. It believes you have the strength to wield its power. And those who command the relics, rule the House tied to it."

The hairs on my arms stood up.

The axe vibrated softly against my palm, humming as if it agreed with her, as if it recognized every word spoken about it. Ehlark finally found his voice, stepping closer as he looked at Eryndra, then at me.

"What she means," He swallowed, eyes dancing between me and the relic in disbelief. "Eleni, the relic has chosen *you* to be the new ruler of the House of Earth."

Well . . . *fuck.*

29

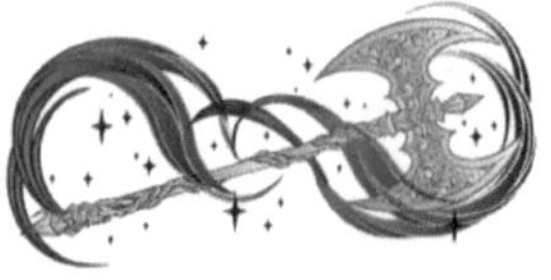

KINDNESS

I blinked, unsure if I'd heard her right. "There must be a misunderstanding." I took a step back, scrambling to process the news.

This can't be happening.

No way. Not now.

Eryndra's gaze didn't waver. "The relics have been passed down through generations. None have awakened for any elemental in hundreds of years. They've simply been handed from one royal family to the next. But it is said that if a relic should awaken, no matter who the being is, they become the new ruler of that House."

I scoffed. "No. I'm not a ruler. Hell, I can't even keep an organizer organized." My gaze dropped to the axe as it dissolved back into the necklace. "I don't belong here. I'm just a regular person trying to keep from losing my grandmother's ranch. I just want to go home." The last words came out softer, the weight of them pressing against my chest. And somehow, I knew this new revelation had made getting home that much harder.

"But it chose *you*, Eleni," Eryndra exclaimed as she wiped the tears from her face. "Do you understand? A relic—a sentient being in its own right—found only *you* worthy of its power. That must mean something."

An ache surged behind my ribs, somewhere between fear and grief, and I clenched my fist. I couldn't believe this. I *refused* to. Not now. Not when I was so close to finding a way back home.

"Then here," I said, my voice shaking. I lifted the necklace over my head and shoved it into her hands. "Take it. Have someone else rule. I'll find my own way home." Before she could respond, I stormed out the door.

I stood outside her cottage, my hands clenched, and I tilted my head back toward the sky, taking a deep breath before letting out a low, frustrated groan.

The last thing I ever expected happened.

Am I ever going to get out of this world?

Or was I meant to be trapped here forever? Was this what Gram went through?

That was terrifying enough to think about.

If they saw my life up close, they'd be asking the same thing. I barely kept my own life together, and handling the responsibility of the ranch was going to make things even harder. What was the relic even thinking, deciding I was worthy of being a ruler?

I laughed dryly.

This whole thing was absurd.

I spotted Velorn and Terryn near the pillars a few yards from the cottage, both looking equally annoyed, standing so close to one another. But Velorn's eyes didn't wander; they remained fixed on the cottage. On me.

Wait a minute.

I hadn't been able to piece it together before because I was so focused on escaping, but now it all made sense—why Malakar wanted me so badly and why he was so obsessed with seeing the relic.

Anger rushed through me as I stormed toward him.

Terryn said something, but I strode right past him, hands already on Velorn as I shoved him back against a tree.

"You knew all along, didn't you?" I seethed. "That's why you never killed me. That's why you brought me to Malakar!"

Before Velorn could answer, Terryn grabbed my arm and yanked me back. "You are not to speak to him unless Ehlark allows it, you skath."

I twisted, trying to free my elbow from his tight grip. "Let me go!"

One heartbeat, his grip was unbreakable. The next, Terryn lay crumpled on the ground, unconscious.

Velorn now stood between us, his presence a solid wall.

"Why did you do that?" I fumed, kneeling beside Terryn. I reached out a hand to check his pulse for a sign of life.

"My contract requires me to protect you. He intended to harm you."

Oh, right.

I could feel myself teetering on the edge, my control hanging by a very thin thread. "Then break the contract, Velorn. That way, you're not required to protect me. Oh, wait," my voice sharpened, "I forgot. You only do what Malakar orders."

I was fed up with this.

All of this.

"You act like this untouchable, tough guy, but deep down? You're lost. Letting everyone else make your decisions for you."

He moved toward me. "I'd be careful with your words."

"Or what? You going to hurt me? Then break the contract." I took a step toward him, closing the space between us.

"Go ahead, Velorn. *Hurt* me."

Logic had left the building. All that was left was the heat in my chest as I glowered at him, daring him to break first.

A low groan from the ground pulled both our attention. Terryn was stirring, rolling slowly onto his side.

"Eleni!" Ehlark's voice carried from beyond the cottage. I turned to see him sprinting.

Velorn moved back against the tree, casual as if nothing had happened. But when Ehlark spotted Terryn still struggling to sit up, he went straight for Velorn.

"Ehlark, don't!" I stepped in front of him, planting myself between the two.

"It's my fault. Because of our contract, he's required to protect me."

I wasn't sure how Ehlark would react to me stepping in. I half expected anger, disappointment, even. But when I caught his expression, his attention wasn't on me at all.

It was on Terryn, who was wiping the blood from his face.

"What did you do?"

"This skath and her guard dog are a disgrace here," Terryn spat, trying to get his bearings.

Ehlark bent down until he was eye level with Terryn.

"Touch her again, and my fists will be the last thing you see. Understand me?"

I remained quiet, stunned by Ehlark's threat.

Terryn didn't answer, his hateful gaze cutting to me for the briefest moment before turning his attention back to Ehlark. "Understood."

❖

Ehlark and I walked along one of the main paths collecting supplies for the healer, Lythara. It had been two days since my visit with Eryndra at her cottage, and I was left in this funk, so Lythara thought it best to assign me tasks.

Which I appreciated.

The fresh scent of baked goods mingled with the rich aroma of the soil pulled my thoughts away as we headed down the trail. People moved purposefully, weaving baskets, repairing tools, or tending to the fields.

No one wore chains. No one looked starved except Velorn, whose ever-present restraints made him an outlier. For the most part, everyone here seemed content, as if they had finally found a place where they belonged.

A home.

Something that seemed to be slipping through my fingers a little more each day. My life back home felt like it was drifting further away.

I wasn't built for this.

I wasn't a knight in shining armor here to save the day. Save these people. They needed someone who understood them.

Someone who grew up breathing this world's air and carrying its burdens. Someone willing to throw themselves into danger without hesitation, someone born to protect their people, like Ehlark.

Not me.

Children's laughter rang out as they darted past us with bright, infectious smiles. Colorful decorations swayed in the breeze, and the sound of lively chatter reverberated. My curiosity must have shown because Ehlark leaned in as his breath touched against my ear. "They're preparing for a soul-binding ceremony tonight."

"A soul-binding?" My eyes drifted to the cheerful flurry of preparations around us.

"Yes," he smiled gently. "It's a rare ceremony where two souls and hearts are connected for life. Not many choose it anymore because of the risks, but it's beautiful to see."

"Risks?"

I imagined it like a wedding back home, though the biggest risks there were usually heartbreak or divorce.

He nodded, his smile fading a little. "During a soul-binding, the pair shares their powers. Each gains the other's and can use both at once. But if one dies," His voice dropped. "The other dies too. That's the price of being bound."

My brows shot up. "So, if one of them trips and falls off a cliff, the other just—what? Drops dead, too?"

He gave a quiet laugh, though it didn't quite reach his eyes. "Not usually that dramatic. But yes. Their lives are tied. If one's flame goes out, so does the other's."

"That's," I hesitated, glancing at the colorful banners strung across the square. "Beautiful. And also, completely insane."

"Some call it the highest form of devotion. Others call it foolish." He shrugged, as if he, too, questioned its logic. "Depends on who you ask."

"Mmm," I mumbled, crossing my arms. "Devotion, sure. Sharing my soul? Might be a bit too bold for my taste."

That earned me a soft laugh. "Well, that's why not everyone is cut out for it."

"Yeah, count me out on that one."

Ehlark turned to me with raised brows. "Really? Do they not have ceremonies like this where you're from?" "

"Not like what you described." As extreme and absurd as this whole soul-binding thing sounded, I couldn't help but feel a small pang of envy. To love someone so deeply, so fiercely, that you'd rather die than live without them . . . Part of me couldn't help but wonder what that felt like.

"Well," Ehlark said, "you're in luck. You should join the festivities tonight." He suddenly stopped, turning to face me with a dramatic flourish. "I'll be your guide." He bent low in a mock bow and extended his hand toward me.

"Lady Eleni," he said with exaggerated formality, "it would be my greatest honor to escort you to the ceremony tonight."

Heat rose to my cheeks, and despite myself, I softly laughed, glancing around to ensure that no one was watching. "Stop it," I said, swatting lightly at his arm. "What if they find the Kortika?"

I told Ehlark I would search for the Kortika myself once we left Eryndra's cottage, but he shut that down fast. He said the Wispwoods were *too unpredictable,* and I was *too important,* and he was *not about to let me get myself killed over stubbornness.*

He insisted he'd send people who knew the forest to look instead and that I should stay put.

I hated it.

Every part of me wanted to argue, but when he reminded me about our contract, something in me eased.

Reluctantly, I agreed.

And honestly? I needed time. I still had no idea what to do about my contract with Velorn, but I knew one thing for certain. I wasn't going to kill him.

"Even if they do find the Kortika, it won't be going anywhere soon. You will be fine to take your mind off it, at least for tonight." He gave me a flashing smile. Whenever I saw that smile, it felt genuine. Like it was only meant for me. It had a way of completely disarming me and melting away my nerves.

"Fine," I replied. "But I don't have anything to wear."

"Oh, that? Don't you worry, I'll send someone to ensure you're properly dressed for the occasion."

I noticed then how his smile transformed his face. The thin creases at the corners of his mouth deepened into dimples, softening the sharp edges of his features. My heart skipped a beat, and I quickly looked away, afraid that meeting his gaze again might betray my thoughts.

"Well," I said, forcing a casual tone, "if you insist, I guess I can't say no."

"Perfect. I'll send for her."

For a brief instant, I experienced a spark of excitement. The pull towards him was undeniable and quite perplexing. Though I had only recently met Ehlark, being with him seemed natural and personal, as if we shared a long history.

It was easy to talk to him. Easy to be near him.

And that's what frightened me most. Because beneath it all, there was a quieter, more dangerous thought, one that wondered what it would be like to stay.

When I reached the healer's house, I saw a different guard securing Velorn to the tree. He slumped heavily, sliding down until his back rested against the rough bark.

His usual guarded demeanor was now gone. Instead, his frame showed signs of tension and exhaustion. I winced at how his head was slightly drooped despite his struggle to hold it up.

Had he even slept since they brought him here? Or was the exhaustion due to the cuffs he had to wear?

My gaze fell to his arm, at the angry red imprint of the burn. It looked worse now—more inflamed, possibly infected.

That was odd.

If I recalled correctly, he'd had that burn mark before the cuffs were placed on him. Shouldn't it have faded by now? He should have healed before those restraints ever touched his skin.

So why hadn't he?

Leave him be, Eleni. He doesn't want your help.

But the nurse in me pushed back, telling me to set my feelings aside and treat him like any other patient.

I walked into the house and spotted the healer, busy cutting dried herbs and cloth into squares at her workstation. "Lythara," I started awkwardly. I was out of my element and unsure how to ask for help here. "Do you have anything that might help with burns?"

"I do," she replied.

She walked over to a large cabinet filled with neatly organized bottles, herbs, and clothes. She pulled out a folded green leaf and handed it to me. "Will this size work?"

I carefully unfolded it and discovered a sticky, resin-like substance inside.

Clever. She'd prepared this herself.

"Yes, this is perfect. Could I also have a wrap?"

"Here you go." She handed me a strip of clean cloth. "Did you burn yourself?"

"Me? No, it's for someone else," I said quickly, and hurried back out before she could ask more questions.

"Give me your arm," I said as I kneeled in front of Velorn.

"What for?"

I let out a sharp sigh. "For once, Velorn, can you stop being a stubborn *son-of-a-bitch* and give me your arm?"

He looked at me, suspicion in his expression, before hesitantly handing it over.

"Thank you."

His burn was worse than I expected. The skin was badly blistered and oozing, angry and raw, resembling second-degree burns. I applied the salve Lythara had given me, working it in carefully while trying not to think about how his gaze was fixed on me.

I secured the wrap, tying it into a small bow.

"Not my best work, but it should help." I stood and brushed off the dirt on my pants when his hand grabbed my wrist.

"Why?"

I froze as his eyes held mine. They had softened into that warm honey hue. Yet behind them, a deeper search stirred, more than curiosity, as if he too was trying to decipher a puzzle within my eyes.

"Sometimes even monsters deserve a little kindness."

His lips parted as if to speak, but then closed again without a word.

When he finally let go, the warmth of his touch disappeared instantly, leaving an emptiness I hadn't realized until it was gone. Suddenly, I felt the urgent need for space and stiffly turned toward the house when his voice stopped me.

"You're wrong,"

I glanced over my shoulder. He was still watching me with that soft gaze.

"Not everyone deserves kindness."

30

SACRED SCARS

Lythara opened her door, and a young woman stepped inside, her arms overflowing with dresses in earthy tones accented by hints of blue and red. She was about my height, with a tan complexion and dark brown hair that fell in soft waves around her face. Her warm, inviting brown eyes met mine as she stepped forward.

"Thalena, perfect timing," Lythara said, motioning toward me. "Eleni's helping me cut herbs, but try not to leave my place in disarray."

Thalena gave a polite nod. "You must be Eleni," she smiled. "I'm Thalena." Her sweetness was contagious, and I couldn't help but smile back. "Nice to meet you."

"Let's figure out your size, and we'll go from there," she chirped, laying out dresses on a nearby chair with detailed enthusiasm.

Her energy was a welcome distraction from my wandering thoughts about the Kortika.

A short while later, I stood in my undergarments as Thalena held up various dresses. She paused, then picked up a soft blue one and examined it.

"This one," she decided, feeling confident. "What do you think, Lythara?"

Lythara glanced up from her worktable, her hands busy sorting herbs. "I like the blue. It brings out her eyes."

I slipped the dress on, the fabric soft and light as it brushed against my skin. It fit well, hugging my frame without feeling restrictive. Compared to the layered monstrosities Malakar had forced me into, this was a dream—simple, comfortable, and tasteful.

Thalena stepped closer, her fingers dancing as she skillfully adjusted the waistline. "How long have you known Ehlark?"

"Not very long," I admitted, fidgeting with a loose scrap of fabric in my hand.

"Really?" Thalena's brows lifted. "Forgive me, but the way he talks about you, I assumed you'd known each other for years."

I hesitated, unsure how much truth she knew. "He saved my life. Helped me escape when I was imprisoned."

She tilted her head with a devilish smirk. "That's not how he tells it. According to Ehlark, *you* saved him and the other prisoners."

I gave a short, awkward laugh. "Pretty sure he's got me confused with someone else. I just helped."

"Either way, thank you. For helping him and the others."

My reply failed me. So instead, I let my gaze drift to her wrist, pausing when I noticed it was bare.

No House mark.

"Is everyone here unmarked?" I asked, glancing between her and Lythara.

"Not all of us," Lythara replied. "Some of us remain loyal to the House of Earth and refuse to swear loyalty to the others."

"If it's true that the other Houses destroyed the House of Earth, then why can't it rebuild? Don't they have the right to stand with the others?"

Thalena glanced at Lythara, and even she looked caught off guard by my question. "Do you not know what happened that night?"

I shook my head. Not the details, at least.

"It was supposed to be a night of unity," Thalena said softly. "A celebration—the official joining of House of Earth and House of Air's young heirs. But it was a trap. House of Air and Fire massacred everyone that night. It was . . ." The words caught in the back of her throat. "It was horrible."

My hand drifted to my chest, seeking the necklace without thinking. But my heart sank as my fingers met only the fabric of my shirt. Forgotten that I'd given it to Eryndra when I'd stormed out of her cottage.

"Because the House of Earth was accused of stealing the relics, the other Houses made their terms clear—if we return all four relics, they will recognize us again. Without them," Lythara shook her head. "We remain nothing more than ghosts of a forgotten House."

Why did they blame the House of Earth for stealing the relics? Gram only had one, so where were the others?

"Ehlark and his brother were lucky to escape that night—especially with Ehlark being so young," Thalena said, her fingers never pausing as they worked the waistline of the blue dress.

"Escape? Ehlark was there?"

Thalena blinked, surprised by my reaction. "Yes. Ehlark and his brother are the last of the royal bloodline from the House of Earth."

I stared at her in shock. The words didn't register at first, like my mind was refusing to accept them.

Ehlark? Royal?

If he was royalty, and if I stayed here, wouldn't that mean I'd be taking his place as ruler? Something about that felt wrong. Really wrong.

Why didn't Ehlark tell me any of this sooner?

The more I replayed his expression and how stunned he looked, yet relieved he seemed, the more confused I became. He hadn't looked disappointed or jealous. If anything, he looked like a man who had been waiting his whole life not to be the one chosen.

Why?

From what I'd seen, Ehlark was a natural-born leader, and his people respected him. He led the efforts to save prisoners, and everyone trusted him. So why would he be relieved to give such a pivotal role into the hands of a stranger?

"They were so young," she continued. "Ehlark was barely two. His brother was only fourteen."

A knot twisted in my stomach. To experience such a thing as a child . . .

"Since that time, Ehlark and his brother have been searching for the missing relics and individuals, whether marked or unmarked by the House of Earth, and bringing them to this sanctuary. It's the only place we can live freely, without the pressure of pledging to a House."

I almost told them I had one of the relics. If I gave it to Ehlark, he and his brother would have a fighting chance at getting their House back. But the other part of me felt like it wasn't my place. I was an outsider, after all. And if Ehlark hadn't told them I did have the relic, then there must be a good reason for it.

"Where is Ehlark's brother now?"

"Last we heard, he was searching for the relics," Thalena said. "He took a few other elementals with him, traveling across Thysia. They're usually gone for months at a time, so we don't see him as often as we do Ehlark. That's why Ehlark focuses more on rescuing those who are unmarked or those who remain loyal to the House of Earth."

Ehlark handled all this responsibility while remaining resilient enough to support others. I could see now why so many acknowledged him or paused their activities to pay their respects.

He should be the one wielding the relic.

Not me.

"He won't admit it, and neither will his brother, but everyone here believes those two can bring back the House of Earth. They've rescued most of us and reunited families that were torn apart. This place wouldn't exist without them."

My mind raced, imagining all the dangers Ehlark must have faced to bring others here. The importance of his actions sank in, and my respect for him grew deeper. He wasn't just surviving; he was fighting for everyone, for his people.

For the hope that one day their House will be recognized again.

"Did you have any thoughts on how you want to do your hair?" Thalena asked, shifting the subject.

"Oh, I was going to leave it alone."

"Oh, you most certainly won't," Thalena replied, her eyes glinting. "I have an idea."

Two hours later, my hair was finally done. I stood before the mirror and could barely recognize myself. My hair, normally wild and unruly, had been tamed into a half-up, half-down style. Loose, delicate braids framed my face, softly blending into the rest of my hair, which cascaded in gentle waves down my back. The braids were adorned with tiny sprigs of blue flowers and thin silver threads that glistened in the light.

"Thank you, Thalena."

She smiled as she slipped into her dress, getting ready in less than half the time it took me, which I blamed on my hair.

I glanced over at Lythara, who was seated at the table, folding fabric. "Are you not joining in the festivities?"

"Oh goodness no," she replied. "I've seen more than my share of ceremonies, and I know my services will be needed once the drinking and dancing begin." She arranged extra bundles of cloth and herbs while Thalena and I were getting ready. She wasn't folding laundry; she was preparing supplies for the inevitable aftermath of the celebration. It struck me how methodical she was, anticipating what others would need before they even realized it themselves.

A wave of admiration warmed me.

She would have made an excellent nurse back home, demonstrating calm focus, efficiency, and kindness.

"Shoo now, girls," she said with a knowing smile. "You don't want to be late."

315

31

SOUL-BINDING

We stepped out of the house, the evening air still warm, carrying the traces of wildflowers and freshly made dishes. Thalena looped her arm through mine, her steps light as we descended the winding path.

As we passed the edge of the sanctuary, I caught Velorn standing with the guard. When our eyes met, his usual brooding intensity was absent.

He appeared unusually calm, as if he were at peace.

The change in his expression threw me off.

I shook off the thought and went back to the path Thalena was guiding me on. Along the way, white ribbons fluttered in the soft evening breeze, tied to tree branches and posts, their ends trailing gracefully toward a meadow. The path was lined with small clusters of flowers, their colors vibrant under the evening light.

The meadow was breathtaking. In the center stood an archway draped with flowers of every color and size, flowing like a waterfall of petals. Lanterns hung from the surrounding trees, casting warm, golden hues over the gathering. It looked like the entire village had come together, everyone dressed in outfits suited to the ceremonial occasion—flowing dresses, tailored tunics, and intricately woven shawls.

Out of the corner of my eye, I spotted Ehlark standing with a group of young men. They were engaged in conversation, but as Thalena and I approached, their chatter ceased, and all eyes turned toward us. My body suddenly stiffened.

Did Ehlark tell them about the relic and what it meant? That I was destined to rule the House of Earth?

My anxiety increased, my palms becoming sweaty thinking about it.

"Ehlark," Thalena greeted cheerfully.

Ehlark halted suddenly, his gaze lifting slowly before his lips curved into a smile. The dark green tunic, paired with those fitted beige pants, suited him too well, highlighting the span of his shoulders and the quiet strength in his frame.

"Thalena," He replied, keeping his focus on me. "You out-did yourself."

"Oh, stop it," she giggled, leaning conspiratorially toward me with a grin. "She was actually quite fun to dress up."

I looked away, feeling suddenly shy. My heart betrayed the calm, collected demeanor I struggled to maintain. I hoped he wouldn't notice the heat rushing to my cheeks.

"Come on," Ehlark said, extending his arm. "The ceremony's about to start."

He led us toward the group gathered beneath the archway, where a few young men and others waited.

I leaned into him. "Did you tell anyone about, you know, the relic and what Eryndra said?"

He turned to look at me. "Your secret is safe. It's only yours to tell." My body relaxed at his words, and I was glad I could be myself tonight.

My eyes fell on Kaelira. She wore a deep forest-green dress that hugged her figure as if it were sewn onto her. Elegant, composed, and clearly displeased to see me. Her posture was painfully straight, arms folded tightly in front of her, and that judging, assessing glare she did so well. Not openly hostile, but definitely not friendly.

I swallowed, the back of my neck tingling.

Fantastic.

Going to try to steer clear of her tonight.

I glanced down at my arm wrapped around Ehlark and noticed Velorn's marks weren't burning.

He must be nearby.

I scanned the area until I spotted him leaning against a tree, flanked by his two guards. My attention shifted back to the archway as the crowd around me quieted. In the center of the arch stood Eryndra, dressed in a golden robe that fell past her ankles. Next to her was a man dressed in elegant ceremonial attire that made him appear as distinguished as the occasion demanded.

Then, right on cue, all heads turned toward the aisle.

A young woman stepped forward, her cream lace dress hugging her figure perfectly before flowing into soft layers that brushed the ground. Tiny, intricate patterns of leaves and vines were stitched into the fabric, catching the light with every step. Her dark hair was styled in loose waves, interwoven with fresh flowers in shades of blush and ivory, the petals framing her face like a delicate crown. She moved elegantly, her steps slow and careful, as if the earth itself guided her. When I looked down at her feet, delicate vines unfolded beneath her, blooming briefly with sparkling petals before fading into the soil with each step. The ground seemed to welcome her, each movement in perfect harmony with the elements surrounding her.

There was something deeply captivating about her presence. Her eyes shone with a dark green glow, like moss catching the first light of dawn.

She approached the altar, her hands trembling slightly as she reached for his. They appeared nervous, their smiles were shy but bristling with unspoken excitement—it was adorable.

Eryndra stepped in between them, lifting her head towards the audience. "Today, we witness a bond that has grown through shared trials and quiet moments of joy. These two souls, who have walked separate paths, now choose to walk as one, bound not only by love but by the strength they bring to each other. In a world often marked by conflict and uncertainty, their union is a reminder of what endures: trust, resilience, and the promise of a brighter tomorrow. Let their love be a light that guides them, and may their journey together bring them peace and purpose."

Her words emitted like a blessing; even the breeze felt warmed by them.

"Tonight, these two have chosen to form the soul-binding, as our ancestors did when they committed their lives to one another, sharing each other's elemental strengths. From this moment on, they will be as one, sharing the harmony and balance of their journey together."

Eryndra stepped closer to the couple. "Now, repeat after me." With her hands outstretched, she chanted.

"Strengthened by Earth, freed by Air,
Cleansed by Fire, nourished by Water,
Bound by love, sealed by blood,
Together as one, our souls intertwine and forever burn bright."

The couple spoke in unison, their voices steady but filled with emotion, each word resonating through the audience.

As the final line of the chant faded, the man stepped closer, his hands raising to cradle her face. A mint green light bloomed in his palms, soft at first and then brighter, more vibrant, until it spilled into the veins of his forearms, tracing glowing patterns beneath his skin. Even his eyes reflected the glow, locking onto hers with a fierce, primal focus. Then he leaned in, his lips brushing her neck before his teeth sank in—not cruel, but desperate and passionate. The glow in his veins flared as her breath hitched, her hands clutching his shoulders. Blood welled where his teeth broke the skin, leaving a thin line running down to her collarbone.

Her eyes fluttered shut, her chest rising abruptly as his energy was absorbed into her, flooding her veins with that same mint light. When she opened her eyes again, she met his gaze with a mix of defiance and desire intertwined. Then she mirrored him. Leaning forward, she bit into the strong curve of his neck, and his breath escaped in a low, shuddering groan as her own power mingled with his, until both of their glows slowly faded.

It reminded me of the time Ehlark had used his canines on me. The mark he left still carried a tingling sensation that never entirely faded. Velorn's bite felt similarly intense, but the way this man sank his teeth into the woman before him was different. It wasn't just a mark; it was deliberate and passionate, like a lover's embrace.

There was something intimate and raw in the act, a primal energy that resonated between them, unspoken yet undeniable. The air stirred with a charged, powerful force. The breeze came to life, swirling gradually through the meadow as if nature acknowledged the moment's significance. It was powerful, magnetic, and impossible to look away from.

I don't know what compelled me to do it, but for some reason, I glanced at Velorn. His rough features had softened, and something else wavered in his eyes. An expression I had never seen him wear before.

He observed the couple beneath the archway with an intensity that felt out of place, his usual stoic mask slipping to reveal a quiet, unguarded curiosity, as if he were witnessing something like this for the first time as well.

Had he ever felt love before?

An ache tugged at my heart.

Then, as if sensing me, Velorn shifted his attention. His gaze sent heat to my cheeks, making me feel like I'd been caught watching something forbidden.

What is this feeling?

I shook myself out of the daze, and I turned back just in time to catch the final moments of Eryndra's words. Her voice commanded the attention and respect of everyone gathered here.

"With this ritual, your souls are entwined, your fates bound." Her eyes reflected the dancing light. "May you walk this path in strength, love, and unwavering unity."

The crowd erupted in cheers as the couple embraced, sealing the ritual with a passionate kiss that seemed to ignite around them. The music swelled, the rhythmic beat of drums and strings blending into a lively tune. People moved gracefully through the crowd, carrying trays of drinks that reflected the festive energy of the gathering.

"Come," Thalena said, grabbing my arm again with that mischievous grin. "Let's dance with the others!"

Before I could protest, she pulled me into the center of the clearing where a group of women had gathered, their laughter bubbling over the lively music. The bride stood in the middle, her radiant smile outshone only by her gown's vibrant scarlet and gold embroidery. It was electric, the beat of drums and flutes weaving a rhythm that seemed to carry everyone along.

"I have no idea what I'm doing!" I laughed, half-panicked, but Thalena winked and spun me toward the others.

"Follow the rhythm. And don't fall!"

We formed a circle around the bride, our hands intertwined as we swayed and stepped in sync. At first, I stumbled over my feet, but as the music's rhythm quickened, so did my confidence. The women started spinning faster, their brightly colored skirts fanning out. Laughter blended with the music as our circle rhythmically tightened and loosened, creating a complex dance of connection and celebration.

The drumming intensified, the beat urging us into a frenzy. My heart pounded harder, my breath quickened, and I couldn't stop smiling. We spun and wove through the steps, arms linked and feet barely grazing the ground as we moved in perfect unison. The faster the music, the more exhilarating it became, as if we were chasing the sound.

All the worries and doubts that had followed me faded away, leaving only the wild, liberating joy of the dance. It felt freeing, like breaking through the water's surface after being held under for so long.

The drums faded, and the women gradually slowed their rhythm, laughter, and flushed faces, signaling the end of our turn. As we stepped back to catch our breaths, Ehlark and the other men, along with the groom, entered the circle. Their confident strides invited cheers and teasing whistles from the women. The men moved to the steady beat of the drums, their steps intentional and their energy contagious as the tempo picked up once more.

We gathered at the outer edge, clapping along to the rhythm.

Thalena returned with drinks, handing me a large mug filled with frothy amber liquid.

"Sharzaa!" she shouted, raising her mug high.

I lifted an eyebrow, not entirely sure what *sharzaa* meant, but from the way she raised her mug, I guessed it was their version of 'cheers.'

"Sharzaa!" I repeated, tapping my cup against hers. The drink was surprisingly light and refreshing, its crispness a welcome relief after the whirlwind of dancing. It tasted closely like beer from back home, but with a woodsmoke undertone that gave it a unique twist.

The music changed to a livelier rhythm. The men advanced toward the outer circle, each extending a hand to someone on the edge, inviting them to join. Laughter bubbled up as couples formed, and the crowd buzzed with anticipation.

Ehlark approached me, his eyes glinting in the firelight. He stopped a step away and gave a small, respectful bow. "May I have this dance?"

I opened my mouth to protest, but Thalena snatched my mug and shoved me forward with a wicked grin before I could say anything. "Of course she would love to!"

I stumbled slightly, catching myself in time to glare at her, but she only wiggled her eyebrows before disappearing into the crowd.

"What a troublemaker," I murmured.

Ehlark laughed, extending his hand once more. "Shall we?" His voice was warm, but a hint of challenge appeared in his smile, like he already knew I'd say yes.

"I'm going to be completely honest with you," I said, nerves creeping in. "I'm a terrible dancer."

I could already feel eyes on us, and the thought of being the center of attention made my stomach turn.

"Follow my lead," he grinned. "Don't worry, I won't let you fall."

Hesitantly, I placed my hand in his. His grip held me firmly, and before I realized it, he was guiding me back into the circle, the music urging us onward. "Trust me, okay?"

I nodded nervously.

His hand slid to my waist, pulling me closer until our skin touched. My breath caught at our closeness, and he beamed—a playful, daring smile that sent a swell of heat through me.

In one smooth motion, he lifted me off the ground, twisting us into a graceful turn before lowering me. My head spun as we moved into the following steps, his confident strides guiding me through the intricate dance. Everything became a blur of quick movements and rhythmic steps, leaving no room for hesitation. No space for my thoughts to drift. I stayed in this moment, and I didn't want it to end.

Every time he lifted me, it felt effortless. I kept expecting him to slow down or show signs of fatigue, but he didn't. Instead, that irritatingly charming smile widened, and the corners of his mouth quirked up, making my heart race.

I couldn't help but smile back, caught up in the exhilaration of the dance. The nervous energy I'd felt earlier had melted away, replaced by pure, unrestrained joy.

When the music finally stopped, I stumbled slightly, breathless but grinning from ear to ear. My cheeks were flushed, my pulse pounding in time with the fading music.

"I need a drink," I gasped, laughing as I leaned on Ehlark for balance.

He chuckled, pulling me out of the circle. "Let's go find Thalena."

We found her a short distance away, laughing with a small group. She was still holding my drink, and I snatched it back, downing the whole thing like my life depended on it.

"You looked like you danced through fire," she teased, her smirk widening.

"Want another?" Ehlark asked, taking my now-empty cup.

"Yes," I replied, still trying to catch my breath.

Ehlark stepped away toward the table of pitchers, leaving Thalena and me. She shot me a sly look. "You two appeared like you were having fun. Someone, however, doesn't seem so happy about it." She tilted her head toward a group of girls nearby. Among them was Kaelira, her striking features marred by the hateful glare she aimed directly at me. A chill ran down my spine. Her deadly look reminded me of someone standing across the meadow.

I followed her gaze as Kaelira sauntered toward Ehlark. Her intentions were obvious—leaning in closely, caressing his shoulder, her laughter a bit too sweet.

I wasn't sure why the sight twisted my gut and left me perturbed. They were just talking. Right?

"Do they . . . have a thing going on?"

I disliked the quiet sting it sent through me, the kind that whispered maybe I was beginning to care about this place, about these people.

About *him.*

Thalena let out a snort, almost spilling her drink. "Oh, goodness, no. She likes him, but it's one-sided." She leaned in slightly. "Trust me, I've seen the way he looks at you. And it's not how he looks at anyone else. Not even her. And believe me, Kaelira's very popular around here. If he wanted her, they would already be a couple."

I could see why. She was petite with all the right curves that made her look elegant and feminine. Her long, silvery hair flowed down her back like silk, and her delicate features gave her an ethereal quality. Yet despite all this, Ehlark's focus wasn't on her; his emerald eyes kept lingering on me, even while he was talking to Kaelira.

Kaelira stayed where she was, her gaze still focused on us as Ehlark approached, both hands carrying our drinks. Her expression made me feel like I was walking into a storm I hadn't prepared for, but I pushed the thought aside.

"Want to take a stroll?" Ehlark asked as he handed me my drink.

"Sure." Anything was better than risking another dance under Kaelira's watchful glare.

We wandered toward the edge of the festivities, where the music and laughter faded into the trees. The cool night air kissed my skin as we walked, eventually stopping by a wooden fence. Ehlark relaxed against it, and I joined him.

We sipped our drinks in silence, with the twinkle of firelight and distant chatter creating a comforting backdrop. I hadn't realized how much I needed this moment of peace and how deeply my soul craved it.

"You know, you don't have to leave if you don't want to."

I blinked, caught off guard.

It was the first time he asked if I could stay.

"I think you could make a difference here if you stayed," he continued, turning to look at me. "With us. With me."

My heart was pounding out of my chest. I wasn't sure if it was from the dance or his presence. "As a ruler? Definitely not." I took another sip, letting the drink calm my spinning mind. "You know I don't belong here," I said finally. "I'm not like you. Other than my ability to throw an axe, I don't have elemental powers. I don't even age as you do. You're probably over a hundred years old or something."

Ehlark laughed, a rich, genuine sound that sent a soothing feeling through me. "I have a long way to go before I reach my prime. I'm still only twenty-seven."

My head snapped toward him. "You're what?"

"Twenty-seven," he repeated.

I glanced across the clearing at Velorn, who seemed to radiate a timelessness that Ehlark didn't. "But Velorn—"

"He's much older," Ehlark admitted. "When our elemental powers awaken, our aging slows. But I was a late bloomer. Mine didn't awaken until I was seventeen."

It made sense now why Farna had studied the bite marks so closely, why her expression had shifted when she saw the difference. Ehlark was practically a pup compared to Velorn. And yet, Velorn didn't seem much older than the rest of us, at least not in the way that time typically reveals.

Ehlark stepped in front of me, closing the distance between us. His presence was magnetic, and I couldn't move away. "Eleni, what if I asked you to stay? Would you?"

My heart ached, and I suddenly felt caught between two worlds.

Part of me wanted to stay, to embrace the strange, unexpected sense of belonging I had found here, with these people, with *him*. Because it was the first time in a long while, I didn't feel entirely alone.

But the other part of me, the more practical, more logical part, knew I had to go back home. I'd been away for almost a month—a month gone without a word. A month with the ranch unprotected. That Strator guy could have taken it by now, and I wasn't there fighting to keep it.

"I can't."

Ehlark set his mug on the fence and gently cupped my face in his hands, his warm thumbs brushing my cheeks as his longing bore into mine. "I'll beg if I must. We need you, Eleni. The House of Earth needs you. . . *I* need you."

Before I could process his words, his lips met mine, stealing my breath. His kiss was warm, intense, and filled with a silent plea, as if he was revealing a part that he kept hidden. His hands cradled my face, his touch gentle yet possessive, anchoring me in the moment.

A surge of emotion swept over me, an overwhelming tide that washed away my worries and the weight of the world beyond this moment. All that mattered was the raw, magnetic pull between us, a connection that defied logic.

I kissed him back, my hands instinctively gripping the fabric of his shirt, pulling him closer. His heat surrounded me, his breath mingling with mine as time seemed to slow. Every brush of his lips was intentional, every movement silent and meaningful, as if he were communicating everything he couldn't say with words.

We stumbled past the fence, our lips still tangled in a desperate kiss. He led me deeper into the trees, farther from where anyone could see. Maybe it was the alcohol, or possibly something else entirely, but everything felt hotter. Hungrier. It was as if every nerve in my body had come alive for him.

There was no before. No after.

Only him.

Only us, caught in this raw, unguarded moment.

Witnesses be damned.

His oakmoss scent wrapped around me, rich and dizzying, pulling me under until thought itself unraveled. I kissed him harder, tasting the hunger between us, my fingers slipping beneath his shirt. Hot skin met my palms, muscles flexing beneath my touch as if my hands alone controlled them.

His hands were everywhere—possessive, searching, and sliding under the hem of my dress until they skimmed bare skin. He gripped my thigh, hiking the fabric higher until my leg hooked around his waist, and he drew me into the hard, undeniable proof of his want.

The world narrowed to the sound of our ragged breaths. His mouth tore from mine, not in retreat but in deliberate descent, trailing along my jaw, tracing heat down the side of my neck. My pulse thundered beneath his lips as they slowly, tenderly, and dangerously moved down.

He lingered at my clavicle, letting his breath mark me before continuing until his mouth found the swell of my breast. His voice was a low moan against my skin.

Something's not right.

The thought flashed in the back of my mind, faint but insistent, like the first crack in glass.

I pushed it away.

"You have no idea," Ehlark groaned, "how much I've desired you, Eleni."

The sound of my name on his lips was my undoing.

I curled my fingers in his hair, holding him to me, as if letting go would shatter whatever spell we'd fallen into. His hands tightened at my hips, and for one dizzying heartbeat, it felt like the world tilted, like nothing existed beyond the heat between us. Not even the slight burn in my wrist.

He grabbed my other leg, forcing me to wrap it around him. He lifted me, carrying us farther from the music and prying eyes, including Velorn.

Something's wrong.

My arm started to burn hotter, the pain slowly traveling up my arm the farther we moved.

"Ehlark, wait—"

The rest of my words broke into a gasp.

Searing pain erupted from Velorn's mark, so sharp and sudden, spreading like wildfire under my skin, burning in relentless waves that coiled up my arm and stabbed deep into my chest. Last time, it had crept in slowly, a warning. This time, it struck like a thousand furious flames, igniting me from the inside out.

"My arm!" The pain came again, stabbing through the haze of the moment, snapping me back to reality. Our shared connection faded as the pain anchored me in a truth I couldn't escape. I abruptly pulled away, my breath wild and my heart pounding excruciatingly. "I'm sorry, Ehlark," my voice trembled in pain. "I can't do this."

His emotions wavered. Surprise? Pain? Perhaps even desperation?

He looked as if he wanted to speak, to reach for me, to undo whatever had broken between us. But I didn't let him. I spun around quickly, forcing myself to run to reduce the pain. It felt like my heart was breaking into pieces as I kept running toward the pull of Velorn's mark, trying to relieve the unbearable sensation.

Why hadn't I told him it was because of Velorn's mark?

Was it because, deep down, even with this searing pain, I was still protecting him? Because I knew the moment Ehlark learned his contract could hurt me, he'd find any excuse to kill him.

Music continued to play, and people laughed over their drinks as I ran past the meadow. The pain started to fade, leaving only a dull ache beneath my skin. It lessened with each step until I reached the far side, where Velorn should have been.

Only . . . he wasn't.

Drawn forward by the pull of the mark, I followed the path. Halfway up, I found him pinned to the ground by three guards. But his attention wasn't on them.

It was on me.

The deadly smirk on his face said it all.

Bastard.

He's taken off on purpose. He's seen Ehlark and me leave together.

"Why?"

The guards kept him pinned even after he stopped struggling. "To remind you of *our* contract."

I stood there stunned. Had he seen us kiss? Heat rushed to my cheeks at the memory. Ehlark's hands on my body, his lips caressing down my collarbone.

I opened my mouth to argue, but then his gaze migrated over my shoulder, and the smirk disappeared. His eyes darkened, with anger sharpening every line of his face.

I looked over my shoulder, dread crawling up my spine, and found Ehlark standing there.

32

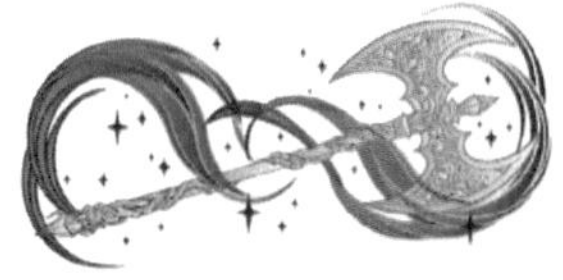

PROPOSITION

"Here, drink this. It'll help with the headache." Lythara placed a cup beside me. The sharp, acrid smell coming from it nearly made me gag.

I sat at her table, wrinkling my nose. Yet, I knew better than to complain. I tipped the cup back and swallowed it in one agonizing gulp, shuddering as the bitter liquid burned its way down.

A hazy memory came flooding back. After whatever Velorn had pulled last night, Ehlark nearly killed him on the spot. Guards and bystanders had to drag Ehlark off before he finished the job. It felt childish, like some brawl between teenage boys, and I wanted no part of it.

Instead, I told them both off and walked away, wandering until I stumbled across a pitcher of something shimmering in the torchlight. It called to me, and without thinking twice, I snatched it up and carried it with me.

The rest of the night was a blur. I vaguely remembered making it back to Lythara's place, after I'd knocked on a few wrong doors, before finally stumbling into the right one.

"Did you have a good time last night?" Lythara asked. She didn't wait for an answer—she already knew what I would say. With a groan, I sank back into the chair, cursing my lack of restraint.

"That poor man hovered near the door all night; I don't know what you did to him. I finally had to shoo him away when daylight was approaching."

I frowned, pressing my fingers against my throbbing fore-head. *Who was she talking about?*

"He's a good man," Lythara added with a sigh, shaking her head. "Just a young, love-struck idiot sometimes." She glanced at me, and whatever expression I wore must have been evident when she raised an eyebrow in confusion.

"Ehlark showed up while you were asleep," she explained. "Wanted to make sure you were okay, even though he knew you were in the safest place possible." She rubbed her eyes, looking like she had gotten little sleep.

"Last night?"

"After the festivities died down, I guess, like you, he had one too many drinks." She let out a small groan. "That damn boy. He has good intentions, but sometimes he doesn't think things through. He's so much like his brother."

Lythara looked at me as she stood and prepared tea, setting the pot over the fire without saying a word.

We sat in silence, the quiet interrupted by the soft crackle of the fire. As the heat seeped into the room, memories of last night stirred. My fingers brushed my lips, finding the swell left by Ehlark's kiss last night.

His touch had ignited something inside me, something I hadn't felt in a long time. I had dated before and had slept with a couple of guys, sure. But always told myself I didn't have time for anything more. Between endless shifts, emergencies, and the exhausting routine of hospital life, it was easier to keep things simple and to keep people at arm's length.

I convinced myself it was enough, that staying busy and immersing myself in work were better than risking something that could end in heartbreak.

But Ehlark was someone I couldn't ignore. He was something more. Whatever *this* was between us, it didn't follow any rules. It was unexpected. Disarming in a dangerous way. I knew if I kept toying with this idea of us, it would make going back home even harder.

"Eleni, be a dear and take some stew to the guard watching over the Tracker." She handed me two bowls instead of one; I caught the subtle hint—she knew I'd probably deliver one to a Velorn.

I stepped outside, balancing steaming bowls in my arms. Lythara had prepared a hearty stew in the morning. She'd made enough to feed an army, far more than the two of us.

As I made my way across the yard, my thoughts drifted to Lythara. The more I observed her, the more I admired her.

Regardless of who came seeking aid or answers, she never judged and never let a sharp word slip.

Even with me, she had shown nothing but quiet understanding. She had given me ointment for Velorn's burn without hesitation and now made extra stew, knowing I would bring it to him. Not once had she displayed disdain or questioned my decisions. I respected her patience and unwavering kindness.

If I stayed here, perhaps I could become her assistant and learn from her. Her role as a healer wasn't so different from mine as a nurse.

I shook my head, dismissing the idea before it could take hold. *No, Eleni. Focus.*

I kept telling myself I wanted to go home, but it felt like I was arguing more with my own conscience than anything else. I'd hated this place when I first arrived, yet the kindness I'd been shown and the people I'd met were making it harder to want to leave.

But if I stayed, what would it cost me? Would I be shaped into something I never chose to become?

I gathered the bowls of stew and handed them to the guard, offering to keep an eye on Velorn while they took their break. After the last incident, Ehlark had reassured them that I was safe around him, as long as the cuffs stayed on.

However, last night changed that. The guard agreed to move further away but still kept a close watch.

Velorn stayed as stoic as ever, his head tilted back against the tree, eyes closed. I might as well not have been there at all. Still, I held out the bowl for him. "Why must you be so damn stubborn?" I muttered. "Just eat it."

He didn't budge.

I sighed in frustration. "Look," I said, taking a spoonful from his bowl and shoving it into my mouth. Immediately, I regretted the decision. I choked, coughing and waving a hand in front of my mouth, my eyes watering and my tongue feeling practically on fire.

"Okay," I managed between sputters, "it's still hot, but see, it's not poisonous."

When I glanced at him, his eyes were open, and I could've sworn there was a slight twitch.

Good.

It wasn't much, but it was still better than the state he'd been in last night, especially after Ehlark had thrown some not-so-nice words his way.

In the end, hunger won. He sighed and finally reached for the bowl.

"Are you going to watch me eat?"

"My bad." I put my arms up in surrender, stepping back and perching myself on a nearby rock.

"You want to talk about what happened last night?"

Velorn continued holding the bowl, letting the steam drift towards me, making my stomach growl.

"What is your contract with that elemental? Did you have a Seer present for it?"

The question triggered a wave of guilt inside me. It felt wrong, like whatever Ehlark and I shared was something no one else should interfere with, let alone know about. Then again, when Ehlark asked me the same thing, I felt the same strong urge to protect my agreement with Velorn.

"He promised me protection in exchange for helping him free the prisoners." The words sounded heavier when spoken aloud. "And no, there was no Seer."

He grunted, then took a bite of the stew.

"Each blood contract is a sacred tie," he said slowly, taking another spoonful to his mouth. "A bond that connects you to another's feelings and desires, in ways far stronger than most can understand."

I remained on the rock, still not entirely following.

"Blood contracts require a Seer," he said, "because they can mediate the bond and strip away any bleed-over of feelings or desires."

My eyes narrowed slightly as the words sank in, and a knot of unease formed in my stomach.

"Because you didn't have a Seer for his contract, your feelings for each other are intensified. Every desire, every pull between you—magnified. The longer it goes on, the more powerful it becomes." His eyes stayed on mine as he continued. "And that can be dangerous."

He had to be wrong.

There was no way that could be true because if it was, then my feelings for Velorn were—

"That's not true," I cut in. "We didn't have a Blood Seer for ours, and I have no feelings towards you whatsoever." The lie sat heavy on my tongue, but I refused to let him see otherwise. He could never know.

"Is that so?" His voice was low, almost amused.

It couldn't be true.

The feelings I had for Ehlark came from what he did for me—keeping me safe, promising to get me home, and spending time together. But in the back of my mind, a quiet voice whispered that Velorn wasn't wrong.

"How about our contract then?"

That gave Velorn pause.

"We didn't have a Blood Seer for ours, Velorn. So, are you saying you're catching feelings for me?" It sounded ridiculous even as it left my mouth. Velorn having actual feelings? Yeah, right. But the question piqued my curiosity. If there was even the tiniest bit of truth to it, did that mean I had feelings for him, too?

Absolutely not.

Hell would have to freeze, thaw, and freeze again before I'd let myself fall for Velorn. Yet the image of him watching the soul-binding couple kept replaying in my head. The way he looked at me afterward sent an ache through me.

His focus was on the bowl of stew, scraping out the last bits at the bottom. "I have a proposition for you," Velorn said, completely ignoring my question.

I looked at him in contemplation. "Go on."

"If you break your contract with that elemental, I'll break mine with you."

Was he serious?

There had to be a catch. No way was he willing to let me go.

"You think I'm going to take your word for it?"

He shrugged. "I guess you'll just have to trust me."

"Yeah, right. You think after everything that's happened, I'm going to trust you?"

"You were the one who told me to let my walls down and trust others. Well, here's your chance."

No. I'm not falling for his little game.

I knew exactly what he was doing. He was using Ehlark's duty to protect me as leverage to maintain the upper hand. But then, why did the thought of breaking my contract with Ehlark feel so wrong? It wasn't just strategy. The idea alone made something twist inside me, as if I could already feel the loss. Had I relied on him so much that the thought of standing on my own now felt impossible?

Out of the corner of my vision, I caught sight of Ehlark heading up the path, Kaelira right behind him.

I immediately stood up from the rock I'd been sitting on. "Hey," I said, brushing out the pretend wrinkles from my pants.

Ehlark's eyes met mine. "Hey." The silence that followed was awkward. I didn't know what to say, and it seemed neither did he. Kaelira rolled her eyes, breaking the moment with an impatient sigh. "Are you ready, Ehlark?"

My head tilted slightly. "Ready for what?"

"Kaelira's going to take me to the Wispwoods," he explained. "We haven't heard back from the others, so we're going to search for them and the Kortika."

"Okay, let me change. I can be ready—"

"*You* are not coming," Kaelira cut in. My eye twitched a little as I directed myself to Kaelira.

The more I looked at her, the more she started to irritate me. Especially when she was so close to Ehlark. She may be beautiful, but damn, she needed an attitude adjustment.

"Since you can't stray too far from the Tracker," Ehlark said, adjusting the pack on his shoulders, "I think it's best if you stay. Once we find it, we'll try to bring it back here."

I don't know why I turned to Velorn. Why I thought he'd say something helpful in that moment. But his expression seemed more like a provocation—an invitation for me to challenge what he said earlier.

I should prove Velorn wrong and break my contract with Ehlark. To show him that what I felt was real. But the thought of breaking the contract still felt wrong. It no longer felt like an agreement; it seemed sacred, almost taboo. Like breaking it would betray something deeper than a promise.

"Kaelira, can you give us a minute?"

She clicked her tongue and stalked off, but not before shooting me one last dagger-eyed glare.

Ehlark reached for my hand, weaving his fingers between mine. "We won't be gone long. I promise." His touch drifted up, settling at the back of my neck, his thumb brushing slow circles that sent sparks racing down my spine.

Relief eased within at those words because the truth was—I did have feelings for him. I cared for Ehlark. For these people. And every day I stayed here, those roots grew deeper, binding me to this place I once desperately wanted to escape.

Should I stay?

If I did, maybe I could actually help. I could aid in rebuilding the House of Earth and forge something good from all this chaos, carving out a life here that had purpose. Perhaps this could become home.

Home.

That single word belonged in two worlds.

Because staying meant never seeing the ranch again. No fond memories, no reading Gram's books. No future to repair the barn and bury Eddie with Gram. No working in the hospital or seeing my coworkers. It meant throwing away the life I'd fought to build, the one Gram raised me in, for a future I couldn't predict.

My heart twisted painfully at that thought, then softened as I watched Ehlark walk away in the fading light.

And then I looked at Velorn.

He was already staring at me, his golden eyes gleaming with smug satisfaction. Like he'd peeled back my thoughts and found precisely what he was looking for: me fantasizing about Ehlark and this future I was desperately trying to deny.

Bastard.

I'd prove him wrong. My feelings for Ehlark were real.

It's not because of the contract.

It's not because of the contract.

God, please . . . not because of the *damn* contract.

33

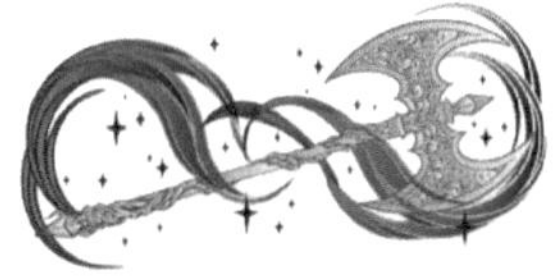

TEMPORARY PEACE

I knew that standing around waiting for Ehlark to come back would drive me crazy. So instead of pacing in circles, I threw myself into anything to stay busy. Helping Lythara with her daily rounds felt like the best option. I followed her from one end of the village to the other, shadowing her through a blend of routines and simple acts of care. Some stops were regular visits, like checking on the sick and offering tinctures or salves for chronic aches. At other times, we knelt in the herb gardens, gathering what she needed for the days ahead.

And, of course, Velorn wasn't far behind.

Lythara asked the guard assigned to him to keep him near the outskirts of the village, measuring the distance by the sting in my wrist to see how far she could push him back. Most of the villagers still feared him, and it wasn't hard to see that his sheer size and the brooding, scarred face were enough to keep anyone on edge.

Which reminded me, was Malakar out there looking for him? For us?

Were we really safe here?

Over the past few days, I'd watched the people around me, and they seemed at peace. No one acted on edge—at least, not when Velorn wasn't nearby. That had to mean we were hidden well enough, tucked away where Malakar couldn't reach us.

Yet the memory of his expression in the dungeon still prickled at me, a warning I couldn't shake.

No, I was safe. We were safe.

Ehlark had said this was a hidden village, one Malakar and his men could never find.

Shifting my attention back to the people here, I figured it was the perfect chance to learn more. Curiosity got the better of me, so I asked Lythara how healing worked in this world. I'd noticed that most people recovered far quicker than I was used to, which made little sense by my standards.

"Healing comes from your core. If you have a strong core, you'll heal faster," she explained as we walked the path to the next house. "But it comes at a cost." She knocked, and the door swung open to reveal an elderly man missing a leg. "Good day, Marcin. I come bearing gifts." Lythara lifted her basket and handed him a jar of salve and a bundle of leaves wrapped in cloth. "How's the leg today?" she asked.

"Oh, you know—the usual pain and discomfort, but nothing new." His smile was genuine, and they chatted for a moment before saying their goodbyes and moving on.

"You said it comes at a cost. How come?" I asked.

"When you use too much of your power in a short amount of time, you drain your core." She pointed to the center of her sternum. I wondered if she meant a person's core was like their inner strength.

Lythara must have noticed my contemplation.

She stopped in the middle of the path and placed her hands against my chest. "Your core is here," she said, then moved her hand to my stomach. "Here." Finally, her fingers touched my forehead. "And here. When we draw on our core, our bodies glow with its color, releasing that magical energy outward. That's why when you see someone using their core, no two glows are the same."

So, it wasn't strength alone.

The mind and body had to work together for their magic to work.

She turned, walking on the path again. "Your core is also drawn to certain elements. That pull is what determines your affinity. Earth, flame, water, air—your core chooses what it resonates with, and that resonance shapes what you can control."

I thought back to the first time I met Ehlark—the way that glowing green light had poured off him, alive and pulsing, his core burning so bright it seemed to breathe with him. I remembered, too, how he'd asked me to share some of my energy. At the time, I'd had no idea what he meant. Now, I wasn't so sure I wanted to know.

"Can an individual share their core with someone else without having to do the whole soul-binding thing?" I asked.

"Yes," Lythara said, not looking up from the basket in her arms. "Although they must be careful. Sometimes, the one receiving can unknowingly take too much."

"And if someone were to use up all of their core?"

Her steps slowed. She drew in a deep breath and let it out like she was setting down something heavy. "It's rare, and usually only in the most desperate situations, but if you drain your core completely, you may never regain it. Or you could die. Most of the time, you'll feel it happening—the slow pull, the exhaustion—but there are moments, life-or-death moments, where you won't recognize the loss until it's too late."

On one hand, it was incredible that a person's core could naturally release energy attracted to a specific element. On the other hand, I couldn't help but wonder what it would feel like to control that kind of power.

Would it be anything like the rush I experienced when I summoned the axe?

Every word from Lythara felt like opening another page in a book I didn't know I was desperate to read. She seemed to enjoy my curiosity.

Each time she pulled something from her basket or pack, she explained its use, the common ailments it treated, and the way certain mixtures worked better together.

Some liquids carried a sharp, alcoholic bite that made my eyes water; others released a sweet, floral aroma that clung subtly. I leaned in to breathe each one in, trying to pin the fragrances to memory, as if knowing them might help me piece together this new world I was beginning to grow fond of.

It felt like being back in pharmacology class—learning all over again about medicines and their uses. Only this time, it wasn't synthetic drugs from a lab; it was real, traditional herbs pulled straight from the earth.

And honestly, this was way more exciting.

My hands worked with the plants, crushing leaves and mixing tinctures, while my eyes lit up with fascination. It was way better than staring at a textbook and trying to memorize endless definitions for a test I'd barely slept for.

Back at Lythara's home, she was teaching about an herb when a loud knock came from the front door. Lythara approached and opened the door. A young boy stood there with tear-filled eyes, clutching his arm. Another boy lingered behind him, wide-eyed and out of breath.

"What is it, child?"

"It's my arm," the boy said, his voice quivering. "I can't move it."

"Come in, little one. Your friend can come too."

She guided them both inside and had them sit at the table. I knelt beside the injured boy, carefully examining his arm. The unnatural bend twisted my gut—it was fractured.

I quickly arranged a few pillows beneath it to support the weight.

"How did you manage this?" I asked, trying to keep him composed.

"We were just playing—I swear," the other boy blurted out before the injured one could respond. His guilt was apparent on his face.

"It's okay, you're not in trouble," I reassured. "Did you fall?"

The injured boy nodded.

"Did you hit your head when you fell?" I asked, already examining his scalp with my hands. He shook his head, and aside from a few abrasions on his legs and arms, he seemed clear of any other injuries.

Lythara returned with a small vial. "Here. A few drops of this will help with the pain."

She didn't wait for his answer as she placed a few drops beneath his tongue. Within minutes, his tense shoulders relaxed, and his face softened as the stress faded away. He sank into the chair like someone who'd received a mild dose of morphine.

"For an injury this bad, couldn't he use his powers to heal himself faster?"

She shook her head. "Children who have not awakened their magic cannot access their core. Until then, they're more vulnerable to injuries and illness, making them a considerable risk to mortality."

Awakened.

I recalled Ehlark mentioning that he didn't come into his powers until he was seventeen. Puberty, perhaps? That had to be what she meant. A sort of magical coming-of-age.

It made sense. However, it also made me realize how unprotected kids like him were in a world that revolved around power.

"In this situation, Eleni, what would you do?" she asked, watching me closely.

"Me?"

"You seem knowledgeable about medicines and their functions," she continued. "I'm curious; what would your approach be?"

I traced back to the ER. Typically, we'd stabilize the injury, take X-rays to confirm the break, and possibly reduce the fracture if necessary. We then splinted it until the patient could follow up with an orthopedic surgeon.

But none of that existed here. There was no imaging, no modern-day supplies and orthopedic team.

"Stabilize the arm and secure it to limit movement," I said. "Make sure circulation isn't cut off. It won't heal the break, but it'll stop it from getting worse."

Lythara gave a slight, approving nod. "Ehlark was right about you."

I glanced at her, my eyebrows knitting together. "What do you mean—?"

But before I could finish, she stepped in front of the child, her hands hovering above his injured arm. A glow resembling sage color pulsed from her veins, initially delicate, then intensifying, spreading into the boy's skin like ripples of light.

He winced but didn't pull away—the tincture was taking effect. I stood there, watching like a student as the broken limb shifted. The bone was now realigned, the swelling had decreased, and the skin had settled. Within minutes, it looked completely normal, as if it had never been broken.

So, this was what she meant when she talked about sharing your power and pouring part of your own core into someone else. This was what Ehlark asked me to do in the cave.

It all made sense now.

Lythara stepped back, her eyes scanning her work with the practiced observation of someone who had done this a hundred times. "Being a healer isn't just about making medicine," she said. "I spent years learning how to channel my ability to mend injuries. But it comes at a cost."

She exhaled, a slight tremor in her hands now that the glow had faded. "It drains me—sometimes deeply. That's why I use it only when necessary, like today."

Admiration spread through me as I watched Lythara work. She was always gentle, controlled, and powerful in a way that deepened my respect for her.

Part of me felt a pang of envy, wishing I could do what she did, wishing I had that kind of gift. She didn't just heal; she offered comfort and compassion. She belonged to this world in a way I never could.

And that caused the ache in my chest to bloom even deeper.

No matter how hard I tried to ignore it, the truth was creeping in. This place was beginning to feel less like somewhere I'd stumbled into and more like somewhere I truly belonged.

It was starting to feel like . . . *home.*

34

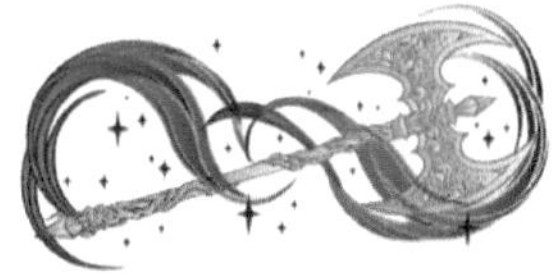

TIDAL PEARL

Not long after dinner, another knock came at Lythara's door. Thalena stood in the doorway, holding a basket covered with cloth, its warm, sweet aroma inviting.

"Eryndra asked me to stop by," she said with a smile. "She made these for Lythara and also requested your presence."

Pulling back the cloth, she revealed a stack of dark, rich-looking squares. The sugary aroma hit me, and my mouth nearly betrayed me.

"What are those?" I asked, trying not to drool like an idiot.

"Eryndra calls them Moonmelt cakes. Sweetleaf and duskroot were the spices in her recipe. Careful, though. They're addictive."

Following Lythara's lead, I immediately took a square. As soon as I bit into it, it melted in my mouth.

These would be devoured instantly if ever brought to work. It was like a brownie, although richer with cinnamon and a lingering spiciness. There was a slight crunch, perhaps from crushed nuts or some seed I couldn't identify, but the combo of flavors worked.

I had to be cautious with these. Moonmelt cakes were dangerous—in the eat-the-whole-basket-and-regret-it-later kind of way.

Even though Thalena said they were for Lythara, I sneaked another Moonmelt cake before slipping out the door and heading toward Eryndra's.

Avoiding Velorn's gaze, I nodded to the guard, indicating my direction.

In the evening, the path to Eryndra's cottage seemed even more beautiful. The soft flames of the lanterns tucked into the trees, the shimmer of dew catching the fading light, it all felt like something out of a dream. Whimsical. Fantastical. It made me slow down without intending to, wanting to savor every step.

Once I'd reached the stone pillars near Eryndra's cottage, I paused and turned back toward the guard and Velorn. With the Moonmelt cake still in my hand, I broke it in two and offered each of them a piece.

Evidently unimpressed by having to share, the guard briefly looked at Velorn before turning to me with a small smile. "Thank you."

As expected, Velorn offered nothing in response.

Did anything make this man happy, or did he prefer to suffer in silence all the time?

On the cottage's porch, Eryndra sat watching the path, seemingly waiting for me.

I sat in the empty seat next to her, letting my gaze follow hers.

From up here on the hill, the village below vanished behind the rise, taking the stone pillars and Velorn with it. All I could see was the sweeping expanse of forest, with towering trees stretching into the horizon and the soft hush of nightfall settling in.

As the sun dipped below the horizon, painting the sky with gold and orange hues, the world seemed to soften. Those moments had a way of quieting the chaos, as if nothing else mattered.

Now, sitting here, I felt that same stillness and comfort under the sky of this different world. As time passed, we watched the fading light together.

"Tell me about your world." She didn't look at me, and I didn't look away from the view. I started talking and told her everything.

About Gram and the ranch, as well as what happened with Eddie.

"Losing them left me hollow." I finally admitted. It felt relieving to tell someone about what happened. Losing Gram and Eddie felt like the ground was ripped from under me, like a gaping hole had been carved straight through my chest. Eddie had been with me practically my whole life. He was the last piece of normalcy I had after Gram passed. And Gram, she was everything. My anchor. My history. My home.

"And what of your parents?"

My parents were never really a topic of conversation for me. Not truly. "My mother died giving birth to me, and Gram never knew who my father was."

They were ghosts in my story, faces I never got the chance to remember. They died when I was too young to hold on to anything meaningful. Gram stepped in without hesitation, raising me with calloused hands and a warm heart that had witnessed too much grief and still chose love anyway.

She was the only genuine family I'd ever known.

But with her and Eddie gone, what was I left with to go back to? I had no family. I mean, yeah, sure, there was Mooch, who I was certain would be fine on her own, and my roommate and coworkers, but they all had their own lives and their own families they still needed to take care of.

What did I have there that I couldn't have here?

The more I thought about it, the more I felt my heart pulling me here—urging me to stay, to learn everything I could about this strange, magical place. I might not have their elemental abilities, but I could learn to heal like Lythara. It wasn't so different from what I did as a nurse back home, just a different set of tools and medicine.

"No matter which path you choose, Eleni," Eryndra's tone was soft as she continued. "Know that each step serves a purpose. Nothing in this world, or yours, happens without meaning. Even the smallest choices can resonate louder than you realize. Fate may place crossroads before you, but it does not bind your feet. You are never without a choice. Never let the world convince you otherwise."

Eryndra pulled something out of her pocket and held it up to the light. "The relic could have chosen anyone," Eryndra said quietly, letting the necklace sway with the wind. "But it chose you."

I felt the subtle pull, as if gravity were bending me towards it. I hadn't noticed it before, but now, with it sitting there, separated from my skin, it called to me.

I raised my hand, hovering under it.

If I took the relic, it meant accepting my fate. It meant taking on a responsibility I wasn't ready for, wasn't trained for, and wasn't prepared for.

My hand slowly withdrew as my fingers curled back.

"I can't, Eryndra."

With a sigh, Eryndra enclosed the necklace in her hand and returned it to her pocket.

"Think about it. Stay here long enough to decide not out of fear, but with certainty."

She was right. If I truly wanted to stay, I needed to be confident about my choice. "Eryndra, if I stayed, could I choose not to rule?"

She was quiet for a long moment, her expression telling me she understood my struggle. "There is a possibility. But before you can even make that decision, we would have to find the other relics first."

"Why is that?"

"The other Houses blame the House of Earth. They believe someone stole the relics, which has caused too much tension between the Houses. War is coming, and if we have any chance to prevent it, we must find and return the relics to their rightful Houses."

The idea of this world falling into war made me shift in my seat. I've read enough history to know how brutal and horrible war was, and I would do anything to prevent one from happening.

"What do the other relics look like?" If I helped Ehlark and his brother recover and return the relics, maybe that could be my purpose here. I could stay a little longer here, with Ehlark.

"Similar to the *Heart of the Mountain*. Each one holds its own unmatched color and power."

Color and power.

For some reason, my mind jumped to the hidden box. The one with the mysterious coins, the jewelry, and the gemstones. My heart picked up speed. "Eryndra, did the other relics look similar to the *Heart of the Mountain*? Was one of them blue?" Memories flooded back—the deep sapphire gemstone, which had the same golden streaks as the green one, but unlike the green relic, it wasn't attached to a chain. Still, it had that strange allure whenever I held it.

Eryndra's eyes sharpened. "Yes. That is the *Tidal Pearl*. It belongs to the House of Water."

Realization hit me like a punch to the gut.

Gram had the relics. At least two of them. My thoughts spiraled, colliding in shock, confusion, and a thousand questions about how it was even possible.

Gram was the one who stole the relics.

"I think I know where the *Tidal Pearl* is." The words tasted unreal on my tongue. My thoughts spiraled—how could Gram have had them? Questions collided in my head, fear pressing hard against my ribs. "Eryndra, I—I have to return home."

Her gaze met mine, and her lips parted to speak, but she didn't get the chance as a deafening explosion reverberated through the trees.

With wide eyes, Eryndra and I both sprang to our feet.

In the distance, flames erupted from below. Bright, hungry fires illuminated the night sky, transforming the peaceful forest into a blazing nightmare.

35

SHATTERED FRIENDSHIP

The flames erupted everywhere, casting the village in a hellish light. Eryndra and I rushed off the porch and sprinted toward the fires before sliding to an abrupt stop.

Velorn stood next to the large pillars.

In his arms hung the limp body of the guard. His expression was unnervingly calm as he reached down and slipped the keys from the man's belt, unlocking his cuffs.

No.

I had vouched for him. I believed there was good in him. But watching him now, I saw how wrong I'd been.

"Go, child!" Eryndra said. "Save the others. I'll hold him off."

"What? No—what about you?" She was older and wiser but not built for combat, and Velorn wasn't someone you *held* off.

I stepped toward her, ready to argue, to stay and fight by her side. But the earth around her garden surged to life. Vines, flowers, and thick roots sprang up, twisting and weaving until a living wall separated us.

"Eryndra!" I shouted, pushing against the barrier. "Don't do this—please!"

She didn't answer.

Through the changing leaves, I took one last look at her standing her ground, facing Velorn alone, before both disappeared.

Terrified screams echoed from below, pulling me back to the chaos in the village.

I glanced one last time at the wall of vines and roots separating me from Eryndra. I'd never forgive Velorn if he laid a hand on her.

But she had asked me to do something.

And I would not fail her.

I wasn't sure how far I could go before the mark on my wrist would start to burn, but I had to try. Gritting my teeth, I turned and ran toward the fires—toward the people who still needed saving, even though it tore me apart to leave Eryndra behind.

Flames roared on both sides as I charged down the hill, heat licking hungrily at my skin. The pain in my wrist crept higher, a dull throb turning into a searing line up my arm, but I shoved it back down. Smoke curled into my nose, yet I kept pushing through. People scattered in all directions, running and searching for safety.

Then I saw them.

Through the thick haze, soldiers stormed into the village, hundreds of them. Clad in dark armor, wielding swords and spears covered in fire. My heart sank.

It was Malakar's men. He had found us.

I veered off the main trail, leaping over roots and weaving between trees, staying out of sight. The burning in my arm felt like fire beneath my skin, but I forced myself to keep moving. I didn't have time to fall apart. Not now.

I needed to get to Lythara's cabin.

When I finally reached it, I pushed open the door. Inside, a group of women and children huddled in the corner, with Lythara among them, her arm wrapped around a frightened little girl. Thalena looked up, and as soon as she saw me, she jumped to her feet and ran straight into my arms.

"Eleni, you're alive!" she cried, wrapping me in a fierce hug.

I held her tightly. She was safe. They were safe.

"We need to find a way out of here," Lythara said. Her voice remained steady despite the rising panic in the room. She moved with purpose, placing herself between the frightened women and children, anchoring them with her calm.

"Those of you with elemental shields—move to the back. Protect our rear as we go. The rest form a line up front and create barriers as we move. We'll use them for cover."

"How did they find us?" A trembling woman holding her child asked.

As they prepared shields, the burn in my wrist slowly diminished. The pain receded, inch by inch, until there was nothing.

Oh no.

"We need to go. *Now!*"

Lythara led the frightened group through the back door and into the forest.

We moved carefully as vines, roots, and thick flowering bushes sprang up around us, woven to shield us from sight. It was working; no one saw us. But something didn't feel right. The farther we moved, the more wrong it seemed, and the burn in my wrist was still gone.

"Eleni, what are you doing?" Lythara's voice cut from behind me.

Velorn was following.

Tracking.

And by staying with them, I was putting them in danger.

"Go," I said, forcing steel into my voice. "I'll catch up—I promise."

"We can't leave you behind," she argued, stepping closer. "If they find you—"

The hairs on my arms stood up. A pull, deep and magnetic, tugged at my chest, wrapping around my wrist.

"Lythara, go! There isn't—"

In the blink of an eye, darkness erupted from the trees, sliding around the throats of everyone in our group. Gasps turned to silence as the dark tendrils constricted, cutting off their air.

The glowing shields around them dimmed—then vanished.

I rushed to Thalena's side, instinct taking over as I reached for the shadows wrapped around her throat. But it was like trying to grab smoke. My hands couldn't grasp anything solid.

"Velorn!" I screamed, my voice cracking with desperation. "Let them go! Please!" Tears blurred my vision. I couldn't lose them, not them.

The shadows stilled, as if obeying an unspoken command. Then a menacing figure stepped forward from the treeline.

Velorn emerged from the veil of darkness as if he had been part of it all along, his eyes now burning molten gold, penetrated mine.

"I told you, little *Viri*, their blood is on your hands."

Thalena, Lythara, and the others were helpless and unable to use their magic. One flick of his wrist, and they would be dead.

"Please, Velorn . . . I'll go with you. I won't fight. Just let them go." I no longer cared what happened to me. Not if it meant saving them.

"I could kill them right now and still take you with me," Velorn hissed. "Their lives mean *nothing* to me. We have a contract to fulfill, and I intend to see it through—so I can finally be rid of you."

His words struck deeper than any wound, delivering a cold, gut-punching truth.

He didn't care about anyone.

Not them, not me; it was always about the contract.

I clenched my fists, rage and grief burning inside me. I thought about summoning the axe, but my heart dropped.

Eryndra had the relic, and if Velorn was here, she was gone, along with the relic.

It couldn't end like this.

I kept my gaze fixed on Velorn and took a steady breath.

Each footstep felt heavier than the last, but I didn't waver. I didn't dare look away from him. I wanted him to see my choice, to know I wasn't running.

I knew this battle was lost.

The hope of getting home, of escaping all of this, had always felt too good to be true. But if staying meant saving them, then I would gladly do it.

I grasped his hand into mine. "Take me. Spare them. You got what you wanted."

The cold, emotionless mask he always wore didn't show a single crack, but his eyes . . . they revealed him. Was it confusion? Regret? I couldn't be sure, but I *saw* it—the faintest softening, a glimpse of something human.

And then, it was gone.

Thump.

Thump thump.

I spun around and saw Lythara collapse to the ground. Then Thalena and the others followed. Every one of them, including the children, fell lifeless to the ground.

"*No!*"

I lunged to run back to them, but Velorn's grip tightened around me. I fought it, twisting and thrashing, but he was a wall.

A stone-cold, murdering wall.

"*Let me go!*"

With a grating pull, he yanked me into him.

His arms wrapped around me, trapping me against his body, preventing me from escaping. His shadows rose around us in swirls. I caught one last glimpse of their still bodies through the haze before the darkness consumed everything—

Erasing them, erasing the light, erasing my scream.

36

FULLFILLED TIES

The swirling darkness unraveled around me, fading into the shadows that disappeared into nothingness. I felt the weight of my body return all at once, my feet hitting solid ground with a jarring thud.

My cheeks were hot with the tears still streaming down my face. Velorn's grip remained on me, even after his powers disappeared.

I shoved my hand into his chest. "*You monster!*"

He didn't move. Didn't flinch. Just held me. My fists struck his chest again, each hit landing harder than the last. I punched and screamed, trying to hurt him, trying to make him feel something.

He remained as immovable as stone, allowing me to hit him, letting me break against him. It wasn't until my punches stopped that I felt his release. My body finally gave way, and I collapsed to the ground.

"Why?" I choked out, my body shaking. "Why did you have to kill them? They were innocent! I came to you willingly, and you—you still murdered them!"

I couldn't breathe, couldn't think.

All I could do was shatter into a million pieces.

Then, I felt a tingling sensation spread across my wrist. The initial feeling intensified, a searing sensation like something ripping from beneath my skin.

I looked down and saw that Velorn's bite mark was disappearing. The jagged scar that had bound us, the proof of our contract, vanished as if it had never existed at all. I traced my finger over where the mark used to be; the familiar feeling now felt like emptiness.

Almost as if I had lost something. An icy chill settled in my chest as the truth clicked into place.

I looked around, taking in the unfamiliar stone walls, the rough ground, and the cruel silence. He brought me to the place Malakar wanted him to take me, which meant only one thing—our contract was finished.

No tie.

No obligation.

No reason to stay.

And yet, he stood there.

I remained crumpled on the floor, my body too heavy with grief and pain to get up. Any feelings I had toward Velorn, that magnetic pull that seemed to linger when he was nearby, had died the moment he brought me here, and I wanted nothing more than to see him dead.

My eyes wandered from him to our surroundings. The atmosphere felt thicker here, damp and heavy with something else. The darkness pressed in, broken only by the occasional flicker of torchlight along the stone walls.

Behind Velorn, rows of metal bars stood.

A bitter laugh escaped me. All the fight drained out of me in an instant, like someone had swung a sledgehammer through my chest and ripped it open.

"Well," I finally spoke, "you fulfilled our stupid contract. Congrats. Now you will never have to see me again." I dragged myself back until I hit the cold, damp wall. Tilting my head back, I closed my eyes.

I heard the shuffle of Velorn's footsteps and the soft scrape of movement getting closer, followed by a cold chill.

Something fell beside me with a soft clink against the stone.

Slowly, I opened my eyes.

Velorn was gone.

I knew what he dropped, but I still turned my head, needing to see it with my own eyes and confirm it.

The necklace was there, its magnetic force pulling me toward it.

I pushed it away.

How could it choose me?

I failed them. All of them. I couldn't save a single person who needed me. So why would a relic bind itself to a failure?

I drew my knees tight to my chest and buried my face against them. The weight of everything finally crashed down on me.

And I wept.

⸺◈⸺

I didn't know if it had been hours or days.

Down here, time bled into itself—one breath stretched into the next until I couldn't tell if I was still breathing at all. The dungeon swallowed everything: sound, light, and even the shape of my thoughts. The only movement came from the torchlight in the distance, sputtering as if it, too, were trying to die.

They left food once, maybe twice. I don't remember. The stench alone turned my stomach; I wasn't hungry. Hunger was for the living. I was something else now, somewhere between fading and forgotten.

Down here, only the echo of my unraveling kept me company.

My head twisted in circles, chewing on guilt, gnawing on names I couldn't save. I clung to memories as if they were still warm, only to find them cold and stiff like corpses. I wanted to scream to prove I still could, but even my voice had abandoned me. Perhaps it was better that way. What good was the sound in a place like this?

I heard footsteps. They were slow and unhurried, almost as if they existed only in my thoughts. But as the figure emerged from behind the bars, I realized they were real.

I looked up to see Malakar standing on the other side of the cell. Beside him was another figure—one I didn't dare look at.

I knew those shadows like I knew my own heartbeat. But I refused to turn. If I looked, it would become too real, and I wasn't ready to break again. So, I kept my gaze fixed on Malakar. My muscles were too tired to tremble, and my heart was too dulled to race. But my eyes remained open, even if everything inside me begged to close.

"You know," Malakar drawled, "all of this could've been avoided if you had come with me willingly when I asked."

He stepped closer, letting the shadows stretch behind him. "Those lives could have been spared. Could've saved yourself the guilt. But you had to play the hero. And now all that blood? That's on you."

I didn't blink or flinch. My eyes remained on his, devoid of any emotion.

What he couldn't see was that I had already relived those choices over and over in this rotting cage. I had already blamed myself for every scream and every soul left behind. I had heard their names in the silence and felt their blood on my hands long before he ever said the words. He thought he was twisting the knife in me. But I'd been tearing myself apart since I was thrown down here.

So, I said nothing.

Because there was not a thing he could say to me that I hadn't already screamed at myself in the dark.

"I came down here to remind you what happens when you defy me. You follow my orders, or you deal with the consequences. I think a few more days down here should help you reflect." He turned to leave, the torchlight catching on the crimson edges of his coat until he paused, glancing over his shoulder.

"Oh, I almost forgot," His smile deepened. "Velorn told me everything, including the knowledge of the Kortika. About how you and the others were trying to find it in the Wispwoods."

That caught my attention. I turned toward the shadowed figure beside him, no longer caring how much it hurt to look. Velorn stood there, half-veiled in the darkness.

He had been listening to every conversation I had with Ehlark and the others.

I am such an idiot.

At that moment, I didn't care about Malakar. Not his threats. Not his games.

It was Velorn I wanted to destroy.

The betrayal burned hotter than any fire, flooding my veins with rage as I fixed my glare on him. The necklace I'd refused to wear—my symbol of failure—pulsed with heat, humming to life, urging me to grab it, wield it, and end the two assholes standing before me. The temptation was there, my fingers twitching to obey. But it was far in the corner, hidden from sight. They'd kill me before I could get to it.

"I would've loved to send my tracker to find the Kortika," Malakar's voice dripped with mock disappointment, "but unfortunately, he had to use his shadows from quite a distance. Depleted most of his strength." He glanced at Velorn before turning back to me.

"Velorn also told me you foolishly discarded the necklace. It amuses me to think how you must be regretting that decision now."

I frowned.

Why didn't Velorn tell him I had the necklace? He must be playing some angle I couldn't figure out.

Malakar strode back down the hallway, as Velorn remained in the dark.

Using the little strength I had left, I rose to my feet and staggered toward the bars, glaring into the darkness. "Make no mistake, Velorn," I warned. "Before I die, the last blood on my hands will be yours."

He didn't reveal himself. In the darkness, only his eyes gleamed.

"I'm looking forward to it."

369

37

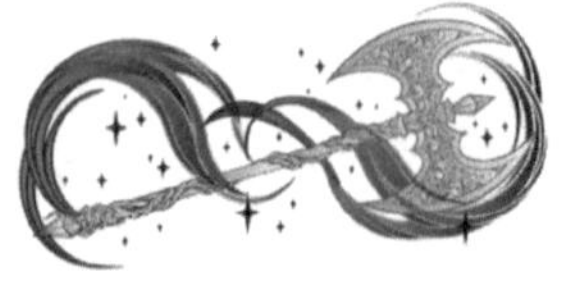

SHADOWED TRAP

My mind careened between despair and desperation, like a pendulum I couldn't stop. One moment, I was drowning under the weight of everything I had lost, everything Velorn and Malakar had taken. And the next, I clung to fragile hope.

I kept praying that Malakar's men wouldn't find Ehlark and the others. That somehow, they'd escaped and returned to Cedarvale. To take care of what was left there. But another part of me, quieter and more terrified, hoped they wouldn't do something foolish. That they wouldn't jeopardize everything by coming to look for me.

When I finally heard footsteps again, I didn't bother to lift my head. I knew it would be a soldier.

"Malakar has summoned you." The soldier tossed a pair of the familiar golden cuffs through the bars. They hit the floor with a sharp clang, the sound echoing off the cold walls. "You're to put those on before leaving your cell."

I stared down at the miserable things.

Out of the corner of my eye, I saw the necklace. It felt as if it had been patiently waiting, reminding me that it was always with me, ready to unleash its power. To eliminate the two men I hated more than anything else in this world.

When the soldier wasn't looking, I hurried and grabbed the relic, slipping it back on. The magic came flooding back, reigniting something within my soul that I thought I had lost.

It felt like breathing life back into me, as if it remembered who I was, even when I didn't.

I looked down at the cuffs still resting in my hand, their gold edges reflecting in the dim light.

Was this it? Was this the end for me?

Looking closer at the shackles, something inside me stirred. A deep-seated desire, a spark that refused to die.

Not yet.

I placed the golden cuffs around my wrists, careful not to let them click into place. The soldier unlocked the cell and stepped aside as I walked out.

I paused in front of him, waiting. Watching.

When he shut the cage door behind me, I let the cuffs drop from my wrists against the stone floor and summoned the axe.

It appeared with the pulsing green light, heavy and alive in my hands. Its energy vibrated through my bones, awakening my senses.

The soldier froze, his eyes widening in terror as he stumbled back a step. "I—I was only following orders."

My grip tightened around the axe. "Get in the cage, and I might let you live."

He whirled, stumbling to unlock the door and step inside. He slammed it shut behind him and tossed the keys at my feet. I grabbed them and ran through a narrow, winding tunnel that led me straight to the surface.

The sudden cold felt like a harsh blow. I paused past the exit, scanning my surroundings. This place wasn't anything like Cedarvale. It looked like the grounds of a fortress. Towering stone walls enclosed everything, and the sparse trees made it feel even more exposed. The sky, however, was dark. Dark enough to keep me hidden if I moved slowly.

As much as I wanted to go after Velorn and Malakar, revenge wouldn't save me. I had to be smart.

Survive now, revenge later.

But as I moved forward, I heard footsteps.

I dove behind a row of barrels stacked against the wall, holding my breath as a group of soldiers entered my view. My blood ran cold when I saw who they were escorting.

Two figures in cuffs followed behind them, their heads bowed as they walked.

No. No, no, no.

I recognized Ehlark immediately. Beside him was Terryn, who had accompanied him when he set out to look for the Kortika. I felt relieved but also a little stressed because I had to figure out how to save them, too.

My heart pounded as three soldiers broke away and escorted them into the dungeon, the very dungeon I had escaped from.

The same dungeon where I had left that soldier cowering inside a locked cage.

Shit.

If they found him, they'd know I escaped.

I waited until the last soldier disappeared. I moved from my hiding spot, my boots hitting the ground silently as I headed toward the dungeon entrance.

Carefully, I moved toward the archway, leaning against the cold stone. I tightened my grip on the axe. Peering around the corner, I saw three soldiers, with their backs to me, escorting Ehlark and Terryn further inside.

With a slow, deep breath, I swung the axe in a high arc, aiming it at one of the soldiers. The air whistled as the axe soared, striking the back of the nearest soldier's head. He grunted and then collapsed. Before the others could react, the axe reappeared in my hand.

Everyone turned to face me. Ehlark and Tarryn's eyes widened in disbelief. Ehlark's lips parted, and a flicker of something unspoken passed between us. He was alive, bruised, but not broken.

"You've got a lot of nerve," growled the soldier nearest him, his hand already reaching for his sword. "Think you can take all of us on?" But the second soldier hesitated. His face turned pale, and his eyes dared from my axe to the fallen man.

"Cadry," he hissed to his partner, panic creeping into his voice, "It's her. The one I told you about. The elemental with the axe."

The first soldier scoffed. "I don't care what stories they've told. I'm not letting some girl with a glorified hatchet scare me."

He took another step toward me, rage flaring in his eyes, his grip on his sword tightening.

The soldier lunged with the blade raised, aiming to strike me down. As he closed the distance, Ehlark collided with him from the side, hitting the soldier with the force of a battering ram and knocking him to the ground. He twisted the soldier's arm until something snapped, then drove his elbow into the man's throat to silence the scream. The soldier's sword clanged as it hit the stone floor.

The second soldier stared in shock. Immediately, he raised his hands and let his weapon drop. "I don't want trouble," he stammered, stepping back until his back touched the wall.

Ehlark didn't hesitate. With the golden cuffs still on his wrists, he ran straight to me and pulled me into his arms. The fear, sadness, and guilt I had carried slipped from my shoulders the moment he held me.

I buried my face, gripping the fabric of his tunic as tears cascaded down my cheeks. We stayed like that—clinging to each other as if the world might fall apart if we let go.

"I failed them, Ehlark," I wept, too ashamed to meet his gaze. "It's all my fault. I should have listened to you."

"Shhh. It's okay." He held me tight, his hand stroking my hair.

After a moment, Terryn stepped forward and fiddled with Ehlark's cuffs, finally unlocking them.

It was like standing amid a storm, the ground vibrating beneath our feet. His power reached for me, wrapping around as if it remembered me, too.

Ehlark stepped back, cradling my face in his hands, his thumbs brushing over my cheeks. "Are you alright?"

I nodded.

"What happened? Why are you here and not in Cedarvale?" Terryn asked, snatching a sword from a fallen soldier.

"They found us," I whispered. "Malakar's soldiers. They attacked right after dusk. We never saw it coming."

The color drained from Ehlark's face. I felt the tremor run through him as he stood there. I turned to Terryn and caught the flash of anger in his eyes, his jaw tightening as his grip closed hard around the weapon.

"Velorn, he—he killed everyone. The Eldryss, Thalena, and Lythara—they're gone. All of them." My voice broke, ashamed knowing it was all my fault.

"I regret not killing that bastard when I could have," Tarryn cursed.

I grabbed Ehlark's hand. "What about Kaelira? The others—did they escape?"

"They did," he said, his voice still tight. "Kaelira managed to get the others out of Wispwoods. The soldiers only grabbed us." He hesitated, his gaze dipping for a moment. "We were close, Eleni. So damn close to capturing the Kortika. But the ambush ruined everything, and it slipped away."

A shaky breath left my lips, and I reached up to touch his cheek. He leaned into my hand, closing his eyes. "I'm relieved you're alive," I whispered.

"Me too," he sighed in relief. "More than you know."

"As much as I love this reunion," Terryn said, wiping blood from his temple as he shoved the surrendered soldier toward an open cell nearby, "we still need to get back to Cedarvale. Or whatever is left of it."

We slipped into the night, pressing close to the crumbling outer wall. Moonlight finally broke through the clouds and washed everything in a cold silver blue, which offered practically no cover as we cut between hay bales and wine barrels. The fortress spread out around us, with guards posted at every exit. I scanned the ramparts for loose stones or an overlooked gap, but there were none. This place was going to be a lot harder to escape than I thought.

"There," Ehlark whispered, drawing my attention to where he pointed. "That's our way out." A half-open door, tangled with vines, stood in the shadows.

"Seems way too good to be true," Terryn muttered, picking up on the unease in his voice. "Feels more like a trap."

No guards watched the door; only stone and the promise of freedom swayed in the trees beyond. But there was too much open space between us.

As much as I hated to admit it, Terryn was right. It felt far too easy.

"I might be siding with Terryn on this one, Ehlark."

Ehlark ignored both of us. He crouched low, pressing his palms into the dirt until his fingertips disappeared beneath the soil. A green light came to life, pulsing through the ground and creeping up his arms. "This isn't a good plan, Ehlark," Terryn warned.

But it was too late.

A crash of snapping branches sounded from the far side of the fortress. Alarm bells rang out everywhere. Soldiers shouted from atop the walls, rushing toward where Ehlark had set a trap.

Ehlark pulled his hands from the soil. "Stay low. Run fast."

Our boots hit the dirt as we took off running. Every step felt louder than it should have, but the gate was getting closer. Only a few more feet, and we'd be beyond the wall, swallowed by the forest.

But something didn't feel right, as a creepy chill swept across the ground. Shadows loomed over the dirt like black oil, spilling, twisting, and coiling into a tall figure ahead of us.

Velorn appeared between us and the gate, his shadows swirling around him, alive and restless. The moonlight reflected off the amber glow of his eyes.

We skidded to a stop. Ehlark flung himself in front of me, his hand reaching for the weapon he had taken from the soldier.

Above us, a whistle rang out.

Dozens of soldiers emerge from the wall towers, crossbows raised, and long spears pointed down at us. We were surrounded, trapped in the middle of the courtyard.

Then, a slow, mocking laugh boomed down from the top of the wall.

38

DARK SURRENDER

Malakar emerged from the top of the staircase, descending with that same maddening calm that made my skin crawl. His charred black coat flared with each step like smoke curling from a slow-burning fire, and the silver accents on his boots caught the moonlight.

That horrible smile spread across his face, and I wanted nothing more than to punch the shit out of him.

"Bravo." His voice was slick with mockery as he offered a slow, theatrical clap. "Eleni, you never cease to entertain me. Hours ago, you could barely stand without trembling. And now," he halted a few feet away, soldiers spreading out behind him. "You look almost dangerous."

A sudden gasp pulled my attention to the side, freezing me in place.

Velorn's shadows had already slid between us, wrapping around Ehlark and Terryn's throats like a noose, as he did with Thalena, Lythara, and the others.

Back then, I hadn't been able to do anything. I see that now. I was a damn fool for thinking Velorn had a heart—some scrap of feeling buried beneath all that shadow and hard exterior, but looking at him now? Nothing existed. No remorse. No hint of doubt. Just a cold, empty void where a soul should've been.

I'd had enough.

Anger surged inside, fueling the warmth and hum of the necklace resting on my chest. I could feel the magic pulse through my veins and into my hand until the axe materialized. My hand gripped the handle as I adjusted my stance, prepared to strike. My eyes fixed on Velorn, and with all my rage and fury, I threw as hard as I could.

It moved with lightning speed, cutting through his shield of shadows like a spear of light through smoke.

Velorn dodged, the blade barely skimming the side of his face. It went through the fortress wall, tearing through anything in its path.

The soldiers shifted uneasily as they stared at the gaping hole in the fortress wall.

Velorn had already recovered. His golden eyes locked onto me, radiating brighter and wilder. Blood trickled down his temple, catching the light as it ran down his jaw.

He wasn't close enough for me to read his expression, but I could've sworn his lips twitched.

Was he smiling?

The axe formed in my grip, its weight settling into place.

I wouldn't miss this time.

Malakar had said Velorn's powers were drained from bringing me here, and now I could see it. He was forcing more strength than usual, pushing past his limits. If that was true, then he might not be able to dodge the next strike.

I lifted the axe, steadying my breath.

"I wouldn't do that if I were you, little *Viri*."

"Velorn," I threatened, "if you kill them, my axe will be the last thing you feel before I kill you."

His lips moved upward, as if he relished the threat.

"Eleni, Eleni," Malakar cut in. "Let's not get dramatic. Velorn won't kill them—at least, not while I'm ordering him not to."

I stayed in place, keeping my focus on Velorn.

"Now put your axe away so we can have a civilized conversation. Or do I need to put the golden cuffs on you?"

I kept the axe tightened in my grip, running the odds in my head.

Sure, I might land a killing blow to Velorn, but would his shadows kill Ehlark and Terryn first? And then there was Malakar and his soldiers. They would be on us in seconds, and three against dozens wasn't exactly in our favor.

Frustration burned as I drew a deep breath and let the axe fade. It shimmered before disappearing back into the necklace. The hum still lingered against my chest, as if whispering that it was still there. Waiting.

"Good girl," Malakar said smoothly. "Though I do recall the last time I saw you, you didn't have that necklace. Which makes me wonder," His gaze slid to Ehlark, then Terryn, before settling again on me. "Who gave it to you?"

He didn't know.

He had no clue that Velorn had slipped it to me. The thought tempted me to expose him and let Velorn face the punishment he deserved. But I held my tongue. Holding onto this information might prove useful later.

"What do you want to talk about, Malakar?" I forced myself to keep my voice steady, steering the conversation away from dangerous territory. The last thing I needed was to give him an excuse to torture Ehlark and Terryn for something they hadn't even done.

"Let's go to my study and talk." His tone left no room for debate. He turned and walked toward the fortress, fully expecting us to follow like obedient dogs.

Velorn's shadows stirred behind me, pushing us onward. I swatted them aside, glaring at Velorn in warning before I followed behind Malakar.

Ehlark stayed close to me as they led us out of the courtyard and into the fortress. Every now and then, I felt the comforting brush of his hand against mine.

We paused before a massive set of double doors that creaked open into what seemed to be a grand study, or perhaps their version of an office. The walls were lined with towering bookcases that stretched toward the vaulted ceiling, filled with scrolls and books of various sizes and thicknesses. A few deep leather chairs were scattered in the corners, and in the center, a broad dark wood desk dominated the space. Malakar stood behind it, opened one drawer, and pulled out a dagger and a roll of parchment.

"When I first laid eyes on you, I knew there was potential," Malakar said. "That storm in your eyes, that unshakable drive. That same determination you're showing me now." He stepped around the desk, the dagger still in his hand. "I need potential like yours fighting beside me when the time comes. War is coming, Eleni. It's an inevitable truth. And I intend to be ready."

"I will never fight for you, Malakar," I bit out. "I know why you want the power of the relic, and that's the only reason I'm still alive."

Malakar arched a brow. "I'm glad you're catching on to why I've kept you alive. But that isn't the whole reason. I'm sure you've wondered why I don't take the relic from you and kill you all right here."

I hated to admit it, but part of me had wondered exactly that.

"You see," he continued, "no relic has awakened in hundreds of years. They don't stir for just any elemental. They choose. *The Heart of the Mountain* chose you, which means you carry power strong enough to shift alliances and the future of Thysia itself. If I ripped the relic from you now, it would be nothing more than a gem. It would never accept me as its master, and therefore it would be useless."

To him, the relic was only a jewel, as Eryndra said. Unless I wielded its power, it had no worth to him at all.

"Since the other relics are still missing, getting caught with one aligned to the House of Earth would make me a thief and a traitor."

"Then wouldn't the other Houses also assume I stole the relics? If they were to see me with the axe?" I shot back. It was precisely what would happen. And worse, I'd probably be killed for theft.

Still, if my hunch was correct and Gram somehow stole the relics and hid them in that box, I knew where the other relics were. There was a slim chance, maybe a stupid one, that if I gathered them all, I could stop a war.

"Yes," Malakar replied. "But they would not dare challenge you if you showed them the relic's power."

I chewed on his words.

Technically, I had the advantage. He needed me. He needed me to prove to the Houses that a relic had chosen me and that I could wield its power.

"So let me make this simple. Bind yourself to me. Vow your loyalty, your strength, and I will spare your friends."

"Don't do it," Ehlark choked out, the shadows coiled tighter around his throat, silencing him.

"Eleni," Malakar said in a coaxing voice, "I know you're a smart girl. Don't make a foolish mistake."

I looked at Ehlark; his face was turning red, he was struggling for air, but his eyes remained on mine in a silent plea.

Suddenly, a blue, liquid-like dagger sliced between Ehlark and me. It shot past Malakar and buried itself in Velorn's chest.

He staggered forward, a spray of blood erupting from the wound. His hand clamped over it, crimson pouring through his fingers. The shadows that had bound Ehlark and Terryn vanished, dissipating like smoke blown away by the wind.

Ehlark collapsed to the ground, gasping for breath, his hands already glowing with a soft, pulsing green light. Beside him, Terryn also radiated light, but it wasn't green. It was a deep, rippling blue, sparkling like moonlight on dark water. My eyes caught on his wrist, and I saw the mark. At first glance, it resembled the House of Earth's crest, but the shapes weren't petals at all. They were waves—curling, crashing, engulfing the painted shape C at its center.

He belonged to the House of Water, the same House that Vyria pledged herself to with Lady Anira.

How had I missed this before? I remembered him work-ing with Ehlark in the dungeon, digging that massive hole. Perhaps that's why I didn't notice. Or maybe it was because I deliberately avoided him, unable to tolerate the recurring disgust in his eyes whenever they fixed on me.

Water rose from the scattered bottles in the room, forming clear, sharp-edged daggers that hovered around him in a silent threat.

"Eleni, take Ehlark and get out of here!"

He turned to me, not with his usual disdain, but with the fierce, unshakable resolve of a man who knew I was their only chance.

Terryn raised his hand to strike, but Malakar raised his in defense. A blazing spear of fire shot forward, tearing through Terryn's body. The blue glow in his veins faded so quickly, like it had never been there at all. His body crumpled, and the water-forged daggers fell across the floor like shards of broken glass.

"Terryn!" Ehlark cried out as he fell to his knees, pulling Terryn into his arms.

I spun to face Malakar. His arms were still raised, molten-red veins glowing down to his fingertips as he held a flame-like dagger in his palm. The relic's magic surged down my arm, eager to awaken and strike him where he stood. But I was too focused on Malakar to notice the soldiers swarming Ehlark until it was too late. They forced him to the ground, the side of his face grinding into the floor as golden cuffs snapped around his wrists. I saw the fight drain out of him.

More soldiers stormed in from every direction, surrounding us and aiming their weapons at me now.

"You're surrounded, Eleni," Malakar warned. "You won't make it out of here alive if you fight. Neither of you will." His flaming dagger hovered between us, pulsing with heat and warning. "I don't want to kill you, but make no mistake that I will kill your friend in an instant if you try to fight."

Anger and frustration burned in my chest. I found myself completely out of options.

Ehlark was shackled in golden cuffs, and Terryn lay lifeless next to him. My gaze dropped involuntarily to Velorn.

He was still crumpled on the ground, blood pooling beneath him, the gaping wound in his chest refusing to stop spilling. Part of me expected his veins to ignite, for that dark power coiled inside him to flare and knit him back together in an instant. But no glow came. No surge of strength. Only his shadows. They intertwined across his body, shielding their master.

Come to think of it, Velorn never glowed when he used his power; his veins never changed color, only his eyes.

Why was that?

"Are you going to cooperate, or do I have to force you?"

I stared into Malakar's dark eyes and knew he wouldn't hesitate to kill Ehlark if I fought back. I couldn't live with myself if I watched Ehlark die because I refused to back down. I lowered my hand to my side as the relic's magic slowly faded away, slipping back into the necklace.

Malakar's shoulders eased as the glow from his veins faded from his arms, his power retreating beneath his skin. "This," he muttered, rubbing his temples, "was not how I wanted tonight to go."

39

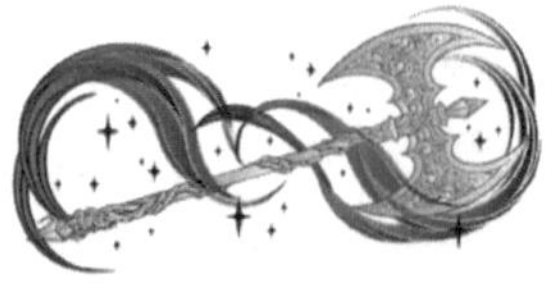

RED BONE

Malakar sat behind his desk, pulling out a bottle of dark amber liquor and an etched glass. He poured himself a drink, watching the liquid swirl, then downed it all in one long, silent gulp.

Ehlark and I stood there, watching.

Velorn's shadows still hovered around him, twisting like smoke to ward off the healer who had been foolish enough to approach. No one dared to come any closer since.

Malakar refilled his glass, his movements unhurried, before finally breaking the silence.

"This is my final warning, Eleni," he offered. "Bind yourself to me, and I won't harm your friend."

If I refused him, he would kill Ehlark right there. I could not stomach the thought of his blood on my hands, not Ehlark's. If I stayed and played along with Malakar's plan, at least Ehlark would have a chance.

"How do I know you won't go back on your word?"

"I'm a business elemental." He responded. "Lies are tools for the weak. And I am not weak." There was no smugness in him. No cocky smirk on his face, only a calm certainty. "I don't break my word. Ever."

I squeezed my hands into fists at my sides, hoping that the choice I was about to make would be the right one.

"Fine."

"Eleni—" Hearing the pain in Ehlark's voice hurt more than I wanted him to see. I raised a hand to him, my eyes trained on Malakar. I couldn't let Ehlark see me break. Not here. If I turned and met his gaze, I knew I would see the hurt in his eyes and would start second-guessing my decision.

"If I'm to bind myself to you," I said evenly, "then I have terms of my own."

His brow lifted in interest. "Do you now?" He leaned back, swirling his drink. "And who says I'll allow it?"

"You will either agree," I replied, "or I won't accept the contract. The choice is yours."

He said nothing as he examined me, trying to peel back layers to find out what I might be hiding up my sleeve.

"You said you are a business elemental. So, let's negotiate."

Malakar finally gave me a satisfied look. "All right. What are your terms?"

"You will not harm Ehlark or his people. And you will allow me to visit my home."

Malakar let out a sharp, amused laugh. "I'll agree not to harm him, but you'll need to be more specific about which people. And your second request? I'll allow it—accompanied, of course."

"Then hear this," I said. "No blade, no fire, no order you give will ever touch the House of Earth."

He took another slow sip from his glass before setting it down with a soft clink. He then reached into a drawer and pulled out what appeared to be an ornate pen. Its silver tip reflected the light as he wrote on the parchment he had set aside earlier.

The room was silent except for the soft scratching of ink on paper. Minutes went by. Then, at last, he set the pen down and looked up at me. "Deal."

With his order, one soldier pushed me forward towards the desk. I stepped closer, glancing down at the parchment. It was the same foreign language I had seen in Hollows Mountain. The same swirling symbols that I couldn't understand.

How would I know he actually wrote what we agreed? I could not trust him. I needed a way to see the words without making it obvious I couldn't read them.

"This is our contract," Malakar spoke. "You vow your loyalty to me. Your strength is mine to command. And in return, no blade, no fire, no order I give will touch the House of Earth. Including your friend. I will also permit you to visit your home."

"I don't come from royalty. Contracts aren't my specialty. So before this is sealed, I want a second set of eyes . . . Ehlark." My gaze stayed on Malakar's, making it clear he wasn't going to fool me with this. He gestured for a soldier to bring Ehlark to the desk.

After a few minutes of Ehlark reading the parchment, he nodded. "It is what you both agreed upon." I could feel Ehlark's eyes
on me, but I kept mine on Malakar's.

I have to do this.

It was the only way to save him.

Slowly, I took the pen and signed my name at the bottom.

After examining my signature with a questionable look, he
reached for the dagger at his side.

At first, it appeared ceremonial—ornate, perhaps even decora-
tive. But as I examined it more closely, a chill ran through me. A
dark crimson surface etched with strange, jagged symbols. This
was no ordinary blade. I shifted my position, unease prickling
down my arms.

"I've never been one to put much faith in Blood Seers or their
magic," Malakar explained, turning the blade in his hand. "So
instead, I had one of their bones forged into this."

Did he kill a Blood Seer?

Or had Velorn done it for him, like back at Hollows Mountain?
And if he'd had this dagger all along, why hadn't he used it then?
Was it a secret weapon he kept hidden from the other Blood
Seers?

I looked past Malakar and caught sight of Velorn's shadows
swirling faster, swallowing him whole until he was gone. I
shouldn't have cared where they carried him. I should have been
relieved he was no longer my problem. But my mind refused to
let it go. I still wanted vengeance for what he did.

I will be seeing you again, Velorn.

Malakar set his glass down, bringing my focus back to him.
"Velorn will be fine. This is not the first time something like this
has happened. He will return once he is healed." His tone was

so casual, so practiced, it was clear Velorn had vanished like this more times than Malakar could be bothered to count.

My gaze stayed on the blade in Malakar's hand, unease creeping deeper the longer I stared at it.

"You see, Eleni, back at Hollows Mountain, the Blood Seer would have forced a contract between us, binding your loyalty to me. They have a way of making sure our feelings towards each other don't grow stronger. But Velorn, with his hatred for them, killed her before she had the chance. Without her, I couldn't risk letting feelings interfere, not until I had this dagger to forge the contract myself."

Feelings?

My stomach dropped.

Was Velorn being truthful then when he asked about Ehlark and my own feelings? Without a Blood Seer to regulate the bond, our emotions grew stronger the longer our contract lasted. This meant the pull I felt toward Ehlark, the same pull I once felt toward Velorn, wasn't entirely mine. It *was* the contract twisting them.

I looked down at my wrist, dread sinking in.

What were my *real* feelings then?

I didn't understand because every part of me longed to be near Ehlark. I still craved his touch and protection. I looked to him, hoping he'd say it was real, that our time together meant more than magic. But the look in his eyes told me he had known. He had known the whole time and had not told me.

"Did you know?" My voice faltered because even now, I wanted to touch him, hold him, and say it was genuine. Every feeling. Every emotion was real between us.

Ehlark opened his mouth, closed it, and opened it again, struggling with the words. "I—" he stammered, then forced the rest out. "It is not the contract, Eleni. I care for you. Contract or no contract, my feelings for you are real. If you want, we can break it now. Let me prove it to you. Let me show you that I want you for who you are, not because of some magical binding."

His words sounded empty because, for the first time since meeting Ehlark, I felt betrayed. I felt hurt that he hadn't been honest with me from the start.

Part of me wanted him to break our contract, to prove to everyone that our feelings were true. But deep down, I already knew. I knew because I had felt the same pull toward Velorn, maybe even stronger. And when our contract was fulfilled, all that remained was hate. No desire to be near him, no passion, no urge to feel his touch on my skin.

Only anger.

Only the need for him to hurt the way I did.

"Oh, I do indeed like where this is going," Malakar cut in, his smile never reaching his eyes. "By all means, I would love a fresh start with you. No existing contracts in place." He nodded toward Ehlark and me, daring us both to comply.

"I'll even sweeten the deal. Break your contract with each other, and I will release Ehlark immediately. He doesn't even need to be present for the binding. Once you break your bond, my guards will escort him outside the gates."

I watched Malakar, searching for any hint of deceit, but his dark eyes showed none. Ehlark met my gaze. "Eleni, let me prove to you that what I feel is real."

"Yes, Eleni. Let him prove his feelings," Malakar droned, dragging the words long enough for me to see he was curious too.

I closed my eyes and drew a slow breath. I had to know. I had to find out if what I felt for Ehlark was real or if it had all been a lie.

Like how everything about Velorn was a lie.

"Okay."

Malakar ordered the soldiers to unlock the cuffs. "Try anything, and I will have you ashed in seconds."

Ehlark slid his hands into mine.

They were a familiar warmth and comfort I didn't want to let go of. He pressed his forehead to mine and whispered, "Do you trust me?" His voice was calm, and I wanted to believe him wholeheartedly.

"Yes."

"Then repeat after me." His forehead stayed pressed against mine as he closed his eyes and spoke.

> *"By vow and word, I sever the chain.*
> *What was bound is bound no more.*
> *Your oath to mine, and mine to yours,*
> *Broken now, forever sworn."*

I repeated the words, each phrase sinking deeper than I was willing to admit. When the last one left my lips, a tingling spread across my wrist. The same sensation I had felt with Velorn's bite when it faded now arose again with Ehlark's.

The contract was broken.

Our tie was broken.

I kept my eyes shut, refusing to accept that everything had been distorted by a lie, that what I had experienced was truly mine alone. But eventually, I had to face it.

I slowly opened my eyes.

Ehlark was beautiful, impossibly so, like the first time I met him in the prison carriage, but the strong pull I once felt toward him, the need for him to be near me all the time and to protect me, was gone.

And the way his eyes met mine told me he felt it too.

"Great. Now that we have that settled, I will have my guards escort your friend out," Malakar stated.

A part of me still hoped Ehlark would speak up, that he would tell me what we had was real, and prove to everyone watching that his feelings were genuine. But his silence spoke louder than words. It confirmed what I already feared—that our feelings were only because of the contract.

I didn't feel anger like I did towards Velorn, only emptiness. It was as if a part of me was gone now.

Ehlark seemed to be drowning in the same emptiness, wanting to say something but knowing it would sound hollow. The guards took him by the arms and led him away, their steps echoing as the doors shut behind them.

He didn't even say goodbye.

"Leave us," Malakar ordered the remaining soldiers. One by one, they filed out until he was the only one left. My eyes stayed fixed on the door, waiting. Hoping Ehlark would come rushing back. Say something to prove that he still cared, that he would still search for the Kortika.

But the longer that doorway remained empty, the harder the truth settled in.

Maybe he was finally realizing that I was the reason his home burned down and that Cedarvale fell because of me. All those lives, all that blood, pointed directly to me. All because I didn't kill the man I believed was actually good.

The quicksand was rising, and I couldn't escape.

Please, Ehlark. Come back.

But he didn't.

A glass was placed in front of me, and I finally tore my gaze away from the door. Malakar stood there, offering it, a second glass balanced in his other hand. I snatched it and drank it in a single go. The taste was sweet, fruity, and deceptively harmless. But I remembered it. The same liquid Velorn had given me that first night in the kitchens.

"Shall we?" Malakar gestured toward the table where the blade waited.

We both stepped closer to the table, and upon a more careful look, I could see the blade more clearly. Instead of the usual ivory color, the bone was a deep crimson, as if blood had seeped out and dried on the surface.

"It carries the same binding power. Only now, can I choose how I want to create my contracts." He reached for another parchment, this one weathered and wide. When he unfolded it, it had symbols and pictures of trees, mountains, and bodies of water. It was a map.

"And this," he said, tapping a marked spot with the tip of the blade, "this ensures I'll always know where you are."

The pieces suddenly came together. Velorn had told me once that he was bound to Malakar by a contract. Which meant . . .

Malakar had known where Velorn was all along; he was aware of Cedarvale's location because he could track Velorn. That's how he found us. That's how all of this started.

A nauseating feeling swept over me because it only confirmed it was my fault.

"Your hand, please."

My body and soul felt hollow as I stared at the dagger.

Was this really where my future led?

Perhaps this was what I deserved.

I lifted my hand and placed it in his. He held it steady over the two parchments and dragged the blade across my palm, causing a sharp pain to tear through my skin. I sucked in a breath as the burn flared up my arm, deeper than flesh. Something in my blood stirred as the first drops splattered onto the parchment. The symbols shone faintly where they touched.

Malakar raised his hand and did the same, slicing across his palm. That's when I noticed his mark. It was a facing-up *C* with what looked like flames in the middle.

House of Fire.

I thought this would feel like the other contracts, like with Ehlark, with Velorn.

Those felt raw and more personal.

But this felt like a transaction.

Malakar reached forward and gripped my hand in his, his bloody palm pressing against mine. The handshake was firm. Final.

Heat surged between our joined hands, not from the blood but from something deeper, older. A current of magic sparked beneath my skin like a live wire, racing up my arm and through my chest. It wasn't comforting as Ehlark's or personal like Velorn's had been. They felt like chains latching on, tethering me to something beyond my control.

The parchment below us glowed, the symbols pulsing once, then fading as if fulfilled.

It was done.

The contract was sealed.

40

ANNOUNCEMENT

The following week passed in a blur.

Malakar allowed me to wander anywhere in the fortress, but most days I sulked in my room. It was spacious and luxurious, with fresh fruit on a small table, a bed covered in soft sheets, and a balcony overlooking hills and skies. Yet, despite its luxury, it still felt like a cage.

The other day, I tried to find the kitchen, but the stares that followed me down the hallways weren't very friendly, some even hostile. After that, I stayed put. A few times, there were knocks at my door, offering to dress me and bring a plate of food, but I always refused. I told them to leave the tray by the door and nothing more.

Malakar had invited me to dine with him several times, but I refused each invitation. I had no desire to share a table with that man, and I would do anything to avoid him.

My mind spiraled. Replaying different paths I could've taken and decisions I should've made. A thousand what-ifs circled like vultures, tearing at the remaining pieces of hope I had left. In the end, it didn't matter.

I was stuck here in Thysia, bound to Malakar until he fulfilled the second part of our agreement and allowed me to visit home. Even that wasn't easy. I had to find the Kortika first. If I couldn't find it, there'd be no way of going home.

I cried myself to sleep most nights. I hated feeling trapped. Hated knowing I'd been lied to. Hated myself most of all for failing to protect Lythara, Thalena, and the others that night.

My thoughts wandered to Vyria. I hoped she was doing better than I was, that Lady Anira was kind to her, and that she was safe. Then my mind drifted home. To the ranch. To work. To the comfort of modern food and familiar routines.

There were so many things I couldn't stop thinking about, and each one reminded me of how distant I was from the life I'd lost.

I sat perched on the windowsill, watching people stream in and out of the fortress gates. There were more today than I had seen all week.

Was something important happening?

Knock. Knock. Knock.

The abrupt sound startled me; no one had ever knocked that loudly before. I stood up and approached the door. "Leave the food outside, thank you."

"My lady, may we come in?" a female voice asked from the other side.

No, I thought immediately.

The room was a mess, and I looked half-deprived. The last thing I wanted was for anyone to see me like this. But after a beat, I sighed. "Sure."

The door opened, and three women stepped inside. Two younger ones carried bundles of clothing, while the older woman in the center carried herself with an air of composure that set her apart. She met my eyes directly as she spoke. "Prince Malakar requests your presence this evening."

"Well, you can tell Malakar I refuse." I kept my tone politely firm.

"He thought you might say that," the older woman replied. "He also told me that if you refuse his offer, he will have no choice but to send soldiers to drag you down in golden cuffs."

Indirect threats now. Interesting.

I studied her more closely. Her bearing was proper, but there was something regal in the way she carried herself, something that made me wonder if being sent here with this message was beneath her. Maybe she was also bound by Malakar's threats, unable to speak of them. Either way, if I were going to be forced, I would rather these women dress me than a squad of soldiers.

"Fine. I will do as Malakar says," I muttered, stepping aside to let them in.

"It is *Prince* Malakar," the older woman corrected, her tone clipped. Clearly, she did not like me.

I arched a brow. "My bad. I will do as *Prince* Malakar says." I wasn't usually in the habit of studying people's wrists, but curiosity got the best of me. I stole a glance and saw her mark. She was bound, not to the House of Earth or Water, but to the House of Fire.

The two younger women laid the bundles neatly across the bed, each one more ornate than the last. "Am I required to wear one of these?" I asked, pointing at the dresses.

"It would be wise," the older woman replied. "There is an important event tonight."

Important event? I didn't like the sound of that. "And what, pray tell, is this *important event* the prince insists I attend?" Because God forbid a girl just wants to stay in her room and be a hermit.

"He did not say. It is not my place to ask. But other Houses will be present for tonight's festivities."

Interesting.

Why was he inviting the other Houses? Wasn't there tension looming between them because of the relics?

"Since you are now representing the House of Fire, it would be wise to look your best." Her gaze moved over me slowly and intentionally, as if trying to hide her disgust.

"News flash, I don't belong to any House." I lifted my wrist in front of her. "I'm not marked. I only have a contract with Malakar, and that's it." She had been judging me from the second she walked through that door, and I was done.

"Marked or not, you are under the protection and roof of the Prince of the House of Fire. That is considered an honor among all. You are his guest, and as a guest, it would be disrespectful to ignore the generosity he has shown you."

God, she sounded like she had walked straight out of a medieval drama, all highborn poise and rehearsed dignity. Her chin never dipped, her composure never cracked.

I rubbed my temples, already feeling a headache brewing from arguing with this woman.

"Ugh, fine. I'll wear whatever the damn prince wants me to wear."

The older woman gestured toward the younger one, who stood beside the bed. "Ravina will help you get ready." The younger girl, no more than a teenager, stepped forward. Pale skin, dark hair, and freckles scattered across her nose. She dipped her head and offered me a shy smile. I found myself returning it.

It was the first genuine smile I had seen since I arrived here, and it meant more than I expected. Her quiet kindness touched me in a way I hadn't realized I was starving for.

⚬

After what felt like hours of getting ready, most of it spent combing out the knots in my hair, Ravina finally led me down the corridor toward the source of muffled voices and soft light.

The evening air was cool enough to awaken my senses as we stepped into the massive courtyard. The long, flowing dress covered most of my skin, and I was grateful Malakar had chosen something more conservative for once. Well, *mostly* conservative. The puffed frills at the ends of my sleeves and the gaudy neckline? Yeah, I snipped those off. Ravina almost had a full-blown panic attack when she saw what I'd done.

The gown was a deep burgundy, rich like red wine, adorned with delicate golden flames beaded along the hem. It gleamed in the torchlight as I walked, almost as if it were trying to ignite itself. Before stepping any further into view, I slipped my hand beneath the neckline of my dress and pulled out the necklace.

It was the only thing that ever truly calmed my nerves. Ever since I arrived, it had been my anchor. And tonight, I had a feeling I'd be clutching it more than once.

Ravina guided me through the courtyard until we reached Malakar. He stood among a group of well-dressed figures, already deep in conversation. As we stepped closer, unease settled in me. I recognized some of them. There were several of the same people who sat at those long stone tables in Hollows Mountain, watching and judging those who weren't marked.

I slowed my pace, steeling myself for whatever game Malakar was about to play.

"There she is," he said smoothly, breaking from the group and walking toward me.

His hand pressed against the small of my back, guiding me forward. I tensed up. The contact felt more personal than I was comfortable with.

Something about it felt wrong.

All of it was wrong—the dress, the stares from the people around us, and Malakar's warm hand stroking my back.

What the hell was this? What angle was he playing?

"Everyone, you remember Eleni," he announced, as if presenting a showpiece. "She's come a long way since you last saw her." The way he said it made my skin crawl, like I was a prize hound being paraded at a kennel club.

He started introducing me to the others one by one. I maintained a neutral expression, careful not to reveal anything, especially not the disgust on my face.

The next man I was introduced to, I recognized immediately. It was the same lecherous man from under the mountain, the one who'd leered at Vyria with roaming eyes and a voice that oozed like oil. And now he was looking at me.

His gaze slowly and shamelessly swept over me. My stomach clenched, and bile rose in my throat, making me wish I could vomit all over him right then.

"Lord Fren," Malakar said, his tone light but unmistakably pointed, "I believe your wife is soon to be with child?" He stepped closer beside me, close enough to block Lord Fren's line of sight, redirecting his attention.

I wasn't sure if he did it on purpose, but it worked. Lord Fren's eyes snapped back to Malakar. The hunger that had been behind them vanished in an instant.

"Uh, yes," he replied, clearing his throat. "She would have come tonight, but our healer advised against it. The journey would have been too dangerous. Still, we hope our gift will reinforce the friendship between our homes. I know the King will need as many allies as possible, since the tension between him and the House of Water has been strained."

I went still—support for the King.

And because Malakar was a prince, that could only mean his father. A cold realization sank in. This was what tonight was truly about: forging alliances against another House. The same House that Lady Anira and Vyria were tied to. Were they preparing to go to war with them?

"I don't recall receiving a gift." Malakar's face was calm, but something shifted in Malakar. It was subtle enough that I don't think the others noticed, but I did.

"Well, it was a bit of a struggle to acquire it," Lord Fren answered, his expression curling with satisfaction. "But it should arrive soon." He looked far too pleased with himself, as though he couldn't wait to see Malakar's reaction.

"Well, do let me know the moment it arrives," Malakar replied, voice even, though his suspicion matched mine. His composure never faltered as he faced Lord Fren.

I needed to leave. Head back to my room, escape this suffocating dress. "Excuse me, gentlemen, I have to powder my nose." It was the only excuse I could come up with, and saying I'd rather piss off than stay another second probably wasn't a good idea.

"Don't be long," Malakar warned. "I have an announcement to make, and I will need you at my side when it comes."

Announcement?

The word made my hackles rise. What could he possibly have to announce that involved me? Unless . . .

Unless he planned to reveal everything.

Tell everyone that I had the relic and could summon it. Panic was settling in.

I forced the fakest smile I could muster and gave a sarcastic bow. "As you wish." I veered away, slipping through the crowd, putting as much distance as I could between myself and the courtyard noise. I needed to leave before his announcement. There was no way I would stand beside him for it.

As I moved through the crowd, I caught a familiar wintery musk scent and my body froze.

I turned and saw Velorn standing a foot away, clad in black from head to toe. His fitted shirt traced every line of his frame, and his dark trousers were tucked neatly into worn boots. His long hair hung loose, a shadowed curtain that partially veiled the scars across his face.

"I see you're not dead."

The sight of him made my heart stagger. I wasn't sure whether to feel relief that I finally had the chance to take him down or the sinking dread that killing him would be much more complicated than I expected.

The last time I saw Velorn, blood was pouring from the gaping hole in his chest before his shadows swallowed him whole and carried him away. And now, here he was, standing as if none of it had touched him. If anything, it only confirmed what I already suspected: he wouldn't go down easily.

"I see Malakar got what he wanted." His voice didn't match his stance. The cold steel I'd come to expect was softened enough to catch me off guard.

Was he concerned?

"Yep," I said flatly. The necklace hummed beneath the dress as if it too wanted blood. But not tonight. There were too many bystanders I could potentially hurt, and I didn't like that. "If you'll excuse me, I have an appointment with a comfortable bed I'd very much like to get to."

Velorn's eyes darkened.

In an instant, his hand grabbed my shoulder, pulling me close until his face was inches from mine. "Whose bed are you going to? Did Malakar order you to his chambers?"

I yanked my arm free from his grip. "What? No! Malakar wanted me here, but I'd rather be in my room."

Velorn blinked once. Twice. Then he straightened to his full height. The cold, unreadable mask he always wore like armor slipped, and something else wavered beneath it. Not anger. Not disdain. Something I had never seen in him before.

In the span of minutes, Velorn had given me more mixed signals than he had in the month I'd known him, and that troubled me. When he brooded, it was easy to hate him. When he wore that mask of indifference, it was easy to see him as a monster. But now, to see his amber eyes softened into warm honey, I didn't know what to think.

"I am glad to see you back in full health, Velorn." Malakar's voice cut in.

Both Velorn and I turned, startled by Malakar's sudden appearance. The sounds of conversation filled the silence between the three of us until Velorn finally spoke. "Yes."

"Perfect," Malakar replied. "Since you are here, you will hear my little announcement as well."

Fuck.

I glanced at Velorn and caught his brows furrow. Subtle, but enough for me to realize he was as in the dark about Malakar's plans as I was. It did nothing to ease the knot of nerves in my stomach.

"Eleni." Malakar extended his arm toward me. "Shall we?"

Every part of me wanted to refuse. To run to safety and get the hell out of here, but I had nowhere to run, no safety net. This was it. My end. Once everyone knew I had the relic, I would surely be dead.

Or maybe I was overthinking this whole announcement thing, and it was something else.

I had to be smart. I had to play along.

I stepped toward Malakar and slipped my arm through his, letting him lead me forward. I wasn't sure why I did it, but I glanced back at Velorn. His face returned to the mask of cold indifference I had come to know. Yet his left hand was clenched into a fist.

Malakar led me up a flight of stairs. At the top, he turned, facing the crowd. From up here, I could see the full scope that there were far more people than I had realized. My eyes swept the sea of faces, desperate for one I recognized, something familiar to anchor me. But all I felt was the creeping dread. I kept running through possibilities, trying to rationalize this *announcement*, but every path circled back to the relic. To its power.

"I want to thank all the Houses who came here tonight for this special occasion," Malakar began. "I will keep this brief, since I know most of you only came for the food."

The crowd chuckled through the courtyard.

We all know war looms on the horizon with our neighboring kingdoms. Recent history has only increased the unrest between our Houses. And so, in light of these dark times, I wish to bring forth something brighter."

He paused, his eyes sweeping the audience before landing on me.

This was it.

He was about to out me and tell everyone I had the relic, claiming I stole it, so I would be exposed, and my downfall would be for all to see. I braced for the following words, preparing for the worst.

"It is my honor to announce my future wife."

41

AWAKENING

It was as if the very air had been ripped from my lungs. I stood still as Malakar's words echoed in my ears. The clapping and cheers from the crowd reverberated through the courtyard, each sound hitting like nails to my coffin.

Future wife.

Malakar's future wife.

My body felt as if it were no longer standing on solid ground but hanging over a cliff. I turned to the crowd, praying and begging that this was some twisted dream. I would wake up back in my bed, with Gram calling from the kitchen, and this nightmare would end.

I dug my nails into the soft flesh of my forearm, pressing harder until I felt blood. But the pain didn't save me. It only proved this was real.

Faces blurred as I scanned the crowd, horror pressing down on my chest like a vice, until I found a pair of bright golden eyes staring right at me.

I should have turned away. I should have broken the connection. But I couldn't. And neither could he.

Hatred burst through every inch of my body. I despised the pain he had forced me to suffer, every wound. Every scar. Every bit of loss his presence had entangled me in. I loathed him more than I loathed Malakar. If I had landed anywhere else on this damn planet, with anyone else but *him*, none of this would have happened.

From the very first day I arrived, he had been my undoing.

My ruin.

And yet, I clung to his gaze because if I looked away, I would shatter. I would fall apart under the weight of their cheers, Malakar's claim, and the invisible chains he kept adding to me.

So I held his stare, letting the hatred burn through the panic. I forced the tremble out of my hands and steadied my breath.

I would not break.

Not here.

Not in front of *him*.

"*Dear.*" Malakar's hand closed around mine, jolting me out of the hatred I had sunk into. My gaze snapped to him. "Lord Fren is trying to get our attention."

I tried to suppress my anger and turned to the bottom of the stairs. Lord Fren was speaking, his lips moving, but his words barely registered. My mind was dulled, ignoring everything around me. It wasn't until I saw the gesture he made toward the far gates that my attention shifted. Soldiers were dragging something—no, someone—into the courtyard.

My body almost gave out.

The guards pulled Ehlark's body into the courtyard until they reached the center. They forced him to stand against a stone pillar, yanking him upright. Chains clanked as they shackled his wrists high above his head, keeping him in place.

I stood there, staring at him in stunned horror.

No.

His face was unrecognizable. It was swollen and bloodied, one eye shut, the other barely open. Deep purple bruises stained his jaw and cheekbones, and dried blood had cracked along his temple. The crimson blood caked the torn skin of his split bottom lip.

My eyes drifted towards the rest of his body. There were dozens of stab wounds on his thighs, some fresh and bleeding, others jagged and hastily wrapped in a blood-soaked cloth that had long since lost its purpose. Long, shallow gashes streaked down his arms like someone had done it to watch him suffer.

My heart broke into pieces the longer I stared.

"This elemental," Lord Fren declared, his voice carrying over the crowd, "is the one responsible for freeing the prisoners beneath the mountain. The one who aided thieves, murderers, and traitors in escaping justice. This—" he drew the pause out like a noose tightening, "is the *Earthshaper*."

A wave of murmurs swept through the crowd. "He's loyal to the House of Earth. Kill the traitor!" shouted another voice from the audience. Lord Fren's mouth curled as he turned back to

Malakar. "This is my gift to you, Prince Malakar. Proof of the justice that awaits those who cross the House of Fire."

My eyes flew to Malakar.

He swore that no harm would come to any elemental of the House of Earth. He had to stop this.

He *had* to.

But instead, he inclined his head. "I am pleased with your gift, Lord Fren. Let us ensure this Earthshaper receives the justice he deserves tonight."

No.

We made a contract. It was our agreement. He swore—

"It is my pleasure to serve you, Prince Malakar." Lord Fren bowed low before stepping back into the crowd, smug satisfaction etched across his face.

And then it hit me like a stab in the back. Malakar had kept his word, technically. *He* had agreed not to harm them. But he hadn't said anything about letting others do it for him.

Fuck.

I bolted down the stairs, already feeling the magic of the necklace humming through my veins. The crowd blurred around me as I shoved past bodies, witnesses be damned.

A hand shot out and grabbed my arm, holding me in place. "It's too late, Eleni. There's nothing you can do for him now." It was the first time Velorn had ever said my name.

"I need to save him! I can't just stand here and watch him die! I refuse!"

"If you do this, there will be consequences."

"What's worse than watching the person you care about die?" I snapped. "Oh, that's right—you wouldn't understand. You've never cared for anyone but yourself!"

He leaned in closer to me, too close, his eyes searching mine. His lips parted, but no sound came out.

Slowly, he released his hold and stepped back.

I sprinted toward the center of the courtyard. All I could focus on was Ehlark. I had to reach him to get him out of those golden cuffs.

When I reached the guards, their stances changed, ready to stop me. But then they suddenly shifted their positions and moved out of my way. I don't know why they did it, but I was too distracted to care.

Everything inside me broke at the sight of Ehlark.

My fingers shook as I reached for him, slipping a hand under his bloodied chin to lift his face. His single eye fluttered open, unfocused at first, but then it found mine. His lips parted like he wanted to speak, but all that came out was a strangled cough and a trickle of blood that slid down his chin.

"What did they do to you?" I whispered. "I thought they let you go?"

He forced his eye open, and the sight shattered me. That familiar green, once bright as spring, was now clouded, bloodshot, and drowning in pain.

"When I left," his jaw worked to find the words. "I didn't know what to do. I was about to cross the border when I realized my feelings for you were real. I couldn't explain them that night. It felt different then—an ache I couldn't name, like a hollow void where I had lost someone I cared about deeply." His words faltered. His lips trembled as blood streaked down his mouth. Still, his gaze held onto me. "But I couldn't get you out of my mind," he whispered. "The feelings came back to me, the ones that proved I do care for you, Eleni. More than you know. More than any magic could ever give."

His chest hitched, and a wet, gurgling cough came out. Blood was filling up in his lungs, each breath more labored than the last.

"*Shhh.* I'm going to get you out of here, okay?" I meant every word. I didn't know how. I didn't have a plan, but I had to get those cuffs off him.

If I could free him, if he could heal—

"Eleni," he rasped. "I want you to know I came back for you. I was trying to find a way to break you free from Malakar's contract. To bring you home."

Home.

A word I'd grieve like death. One I thought I'd never hear again. And hearing it now, on his lips, felt like a promise that made my heart unravel.

"Somehow, they were waiting for me at the border. Like they knew I was coming."

I cradled his face in my hands, forcing his fading gaze up to mine. "We'll worry about that later," I whispered, trying to hold back tears. "Right now, I need to get these cuffs off you."

"No." His voice was strained, like every syllable cost him pieces of himself. "It . . . It's too late for me now."

"No." I shook my head. "Stop. I won't accept that. I can't. You need to hold on a little longer, okay?"

"Eleni, please . . . listen to me." He coughed, more blood spilling from his lips. I attempted to wipe it away with my dress, but the blood was coming out faster.

"You can save . . . this world. You can save . . . the House of Earth. Our House. Your home."

My heart broke into a million pieces.

Our House. As if he had already accepted me, claimed me, as if I belonged here. But I couldn't accept that. Not like this. Not with him slipping away in my arms.

I had to save him.

His head slumped, but he pushed it back up again. "Find my brother—Kelstro. Tell him you have . . . the relic. He'll know what to do."

"I can't do it, Ehlark." I continued to fight the tears running down my face, but they kept coming.

He lifted his gaze to me, every movement costing him more than he had left to give. His lips quivered as he spoke. "I love you, Eleni. Maybe in the next life . . . we can share a ceremony . . . togeth—"

His head dropped forward, and with it, the last breath left his body.

"*No.*"

"No. Ehlark, fight—you hear me?" My voice cracked as I grabbed his face and forced it up toward mine. "Stay with me!"

But the light was already fading from his eye. I searched it, desperate for any spark of life, any glimmer that he was still there. But there wasn't.

Ehlark was gone.

I reached up, my fingers fumbling as I unhooked the chains and pulled him into my arms.

The guards didn't move. No one did.

I sank to the ground, holding him close, as if keeping him near might bring him back. But his body was still. Too still.

Blood continued to drip from his mouth and onto me. I pulled him closer to my chest, pressing my forehead to his, as my tears fell onto his bloodstained face. "Please, don't leave me." I breathed. "Not you too."

I cradled him in my arms, drowning out the voices coming from the crowd.

How could this happen? How could I let him die?

I squeezed him tighter, refusing to let go, until something inside me completely shattered. It wasn't just grief. It was a raw, primal wrenching that ripped through ribs and reason, a soundless scream yearning to tear the world apart.

Heat flared in my chest as the necklace thudded against me, its soft light pulsating, until I realized it wasn't glowing; it was bleeding. Its light spilled into Ehlark's blood, where it stained my skin, before melting into me. The warmth and hum of the relic suddenly thundered to life, consuming every vein and every nerve within me.

I gasped as the relic's glow faded, sinking into my chest as if it had been waiting all along to find its way home.

The flow of power changed. It was stronger. More alive than before.

It no longer pulsed in my arm. It was everywhere, flowing wild and furious through my entire body. And it wanted out. It wanted to be free, to rip through the world and unleash its fury.

My fury.

The courtyard stirred uneasily, people moving and whispering as the stone beneath me shook. A low groan vibrated through the ground, swelling into a sharp, splintering crack that traveled the entire courtyard.

Lightning exploded from the earth in jagged veins, ripping open the courtyard. The crowd screamed as the bolts snaked outward, cracking stone and sending sparks into the night.

Each fracture struck like a heartbeat, brimming with raw energy. My fingers sparked with unfamiliar light I hadn't seen or felt before. This wasn't the same power I felt with the axe. No. This was older—something ancient, sealed away for too long, now yearning to be free.

It had been waiting for me.

Waiting for me to break its slumber.

I rose slowly, every movement pushing the power inside me to release.

It wanted out. It needed to be out.

I drew in a single breath.

And let it go.

The world erupted in a brilliant light. It coursed through me, flooding every vein, nerve, and bone until I was nothing but its radiance. I was no longer flesh, no longer breath. I was fury. I was fire. I was the earth itself awakened.

The sky above churned in response. The clouds swirled with unnatural speed as electricity danced across my skin. My hair lifted, floating as the static built around me.

The crowd stumbled back, screaming. Some soldiers raised their shields, while others dropped them in terror and ran.

Power ripped through me, spilling from my fingertips in crackling arcs of lightning that grasped at the storm above. It was as if the sky itself responded to my call; thunder echoed like a war drum, clouds churned in a frenzy, and the wind whipped around me.

I beheld the crowd. The faces of every single person who had stood there, silent and complicit, as he died.

I saw Lord Fren among them, looking as dumbstruck as everyone else. He was the one who caught and tortured Ehlark. He was the one who dragged him back here to be displayed so others could see him suffer in horrible agony.

Rage burned inside me, and the power obeyed. Bolts of intense energy burst from my hands, piercing into the crowd. In one heartbeat, they were there—eyes wide, mouths open in fear, feet scrambling to run. In the next, they were gone.

Not a shred of clothing. Not a sound. Only scorched stone and the smell of singed flesh.

More screams erupted as people fell into chaos trying to escape. But it was useless. The electric power inside me didn't stop; it only grew, feeding on itself, constricting tighter in my chest until my skin felt too small to hold it. My veins burned like molten metal, and my heartbeat thundered.

It wanted release.

And for the first time, I understood. Not what the relic was, but what it desired.

This was the *Heart of the Mountain* in its purest form.

It was raw, wild, and utterly unforgiving. The power didn't fill me; it consumed me, burning through doubt as if it had never existed, stripping me down to the brutal truth.

Its purpose was survival.

Its intent was justice.

Its hunger was vengeance.

I felt its grief as it felt mine. Centuries of silence, loss, and a kingdom reduced to nothing. When I let that power in, I felt what the House of Earth had been. Its pride, its unity, its people, and I felt the hollow absence of everything that had been taken.

Not anymore.

From this day forth, I would seek justice and bring vengeance on those who destroyed the House of Earth.

Ehlark's home.
My home.

42

KAELIRA

"I think that's all of them."

I stood beside Kelstro, his hands covered in dirt and ash, as we examined what was left of the remaining bodies. He looked like Ehlark, only older and rougher around the edges, with dark crimson hair.

The fires had long since died out, with smoke fading into the sky. Days had passed, yet many bodies still needed proper burials. Cedarvale had been my home—my sanctuary, a refuge for those with nowhere else to go: the Riftblood, the forsaken, and the last remnants of the House of Earth. For me, it was my family.

Because I was Riftblood.

"How are Lythara and the others?" Kelstro asked.

After Ehlark and I heard that Cedarvale had been attacked, he ordered me to mistweave here to see if anyone remained. But when I arrived, everything was ashed. It wasn't until I heard a child's cry in the distance that I found Lythara, Thalena, and the other women and children hiding nearby.

"They will be okay." Though the words felt heavy in my mouth, my chest still ached from the smoke I had inhaled. "Some of them are still struggling after the smoke, but Lythara believes with rest and fresh air, they'll recover."

Lythara told me everything. She said they should all be dead. Malakar's Tracker, the shadow-wielding elemental that tore through the village with a force that should have left no one standing. She felt it in her bones, the way the darkness swallowed them whole. Yet, they woke hours later, shaken but alive. Not one of those who tried to escape with her had been killed.

Kelstro's brows knitted together. "Lythara mentioned someone else. A woman, an outsider who came with the Tracker but was gone when they woke?"

"Yes," I admitted, unable to hide my disgust. "Your brother went after her to try and save her. But I haven't heard from him since. His last words to me were that she would be in Emberhold."

"You need to mistweave us there, Kaelira. We have to save my brother before he does something he'll regret."

I nodded and grasped Kelstro's hand, drawing in a steady breath as I let the cool mist rise and curl around us. The world blurred, weightless, until the air itself carried us. When the haze thinned, we stood at the edge of Emberhold.

The closer we got to the fortress, the clearer it became. This wasn't just Fire's territory tonight. Elementals filled the grounds, their banners and armor distinguishing them from the other realms in the eastern kingdoms. Most were from the Houses of Air and Fire. None from Water. And of course, none from Earth.

"Why are they all gathered here?"

"Don't know," Kelstro murmured. "But if we are discovered, we will be killed on the spot."

We slipped into the shadows. When two soldiers crossed our path, Kelstro struck quickly, his power rushing through them before they could draw breath. We dragged their bodies into the dark, took off their armor, and slipped into their uniforms.

By the time we straightened our collars and pulled helmets into place, we blended in like the rest of Malakar's soldiers, faceless and forgettable. Taking up their posts, we blended into the sea of enemy bodies, my heart pounding in anticipation.

A crowd swarmed the courtyard, their voices a low hum that made my skin crawl. And there, in the center, I saw him.

Ehlark. He was being held in someone's arms.

I squinted, holding my breath.

It was *her*.

Rage ignited inside me. *How dare she touch him. How dare she hold him as if he belongs to her!*

I lunged forward quickly, but Kelstro's hand grabbed my shoulder, stopping me in my tracks. I whipped toward him, ready to snarl and demand he let me go, but then I saw utter shock on his face, and I quickly turned to see what had caught his gaze.

She was crying as she clutched Ehlark tighter.

Why was she—

"*No.*"

The word broke out of me in a choked whisper as my hands flew to my mouth.

Ehlark's body lay limp in her arms, bloodied, battered, and motionless. My heart split open as the truth struck.

He was gone.

Ehlark was dead. The woman holding him was the reason. Anger welled through me, my power humming beneath my skin, ready to tear her apart from the inside out.

Then the ground shifted. A burst of light erupted beneath her, pulsing up from the earth. The soil rose in bright veins, wrapping around her feet, and the sky lit up with her power. Thunderclouds rolled in as if responding to her call.

What was she?

Ehlark told me she didn't possess the same magic as we did, so I assumed she had none, which was unusual. I hadn't cared to know before. I did now. Whatever her power was, it wasn't ordinary. It carried a kind of wrath that could unmake things.

Things that only came from Riftblood.

She unleashed her power, destroying everything and everyone in her way. I wanted to stay, to at least recover Ehlark's body, but she made that impossible. Anything that came near was reduced to nothing.

Not burned, not broken. Erased.

Kelstro yanked me back before the blast reached us, and I mistweaved us out to safety.

We reappeared in Cedarvale. My nose bled from the strain of magic I had pulled in a single instant. Kelstro's face was cold and furious, a storm gathering behind his eyes. He looked angrier than I felt, and that was saying something. If there was one thing I knew about Kelstro, it was that there'd be hell to pay.

He would stop at nothing to avenge his brother.

"Kaelira, go back to Stonehaven," he ordered. "I'll handle the remains. You need rest."

"I told Ehlark not to trust that woman," I snapped.

From the first time I met her, she felt off to me. Not normal, and the fact that she brought that Tracker with her was more reason we should have left them in the Wispwoods. I should've told Ehlark that the Tracker took that woman back.

My hands trembled, and my body screamed for sleep, but I made a promise. I would not back down. Not now. Not ever.

Kelstro exhaled slowly. "Leave that woman to me. Your priority should be yourself and the survivors." He bent down and picked up a handmade bracelet, half-buried in the ash that

clung to the body it once adorned. The delicate craftsmanship remained visible beneath the soot. He placed it in my palm and closed my hand around it.

"The ones you saved, the ones who escaped, need time to mourn. Time to heal. Time to rebuild their strength. They need a leader. That is your responsibility now."

I clenched the bracelet until the metal left imprints on my skin. The pain was familiar, the kind that awakens the part of you trained to do one thing and one thing only. I took one last, burning look at Cedarvale's ruined bones and at Ehlark's memory turned to ash. Grief tore me apart, but beneath it, the strongest part of me hardened like steel.

His death would not be a whisper in the wind. I would hunt her down. I would drag her into the dirt and make her feel every second of what she stole from us. If revenge became the only thing that kept me breathing, then so be it.

Thank You

I want to thank my sister, Jennifer. This story would never have come to life without her constant support and countless phone calls and texts whenever I needed to talk through a scene. I am grateful for my family and friends who patiently endured the rants about my story. To my husband, Robert, thank you for your patience from the very beginning and for supporting me through every late-night editing marathon. Thank you to my editors for pushing my boundaries and helping elevate this story. And to my beta readers, your encouragement and motivation carried me farther than you know.

Lastly, to the reader holding this book: you took a chance on an indie author, set aside your precious time, and let my world live in your mind for a moment. Your willingness to walk beside me on this journey means everything. Thank you for giving this story space, for listening, and for being part of its beginning.

P.S. If you want a sneak peak into Velorn's POV, subscribe to my newsletter!

About the Author

C.C. Martinez is an author based in Austin and Knoxville who spent seven years working as an emergency room nurse and, prior to that, taught English in South Korea. Her debut novel was inspired by a love of stories that explore resilience, grief, and hope woven into immersive, fantastical worlds. When she is not setting broken bones or handling the occasional drunk, naked patient, she can be found racing motorcycles, running with her dogs, or hunting for the perfect chai latte.

Website: http://www.ccmartinezauthor.com
IG: @ccmartinezauthor

www.ingramcontent.com/pod-product-compliance
Lightning Source LLC
Chambersburg PA
CBHW051128130726
47988CB00005B/1752